P9-EJI-149

FALSE COVENANT

FALSE COVENANT

A Widdershins Adventure

ARI MARMELL

an imprint of Prometheus Books
Amherst, NY

Published 2012 by Pyr®, an imprint of Prometheus Books

Cover illustration © Jason Chan
Cover design by Nicole Sommer-Lecht

Inquiries should be addressed to
Pyr
59 John Glenn Drive
Amherst, New York 14228–2119
VOICE: 716–691–0133
FAX: 716–691–0137
WWW.PYRSF.COM

16 15 14 13 12   5 4 3 2 1

Library of Congress Cataloging-in-Publication Data

Marmell, Ari.

False covenant : a Widdershins adventure / by Ari Marmell.

p. cm.

Summary: Davillon's economy has suffered in the half-year since the brutal murder of Archbishop William de Laurent, but when the new bishop uses trickery and magic to try improve the situation he inadvertently admits an evil creature that only Widdershins and her personal god can stop.

ISBN 978–1–61614–621–4 (cloth)

ISBN 978–1–61614–622–1 (ebook)

[1. Fantasy. 2. Robbers and outlaws—Fiction. 3. Gods—Fiction.] I. Title.

PZ7.M3456Fal 2012
[Fic]—dc23

2012000416

Printed in the United States of America

For Rachel,
who has endeavored to live the sort of world-changing life
that I've only ever had the guts to try writing about.

Beneath the sun, the roads are man's,
His work, his home, his town, his plans.
But 'ware the ticking of the clock:
The night belongs to Iruoch.

—from an old Galicien children's rhyme

"But I don't understand," said golden-haired Adeline. "You told me that you were not hungry this evening."

"I am not," said the Marquis Iruoch.

"And you said I had not offended you in any way," said Adeline.

"You have not."

"Then why do you seek to murder me?"

"Because I may later be hungry," said Iruoch.

"Because you may later offend me," said Iruoch.

"And because I can."

—from "The Princess on the Road of Beasts,"
a popular Galicien fairy tale

CHAPTER ONE

If she hadn't already known, she'd never have recognized the lie for what it was.

She'd been here once before, a guest in the sumptuous manor of the Marquis de Ducarte. Now, as last time, the air was heavy with the strands and strings of music, the floor vibrating with dancing couples. Vests and hose were deep, richly hued; magnificent gowns with hoop skirts resplendent in all the bright colors of spring. The servants—though clad largely in blacks, whites, and grays—were scarcely less fancy than the guests; the tables over which they stood were laden with fish and fowl, pork and pastry, and an array of wines that would have put most vintners and taverns to shame. The breath of a hundred conversations pursued the delectable aromas up toward the ceiling, where they swirled around hanging banners and streamers. On some snapped and flapped the sun-and-crown ensign of Vercoule, highest god of Davillon; on others, the rose petals of Ruvelle, patron goddess of the Ducarte line and its current scion, Clarence Rittier.

In nearly every way, it looked the same this time around as it had six months ago, when Madeleine Valois had attended Rittier's greatest fete ever, to celebrate the arrival of his honored guest, Archbishop William de Laurent. Nearly every way—but not all. The gleam in the eyes of the guests was perhaps just a bit wild, a bit worried; the tone of their friendly laughter and malevolent gossip high and desperate. Banners and streamers, tablecloths and gowns, were immaculately washed and well maintained, but they weren't *new*. Once, they'd have been new, every last one.

No more. Not since Rittier's disgrace—and certainly not since Davillon's. The ball, the joy, the carefree celebration . . . A façade, every bit, a lie rigidly maintained by the city's aristocracy because none of them had the slightest clue of how to live any other way.

Well, almost none of them.

Dazzling in her gown of velvet green, the intricate locks of her blonde wig piled high like a hairy wedding cake in the latest fashion, Madeleine glided through the crowd, a beautiful wraith leaving nothing but a faint breeze and the occasional heartbreaking smile to mark her passage. Her knees grew tired of constant curtseying, her cheeks stiff from carrying that artificial smile, her voice hoarse from the false good cheer.

"Your Grace, so lovely to see you again! Are you well?"

"Yes, ghastly weather last week. This summer's likely to be just abominable, isn't it?"

"Indeed, it's been a while. I fear family matters have kept me from attending as often as I'd wish. But I'd be delighted to accept your invitation . . ."

And then, under her breath, so quietly that nobody could possibly have heard her, Madeleine said, "Could you please, please, *please* make everyone stop talking for a while? Or you could just strike me deaf. There's a lot to be said for being deaf, I think. At least it's quiet. . . ."

From everywhere and nowhere, a faint ripple of amusement—a voiceless laugh—sounded in Madeleine's mind.

"Well," she huffed, "I'm glad *one* of us is entertained."

Most of the time, her unseen companion's replies of pure emotion and intent could be only loosely translated into actual words. But in this case, the meaning of "Me, too" was unmistakable.

The corners of her lips twitching as she tried to simultaneously scowl and smile, Madeleine drifted past a table of various wines and punches, and just about collided with one of the men responsible for serving said beverages. A chorus of "Eep!" from Madeleine and "Ack!" from the servant—or syllables to that effect—accompanied a frantic dance of skittering feet. Half a cup of citrus punch sloshed across the floor, and it was only the young woman's surprising speed (with perhaps the tiniest hint of divine intervention) that prevented her gown from absorbing the briefly airborne aperitif.

"Uh, terribly sorry, miss—uh, mademoiselle—uh, I mean, m'lady."

Madeleine blinked at the flustered fellow, who didn't sound much like any professional servant *she'd* ever dealt with. "No harm," she murmured. And then, forcing her voice to squeeze itself into a more haughty outfit for which it was ill suited, "But do take more care in the future, yes? Not everyone here is as quick-footed as I am—nor as forgiving."

"Of course, miss—uh, m'lady."

"What the happy hopping horses was *that* about?" Madeleine demanded of her silent partner. Then, when the response was something about the overall clumsiness of human beings in general, she could only wait until she was sure nobody was watching and then blow her unseen friend a quiet raspberry.

"Disgraceful, isn't it?"

Madeleine about jumped out of her skin, and then twisted to face the speaker. It was another young woman, perhaps half a decade older than Madeleine herself, clad in a golden gown and a wig so pale it was less "blonde" and more "translucent." Madeleine had seen her before, at several of the aristocracy's fetes and balls, but not in some time; if she'd ever known the woman's name, it had long since slipped her mind.

"Um . . . yes?"

"I mean," the woman continued, "I think we all understand the marquis's . . . predicament." It was the closest anyone in the blue-blooded crowd would come to overtly acknowledging Rittier's recent troubles, let alone their own. "So a certain degree of belt-tightening is to be expected, I suppose even commended. But really, I think perhaps he could have afforded to stint a *little* on the refreshments, if it meant acquiring a higher class of server, wouldn't you think? I mean, one expects a certain minimum degree of civilization in one's affairs."

Madeleine—who wanted nothing more than to sigh and walk away, or perhaps smack the woman on the back of the head so hard that her eyes would sprout hair—instead pontificated at length about how right she was, and how it was utterly disgraceful for a man of Rittier's (former) influence to be so lax in his standards, and how it simply wouldn't do at all, and perhaps they ought to consider writing the Duchess Beatrice and ask her to have a word with the marquis before the affair become scandal worthy?

(By the end of it, Madeleine was having serious difficulty keeping a straight face, mostly because her invisible companion was quietly having hysterics.)

Eventually, the other noblewoman wandered off to go find someone else to grouse with (or at, or about), and Madeleine returned her attentions to the task at hand.

Or, most of her attentions, anyway.

"Tell me again, Olgun, why I ever wanted to be one of them?"

Olgun, the invisible presence to whom she'd been speaking throughout the evening, shook a nonexistent head. And then, perhaps troubled by the tone of Madeleine's thoughts, willed a gentle question across her psyche.

"Hmm? No, I'm fine. I just . . ." She stopped, realizing that she was chewing on a loose lock of hair from her wig—a very *un*aristocratic mannerism. She swiftly spit it out, patted it back into place, and sighed softly. "Olgun, that was twice in two minutes something caught me by surprise. The drink, and then that—that *woman* . . . I'm supposed to be more alert than that, yes?"

A moment more to interpret Olgun's unspoken response, and then, "I am *not* out of practice!" she practically hissed, drawing herself up and glaring around arrogantly in response to a few peculiar looks cast her way by those who *almost* overheard her. "I am not out of practice," she repeated, far more softly. "I just—haven't done this in a while."

And again, after a brief pause, "There is *so* a difference! It's a subtle distinction, but an important one! Vital, even! No, I'm not going to explain it to you. You're the god; *you* figure it out!"

Nose held high (making her look rather like half the other folk in attendance), Madeleine lifted her skirts and swept gracefully toward the exit. She passed through pockets of conversation about the general ungainliness and lack of competence among the serving staff—apparently, her own near miss was far from the evening's only unfortunate incident—and muttered a number of polite farewells on her way out.

Only a few even noticed her passing. Not that they were deliberately slighting her at all, no; rather because their attentions were focused elsewhere. In the room's far corner, occupying a bubble all to himself as though his mere presence repelled the spinning dancers or even efforts at conversation, was a middle-aged fellow in the simple brown cassock of a monk. Perhaps as a peace offering to an angry Church, the Marquis de Ducarte had invited Ancel Sicard, Davillon's newly appointed bishop, to his gathering. The fact that Sicard had chosen not to attend, but had sent his assistant instead, was cause for even more gossip throughout the party than the lackadaisical efforts of the servants. The monk, Brother Ferrand, stood, and smiled, and engaged in what conversation came his way, and if he noted the puzzled or hostile glowers, or the angry mutters directed toward him, he certainly gave no sign. Madeleine threw him a final, curious glance—recalling another monk of the same order whom she'd known only briefly but liked to think of as a friend—and then slipped out into the moonlight.

A path of cobblestones wound through garden and orchard, an inebriated earthworm twisting through the grounds of the Ducarte estate as it made its way toward the gates and, from there, the main road. Thick grasses and rich flowers perfumed the night, enjoying the last moments of a fruitful spring before the oncoming summer began to pummel them with fists of heat and sun. Again, Madeleine couldn't help but think of her last visit here . . . of the breaking glass, the quick plummet, and a desperate escape across this same meandering pathway . . .

She couldn't remember what the gardens or the trees might have smelled like, then. She'd been too wrapped up in the scent of her own sweat and blood.

"Okay, Olgun," she announced with a headshake that threatened to send her carefully coifed wig toppling into the dirt. "Enough with the reminiscing." (As though it'd been *he* who'd been doing it.) "Let's get on with it."

Madeleine Valois had done her part; it was time for the noblewoman to take her leave, and the street-thief Widdershins to take the stage.

❋

It was one of her standard techniques, a methodology that had served her well time and time again: use one identity to scout and study the target; the other to relieve said target of just a small portion of excess wealth. Charity was a civic duty and a religious obligation, after all; one could even argue that, as one of the poor who needed said charity, she was actually doing them a *favor*.

(In fact, not only could one argue it, but she had done so, in her time. Oddly, few of the city's wealthy—or the Guard—ever found her logic particularly convincing.)

Her name had once been Adrienne Satti, and though not born into high society, she'd found her way into the aristocracy thanks to the efforts and kindness of the noble Alexandre Delacroix. The apparent fairy tale had not, alas, brought about a fairy tale ending; Alexandre was dead, now, and Adrienne wanted by the city's elite for a series of horrific crimes that she'd never committed. Today she was mostly Widdershins—thief and, far more recently, tavern owner—but she still kept up her presence within the aristocracy under the name Madeleine

Valois. It all might have been confusing enough to make her head spin, if she hadn't had the misfortune to live all of it firsthand.

But at least she wasn't alone. No, Adrienne Satti hadn't been the only survivor of those crimes for which she herself had been blamed. There was one other.

Olgun. A foreigner. A god.

A god few had ever heard of, and only one now worshipped.

A god who now kept careful watch, alert for any interruptions as his disciple and partner disappeared into a shadowed alleyway, gown and wig and other signs of Madeleine Valois sliding into the maw of a black canvas sack. Dark leathers, precision tools, and a blackened rapier emerged from that same hiding place. The young lady—slender and fine-featured, brunette—who scrambled up the nearest wall to perch, staring carefully at the Rittier estate, really didn't much resemble the absent noblewoman at all.

"All righty, Olgun, now it's time for the fun part, yes? You know, the waiting. What? Well of *course* the waiting's fun! Why else would we do so bloody *much* of it? For a god, you're really not all that good at logic."

And then, "I can *tell* when you're making those kinds of faces at me, you know."

After that, Olgun lapsed again into an amused silence, and Widdershins really had nothing to do but wait (which was not, despite her efforts at convincing the god or herself, the "fun part" at all) and watch for the activity at Clarence Rittier's manor to slowly taper off.

❁

Windows of stained glass, worth more than Davillon's average laborer would make in years, cast the sanctuary in a soft rainbow glow. The steady gleam of the moon and stars, augmented by the flickering of a dozen streetlights, threw reflected images of countless holy symbols and scenes across row upon row of pews and kneeling cushions. The most oft-repeated symbol was, of course, Vercoule's crown-and-sun, but here was the golden pyramid of Geurron, the silver face of Demas, the white cross of Banin, the bleeding hand of Tevelaire, and more. Those gods most prevalent in Davillon boasted the largest and most frequent icons, but every single deity of the Hallowed Pact—all 147—were represented somewhere.

Here in the Basilica of the Sublime Tenet, the heart of worship in Davillon, it would have been improper to do any less.

Perfumed censers and waxy candles breathed a pungent, greasy smoke that left a sweet aroma in its wake as it swirled toward the domed ceiling. From the raised dais at the front of the sanctuary, a priest's melodious voice rose and fell through a litany as familiar as his own name.

It was a litany few heard. That the sanctuary should be sparsely populated was no surprise; the midnight mass was never a well-attended function, even at the best of times. But this night—and, for that matter, the past two seasons—could not, for either Davillon or the Church, qualify as the "best of times." Tonight, the priest and his assistants outnumbered the parishioners.

Nor had it been that much better during the day.

From a shaded balcony above the sanctuary proper, all but invisible to the smattering of parishioners below, an old man watched, his eyes red with unshed tears. Ancel Sicard had always loved his Church, and the many gods whom he had the honor and privilege to represent. But in his past six months as bishop of this conflicted city, he'd come to love Davillon as well. And to see the two of them at odds ate away at him, body and soul.

He was a large man, but far narrower of girth now than when he'd arrived. His thinning hair and thickening beard, previously an even salt-and-pepper mix, was now entirely gray save for a smattering of dark patches. It seemed to him that even his white cassock of office had grown dim and discolored, though he knew, in his less emotional moments, that this could only be a trick of the mind.

Bishop Sicard kissed the tips of his fingers and held them up toward the largest of the stained glass windows, then spun on his heel and moved toward the nearest stairway. His footsteps echoed back to him as he plunged downward, a rhythmic counterpoint to the rapid beating of his heart. Through a heavy doorway and along plush carpeted halls he strode, into the small suite of chambers that were his own home here in the basilica.

Here, he paused for only a few moments, long enough to swap out his cassock and miter for the simple tunic and trousers of a commoner—a sort of outfit he'd had little cause to wear in over a decade—and to gather a satchel of yellowed parchments and old, cracked, leather-bound books.

He did *not* pause to question what he was about to do. *Those* concerns he had made peace with long ago.

Then he was off once more, through the halls and out into the Davillon streets. A number of sentinels—both Church soldiers and City Guard—stood watch around the property, just another testament to the growing rift between the sacred and the secular. Yet these men and women, though skilled at their duties, were watching for vandals and other angry threats from *without*; not a one of them thought anything strange of an old man leaving midnight mass, assuming they even noticed him at all.

Once clear of the basilica, Sicard took a moment to orient himself. In the months that he'd been here, he'd done precious little traveling on his own. Always with an entourage, usually inside a coach, he'd had scant reason to learn the layout of the city's streets. He'd *certainly* never traversed the city in the dark, alone.

Unprotected.

A frisson of worry coiled around Sicard's spine like a hungry snake, but he swiftly shook it off. He'd been to the house once before, had memorized the route. He wouldn't get lost, not so long as he paid attention to his surroundings.

As for robbers or other hazards of the city? Well, either he'd make it to the Dunbrick District or he wouldn't; either the gods approved of his actions, or they didn't.

And either the rather disreputable individuals with whom he was supposed to meet would keep their promise of safe treatment, or they wouldn't.

After the relative silence of the cathedral, the hustle and bustle of the city, even so late, was something of a shock. Scattered merchants carried goods across town, making ready for the next morning's custom; somewhat less legitimate vendors hawked stolen, illicit, or simply socially unacceptable wares from dim venues. Sicard grinned briefly in morbid amusement, wondering what some of the dealers, fences, and streetwalkers would think if they knew they were propositioning the city's new bishop.

His route took him only briefly by the Market District or other crowded quarters, so he was bothered only sporadically by Davillon's nocturnal population, troubled only momentarily by the stale sweat, dried horse manure, and other lingering odors of the past day.

Sicard thought, as he walked, of William de Laurent. The archbishop had been one of his teachers and mentors in the seminary, and—though they'd never been *that* close—a friend. He'd survived a lifetime of laboring on behalf of the Church; two wars; half a dozen attempts on his life; and decades of the political infighting that plagued the clergy despite their best efforts to squelch it.

He'd survived everything the world could throw at him, until Davillon.

William would never have approved of what had happened in Davillon since he died; of this, Sicard was absolutely certain. He could only hope that the venerable archbishop would have understood what Sicard had to do to make things right.

The house, when he reached it, was—well, a house. Old but sturdy, small but comfortable, with once-fine paint only slowly starting to peel from the façade. A mundane, commoner's home in a mundane, commoner's neighborhood, it was one of many properties the Church owned throughout Davillon—one that had been left to them in the last will and testament of a devout parishioner, back when the city was on better terms with its shepherds.

A quick glance either way was enough to convince Sicard that he hadn't attracted any undue attention, and then he was across the street and through the door. The carpet and the sofas were thick with dust, save for those spots where the small group awaiting his arrival had seated themselves.

He didn't explain himself; if they were here, they already knew why. He didn't introduce himself; he'd never heard their names, and he had *zero* intention of telling them his. No, Bishop Sicard removed the old parchments from his satchel—parchments that were very clearly *not* liturgical or sacred in nature—and then, after a simple, "Does everyone know what's required of them?" began to read.

CHAPTER TWO

The chiming in the distance, resounding from the intricate clock tower atop the city's Hall of Judgment, informed Widdershins that her long wait had finally ended at four hours past midnight.

Her hopes that the evening might go even vaguely according to plan ended perhaps four minutes after that.

"Here we go, Olgun," she announced in a whisper, rising from a crouch and taking a moment to stretch a few stiffening limbs. "Remember," she continued—even though he already knew all of this, perhaps reminding *herself* of the objective—"we're just looking for loose coin. The marquis was certain to have money on hand in case something went wrong at the ball. Should be more than enough to cover . . ." She trailed off, uncomfortable giving voice to her current problems.

With nothing more than a single deep breath, Widdershins broke into a sprint. Her feet came down with an impossible speed and grace on the shingles of the roof and made not a sound. Thanks to both her own ingrained talent and the aid of her divine partner, a cat made of cloud would have surely been louder. The edge of the roof came up fast, frighteningly fast, and Widdershins didn't so much as slow. A gazelle-like leap, propelled by what felt like invisible fingers interlaced beneath her feet, and she soared across the gap to the next building.

Where she landed with a faint scuffle and a brief stumble—neither sufficient to draw the slightest attention, but enough to make the young thief blush in humiliation.

"Wow," she whispered. "Maybe I'm a little out of practice." Then, "If I get even the slightest *hint* of 'I told you so,' I'm trading you in for a boyfriend!

"What? I don't know *where*. Look how many gods Galice has! I'm sure there's a bazaar somewhere that trades in divinity. I just have to find—Oh, figs."

From her new vantage, on a rooftop nearer the northern end of the property, Widdershins could see what might otherwise have escaped her notice. A band of figures—perhaps six or seven of them, little more than silhouettes in the shadows—were scaling the outer wall of the Ducarte estate. They were good, very good; if Widdershins hadn't already been a master of all the tricks herself, and had her night vision not been ever so slightly enhanced by Olgun's power, she would have missed them.

And if they were that good, that stealthy, it could only mean one thing: She wasn't the only member of the so-called Finders' Guild planning to take advantage of Clarence Rittier's party.

"Olgun?" It was almost a whimper. "Things actually *do* go right for some people, yes? I mean, it's not just a foolish dream I have, is it?"

She was fairly certain that the god more or less shrugged inside her mind.

Widdershins's first instinct was just to leave. She had no real authority to make them go away; there were more of them than her; and she was somewhat unpopular with several factions within the community of Davillon's thieves, thanks to a minor misunderstanding some months ago that had resulted in the deaths of about a dozen Finders. It hadn't been her fault—not really—and the guild's leader, the enigmatic Shrouded Lord, had cleared her of any wrongdoing, but not everyone was eager to let the matter lie.

On the other hand, Widdershins had spent days planning this heist, there might not be another plum opportunity to match this one for a while, and—most importantly—there was more than just her own avarice riding on this.

With a grumble, a sigh, and an angry pout (which, she would have been mortified to learn, was really far more cute than it was menacing), she dashed once more for the roof's edge.

Not even a boost from Olgun would have allowed her to cross the entire boulevard separating the estate from her current vantage. Instead, she dropped over the eaves and clambered down the wall, her fingers finding holds as easily as if someone had placed a ladder for her convenience. A quick dart across the road, so thickly concealed in shadows that they might have been sewn to her outfit, and she was at the property's outer wall. A quick leap, a yank with both arms augmented by Olgun's strength, and she'd vaulted the wall to land smack-dab in the midst of the other larcenous newcomers. This close, she recognized the lot of them, and had no doubt whatsoever as to who the leader was.

"Evening, Squirrel," she said, hands well away from the hilt of her rapier (but near enough for a lightning draw if necessary). "Out for a walk, maybe?"

Simon Beaupre—or "Squirrel," to most people in the Guild or the Guard—very nearly toppled over in a tangle of long, gangly limbs and equally long, black hair. A lengthy stiletto, essentially a prepubescent rapier, was halfway from its sheath before he recognized the phantasm that had just dropped in on them.

"Gods and demons, Widdershins!" He brushed the dangling hair away from a youthful, narrow face and glared as menacingly as he could (which wasn't very). "Are you *trying* to get yourself stabbed to death?" The other miscreants with him—all roughly his age, but of a wide variety of builds and miens—grumbled their agreement and sheathed their weapons as well, all pretending that their hearts *weren't* beating so hard as to bruise the insides of their chests.

"If I were," Widdershins said primly, "I'd have thrown myself at people who were actually, you know, *dangerous*. What are you *doing* here, Squirrel? Little boys should be in bed by now."

The various "little boys"—several of whom were actually older than Widdershins, and none of whom were more than a couple of years younger—glowered at her once more.

All but Simon himself, who, having now recovered his breath, allowed his attentions to roam, as they so often did when the two of them met, everywhere *but* Widdershins's face. She repressed a brief shudder and wished she could take the time to go scrub herself bloody in a hot bath; she swore his gaze left a trail of slime across her skin.

"I'm sure it's the same thing you are, gorgeous."

If Widdershins had rolled her eyes any harder, she'd probably have sprained something. "Enlighten me."

"Well . . ."

"Uh, Simon?" This from a tall, broad-shouldered thug of a thief whose name was—actually, Widdershins couldn't for the life of her remember *what* his name was, and would have to have been unconscious or dead to have cared any less. "What we're doing right *now* is standing around waiting to get nabbed."

"You're right. Go on ahead, guys. Stick with the plan; I'll catch up."

"Wait!" Widdershins hissed, trying to spin to face all of them at once and making herself vaguely dizzy for her trouble. "Don't . . ." But they were already gone. "Oh, figs."

She thought briefly of chasing after them, but Squirrel was still here, eager to talk—and oblivious to how *un*eager she was to listen to him—and besides, what would she do if she caught them, anyway?

"You were saying?" she prompted, her voice chilly as a snowman's backside.

"Well, I mean, it's obvious, right?" He grinned wide, eager to impress. "Gods forbid any of the 'aristo-brats' be reminded of just what shitty shape Davillon's in, so you know all their parties have to be all fancy. This is the first party Rittier's thrown since the archbishop was almost killed here last year, so it's gotta be even fancier, right? This is probably one of the biggest accumulations of wealth the city's seen in months, and at this time of night, most the guests are gone and everyone's tired, so . . ." He shrugged, palms spread wide. "Best time and place for guys like us. You obviously had the same idea, right? So work with us. Plenty to go around."

"This," Widdershins growled through a cage of teeth, "Was. *My*. Caper!"

"I don't see your name on it."

Her jaw dropped. "Did you *really* just say—?!"

"Besides, Shins, you're one to talk about stealing a job out from under someone. Not after you swiped the d'Arras Tower job out from under Lisette."

Widdershins swallowed the bitter medicine of an angry retort, and Olgun—despite the outrage and frustration he shared with his worshipper—couldn't help but chuckle.

"I hate to break it to you, oh master schemer," she said instead, "but you didn't think this through. Yeah, Rittier should have a lot of coin on hand, but not enough to make the score worthwhile once you split it *seven* ways—let alone if you bring *me* in! The risk's not worth it! You—"

"Coin? Shins, who said anything about coin?"

A second time Widdershins's jaw hung loose—this time, she was sure, low enough that she'd probably have to pick soil out from between her lower teeth. "You *can't* be that stupid!" It was barely a whisper; perhaps a prayer.

But she knew, even as she spoke the words, that he could be. And it explained why he needed so many thieves for the task.

"The table settings, the art, the jewels . . . You have any idea what those'll bring, even on the street? Hell, Widdershins, you can *have* the coins if you want!"

She was just about squeaking now. "There's *no way* you can sneak out with that much loot without being spotted!"

"And who," he asked, his hand dropping once more to his blade, "said anything about *sneaking*?"

It was a perfect cue, and sure enough, that last word was punctuated by the shattering of glass and a sudden scream from the manor.

"Come on!" Simon insisted, turning toward the commotion. "We're missing all the—"

He never got to explain *what* they were missing, because at that moment Widdershins hauled off and punched him as hard as she could in the jaw. It wasn't all that impressive a blow, really; young and slight, Widdershins tended to rely more on speed and stealth than on strength. But with Olgun adding a touch of divine "oomph," it was more than enough to drop Squirrel like, well, a squirrel.

"We need to *go*!" Widdershins hissed to her unseen ally. "We do *not* want to be around when this fiasco decides exactly which of the ten thousand possible ways it's going to go bad. Also," she added, shaking her hand, "ow! Ow, ow, ow, ow, ow . . ."

And indeed, she was several paces nearer the outer wall, already tensed to leap, when the next batch of sounds escaped the manor and caught up with her. The sounds not of a forceful robbery or frightened victims, but the clatter and clash and shouts of . . .

"Combat?" Widdershins yanked herself to a halt so abruptly that the muscles of her back and legs twinged in protest, and Olgun let out a startled yelp. "Who in . . . ?"

Then she was running once more, this time *toward* the heavy stone structure—and through an ever-thickening wave of strenuous objection from her divine partner.

"I know, I *know*!" she argued between gasping breaths. "But I need . . . to know what's . . . going on!" And then, grinning despite herself, "Kind of like . . . old times, yes?"

Olgun spent the next moments explaining, in no uncertain terms (well, emotions and sensations), exactly what he thought of "old times." But at least it kept him occupied.

Another leap, a scuttle up the side of the wall that a circus-trained spider would have been hard-pressed to match, and Widdershins was peering in through a window overlooking the dining room.

No trace of the marquis himself, or any of the remaining guests.

Instead, she saw four of Squirrel's compatriots, now wearing masks pulled over their faces, locked in combat with . . .

With Rittier's servants?!

Except that even as she watched, the servants revealed themselves for who and what they really were. She saw hidden weapons appear from within their dull-colored uniforms. Blades, yes, but also "bash-bangs"—flintlocks with stocks of brass rather than wood, weighted to function as brutal head-breakers just as efficiently as they did pistols.

And they were carried exclusively by the City Guard.

Well, if nothing else, it explained why those people were so bad at actually serving food, didn't it?

It made sense, too, after Widdershins thought about it for a moment. If the thieves could figure out that Rittier's party made for the most tempting target in months, it wasn't that surprising that the Guard could come up with the same idea.

It also left the young thief in something of an ugly quandary.

"Yeah," she said absently as Olgun resumed encouraging her to depart with some vague semblance of haste. "But Squirrel and the guys know that I showed up here. If I vanish and they get nabbed by the Guard, who do you think they'll suspect of selling them out? Give you three guesses. What? No, they don't have to *prove* it was me! Just the suspicion would be enough to make my life . . . Oh, rats." She winced at the thunder of a brass flintlock, watched as the first of the thieves fell, his left shoulder shattered by the ball.

"All right, Olgun," she sighed. "Hold on. I don't know, whatever it is you normally hold on to!" Then, unwilling to waste any further time in argument, she burst into motion.

One hand yanked her own hood up over her head; not as good as a mask, but hopefully sufficient to hide her features in the chaos of what was to come. An elbow shattered the glass of the expensive window (Olgun scrambling to keep the shards from drawing blood), and then she was inside.

Two of the Guardsmen—those who hadn't already discharged their pistols—fired at the dark figure that suddenly appeared before them, but Widdershins was already dropping to the floor. The two balls sailed high over her head, missing even without Olgun's extra nudge. She landed in a crouch atop the heavy table and leapt again, once more clearing a height impossible for any mortal athlete, let alone a girl of her size. At the apex of her abbreviated flight, her fingers closed around a thick cloth of darkest green. The banner boasting the red petals of Ruvelle went taut, and then ripped free from its anchor, unable to support even Widdershins's slight weight.

But then, she'd never intended it to.

"Olgun . . ." It was the lightest whisper as she dropped, coming down on one knee, both palms pressed flat on the floor. She hadn't time to explain what she wanted, but then, she didn't need to. She felt the familiar tingle of the god exercising what power he had, and the enormous hanging twisted as it fell.

Twisted so that, impossible as it seemed, it landed atop all four of the disguised Guardsmen. It wouldn't hurt them—though the bruises on their pride wouldn't fade for quite some time—but they were effectively blind and helpless, if only briefly.

"Run!" she hissed at her fellow Finders. "Get out!"

"But . . . but our score!" one of them protested—whined, really.

"You think these are the only constables here, you idiot? They were waiting for you!" She pointed imperiously at the injured man. "Get him and *get*!"

They got, hauling their companion upright and vanishing through the doorway to the front hall.

And, as though in answer to Widdershins's prediction, another door—this one across the ballroom and leading deeper into the house—flew open as though shot. Through it marched another pair of Guardsmen, these two in full uniform: black tabards emblazoned with the silver fleur-de-lis, equally black plumed hat, and medallions showing the silver face of Demas, patron god of the Guard.

One, blond with a goatee, was a stranger to her. But the other, with hair and mustache of rich brown, she recognized all too well.

"Oh, no . . ." She was sprinting, despite an ankle made slightly wobbly by the earlier drop, before she might be recognized in turn.

There were few in the city, and none in the Guard, who knew her face as well as Major Julien Bouniard. She'd always been sure she'd never call one of the Guard a *friend*, but Julien was starting to challenge that certainty.

Unless, of course, he identified her as part of the group of thieves who'd invaded the home of the Marquis de Ducarte, at which point, she was fairly sure, any burgeoning friendship would end with the slamming of a cell door.

From the sound of things, as best she could tell in the thumping, pounding tumult, only a couple of them were following her as she fled. Probably, she guessed, Julien and his other uniformed friend. The other Guardsmen, the ones disguised as servants, were either still flailing about beneath the banner or, more probably, had taken off in pursuit of the other escaping thieves.

Well, Julien was good, no doubt of that. And while Widdershins didn't know the man with him, she had to assume the major had chosen only good people to work with him on this. Nevertheless, the day she couldn't outrun two Guardsmen was the day she *deserved* to be arrested.

She pulled streamers off the wall as she passed, shoved over the occasional chair or unlit candelabra, hoping to tangle the feet of her pursuers. Again, it wasn't that she doubted she could stay ahead of them, but why take the chance that they'd come close enough for a clear shot? She took a small flight of stairs in a single leap and found herself nearing one of the manor's side doors, presumably meant for deliveries and servants. It hung open before her, and Widdershins found herself wondering briefly if some of Squirrel's gang might have already used it as an escape route. Not that it mattered; a few more steps and she'd be . . .

Olgun's cry of alarm warned her a split second before the much more human grunt of pain would have. She twisted in the doorway, slouched uncomfortably so she could keep the hood over her face, and gasped at the scene playing out before her.

Two of Squirrel's thieves—she could tell, even with the masks, that they were not part of the group whom she'd helped escape—were closing in from behind the pursuing Guardsmen. The blond constable she didn't know had staggered back against the wall, his right arm bleeding freely from an ugly gash across the bicep, his bash-bang having fallen to the floor at his feet, discharging its payload harmlessly into the wall when it hit. Even as his face paled with pain, he struggled to draw his rapier, however awkwardly, with his left hand.

Julien himself had dropped into an expert duelist's stance. Widdershins wasn't certain what had happened to his own firearm; he held his rapier unerringly straight, but he was having more than a little difficulty trying to cover both opponents at once.

No, not both. All *three*. Even as Widdershins watched, Squirrel himself—a deep bruise creeping across the lower half of his face like a fistful of grape jelly—stepped from a side passage to join the others.

"You're losing your touch, Olgun," she muttered softly. "Well, of course *your* touch! I mean, you *know* that *I* can't hit that hard. . . ."

Squirrel growled something unintelligible, drew his stiletto with his left hand—and with his right, produced what could only be Julien's own flintlock! Widdershins couldn't begin to guess when or how he'd gotten his hands on it, but then, he was a thief, after all. That's what he did.

Except now he was about to become not just a thief, but a Guard-murderer.

And Widdershins couldn't afford to worry about her own escape any longer.

"Olgun!"

A flash of divine power, a spark from nowhere, and the bash-bang discharged before Simon could pull the trigger, while he was still bringing the weapon up to fire. The ball shot past Julien, ruffling the edge of his tabard rather than punching through flesh and bone, and gouged an ugly hole in the wall behind him.

Multiple astonished stares flickered to the disobedient weapon, and in that moment, Widdershins struck. Her own rapier—currently lacking its defensive wire basket so that the hilt could lie flush against her back—was now out and moving. The thug to Squirrel's left screamed and dropped to one knee, clutching at an arm that was now bleeding far more fiercely than the wounded Guardsman's.

Squirrel and the remaining thief spun, their faces twisting with a betrayed fury, and then recognized their error almost immediately. Squirrel broke into a run even as his remaining friend turned back to face the Guardsmen and received Julien's blade high in the chest for his trouble. Widdershins winced as the body dropped; she'd really hoped that Julien would strike to wound, as she had, even though she knew that wasn't how they were trained. She was only vaguely aware of Simon shoving past her and disappearing out the door.

Olgun shouted another warning, but there was little Widdershins could do. She gawped up, face pale, into Julien's twisted features; felt his fists close with bruising pressure on her upper arms.

"What the hell are you doing here, Widdershins?!" He was screaming at her, furious. She couldn't remember ever having seen him quite this way before, and she'd seen him in some truly ugly situations.

"I . . . Julien, I . . ."

"*What are you doing here?*"

"Julien, you're hurting me. . . ."

His face rocked back as if she'd slapped him; his hands dropped away as though she were suddenly burning to the touch. "I . . . I'm sorry, Shins." His eyes dropped for just a flicker of a second, then locked on hers once more. "Give me a reason."

"A reason . . . ?" Her thoughts were spinning wildly, enough to make her dizzy. She couldn't follow the conversation, didn't know what he was asking.

"Give me a reason not to arrest you," he whispered. "Please, Shins, something. *Anything*."

Widdershins had believed, well and truly *believed*, that nothing else that happened this evening could possibly surprise her. She was wrong. Even Olgun was stunned into silence.

"Please . . ."

Gods, he was practically *begging*. He really didn't want to have to take her in. Widdershins's peculiar sense of vertigo was, if anything, growing worse. She felt sick, her face feverish.

"I . . . I was an invited guest here, Julien. Not 'Widdershins,' I mean, but—uh, someone else. A noblewoman that I, uh, sometimes call myself . . ."

What am I doing*?! I can't tell him this! He can't know this! Olgun, make me shut up!*

But clearly, Widdershins's mouth was a far stronger force than even a god might contend with. Olgun did no such thing, and she kept right on babbling.

"I, uh—not dressed like this, of course. I mean, this isn't exactly, um, the height of fashionable party wear, you know? Maybe . . . maybe next year?"

Oh, gods, kill me now.

"And do you expect me to believe," Julien asked softly, "that you *weren't* here to scout the place?"

"Uh . . . I wasn't . . ." She offered a limp-wristed wave toward the fallen thugs. "I wasn't part of *that*. I swear it, Julien, I wasn't . . ."

"Why didn't you run? You could have kept running."

Widdershins's thoughts finally stopped spinning—froze, in fact, crystallized into a single, solid certainty. She looked up, finally meeting his gaze, and felt her heartbeat quicken even as her breathing slowed.

"I couldn't let them kill you," she told him.

For somewhere between a second and a century they stood, staring at one another—and then Julien took a single step back. "Go."

Widdershins, despite the ghostly chains of questions and uncertainties that dragged at her ankles, obeyed as swiftly as her feet could manage.

❋

Constable Paschal Sorelle, of the Davillon City Guard, pressed a wad of moderately clean cloth to the gash in his arm and, with a pained gasp or two, staggered over to stand at his commanding officer's side.

"Sir? I don't suppose you'd care to explain that?"

Major Bouniard tore his attentions away from the darkness into which Widdershins had vanished and bestowed a disapproving frown on his lieutenant. "Did I miss a promotion ceremony, Constable? Am I *supposed* to explain myself to you now?"

"Not at all, sir." Paschal's tone, though thinned by the pain of his wound, was deliberate enough to suggest that he was choosing his words *very* carefully. "You needn't explain a thing to me. But, ah . . . you *will* have to explain yourself to command, sir.

"That's not," he added swiftly, "a threat, of course, sir. Merely a statement of fact."

"I know that, Constable."

"Just wanted to be sure, sir. You'll write your report as you see fit, of course, sir, but I've also got to write mine, and . . . Well, the operation was overall a success, sir, but I'm not sure this last incident casts you in all that flattering a light." Paschal's face softened imperceptibly in the flickering lantern light. "I don't want to cause you any problems with command, sir. I *really* don't. But—"

"Say nothing more about it," Bouniard ordered, clapping a hand on Paschal's shoulder (on the uninjured side, of course). "You report the events exactly as you saw them. If there's any trouble coming my way, I brought it on myself. First lesson I learned from Major Chapelle, back when I joined up: You don't sacrifice your integrity for anyone, not even a colleague. You hear me, Constable?"

"Loud and clear, sir." Then, after a moment, "She's certainly a unique one, sir."

"She is that, Constable. You *did* note that she acted to assist us, didn't you?"

"Of course, sir. And it'll be in my report, make no mistake."

"I was certain it would be, Paschal."

Julien Bouniard once more turned his face to the darkness; Paschal Sorelle turned his own toward his commander.

"Come on, Constable," Julien said finally, turning away from the door. "Let's get that arm looked at."

❁

Aubert and Osanne Noury weren't stupid. No, really, they weren't, not normally. What they were, however, were newlyweds; Osanne had only *been* a Noury for about seventy-two hours, give or take. So when the couple found themselves up and alert less than an hour before the dawn, they perhaps cannot be blamed, in their distraction, for deciding to take a romantic stroll in the moonlight.

It shouldn't have been all *that* great a risk, really. The new Noury couple dwelt in Rising Bend, one of Davillon's richer (and therefore, safer) neighborhoods. Nor were they planning to go too terribly far from home; the *worst* they could have expected to encounter, unless they were struck by a truly devious misfortune, would have been a desperate beggar or *maybe* a particularly brave robber. So . . . stupid, yes, but not *very*.

Except that the misfortunes of that night were, indeed, truly devious.

It began with a whisper, one that scythed clean through Aubert's and Osanne's soft giggles. They could make out no words at all, just a series of sounds beneath someone's breath, rasped at the very limits of human hearing. Once, the spooked couple might have dismissed it as a trick of the wind; twice, as the foraging of some feral animal digging in the refuse of an unseen alleyway.

But when it continued—indeed, when the sound clearly began to creep closer, despite the lack of any visible movement in the feeble glow of the streetlights and the cloud-covered moon—they could no longer even pretend that its source could be anything so mundane.

"Who . . . ?" Aubert cleared his throat, tried again. "Who's out there?" To his credit, it must be noted that, though armed with nothing more than a small dagger—a utility tool more than a weapon—he did step in front of his unarmed wife, placing himself between her and whatever danger he couldn't quite perceive.

And then the whispers crumbled, breaking apart into a throaty, guttural, liquid laughter. Osanne whimpered; Aubert's dagger twisted and fell from an abruptly sweat-soaked hand.

The laughter grew—nearer, rather than louder—and finally, something moved in the darkness.

It might have been human—*could* have been human, by general shape if nothing else. A dark silhouette, shadow in shadow, seemingly without face or feature. It clambered across the nearest wall, moving sideways yet hanging head-down, some horrible mockery of crab and insect both. And even as it moved, the horrid chafing laugh continued, echoed . . .

Stopped. Even as the shape moved back into the darkness, becoming once again invisible, the sounds utterly ceased.

But only for an instant. The laughter resumed once more, this time from the *opposite side of the street*. Shadows shifted in the lantern light, and the figure seemed to reappear on a building behind the terrified couple without having bothered to cross the intervening space. Osanne swayed on her feet, nearly fainting, while Aubert's hose were suddenly warm and wet.

They ran, then, screaming and crying, both dagger and dignity left on the cobblestones of what should have been a safe and quiet street. The dark figure did not pursue; but the laughter followed them, in their dreams, for months to come.

CHAPTER THREE

Robin allowed herself a deep, heartfelt sigh and slouched briefly against the back wall, where in a more traditional (and wealthier) establishment than the Flippant Witch, a large mirror might have hung. It wasn't a posture particularly welcoming to customers—but then, as there were precious few of those today, and all of them were regulars, it didn't seem particularly inappropriate, either.

The teen and the tavern were quite similar in many respects; both friendly enough, but fairly drab and unremarkable on the surface. She was a slender slip of a girl, lightly dusted with freckles as if by a stingy confectioner, wearing her hair chopped short and sporting nondescript tunic and hose. She was accustomed to being mistaken for a boy at any distance—encouraged it, in fact, when she was traveling the streets of Davillon—though at her age, that was becoming less and less likely with each passing season.

Until about six months ago, Robin had been a serving girl at the Flippant Witch tavern; it hadn't been an easy life, or a rich one, but she'd been happy enough. Now, despite her age, she was one of its managers, carrying enough responsibility to bruise those tiny shoulders of hers. If she hadn't cared so much—about both the tavern's current owner, and the lingering memories of its former—she might have gone to find some other employment by now.

Assuming there was any to be found, these days.

Frowning, chewing on the corner of her lip, she looked once more over the common room. There wasn't much to the Flippant Witch: a squat, hunkering building that, other than that selfsame common room, contained only a kitchen, a storeroom, and a few small, private parlors. Sawdust, firewood, and a mélange of alcohols wafted on the air, laced just around the edges with stale sweat. The scents had soaked into the rafters, the wooden tables, even the small stone altar of Banin. (Neither Robin nor the tavern's owner actually worshipped Banin; they kept the icon out of respect for an absent friend.)

Unfortunately, said scents were finally starting to fade. A chamber that, this time last year, would have been crammed to capacity by multiple dozens of patrons now housed only a fraction of that number. Casks and bottles stood almost full, or even unopened; in the kitchen, cuts of meat hung uncooked, loaves of bread slowly went stale. It was quiet enough in the common room to hear the passersby outside. On occasion, the servers didn't even have to deliver a customer's order to the bar or the kitchen, as Robin and the cook could listen to them clearly enough all the way from the table.

The Flippant Witch wasn't dying, necessarily, but she was most assuredly sick. And Robin hadn't the slightest idea of how to fix it. With a second sigh far too large to have been contained in such a small form, she drifted out from behind the bar and went to go see if she could help at the tables.

"Kinda quiet in here, isn't it, Robs?" The words, though slightly slurred, remained entirely comprehensible. No surprise, really; since the speaker spent more or less every waking hour in his cups, he'd certainly learned how to function by now.

Robin offered a small smile to the man seated at the corner table. Rough, unshaven, dressed in clothes that were more wrinkled than a bathing grandmother—and as much a fixture of the Flippant Witch as the furniture.

"Reading my mind again, are you, Monsieur Recharl?" she asked lightly, and then had to force herself not to laugh at his confused blinking.

No, he hadn't been reading her mind. It was the same question he'd asked every day for the past two months. So, since it always satisfied him, she offered the same answer.

"It's the same everywhere in Davillon, monsieur. Things are bad all over; you know, with the Church and all."

"Right," he said. His blinking continued. "That thing with, uh, with the bishop . . ."

"Archbishop," Robin corrected gently. "William de Laurent. Yeah."

Indeed, ever since the murder of the archbishop last year, many of the Church clergy had made their displeasure with Davillon clear in no uncertain terms. Merchants were "encouraged" to do their trading elsewhere; major liturgical events were held in alternate cities; and priests at pulpits across Galice sermonized on the evils of the nation's newly crowned "most depraved and violent" city.

It wasn't very "Churchly," but it was certainly very *human*.

And the result, in a short two seasons, was an economic downturn of a size Davillon hadn't seen in generations. Several priests had been beaten and robbed in retaliation, souring the city's reputation with the Church even further, and Robin was a little surprised that their newly appointed bishop—what was his name? Sicard, right?—hadn't been lynched or assassinated within weeks of his arrival.

Robin chatted with the tavern's most loyal customer for a few moments, bemoaning the state of Davillon and the pettiness of Churchmen who really ought to know better, reminiscing about how much better everything used to be, and in general making Robin sound older than she was and Recharl as though he had a better memory than he did. Then, finally, she was able to politely slip away, ostensibly to get him a refill.

"Gerard?" she asked the red-bearded figure currently hefting a tray of dirty mugs across the common room. "Could you see about getting Monsieur Recharl another—"

"It's not the Church, you know," he said softly.

It was Robin's turn to blink in confusion. "What?"

"Come on, Robin. I mean, yes, the economy's hurting us, a lot, but it's not the only—"

"Don't! I don't want to hear it."

Gerard frowned, set his tray down on the nearest empty table, and placed a hand on Robin's shoulder. She just as swiftly shrugged it off.

"Robin, we all love Shins. You *know* that, just like we all know that this place wouldn't be here at all if it wasn't for her."

"Yeah, you sound *real* grateful, Gerard."

"Don't be that way. I'm just saying, she's not as good at this as—"

"She's trying!" Robin tensed, glanced around at the bleary stares aimed her way, and then lowered her voice. "She's doing the best she can for us! It's *killing* her that the Witch is doing so poorly!"

"I know that!" Gerard repeated. "I'm just saying, *something* needs to change! She needs to hire on someone who knows how to run a place like this, or—I don't know, take lessons or something. But she can't just keep on doing what she's been—"

"We've got a customer," Robin interrupted, overtly relieved at the sound of the front door. "I've got to go. We'll discuss this later." *Much, much later.*

She spun away from Gerard's glower and plastered a smile once more across her face. "Good afternoon!" she chirped. "Welcome to the Flippant Witch, how can we . . ."

This, she couldn't help but observe, *was* not *exactly your standard tavern-goer.*

The newcomer was a tall man, young, probably about as much older than Widdershins as Widdershins was older than Robin. His onyx-black hair was tied back in an ornate braid, revealing the sharp, narrow features of a well-bred aristocrat. He wore a heavy traveler's coat and one of the brand-new tricorne hats (currently gaining in popularity in Galician high society, but not yet common in Davillon itself), but what snagged Robin's attention was the blade at his side: a long rapier with a brass bell guard, and what looked to be an honest-to-the-gods ruby in the pommel!

This was, without doubt, a man of means—and given how careless he was about *advertising* those means, he was either an idiot or unshakably confident in his ability to defend himself.

In that same corner of her mind, Robin casually noted that most girls her age would probably find the fellow irresistible.

". . . help you," she finished lamely, about eight or nine hours later.

The stranger smiled, a gleaming white expression that might or might not have been genuine; Robin, for all her experience reading people, couldn't begin to tell. "And a fine afternoon to you, mademoiselle. I'd very much like to speak to the owner, if I might."

Robin felt the hairs stand up on the back of her neck. Sure, the request *could* be legitimate—but given Widdershins's past, and the sorts of people she dealt with, the odds were stacked against it.

"I'm afraid the owner's not in just now," she said carefully. "If you wanted to leave me a message, I'd be happy to pass it along."

"Hmm. I'm not sure that would do at all, honestly. Any idea where I might find her? Or when she might be back?"

"I . . . don't think it's my place to share someone else's schedule, I'm afraid. You understand." She glanced around, and was gratified to see that Gerard had sidled over toward the bar—and the heavy cudgel they kept back there for emergencies. "I'm one of the managers here; are you sure there's nothing I can help you with?"

The man's grin slipped, just a hair. "No, you can't. I know the young woman who goes by the name 'Widdershins' owns this place; I've seen the prior owner's will, down at the Hall of Judgment. My business is with her, and no one else."

"I'm sure," Robin said, struggling to keep her voice steady, "that she'll be sorry she missed you."

Just that quickly, the nobleman's smile was back in place. "I'm certain she will. Ah, well. Tell her Evrard stopped by, would you? And that I'll call on her again later?"

"Evrard?" The name didn't mean anything to Robin. "And have you a family name?"

"I do," he said simply. And then he doffed his hat, offered a quick and courtly bow, and turned on his heel with military precision.

Robin watched the door that drifted shut behind him, and then slowly glanced toward Gerard. He could only shrug.

"Do you mind watching the place for a while?" Robin asked him.

The server cast an exaggerated look across the entirety of the common room. "I think I can probably handle the vast hordes for an hour or two, yes."

Robin was out the door before she even finished nodding her acknowledgment. Widdershins needed to know about Evrard; something about the man *really* worried Robin, and she could only hope Shins would have some idea of who he was. Thankfully, even if nothing else was going right that day, she had a pretty good idea of where to find the itinerant thief-turned-tavern-owner.

And she also had to admit, though she hated to do so, that Gerard had a point. Much as she loved Widdershins, they simply hadn't had these sorts of problems—or not often, anyway—when Genevieve was alive.

❁

"Hello, Genevieve."

Widdershins slowly lowered herself to sit cross-legged beside the ornate gravestone. Graven angels lined the marble monument, hunched as though supporting both the name inscribed across its surface and the cross of Banin that adorned its top.

Technically, Genevieve Marguilles had deserved a full-fledged mausoleum, with four walls, an ornate sarcophagus, and room inside for mourners. But the young woman had been estranged—very publicly—from Gurrerre Marguilles, her aristocratic father, and so the demands of propriety (and expense) for her final resting place were somewhat lighter than they otherwise might have been.

Widdershins, for her part, was just as happy this way. Here, she could sit close beside her best friend—and Genevieve herself, Shins liked to think, would have preferred it.

Now, at the tail end of spring, the grasses throughout the entire cemetery were healthy and thick, the trees draped in emerald, the many flowers bright and pungent. But around Genevieve's grave, those grasses were particularly lush. Roses, irises, and poppies intertwined around each other, forming a garland about the headstone and, in a few instances, creeping up the sides of the marble in intricate patterns. The aromas of those flowers, carried by a gentle breeze centered on this spot alone, somehow mixed into a perfect blend that reminded Widdershins overpoweringly of Genevieve herself.

She said nothing for a long moment, only offered a grateful, heartfelt smile through her falling tears. And Olgun, who knew the smile and the thanks were for him, and for the work he had done here, offered in return a single waft of comfort and support before withdrawing into the deepest corners of Widdershins's mind, so that she might be alone with her friend, and her thoughts.

Slowly, Widdershins removed a bottle of cheap wine from the sack she carried at her side. The sound of the popping cork was close enough to a pistol shot that, even though she herself had pulled it from the neck of the bottle, Widdershins couldn't help but jump. She poured a few mouthfuls into the soil beside the headstone, then took several deep gulps herself.

"It's not the best vintage," she apologized, "but I didn't think you'd approve of us sharing the good stuff without some reason to celebrate. And, well, I can't pretend that my being here is a special occasion, can I? You're probably sick to d—ah, sick of hearing from me by now. How many times have I been here in the last . . . ?" Widdershins ticked off days on her fingertips, and then, with a shrug, gave up on the whole notion and took another swig from the bottle. "I just wish I'd bothered to visit you as often when you were still . . ." Again she trailed off, this time with a moist sniff.

"Gen, I'm sorry!" The stone, the flowers, the entire cemetery were beginning to blur. "I'm trying to take care of your place, your people, I'm *really* trying! But I don't know what I'm doing; I don't know how to keep it going. You'd know; you'd know just how to deal with everything that's going on in this stupid city, but me? I was never any good at anything except . . . well, you know. I don't—I don't think you'd approve of me funding the Flippant Witch that way, and I've tried not to, but . . ."

Widdershins lay one palm flat against the marble, dropped her head, and sobbed as quietly as she could manage.

She ignored the distant sounds of footsteps on the cemetery's winding earthen paths. Mourners were constantly coming to visit this loved one or that, and here, if nowhere else in Davillon, everyone was respectful enough to leave everyone else alone. Already she'd noted, and dismissed, several strange faces—a few haughty and irritated, but some genuinely sympathetic—glanced her way during her crying jag.

This time, however, the steps didn't gradually pass beyond hearing. Instead, they grew nearer, ever nearer, and then . . .

"Shins?" The voice was soft, scarcely more than a breath.

Widdershins bolted upright, wiping her tears with the back of a hand as she came up on one knee and spun halfway around. "I—what? Robin?!"

"Shins, are you all right?" the younger girl asked.

"I—I'm fine."

Apparently, whatever she saw on Widdershins's face or heard in her voice pretty well put the lie to that. With a soft cry of her own, Robin darted forward and wrapped her friend in a frighteningly intense hug. (One might have called it a "bear hug," except that Robin could not possibly, in any stretch of metaphor, *ever* be compared to something that large. A "rabbit hug," maybe.)

For a second, perhaps two, Widdershins stiffened, as though she'd pull away—and then she collapsed, burying her face in the shorter girl's collar. "Robin, I miss her!"

"Shh . . . I know, Shins." They stood for long moments, Widdershins practically shaking in Robin's arms, Robin gently stroking her friend's hair. "I know . . ."

Finally, Widdershins straightened up once more and gently pulled away. Robin, after a moment's apparent hesitation, let her arms fall to her sides.

"But . . ." Shins said, blinking her now red-rimmed eyes. "Robin, what are you doing here?"

"Looking for you, actually. It wasn't hard to figure out where you were. You've been spending a lot of time here and with, uh, Alexandre."

Widdershins nodded. Alexandre Delacroix's grave was in a different cemetery—but both graveyards, reserved primarily for the aristocracy and their families, were fairly near one another.

"I've lost a lot of people, Robin," she said, slowly lowering herself to sit once more on the grass, gesturing for her friend to do the same. "But none of them ever hurt this much."

Robin said nothing to that, perhaps with the full understanding that there was nothing she could possibly say.

"So, all right," Widdershins continued some time later. "You were looking for me. I assume for some reason other than you just missed my sparkling wit and engrossing conversation, yes?"

Robin's lip twitched. "Well, those, too. But yes." In precise details—or what precise detail she could recall—she went on to describe the peculiar encounter at the Flippant Witch and the appearance of the man who had initiated it.

"Evrard?" was all Widdershins asked when all was said and done.

"That's what he told me."

"But . . . I don't think I *know* any Evrard!"

"Well, he certainly thinks he knows you, Shins."

"Great." Widdershins idly kneaded the grass between her fingers. "You know, I don't need this. If I was going to make a list of things I don't need, this would be right near the top."

Robin snickered. "You'd put something you didn't know about at the top of a list? How would you accomplish that, exactly?"

Widdershins stared haughtily down the bridge of her nose. "I," she announced, "have talents you cannot possibly imagine."

For reasons that Widdershins couldn't possibly fathom, Robin looked away, her face flushing ever so faintly.

"Um, right," the older of the pair continued, now more confused than ever. "If nothing else, I'd get Olgun to help me."

That, of course, wasn't really the right thing to say, either. Shins had tried, some months ago, to entice Robin into Olgun's worship. Robin had only grumbled something about Banin not protecting Genevieve, and that she'd little use for *any* deities, and refused to speak any more on the topic whenever Widdershins tried to bring it up.

It was, thankfully, Robin herself who provided the subject change for which Widdershins was so desperately casting about.

"Shins, I . . . Um . . . There's, ah, something else we probably ought to, you know, talk about. . . ."

A single dark-brown eyebrow rose at that. "Oh, boy. This sounds serious. You haven't been this nervous since you smashed that bottle of Scyllian red all over the kitchen floor."

"I told you, that wasn't my fault," Robin protested absently. "The label was slippery 'cause it'd been over-waxed, and—"

"Robin? It's all right. What did you want to say?"

"Well, it's just . . . Shins, the Flippant Witch isn't doing real well."

Widdershins's face went stiff. "I know that."

"I'm not blaming *you*!"

A few heartbeats more, and then, "It's all right, Robin." Widdershins's expression softened. "It *is* my fault."

"It's *not*. The city—"

"Genevieve would know how to roll with it. I'm trying my best, Robin. I am." Again she found herself clenching her fists in the grass, as though clutching for the woman who now lay beneath.

"I know you are, Shins," Robin told her. "It's just . . . Well, some of the guys don't seem as sure. Maybe if you were there a little more often . . . If they could *see* you working alongside them, you know? But you've . . . You haven't been around much recently."

Widdershins studied the base of the headstone. "I've been trying to save the tavern my own way," she whispered.

Robin blinked, as though unsure what her friend meant. And then, "Oh, Shins. I don't know if Gen would've wanted you to save the Witch like *that*."

"I don't either." Widdershins sniffed; she would *not* cry again, by gods! "But it's all I know how to do." She shrugged, then, smiling without much humor. "Or at least I used to. It's not as though last week went all that well."

"Last week?"

Her own face flushing now with embarrassment, Widdershins told Robin of the attempted robbery at the Ducarte estate some days earlier, and the fabulous mess that had resulted.

"Bouniard let you *go*?" Robin squeaked.

"What, you think I belong in gaol with the rest of the thieves?" Widdershins's smile was, she hoped, enough to take the sting from her words.

"No, it's just . . . That doesn't really sound like him, does it?"

"He's . . . been coming by the tavern, Robin."

"He has? I never saw . . ."

"Only occasionally, and only when I'm running a shift. It's like he knows. He always says he's just stopping by for a drink, but I think he's keeping an eye on me, yes? I thought, at first, he was hoping to catch me doing something illegal, but . . . I don't know, Robin. I've actually started looking forward to our conversations. They're—I don't know, a little awkward, but . . ."

The other girl, at this point, had tucked her knees up to her chest. "You can't trust him, Shins."

"I wouldn't have thought so, but after that . . . He protected me. I'm not sure what to think anymore."

Robin wrapped her arms around her knees, almost curling into a ball. "It's good that you have friends, I guess," she said dully.

"I don't know," Widdershins repeated, shaking her head. "Maybe he just didn't want to deal with me. I mean, he's smart enough to know that *I'm* not dangerous, so between the other thieves and whatever's been creeping around the streets at night, maybe he's got his hands full."

Robin, who—like everyone in Davillon—had heard plenty of gossip regarding the strange and seemingly supernatural encounters that had terrorized portions of the city over the past week, shuddered briefly. It had never much bothered her wandering around in the dark; she could take care of herself, or at least run very fast and hide in small spaces. But the idea of running from something that wasn't even *human* . . .

"Has anyone died?" Robin asked, her voice suddenly tiny.

"I don't think so. Not that I've heard. Just a lot of scared people, and a few injuries." Widdershins tossed her head, flipping a few stray strands of hair from her face. "I wouldn't worry too much, Robin. I'm positive that if it was *truly* dangerous, whatever it is, it would have been leaving bodies behind by now." It was Widdershins's turn to shudder, given that it was barely six months since she herself had faced just such a nightmarish creature.

"Anyway," she continued, rising smoothly, "I've got a meeting to get to."

"Oh?"

"About last week's fiasco."

"Oh." Robin, too, climbed to her feet—rather more awkwardly than her friend. "*That* sort of meeting."

"Yeah. Robin?"

"Yeah?"

"I'll take care of the Flippant Witch. And you. I promise."

"I know." The girl darted in, gave Widdershins a quick hug and a kiss on the cheek, and then was off and running. "See you later!" she called back over her shoulder.

Widdershins offered a goodbye wave, and then frowned. "What?"

Vague disapproval from some distant point in her mind.

"Don't think at me in that tone of voice, Olgun! I can *so* take care of the tavern! I just need one job to go right, and we're set! Well, for a while, anyway.

"Ooh, you're impossible! I won't *get* caught! I haven't yet, have I?"

Olgun reached directly into her mind, or so it felt, and hauled a memory of Julien Bouniard across her vision. Widdershins's face, which had just returned to its normal color, went red once more.

"*One* time," she muttered. "I won't count on it again. I won't *need* to count on it again! I'm better than that, I was just . . . out of practice. Oh, shut up!"

Still arguing with her god, Widdershins stalked from the cemetery and toward the poor, dilapidated district known as Ragway—and the headquarters of the Finders' Guild.

❁

Dusk crawled across the face of Davillon, dragging the heavier shroud of night slowly behind. And with it, too, came a gentle but pervasive spring drizzle—not even true rain, really, but simply a wetness in the air that transformed itself into drops at the slightest provocation, so that pedestrians grew far wetter than the roads on which they traveled. Some increased their pace, hoping to escape the sudden damp and chill; others welcomed any relief from the warmth of the day.

Not, it should be noted, that there *were* all that many pedestrians on the streets of Davillon after dusk. The tales and rumors of brazen assaults on citizens by apparently supernatural perpetrators, though only a week old, had matured into panic. (The fact that the tales grew with each telling, as such stories always do, only succeeded in heightening the fear even further.) The Guard added extra patrols in those neighborhoods where the peculiar phantasm had struck, but nobody (including, if one were to be brutally honest, the Guardsmen themselves) actually expected it to do any good. People were more than content to go about their business during the day, but as the skies darkened, the streets emptied with dramatic alacrity as citizens retired to their homes, or—in slowly but steadily growing numbers—to late masses at the Pact churches.

But then, there were those who scoffed at the danger, either refusing to believe the rumors or pointing out that the odds were pretty dramatically against any one specific person falling victim. There were those willing to take any risk, if it meant the success of this endeavor or that. And there were those whose livelihoods or objectives simply *required* that they brave the late hours.

Such was the case with Faustine Lebeau. The young woman—just a sliver older than Widdershins, though such a comparison would have meant nothing to her, as the two of them had never met—served as a messenger and courier for several of the city's wealthier merchants. As such, she was a common sight on the streets whenever she was required, day or night; long limbs pumping as she ran, her hair trailing behind her in a streamer of blonde so pale it was almost silver. Tonight, one particularly careless vendor had neglected to pay his supplier of fine textiles—for the third time this year—and had sent Faustine to deliver his last-minute apologies and to assure the good fellow that his fee would be forthcoming first thing in the morning.

A fairly mundane errand, all things considered, but one that kept Faustine out into the late hours of the evening. The walkways and alleys by which she passed slowly emptied, the sounds of footsteps faded into the distance, until she felt—no matter how much she told herself it wasn't true—that she was the only soul left in Davillon.

A moment later, as the soft laughter sounded from above, as some dark silhouette scuttled downward along the side of the nearest home, she *wished* she were.

She ran, then, ran as she never had while on a simple commission, her deep-blue skirts and formal blouse soaking up the not quite rain as efficiently as bath towels. She refused to slow even long enough to look behind, biting back a whimper and speeding up even further—though her legs began to ache and her side to burn—when she heard the chilling laughter still close to heel.

And then Faustine rounded a corner, and couldn't help but scream. The shape had somehow gotten *in front* of her, was now dropping from another wall to land before her in the street. Faustine fumbled for the dagger she kept in her skirts—she carried a small flintlock, too, but even had her hands not been shaking too violently to aim, the drizzle would assuredly have spoiled the powder—and raised it before her in a competent knife-fighter's grip.

The creature only laughed harder. With impossible speed, as though moving between heartbeats, it darted forward. Faustine got a glimpse of heavy black fabrics, covering the form from head to toe, before it lashed out at her wrist. A shock of pain traveled up her arm, and the dagger flew harmlessly from her numbed fingers.

Whether Faustine would have been injured and terrorized, as most victims of the peculiar apparition had been, or whether she would have been the first to suffer a more terminal fate is unclear, because neither occurred. Even as the dark-wrapped figure straightened an arm to strike, the scuff of a boot in the shadows snagged the attention of creature and courier both. Both craned their necks to look, and it was only the assailant's inhuman speed that allowed it to leap away from the path of a whistling blade.

Faustine couldn't make out much about her savior—not between the dark, the drizzle, and the rapid movement. She saw only a tall man in a dark coat, wielding an elegant rapier against the thing that had attacked her. His feet practically danced across the cobblestones, and his sword wove elaborate designs in the air. Faustine had seen more than her share of duels, and though it was difficult to tell when he faced such a peculiar opponent, if he wasn't easily one of the best swordsmen she'd ever seen, she'd *eat* the dagger she'd recently lost.

Still, he was human (or so he appeared, and so she assumed), and his adversary didn't seem to be. The man in the coat launched a series of rapid thrusts from a variety of surprising and sometimes nigh-impossible angles, and each time the silhouette shifted away at the last moment. Yet neither could the phantasm penetrate the woven web of sharpened steel long enough for even a single counterattack.

They settled swiftly, even instinctively, into a pattern that was nearly a dance, with each specific slash or thrust leading to a particular twist; each attempted riposte resulting in a specific parry. Step, step, cross-step, twist; thrust, slash, parry, lunge. Their feet on the cobbles provided a musical accompaniment, and the entire affair was borderline hypnotic.

And then, without so much as a flicker or a tremor to give himself away, the man in the coat broke that pattern. Rather than parry the dark figure's attempted grab, as he'd done half a dozen times now, he instead lunged forward on bended knee, dropping so low as to pass *beneath* the outstretched arm, and drove his blade home. Only the tip of the rapier, the first inch or so, penetrated whatever flesh lurked beneath the heavy black fabrics.

The result was a very human scream, immediately followed by the figure scampering off far faster than any normal person could have pursued. Something about the acoustics of the street and the heavy, rain-drenched air made it sound as though the shriek of pain echoed back at them from a different direction the same instant it erupted from the cloth-wrapped throat.

Faustine darted forward to stand beside her rescuer, who was currently examining the tip of his blade. Although it was already starting to run in the gentle rain, the liquid beading on the steel certainly *appeared*—so far as the feeble lighting allowed her to see it at all—to be normal, red blood.

Even as she opened her mouth to speak, however, the man shrugged and faced her. "Would you, m'lady, happen to have a cloth or a handkerchief you'd be willing to part with?"

Puzzled, she reached into her bodice and removed a scrap of linen. He bowed from the neck, then proceeded to clean his blade. "I can, of course, reimburse you for this . . . ," he began.

"Oh, don't you dare!" She smiled, even as she shouted. "I think I can afford the cost of a handkerchief for the man who saved my life."

He returned her smile, sheathed his rapier, and began casting around as though looking for something. "I'm just glad," he said, "that my own errands have kept me in this part of town. Otherwise, I'd never have been near enough to hear your cry."

Faustine shuddered briefly at the implication—and then knelt as something caught her attention. From the shadows where he'd first emerged, she lifted a sodden tricorne hat.

"Is this what you're looking for?" she asked.

He bowed once more. "Indeed it is. My thanks, m'lady . . . ?"

This time, there was no mistaking the question. "Faustine. Faustine Lebeau. And you, sir?"

"Evrard."

"And have you a family name?" she asked after a moment of silence.

His smile widened, and he chuckled softly, as if at some private joke—or, perhaps, a memory of earlier that day. "I do," he told her.

And just like that he was gone, vanished once more into the Davillon night.

CHAPTER FOUR

For several minutes—actually, rather longer than several minutes, if truth be told—Widdershins stood on the sad Ragway street and just glared at her destination. Her hands were clenched into pale fists, her hair plastered to the side of her face by the gentle but constant rain, and she really wanted nothing more than to turn around and go home.

"No, of course I'm not *going* to," she answered Olgun's concerned query. "They want me to talk to them, I talk to them. I'm not *that* stupid." And then, before even the god could possibly reply, "Shut up."

Olgun responded with wounded innocence—a feeling not *quite* capable of hiding his amused self-satisfaction—and allowed Widdershins to return to her brooding.

The building across from her was a decrepit, dirty eyesore of a structure. Ostensibly, it was home to a rundown business specializing in pawnbrokering, caravan insurance, and similar endeavors, and was always on the verge of shutting down. At this point, though, Widdershins wondered why they even bothered maintaining the front, since pretty much *everyone* in Davillon—or everyone involved in either the law-enforcement or law-breaking communities, anyway—knew what the place was *really* for.

She herself had only been back a few times in the last half year or so, partly because she hadn't been stealing much—she really *had* tried to run the Flippant Witch as Genevieve would have wanted her to, no matter how unsuccessful (and, to be blunt, *bored*) she was at it—but primarily because a rather disturbing number of her fellow guild members were pretty eager to see her dead.

It had been here, six months ago, that Widdershins had come in a last-ditch effort to escape the clutches of a demon (yes, a real one), and the religious fanatic who had summoned it. She'd succeeded in doing so, thwarting their schemes in the process, but the creature had slaughtered over a dozen members of the Finders' Guild before it fell. The Shrouded Lord, leader of the Finders, had decreed that Widdershins's actions had actually saved the city and the guild from something far worse, and the guild's priests had backed him. As such, Widdershins's standing in the Finders' Guild was *officially* just fine, and she should be perfectly safe. Unofficially, not everyone in the ranks was so forgiving.

"Well, fine!" she announced abruptly, startling not only Olgun, but a small mockingbird that had landed for a brief rest on a windowsill nearby. "I'm *supposed* to be here, yes? So if they want trouble, well, they're welcome to it!"

As announcements go, it probably wasn't the most reassuring she could have made, seeing as how she could literally feel the sudden doubt radiating from her divine companion. But by that point, having made up her mind, she was already marching across the street. Chin held high, she pounded heavily on the door.

"Appointment with the taskmaster," she announced as a concealed panel in the door slid aside, allowing the sentry within to get a good look at her.

"Hey!" She didn't recognize the voice, but then, it wasn't as though she could possibly know *everyone* in the guild. "Aren't you the one who—?"

"Yes! Yes, I am. And I don't want to hear it. I'm sorry about whatever happened to you, or at you, or near you, but it wasn't my fault. The Shrouded Lord said so and the priests said so, so *get over it*!" By the end of the brief but heartfelt tirade, she was actually panting.

"I . . . Uh . . . I was just gonna say, you have serious guts coming here. I don't know if I could do it if I were you, even if I *was* summoned. I'm impressed."

"Oh." Widdershins felt her face grow warm even in the chilling rain. *What was that, three times today someone's made me blush? What in the name of Banin's overcoat is* wrong *with me?!* The fact that she could feel Olgun laughing at her certainly wasn't helping matters any. "Uh, thank you?"

"You're welcome."

Silence, save for the faint patter of the rain. Then, "Um, can I come in now?"

"Oh, sure." A loud clatter as several bolts drew back, a single, louder thump as the bar (a relatively new addition) was removed, and the heavy portal swung inward.

The hall beyond was largely as she remembered it, save for certain portions of the walls that had been more recently repainted—hiding bloodstains, for the most part. The door guard, a young man with a scraggly beard and so many acne scars that he looked as though he'd been shot with a miniature blunderbuss, might not have held any animosity toward Widdershins, but the same couldn't be said for a number of the others. As she made her way through the winding, twisting hallways beneath the pawnbroker's—the halls that were the true headquarters of the Finders' Guild—she couldn't help but note that one of every three or four faces went sour at her approach. A few frowned unhappily, but most of them twisted in angry scowls, baring teeth or mouthing profanity-laden threats. A few hands even dropped toward daggers or flintlocks, but invariably the fact that the Shrouded Lord had forbidden any retaliation was sufficient to prevent the potential violence from turning into *actual* violence.

Widdershins, for her own part, marched through the halls as though she were thinking of buying the place (but found it too drab and distasteful to seriously consider), ignored Olgun's worried chatter as best she could, and struggled not to quiver or look over her shoulder every time she turned her back on the angriest of those hostile faces. She briefly considered trying to find her old mentor

Renard, if only for the comfort of a friendly face down here, but she decided, reluctantly, that she couldn't really spare the time such a hunt might require.

Ostensibly, she *should* make a point of stopping by the shrine before proceeding to her appointment. The Shrouded God—patron of the Finders' Guild, member of the Hallowed Pact, and the inspiration for the Shrouded Lord's own title—was not a demanding deity, but the guild still had customs and rituals its members were supposed to follow. The idol itself—mostly stone but with a hood of thick fabric hiding its features, because anyone other than the priests or the Shrouded Lord who looked upon that face was subject to an awful curse—stood in a thick-walled, carpeted chamber at the very heart of the guild's labyrinthine headquarters. Convenient to most of the organization's offices, it would have been a matter of minutes for Widdershins to swing by and offer a few prayers; and Olgun, since he knew full well that she didn't mean a word of them, certainly wouldn't have objected.

Widdershins, however, went nowhere near the heavy metal doors providing ingress to that shrine; shuddered, in fact, when she passed them by, and smelled the faint traces of incense from beyond. Lots of memories lurked within the shadows there, and not a one of them pleasant.

Instead, she moved straight for a door in one of the passages adjacent to said shrine. The wood had scarcely ceased vibrating from her first knock when a voice called, "Get the fuck in here!"

"Well," she said to Olgun as she pushed the door open, "at least he's in a good mood, yes?"

Laremy Privott—or "Remy" to most Finders—had been taskmaster (that is, lieutenant to the Shrouded Lord) since the dismissal of Lisette Suvagne late the previous year. Imposingly tall and broad-shouldered, bald as a stressed tortoise from the neck up but hairy as a northman everywhere else, he looked very much like someone had simply shaved an ape's head. (Though this was not, it should be noted, a comparison that anyone actually made aloud when Remy himself was in the room.)

Today he was clad in heavy trousers, which helped to minimize said simian comparisons, and a white tunic, which *might* have done so if individual hairs hadn't been protruding through holes in the weave.

He also, Widdershins couldn't help but note, wasn't alone in the chamber.

"Taskmaster," she greeted him with a bob of her head. And then, turning to his other guest, "Hey, Squirrel. How's the jaw?"

"Go to hell, bitch."

"Hey!" Remy snarled across his desk—a massive, antique monstrosity that was clearly too nice for the otherwise frugal office and had most probably been stolen from somewhere fancy. "None of that! Both of you, sit!"

They sat. The office contained four rickety chairs (not counting Remy's own); perhaps unsurprisingly, Widdershins and Simon took the ones on the edges, leaving two empty seats between them.

"Good. Now, we're gonna have a couple of words about your little disaster at Rittier's manor last week."

"She ruined—!" Simon began, simultaneous with Widdershins's own, "If that idiot—"

"*Shut up!*"

They shut.

"Widdershins, you haven't worked a lot of jobs since the Shrouded Lord promoted me, so maybe you've forgotten, but we're a *guild*, not a gods-damned social club! That means that if you're hitting a big target —such as, just for instance, anything likely to attract other Finders besides yourself—you *coordinate*! You keep us the hell informed!"

"But I—"

"*That wasn't a question!*"

"Got it," she grumbled.

"And you!" Remy continued, swiveling to face his other victim.

"Wipe that fucking smile off your face before I *carve* it off you! You're a bigger fool than she is!"

"But—"

"What the *hell* were you thinking, you diseased jackass? You bring an entire crew with you? Try to rob a noble estate at knife-point? To take *hostages*?!"

"Finders rob lots of people," he protested.

"Not the *aristocracy*, gods damn it! You want to steal something from one of the blue bloods, you do it *quietly*! You *trying* to bring the whole fucking Guard down on us?!"

"What are *they* going to do? They've known where we are for years, and they haven't . . . they . . ." Simon trailed off, looking as twitchy as the rodent for which he was named, as Remy slowly rose and leaned over the desk.

"I," he said, his voice abruptly calm, "am *this* close to wringing out your brain and using it as a sponge. At which point, I should point out, it will probably become *more* useful than it is right now. Are you hearing me?"

Squirrel nodded. Widdershins, deciding that safe was *definitely* better, at the moment, than sorry, nodded too. Just in case.

"If you'd killed any of the nobles," Remy continued, "we'd probably have handed you over to the Guard ourselves. We *sure* as hell wouldn't even be considering paying bail for your idiot friends."

Squirrel's eyes brightened, perhaps reflecting the escape route he suddenly saw for himself. "Nobody would've been caught at all if it wasn't for *her,*" he spat, pointing. (As if there were any other "her" in the room to whom he could have been referring.)

"Oh? And how's that?"

"She *helped* them, Remy! Helped the damn Guardsmen grab some of my boys!"

"That so?" he growled, turning once more.

Widdershins sat straight in the chair, refusing to cringe or even so much as frown. "Not initially. I actually got involved, even after

Squirrel and his nuts messed everything up, to *keep* them from getting arrested."

"Oh, horseshit!" Squirrel began. "You're such a—"

"Have some of your people ask around about a gaggle of Guardsmen getting a banner dropped on their heads if you don't believe me," she said to Remy.

"I may do that. But even if it's true, you said 'initially.' That sounds to me like an admission that you *did* eventually throw some of our people to the Guard."

Squirrel grinned a tight, evil little grin.

"Well, yeah," Shins said casually. She actually crossed one leg over the other knee and began examining the nails on her right hand. "I mean, given how peeved you are about those idiots threatening a few aristocrats and servants, I can just *imagine* how irked you'd have been if—"

"She's lying!" Simon screamed, rising to his feet.

"—they'd actually succeeded in—"

"Shut *up*, you bitch!"

"—deliberately murdering officers of the Guard."

Simon looked about ready to hurl himself across the room at her, but Remy's abrupt stare effectively pinned him to the floor where he stood.

"They . . ." He swallowed once, then tried again to answer the taskmaster's unasked question. "They were disguised as servants! How could we have known?"

"The first ones were disguised as servants, Squirrel," Widdershins helpfully reminded him. "The ones that you actually tried to stab were in full uniform, though."

"That so?" Remy asked again.

"No!" Squirrel insisted.

Widdershins shrugged. "As I said, I know you have sources in the Guard. Ask around. We'll be happy to wait." She smiled sweetly at Simon. "Won't we?"

Simon might have had a response to that—probably not, though—but either way, it didn't matter. The door opened without so much as a knock, and Remy was immediately on his feet, Widdershins close behind.

There was, after all, only one man in the guild who'd dare to barge in on the taskmaster *without* knocking.

Framed in the doorway, illuminated by the flickering lantern light, stood the Shrouded Lord, unquestioned master of the Finders' Guild. His garb consisted entirely of charcoal-hued fabrics hanging in heavy folds, topped by a full-face hood not dissimilar to that worn by the nearby idol. The result was to make him look vaguely phantasmal (and, in fact, not *too* different from the mysterious figure stalking Davillon's streets, though he had no way of knowing about that unfortunate coincidence). It was a much more successful effect in his own audience chamber, which was kept full of a scented smoke whose color matched the fabrics, but even here it proved impressive enough.

Nor was he alone. Just behind and to the left loomed a tall, severe-looking, hatchet-faced woman of middle years. Her dark skin, her darker hair, and her eyes—piercing and black—contrasted sharply with her cassock of formal whites and grays. Widdershins had had only a few sporadic dealings with the woman, but she recognized her well enough. This was Igraine Vernadoe, the high priestess of the Shrouded God and the clergy of the Finders' Guild.

"Sit," the Shrouded Lord ordered, gliding into the room, the priestess at his heels. His voice was rough, gravelly, and blatantly artificial. None, save the priests themselves, ever knew which member of the Finders' Guild wore the hood of the Shrouded Lord; but of course, the hood did nothing to alter his voice. That, then, was entirely up to him. Widdershins had long wondered just how badly the fellow's throat must hurt at the end of any given day. "What, pray tell," he continued when everyone had done as he ordered, "is all the shouting about? We heard you from down the hall."

Remy glowered one last time at Squirrel, who had the courtesy to cringe, and then repeated the entire exchange to the Shrouded Lord.

"I was," the taskmaster concluded, "just about to start discussing punishments when you arrived, my lord."

The hood rumpled forward in a nod, and then turned toward the priestess—who looked neither at Remy nor Simon, but had kept her attention locked on Widdershins from the moment she entered the room.

Widdershins was trying to return that look confidently without crossing the line into "challenging," and was having a tough time of it. No other priests or worshippers in Davillon—in the *world*, so far as she knew—had the same connection with their deities as Widdershins had with Olgun. But she knew that many priests had *some* abilities that bordered on the mystical, including a surprising degree of insight. As such, she was never sure exactly what Igraine, or the other guild priests, actually knew, sensed, or suspected about her and Olgun. It made her nervous; it made Olgun nervous; and they, in turn, fretted enough to make each other even *more* nervous.

"I think," the Shrouded Lord said slowly, "that Monsieur Beaupre has begun to get some inkling of how displeased we are with his actions, and could use some time to ruminate on that." He slowly faced Simon, who had grown pale enough that even a professional undertaker might have mistaken him for a client. "Couldn't you?"

"Ah . . . yes, my lord."

"Good. Go. We will discuss your punishment another time. Do be prepared to explain what you've learned from this, hmm? It may have some bearing on the severity of your penance."

Simon rose, bowed—no mean feat, given that he was trembling at the time—and made for the door, edging around the room so as not to get too near the Shrouded Lord in the process.

"Well," Widdershins said, standing up as the door clicked shut behind the fleeing Squirrel, "I guess I should be on my way, too. Taskmaster, thank you for—"

"Sit. Down."

"Wow." Widdershins sat. "Did the three of you practice that? Because, I mean, that was pretty much *perfectly* coordinated. I—"

"You should probably stop talking now," Remy warned her.

"Now?" she said. "Probably a while ago, I'd think."

Despite what appeared to be his best efforts to thwart them, the corners of the taskmaster's mouth curled upward in a faint smile.

"We were planning," the Shrouded Lord said, leaning back against the wall and crossing his arms so that the hanging fabrics draped in layers over his chest, "to call you in anyway, Widdershins. So it's just as well the taskmaster summoned you."

Widdershins bristled at the word "summoned," but she managed (possibly with Olgun's help) to avoid blurting out something *really* stupid.

"We would, in fact, appreciate your assistance," the guildmaster continued. "We—"

"My lord?" They all turned to the priestess, who was perhaps the only Finder in the city who would dare to interrupt him. (Or the only one who would dare and could reasonably expect to suffer no serious consequences.)

It was impossible, beneath the Shrouded Lord's hood, to see even a hint of facial features, but Widdershins was absolutely certain she could sense a raised eyebrow. "Yes?" he asked Igraine. It was long, drawn out; more of a *yyyeeeeessss?*

"I wish to protest this, *again*. I don't believe she can be trusted."

"Hey!" Widdershins snapped. "Standing right here, you know!"

Igraine ignored her. "I'd be far more comfortable if—"

It was, this time, the Shrouded Lord who interrupted *her*. "Yes, so you were making clear before Monsieur Beaupre's outburst distracted us. And as I believe *I* was making clear, I understand your concerns, but I do not share them."

"My lord, my counsel is one of the reasons—"

"That'll do, Igraine."

The priestess nodded, then directed her sharp, scarcely blinking gaze at the young woman in question.

A young woman who, frankly, had lost her patience some time ago.

"What *is* it," she demanded of the room at large, "with me and the powerful women in this guild? First Lisette, now you? What'd I do to ruffle *your* holy feathers?"

Remy coughed into his hand, presumably since laughing outright wouldn't have been politic.

Even Igraine smiled shallowly at the comment. "I've nothing against you personally, Widdershins."

"Then what—?"

"I do not understand precisely what happened here last year. I don't know why you had such an unholy creature pursuing you. And I have yet to determine what it is, but there's something *wrong* about you. An . . . aura, if you will. A power that I find distasteful, and possibly contrary to the will of the Shrouded God."

Well, Widdershins groused mentally, *I guess that answers my question about how much of Olgun she can sense.*

"I distrust what I don't understand," the priestess continued, "and I dislike what I don't trust. So unless you'd care to explain . . . ?"

"I," Widdershins announced firmly, "have no idea what you're talking about."

"Of course you don't."

"Are you quite through?" asked the Shrouded Lord.

"I am," Widdershins told him. "I can't speak for Her Eminence."

"That's a term of address for an archbishop," Igraine corrected her with a sniff. "Not a priestess."

"Oh, I'm sorry. Her Insignificance, then."

The taskmaster's coughing fit grew worse.

"Let me rephrase," the Shrouded Lord said. "You two *are* quite through."

"Yes, my lord."

"All right."

"Laremy," the guildmaster continued, "you may wish to have that cough looked at."

"Uh, yes, my lord."

"Good. Now—"

"Uh . . . Excuse me? Um, my lord?"

The Shrouded Lord's shoulders deflated. "Yes, Widdershins?"

"Um . . ." She was chewing on the ends of her hair—and when exactly had *that* become a habit?!—her face suddenly serious. "What *about* Lisette? Any . . . uh, any news?"

Lisette Suvagne—Laremy's predecessor as taskmaster—had been Widdershins's avowed enemy ever since the younger thief had stolen the ancestral treasures from the d'Arras family tower, a job that Suvagne herself had been planning for months. The former taskmaster had made multiple attempts at destroying Widdershins, until she'd finally gone a step too far and been removed from her post for disobeying the Shrouded Lord's direct orders. She'd utterly vanished not long afterward, even from the far-reaching attentions of the Finders' Guild.

"No," he said simply. "Nothing."

"Oh."

"*As* I was saying," he continued, a touch of impatience creeping into his rasping voice, "we have a bit of a conundrum on our hands, and we—that is, *some* of us—felt that you would be an appropriate choice to help us out."

"I would? What'd I do *this* time?"

"Nothing. Other than come dangerously near to annoying your boss."

"Maybe I'll be quiet and let you finish," Widdershins murmured.

"Maybe, but I have my doubts."

Silence, then—perhaps deliberately to prove the Shrouded Lord wrong.

Eventually, he continued, "While I do not share my priestess's distrust of you, she's not wrong in her facts. You were *heavily* involved in a number of mysterious and even supernatural events last year. The demon that pursued you through our halls; the death of its summoner; even the murder of Archbishop William de Laurent, as well as several of your friends."

Widdershins looked to the floor; six months later, the wounds remained fresh.

"To say nothing of whatever power it is that Igraine senses around you. We've all heard tell of your astonishing good luck, enough to know that *someone*—or some*thing*—watches over you."

"Well, I—"

"So, what do you know of the phantom that's been attacking Davillon's citizens over the past week or so?"

Widdershins's jaw clacked audibly shut. She wasn't sure what she'd been expecting, but that was *not* it. "Know? Nothing. I mean, I've heard the rumors, same as anyone, but . . ." She shrugged. "I didn't really think it even involved us."

Igraine made a sound that, had it been any louder, would have been a scoff. "A figure wandering the streets in the dark, attacking citizens, at a time when everyone—even the Finders' Guild—is struggling to make ends meet? And you didn't think this might concern us?"

"Uh, maybe I didn't think it through?"

"Maybe you didn't."

"If this is a mortal," the Shrouded Lord said, "he is acting outside the purview of the guild. If it's supernatural, it will make our own efforts that much more difficult, as patrols increase and travelers *de*crease. In either case, it's likely to bring suspicion down on our own heads, as the Guard casts about for answers—or, if they get desperate enough, a scapegoat." He paused, scratching at his chin through the heavy fabric. "Are you certain this couldn't be the same sort of demon that came after you?"

Widdershins shuddered, but shook her head. "I don't see how. All the rumors I've heard said the thing looked more or less human-shaped, and my demon sure wasn't. And I don't think it would've left *anyone* alive, let alone *everyone*, you know?"

"Fair enough. Well, you may be no expert in the occult, Widdershins, but you've more experience than most of my people. I would appreciate it if you would see what else you can learn about this thing."

"What? Me? I—"

"I'm not asking you to devote your every moment to investigating it. Just keep an ear out, see what you can discover. Consider it," he added, "penance for your own part in the screwup at Rittier's estate, so that Laremy need not assign any additional punishment."

Widdershins grumbled something that the others pretended not to hear, and nodded curtly.

"Good, you may go."

"Oh, *may* I?" Then, realizing that she was probably on the verge of pushing things just a hair too far, Widdershins nodded a second time and made a beeline for the door as fast as courtesy permitted.

Maybe faster.

❁

The hallways of the Finders' Guild didn't provide a great many hiding places. Or rather, those near the outside did, for purposes of defense, but the passages toward the center—such as, for instance, around the office of the taskmaster—were fairly straightforward and unadorned. The torches cast a few pockets of shadow, and some of the doorways provided narrow niches, but it would take a true expert to use such feeble cover for any sort of effective concealment.

Then again, these were thieves, so such expertise wasn't all that hard to come by.

The door opened and Widdershins flounced out, muttering under her breath as she vanished down the long hall. The Shrouded Lord and Igraine Vernadoe emerged a moment later, heading in the other direction. The door closed once more behind them, leaving Laremy Privott alone with whatever thoughts or duties now occupied him.

Lanterns burned. The smoke in the hall grew thick and then faded, puffed away by the random currents making the rounds of the labyrinth. And Simon Beaupre, called Squirrel, emerged from a pocket of shadow not far from the taskmaster's door.

A most interesting conversation, that had been. Time to gather the boys together; if they could learn more about this supernatural creature stalking the streets, that would surely be enough for Squirrel to earn his way back into favor, to avoid whatever unnecessary punishments they were concocting for what was *clearly* a simple misunderstanding.

And just maybe, if the gods smiled and he played the game just exactly right, he might also learn what peculiar secret the enigmatic Widdershins was hiding from her fellow Finders.

Mind afire with plans and possibilities, Squirrel, too, made his way down the many halls and back out onto the rain-slick streets of Davillon. It shouldn't, he was certain, prove all that difficult an undertaking. After all, this strange assailant had been active for over a week, striking almost nightly, and it hadn't killed a soul. How dangerous could it actually be?

❋

Constable Carville raised a hand in salute as Paschal Sorelle, his arm wrapped in a sling, approached the post. Sorelle himself nodded his reply. "Report?"

Carville straightened up and firmly announced that absolutely nothing of any importance had happened. It was a waste of time, and they both knew it, but procedure was procedure.

It was a cushy assignment they'd been given, a chance to relax after a job well done—and, in Sorelle's case, a chance to recover from his injury—though it would have been far more pleasant without the rain. Tradition and law demanded that several of the Guard stand outside the walls of Davillon every night, watching for invaders, smugglers, or other illicit activity, as well as for messengers or other travelers whose purposes were so urgent that they could not wait for the main gates to reopen at dawn. In theory, it was a solid idea and an important duty. In practice, it amounted to several hours of standing around doing absolutely nothing. In the dark. In times past, there might have been a few late travelers to break the monotony, but with Davillon currently suffering the Church's displeasure, travelers of *any* sort, nocturnal or otherwise, were rare.

Carville had been a part of the operation at the Ducarte estate; had, in fact, been one of the Guardsmen dressed as servants, and had been right in the middle of the group on whom Widdershins had dropped the banner. His hair and complexion were both darker than Paschal's—the former by quite a great deal, the latter only slightly—but otherwise they looked identical enough, especially as both wore the black and silver of the Guard.

"So in other words," Paschal said as Carville finished up his non-report, "you're bored as a blue blood without a mirror."

The other snorted, nodding. It wasn't a crack either would have made had Bouniard been present, but as soldiers of the same rank—even if Paschal technically had seniority by a year or so—they could justify a certain breach of decorum.

"All right, Constable," Paschal said. "You know the drill. Whistle if you need anything." And with that he was off, continuing to walk the rounds of the wall so that he might check in with the other nighttime posts under his command. Carville saluted a second time, held the pose until Paschal was gone, and then resumed slouching against the monolithic blocks of the city wall, trying not to wince as the cold drizzle occasionally dribbled off his hat and down the back of his neck.

When the figure first appeared, some cold and soggy minutes later, he wasn't even certain he was really seeing it. It looked, initially, to be nothing more than a denser spot amidst the drops, perhaps whipped up by an errant gust of wind. Only as it neared did it resolve itself into a human form, disturbingly long of limb and even more disturbing in how it moved. Shoulders shifted in an exaggerated gait; legs skimmed, rather than stepped, across the surface of the muddy road. It was less a walk than a ballet; less a ballet than a macabre glide. The traveler's forward movement seemed independent of those peculiar steps.

Even as it—he?—drew closer, Carville could make out few details, save for a ragged coat and a wide-brimmed hat that sagged sadly in the rain.

That and, peculiarly, the scent of peppermint, wafting clearly on the wet breeze.

"Who . . ." Carville stopped, clearing his throat even as he dropped one hand to the butt of his rapier. Gods, but the fellow's bizarre pace must have unnerved him more than he'd realized. "Who goes there?" he tried again, his voice steadier.

The figure halted, oh so briefly, and then twisted toward Carville. He stood several yards nearer, without having taken a single intervening step. The Guardsman could swear, absolutely *swear*, that somewhere in the distance he could now hear the faint giggling of children.

"Just a lonely traveler, sir." The voice . . . It must be the weather and the wind, doing something strange, something awful, to that voice. "A traveler, come to seek his fortune." It sounded very much as though there were two throats—one a grown man, one a young child—speaking in perfect unison. In some syllables Carville heard both, in some only one or the other, but never was there the slightest lack of clarity in the words.

"You, ah . . . You've business in Davillon, then?"

"Oh, yes, yes, indeed! Lots and lots and *lots* and lots of . . . business." And the figure giggled, then—or was it once again those faint voices from so far away? Carville wasn't sure, seemed to be having some difficulty focusing on his duties.

"I . . . You'll have to wait until morning, I'm afraid. And you really ought to go around to the main gate . . ."

"Oh, but I *so* hate waiting!" The figure actually stamped a foot, sending a small deluge of mud and water spraying across Carville's boots.

(*Boots? My boots? Gods, when did he get that close?! I should . . . I . . .*)

"I don't think I want to wait!" The stranger was *singing* now. "I don't think I want to wait, I don't think I need a gate!"

One more step, just one, and he loomed over Carville, less than an arm's-length distant. And the Guardsman, finally, could see beneath the flopping brim.

"Oh, gods. Oh, gods, I *know* you!"

"Everybody knows me." The grin beneath the hat grew wide, an ugly slash of gleaming white in the heavily shadowed face. "Or at least, they *will*."

A lunge, faster than a blink, and the traveler's lips latched onto Carville's own, grabbing with what felt like a thousand tiny hooks. And Carville—*dwindled.*

Skin shriveled against muscles that in turn flattened against bone. Eyes crumpled into little balls, yellowing and crinkling into age-old parchment. Hair and fingernails grew brittle, then fell from their perch, no longer held fast to drying flesh.

The stranger leaned back, allowing the now-desiccated lump of leather that had been Constable Carville to fall, with a dull plop, to the mud. And in the distance, the chorus of children that did not—could not—exist, sighed aloud in joyful satisfaction.

Gliding over the already-forgotten body, the traveler reached the walls of Davillon. Slowly, he extended his hands, hands possessed of inhumanly, impossibly long digits that twitched and flexed like the legs of some horrid spider. Narrow fingertips pressed against the stone and then—his body held rigidly straight, never touching the wall save with those gruesome, scuttling fingers—the newcomer began to climb.

Davillon had called to him, however unknowingly. And he was *so* looking forward to answering.

CHAPTER FIVE

". . . Ulvanorre, who stands upon the highest structures and the highest peaks; Demas, who watches over us, who interposes himself between his people and harm; and, Vercoule, who among all the gods, has chosen this, Davillon, as his favored city. To all these, and more, we offer our gratitude, and our devotion, and our most humble prayers."

A ripple of sighs and similar exhalations washed through the assembly; a sign of piety from some, yes, but of relieved impatience from more than a few others. The bishop had not, in fact, named in his litany all 147 gods of the Hallowed Pact—had included barely a quarter of them, actually—but it certainly *felt* to some of the congregants as though the recitation had gone on interminably.

It would be inaccurate to say that the cathedral was "packed," precisely, but it was certainly far more crowded than at any other time in the past two seasons. More of the pews were occupied than empty. The multihued light of the stained glass gleamed across more than a hundred faces, and the vast chamber sweltered, as though the height of summer had already arrived, due to the warmth of so many assembled bodies.

Standing atop a raised dais before the throng, clad in purest white, Ancel Sicard lowered his hands, which had slowly risen in supplication and emphasis as he listed those deities most important to the city that now fell under his purview. "My friends," he said, his voice a little softer than it had been, "I know that these have been trying times. I know that many of you are frightened of the affliction that has so recently beset Davillon." His stare flitted across the assembly, seeming to settle on each and every individual, one by one. "Fear is only natural, in light of what we must face. Only human.

"But consider, my children. It has been nine nights and ten

days, now, since this phantom, this demon, this fiend, descended upon our streets. In that time, how many of our brothers and sisters in Davillon have been attacked? Perhaps fifteen, sixteen? True, that is fifteen or sixteen more than there should be, but in a city so huge as this one? And of those, how many have been slain, or even crippled? *None*, my friends. Surely, a supernatural, unholy entity such as the one we are clearly facing should—nay, *must*—be capable of spreading carnage far more widely, and far more severely, than we have seen. Can this truly mean anything, *anything*, other than—despite the foibles of mere mortals that have caused the unfortunate rift between our father city and our Mother Church—that the gods of the Hallowed Pact still watch over us all? That they protect us, no matter our sins and our mistakes? Dare we, then, continue to avert our faces from our sacred guardians? No! We must renew our faith, renew our veneration, lest we—all of us, laymen and clergy alike—anger them sufficiently that they withdraw their protecting hand."

Quite a few grumbles and murmurs of disagreement and discontent sounded in the audience—Davillon's bitterness at the clergy's efforts to isolate and punish the city for the death of William de Laurent, having built up over six months, was hardly about to vanish in a week and a half—but said sounds were vastly outnumbered by the nods and sighs of agreement. There could be no doubt at all that the people of the city were afraid, or that the hopeful words of Sicard and Davillon's other priests offered a respite, if only temporary, from that fear. Since the unnatural attacks had begun, attendance at masses and other services across the city had increased several times over, and if the congregations didn't rival their previous sizes, they were far closer than they'd been in ages.

Among those in the audience who were far from convinced was a young noblewoman in an emerald gown, her natural hair hidden beneath a piled and coifed wig of golden blonde. As Sicard continued his sermon—his tirade?—she could only tap her foot and absently wish that she had a lock of hair loose enough to chew on.

"What do you think?" Madeleine Valois (for that's who she was at the moment) asked in a voice so far under her breath that even those seated to either side couldn't hear her.

But then, she hadn't been speaking to them.

Olgun replied with the emotional offspring of a shrug and a scoff.

"Yeah, that's kind of what I thought, too," she agreed. "I guess we shouldn't . . ." She shook her head, making the top-heavy wig wave and bobble. "I wish William were here."

She smiled sadly at Olgun's sorrowful agreement. And then, her decision made, there was nothing left to do but wait courteously for the sermon to end, so that she might depart with the rest of the crowd.

❋

As the congregation slowly dispersed, Sicard smiled and nodded beatifically from the dais, blessing all who had come and all who now ventured forth into the world. All the while, he scanned the crowd, attempting to match sight to the peculiar, not quite natural presence he had detected, something that didn't quite match up with any of the five senses normally available to mortals. It was a quiver in the air, something there and yet . . . not. Something wrong, or at least abnormal, and now was *not* the time for abnormalities. Not with so much at stake.

So where . . . ? *Ah.*

Maintaining his smile and scarcely moving his jaw, precisely as though he murmured prayers over the heads of the departing, the bishop called out for the man behind him.

Brother Ferrand appeared from his inconspicuous post, where he'd waited throughout the mass to provide anything Sicard might have required. "Yes, Your Eminence?"

"Do you see that young woman there? No, to the left. Green

gown, blonde wig? Sort of in the center of the crowd by the far door?"

Finally, after several moments of this—and only shortly before the woman in question would have been through the door and out of sight—the monk bobbed his tonsured head. "Yes, I see her. What of her?"

"Do you know who she is?" the bishop asked.

"I can't say that I do, Your Eminence. Is she important?"

"I'm . . . not entirely certain. There's something about her. A presence, an aura . . . I'm not sure how to describe it. It's not quite what I feel in the presence of omens or other blessings of the gods, nor"—and here he lowered his voice so that Ferrand could only just hear, and *certainly* nobody else could—"does it feel at all similar to other magics with which I'm familiar."

"You think her a witch, then?"

"I don't know what I think, Ferrand—except that I think the timing on this is suspect, and that I need to know what it is I *don't* know. You understand me?"

"I do. I'll learn who she is, Your Eminence, and all I can about her."

"You do that, Brother Ferrand. Discreetly, of course—but do be certain to learn *everything*."

The bishop returned his full attentions, then, to the retreating backs of his congregants, while his assistant slipped from the back of the dais and vanished into the streets of Davillon.

❁

By the time she'd returned to the Flippant Witch, the afternoon had concluded its metamorphosis into early evening, and Madeleine Valois had completed *her* metamorphosis back into Widdershins. (Although the former was brazen enough to make such a transformation in public view of everyone, the latter had required a modicum of privacy in the back of an abandoned leather goods shop.) She wasn't decked out for robbing anyone—she wore a workable peasant's tunic, dark hose, and worn boots, rather than her "stealing leathers"—but the gown and the wig were most assuredly gone, with no trace that they'd ever existed. As always, the only item on her of any apparent value was the basket-hilt rapier that hung at her waist, originally stolen from, and then gifted to her by, the late and very much lamented Alexandre Delacroix.

Widdershins blew through the front door of the tavern, absently returning the occasional wave or shouted greeting from regulars who recognized her. As twilight hadn't fallen, and many workmen and vendors remained at their jobs so long as light remained in the sky, the place wasn't as crowded as it would become in a few more hours. Not that any evening's attendance qualified as "crowded" these days, but Widdershins had enough presence of mind to hope that business would pick up a *little* bit when the sun went down.

Her nose barely wrinkling against the aroma that had become as familiar to her as her own, Widdershins examined the servers and guests until . . .

"Hey, Robin!"

The slender girl looked up from mopping a glistening spill beside the bar. Widdershins frowned for a second at the startled-deer expression, then decided that Robin was probably just worried, as she had been so much recently, about the tavern's financial woes. "So I just attended one of His Emminencialness's sermons," she began, taking the mop from Robin's hands and getting to work on the spill herself (more from a desire to have something to do than any real need to be helpful). "I'd been hoping—"

"Shins . . ."

Whether Widdershins didn't hear or just didn't listen, she bulled ahead as though Robin hadn't spoken. "—that he might be worth approaching as an ally. Might be like William was, you know? Churchmen are supposed to know all about this supernatural stuff, yes? Maybe—"

"Shins?"

"—even tell him about Olgun, at the *least* ask if he has any idea what the bugaboo wandering Davillon's streets might be. Stupid Guild assignment. Oh, *I'm* their big monster expert just because—"

"Shins!"

"—a demon tried to kill me once. Well, all right, twice. But I don't *like* him. He's so—I don't know. Harsh. Arrogant. Everything I *expected* a high Churchman to be before I met William. So now I don't have anyone who knows about this stuff I can go to, and—"

"*Gods damn it, Widdershins!*"

Not only the mop but a great many mugs of various alcoholic libations froze as more than a dozen eyes turned in shock toward the young girl, who was actually *panting*, her face red, her shoulders heaving. After a moment, however, said eyes—and the heads in which they resided—all returned to their prior endeavors; all save Widdershins's own.

"Holy hopping hens, Robin! You don't have to *shout* at me, you know. What could—?"

"Shins," Robin said again; this time it came out in a hiss. "Look, you—you don't need to do this. I've got this." She lashed out, yanking the mop away almost hard enough to send Widdershins stumbling.

"What's gotten *into*—"

"Why don't," Robin continued, this time trampling over *Widdershins's* words rather than the other way around, "you go out. We've got this handled, and the crowd's not all that big, and I know you've had a lot on your mind, so you go and have yourself a nice, relaxing evening somewhere, all right?"

"Are you trying to get rid of me, Robin? What—?" And finally, *finally* Widdershins—who could have kicked herself up and down the entire length of the common room, and retained enough embarrassed frustration left to give herself a good pinch—came up for air through the thick, swirling depths of her own preoccupation and picked up on what should have been obvious from the start. "I," she grumbled, "am *such* a moron."

At any other time, Olgun's surge of agreement might have been offensive.

Widdershins's hand dropped to the hilt of her sword, and she instantly began trying to examine all four corners of the room at once. "Robin? What's going on?"

"He came looking for you again, Shins." Robin studiously examined her feet, or perhaps the soaking strands of the mop. "I didn't want to worry you any more than you already are; I just wanted you to get—"

"Who? Who came looking for me?" For an instant, the hassles of the past few days and the meeting with the Shrouded Lord clouded her memory of earlier events, and then . . . "That Evrard guy? Him?"

"Indeed, 'that Evrard guy,' at your service, mademoiselle."

Robin eeped—that was the only way to describe it, really, as an "eep"—and even Widdershins practically jumped out of her boots. He was simply *there*, offering them a sardonic but graceful bow. But that would have meant he'd been in the tavern this whole time, and she'd *missed* him! She couldn't have just missed him, could she?

She didn't need Olgun's gentle reminder of just how distracted she'd been to point out that, well, yes, she could have.

"Sure, *now* you tell me!" she groused at him. Then, standing tall, keeping one hand on her rapier, and ostentatiously *not* returning Evrard's bow, she methodically examined the stranger who'd apparently been seeking her for some days.

He was pretty enough to look at, she decided. His eyes were deep and twinkling above sharply chiseled features; and he wore his long coat (and, presumably, his tricorne hat, though at the moment it was in his hand) with what could only be described as a graceful panache. But his smile, though friendly, felt false, and even through the coat, Widdershins could see the tension in his shoulders.

Then, of course, there was his rapier. The leather on the hilt was worn far too thin for a weapon of such fine quality. Either he didn't bother to maintain the blade—which she didn't believe for an instant—or it saw a *lot* of use.

For a moment or two he simply stood, as though basking in her obvious examination. And then, "I assume, based on your conversation, that I have the honor to address the woman known as Widdershins?"

"Uh . . . You do. And you are?"

"Evrard. I thought we just covered that. A bit dim, are we?"

Widdershins scowled. (So did Robin, but Shins was too distracted to notice.) "I meant who *else* are you? What's your family name? Or title?"

"And why would you assume I have a title?"

"Because you're either an aristocrat, or someone who wants people to *think* he's an aristocrat. If you were putting on any more airs, the rest of us wouldn't be able to breathe."

"Ah. I see. And of course, if I share with you my full and proper name, you'll do the same in return? I'm fairly certain, after all, that 'Widdershins' is not what your parents chose to call you."

By this point, the entire common room of the Flippant Witch had gone silent, save for the occasional clank, clatter, or gulp of a mug. No one present understood the intricacies of this confrontation—heck, Widdershins herself only halfway grasped what was going on—but nobody wanted to miss a word of it.

"No," Widdershins said through a clenched cage of teeth. "I won't be doing that."

"Shame. Then I fear I shall simply have to remain 'that Evrard guy' for the time being. And you," he continued before she could speak, all traces of his smile sliding from his face, "can remain the same common, slovenly little criminal you've always been."

"Hey! Who are you calling 'common'?!"

"What else would I call you, Widdershins? You can pretend at being a tavern owner, a 'businesswoman,' all you want, but you're fooling precisely nobody. All you've ever been good for is slinking around in the dark, taking coin from those among your betters too foolish to hang onto it."

"Hey!" Robin shouted at him.

Widdershins merely raised an eyebrow. "Now you're just *trying* to make me sound like a whore."

"You hardly need *my* help with that, mademoiselle."

More than a few gasps sounded throughout the common room, and several of the Witch's regulars rose (however unsteadily) to their feet, ready to defend the proprietor of their home away from home. But it was Robin who began a forward lunge, only to be brought up painfully short by Widdershins's sudden grab at her collar.

"Robin, no!"

"But—but he—!"

"I know. It's all right."

"No," Robin muttered, as angry as Widdershins had ever heard her, though at least the girl was no longer struggling to charge headfirst into gods-knew-what sort of trouble. "No, it's not."

"Are you quite done hiding behind your little friend?" Evrard sneered.

Widdershins very deliberately stepped around the now-sputtering Robin. Evrard just about gleamed with some inner light as her hand once more clenched the rapier at her side, and he grinned as she marched over to stand perhaps an arm's length from him.

"Are you planning to challenge me, then, Widdershins?"

"No, not really."

At which point, as Evrard was carefully dividing his attention between Widdershins's face and the arm she would use to draw the rapier, she kicked him square in the groin.

Duelist that he was, Evrard might have dodged or deflected even so unexpected an attack, had there not been a brief surge of power from Olgun that caused the nobleman to "accidentally" slip on the sawdust-covered floor as he spun away. He choked once, all arrogance finally draining from his expression, and crumpled to a heap, clutching at himself.

Robin let out a whoop to match her prior eep, and a round of snickers circled through the observing patrons.

"You . . ." Evrard seemed to be having a great deal of difficulty speaking all of a sudden. "You . . ."

"I'm sorry, what was that?" Widdershins put a hand to her ear. "I'm afraid I can't actually hear your voice when it's that high."

Maybe it was Widdershins's taunts, or perhaps it was being laughed at by the crowd for the second time in half a minute, but Evrard pulled himself together. His face was pale, and he winced with every inch, but he rose slowly until he stood flagpole-straight.

"If you were of noble blood . . . ," he growled, fingers seeming to twitch toward his rapier of their own accord.

"Then I'd probably have died of hypocrisy poisoning by now. Evrard, *what do you want*?"

"I want," he said, his breath coming more easily now, "to inform of you my intentions."

"Your . . . ?"

"As I understand it, Gurrerre Marguilles briefly challenged his daughter's will? Specifically the provision granting you ownership of her tavern?"

Widdershins scowled. "That was dropped."

"Yes, because as the city's trade dried up, Lord Marguilles couldn't afford to waste time and resources on a prolonged legal struggle. But it remains true that 'Widdershins' isn't your legal name, and therefore, the will may not be binding."

"It's how Genevieve knew me, you rat! I have a dozen people ready to testify to that! It's *why* Marguilles couldn't afford to continue his challenge!"

"And do you think he'll feel that way when I tell him that the entire will was forged?"

Widdershins felt as though she was suddenly tumbling backward, down an unseen hole; could barely hear the common room through the sudden frantic pounding of her heart, which must surely be deafening to everyone around her. She could only hope she sounded a lot more confident than she felt when she said, an eternity later, “I don’t know what you mean.”

“Of course not.” Evrard leaned in, as though to whisper, but continued in a perfectly normal tone of voice, “I have connections *everywhere*, Widdershins. There’s nothing you can do that I cannot discover. Genevieve would be ashamed of you.”

The young woman’s whole body went taut as a crossbow string, and there’s no telling whether she’d have actually drawn her blade at that point or simply attacked Evrard with her bare hands (or booted feet), but as she’d held her friend back a moment earlier, it was now Robin who returned the favor.

“Shins, no!”

“I see,” Evrard continued, as Widdershins relented against the tide of gangly limbs pressing against her, “that you’re *not*, in fact, done hiding behind your friends.”

“I won’t let you do this!” Widdershins wasn’t sure if it had come out as more of a growl or a whine; she desperately hoped for the former.

“You’d have to kill me,” Evrard said simply.

“Why?” Robin fell away as Widdershins deflated. “Gods, what did I ever do to you?”

“Maybe, if you really can’t figure it out, I’ll explain it to you someday. In very short words. Have a good evening, ladies and gentlemen. So sorry for the interruption.” He tossed a handful of coins at the bar; they skipped and scattered over the smooth wood, tinkling as they fell, and nobody—employee or patron—moved to pick them up. “A round on me, to compensate you all for your trouble.” With that, and a last sardonic bow, Evrard strode through the door, cloak flapping with an almost deliberate melodrama in his wake.

"It's fine, everybody." Widdershins's tone put the obvious lie to her words, but none of the customers appeared willing to challenge her assertion. "Everything's fine. Please, go back to your drinks." And then she just stood in the center of the room, gazing at nothing at all.

"Shins?"

"Hmm?"

Robin's face, even more pallid than normal, interposed itself between Widdershins and the nothing she was staring at. "Can he actually do that? Can he take the Flippant Witch?"

"I—I don't know, Robin. He has no *proof* that the will was fake, but just the accusation might be enough to spur Gen's father to new efforts. He could certainly make life really, *really* hard for us."

"Right." Robin attempted to force a shallow smile. "Because things were going so smoothly before now." And then, blinking at Widdershins's abrupt turn, "Where are you going?"

"I'm going to follow that—that *snake*! He knows so much about me? Fine! I'll even things up!"

She was gone before Robin could possibly have decided whether to protest or to cheer her on.

❋

"There she is!"

Squirrel followed his friend's pointing finger just in time to see Widdershins, apparently having burst through the door at something of a run, haul herself up short. She took a quick but steady look around, as though searching for something, and then headed off down the Market District's main avenue at a much slower pace. Swiftly she blended in with the crowd, occasionally vanishing completely into pockets of shadow between the glowing lantern posts. (This despite the fact that she wasn't currently dressed in her "business-related" blacks and grays.) Clearly, she didn't care to be detected.

Just as clearly, she was expecting any potential discovery to come from in front of her. She wasn't nearly as well concealed from anyone following behind, especially not anyone who knew most of the same tricks.

"All right, boys," Simon said through a tight little grin. "Let's see what our girl's got going on tonight, shall we?"

And they, like Widdershins before them, moved out into the street and vanished into the crowd, pursuing a quarry utterly unaware of their presence.

CHAPTER SIX

So furious was Widdershins's burning anger, her determination, and yes—though she'd never have admitted to it—her fear, that it took several moments of intense emotional "shouting" before Olgun was able even to attract her attention.

"What? No!" She cast an ugly glance at the nearest passerby, who was currently staring at her, and then continued in a much lower tone of voice. "No, I do *not* think this is a dumb idea. In fact, I think this is the best idea anyone has ever had in the history of anyone ever having ideas!"

That response, if nothing else, was apparently enough to cause dizziness, because she'd pushed through the rapidly thinning crowd—most people were hurrying home, if they were out at all this late in the evening—and had covered another two blocks or so before . . .

"Well, I don't care if *you* think it's a bad idea! You're not the one who's about to lose your best friend's life's work, are you? What would you even *know* about—"

Widdershins actually moaned aloud and stumbled, barely catching herself before careening into the worn and discolored wood that was the nearest wall. She couldn't remember the last time she'd felt something from Olgun that powerful, that overwhelming. She actually found her gut clenching with a shame that very much reminded her of those times she'd bitterly disappointed Alexandre.

"You . . . Olgun, I'm so sorry. I know what you've lost. I had no right to say that to you. Forgive me?"

Acceptance, grudging for an instant, then growing stronger—but still tinged with more than a little anger, and more than a *lot* of worry.

"But you won't lose *me*, not over this. No, I don't know who he is, but you and me? We can handle anything, yes?"

She was moving again, struggling to catch up before she lost Evrard completely, and though she could sense Olgun's grumbling, she could sense, too, that he wasn't about to argue any further.

The street steadily evolved from mud with the occasional cobblestone to well cobbled with the occasional pothole—and even those began to fade as Evrard's path drew him, and Widdershins, ever nearer Davillon's richer districts. Any doubt the thief might have had regarding her adversary's nobility (in birth and blood, if not in demeanor) was swiftly washing away.

So who *was* this guy? And why did he harbor such hatred for her?

Evening had taken her leave of the city some minutes earlier, leaving night to assume its rightful place. The roads weren't empty, not entirely, but pedestrians were sparse, and Guardsmen ever more common. Widdershins found herself with no crowds in which to hide; forced to resort ever more often to shadows, doorways, and alleyways any time Evrard thought to look around, her pace slowed and her quarry began to pull ahead. She realized, with a weight in her stomach as though she'd swallowed a whole goose—and not one braised and roasted, either, but feathered and honking—that she was on the verge of losing him entirely.

She peered briefly toward the rooftops, wondering if the "thieves' highway" might not be a wiser option, but quickly dismissed the idea. She didn't know this part of town well enough, didn't know if she'd find herself stranded before a gap too wide to cross. No, best to keep to the roads, maybe even to sacrifice stealth for speed and just hope that the irritating aristocrat wouldn't happen to check behind him at any point where Widdershins couldn't—

The rest of the thought was lost in yet another surge of emotion from Olgun, but this was not anger, nor was it directed at Widdershins specifically. It was, as best she could determine once she had a moment to gather her scattered wits, an intense puzzlement, tinged with, just perhaps, a tiny sprinkling of fear.

"What? Olgun, *what*?"

An urging, then, as though he was trying to guide her way.

"No! Olgun, Evrard's going *that* way. I'm not . . . *No!* I don't care *what* might be down that way, I'm not letting—"

She felt a surge in the air around her, as well as within her own mind, and recognized the sensation of Olgun's power. The voices of the few other pedestrians in sight resounded in her ears, each word burning itself into her thoughts. She could hear footsteps as clearly as drumbeats, her own heart as though it had crawled up into her skull (perhaps in search of a better view).

Just as swiftly as it began, it faded. No, not faded, *narrowed*. Sounds fell away as though she were moving past them, until she heard only what was occurring several streets off to her right.

Gasps. Running. And the occasional scream, not quite loud enough to carry itself normally to her ears.

"It's nothing to do with us," she insisted, struggling to spot Evrard's flapping coat in the darkness ahead. "I wouldn't even know about it without your stupid jumbo god ears, so—"

She felt, as though it were her own, Olgun's desperate curiosity, his need to know what bizarre power he'd sensed moving through the city.

"I don't care. I've got to learn what Evrard—"

He drew from her thoughts a distinct memory of the Shrouded Lord's directive, to learn precisely what was haunting Davillon.

"*I don't care!*"

Her hearing focused even further, until she could make out little but the ever-increasing shrieks of terror.

"I don't—oh, *figs*!" And with a last, vicious glance toward Evrard's retreating back—though it might just as easily have been directed at Olgun—she was sprinting toward the sounds of fright that nobody else on the street nearby could possibly have heard.

Her senses swiftly faded back to normal levels—there were, she knew, limits to how much power Olgun could exercise on her behalf—but it wasn't long before she no longer needed them. The screams, now clearly incorporating no small degree of pain as well as terror, drew near enough for her to hear on her own. Had she been any farther away, even Olgun wouldn't have detected whatever it was that had attracted his attention; had any of the patrols been nearer, rather than concentrated on the main thoroughfares, they could have dealt with this and Widdershins wouldn't have had to abandon her own pursuit.

"We're gonna talk about this later, Olgun," she snipped at him. Then, once she'd narrowed down her destination to a nearby side street, and realized, further, that there was indeed a building overlooking said street (a glassware shop, if she wasn't mistaken), she swiftly began to climb. Better to approach the trouble, whatever it might be, from an unexpected angle, yes?

In point of fact, the "side street" wasn't much wider than most alleyways she knew. The rear of multiple establishments bordered it on both sides; in fact, had the entire street been this way, rather than just these few blocks, it actually *would* have been an alleyway.

But it was the alley's—that is, the street's—inhabitants, rather than its design, that snagged her attention as she peered out over the edge of the sloping roof, hands itching as they pressed up against the rough, wooden shingles. Two young men—either well-dressed servants of some noble, or rather cheaply dressed aristocrats themselves—crouched, huddled against the shop next door to Widdershins's own perch. One clutched at a red-smeared arm and stomach, and, though there didn't appear to be enough blood to suggest that either wound was especially dangerous, they were pretty clearly *painful*. The other fellow was holding his friend's shoulders, as though that would provide any protection against their attacker. An attacker clad all in swathes of black fabric; he looked, to Widdershins, like the Shrouded Lord's disreputable second cousin.

But from her raised vantage, Widdershins could also see something that the two victims on the ground most assuredly could not:

A *second* dark figure, garbed identically to the first, clinging to the shadow-cloaked wall just beneath the eaves of a building some ways down the street.

"So, Olgun. These guys what you sensed?"

Apparently, the god wasn't sure—she detected more than a touch of doubt.

"Well," she continued as the silhouette on the street produced a narrow blade, laughing as he (it?) made threatening jabs at the two sniveling travelers, "guess we should do something, yes? Care to lend a hand?"

She felt the tingling in the air once again, this time concentrated around her legs and feet. Grinning manically, Widdershins backed away from the edge of the roof, drew her rapier, and charged.

It was, every step of it, impossible—but impossible was a specialty of this particular partnership. With almost inhuman speed, Widdershins cleared the entire length of the roof and leapt, sailing majestically across the gap. She twisted as she flew, the envy of any acrobat, flipping over so that her feet landed against the wall of the opposite shop. She tucked and pushed, propelling herself once more across the street, this time angled and hurtling directly at the dark-clad figure who appeared utterly frozen in shock.

He began to move, and Widdershins had the barest instant to note that he was far faster than he should have been; not that much slower, in fact, than she herself at that moment. But it wasn't fast enough. Her rapier punched through muscle and flesh even as she collided with the target, knocking him, winded and screaming, to the earth. Had she wanted him dead, he'd have been dead. As it was, it would be some time before his perforated shoulder would work properly.

Widdershins rolled backward and came once more to her feet, rapier held before her en garde, but it wasn't necessary. Not only was her target rolling on the street, clutching his wound and screaming in a very human voice, but his presumed partner—the other mysterious silhouette—had plummeted from his perch on the wall. He, too, was doubled over and groaning in pain, though Widdershins could only guess why. Had her appearance so startled him that he lost his grip, causing him to injure himself in the fall?

Well, whatever the case, it was time to learn more about these . . . Guys? Bandits? Monsters? Whatever. Widdershins, taking only a moment to make vaguely reassuring "There, there, it's all right" noises to the two weeping gentlemen, reached down and yanked away the hood that covered her fallen opponent's face.

"Hey! I *know* you!"

And she did, at that. Not all that well; she wasn't even certain what his name was. Ricard? Rupert? Something with an *R* and two syllables, she thought. But that wasn't the point. The point was *where* she knew him from.

Monsieur R-and-Two-Syllables was a member of the Finders' Guild!

But hadn't the Shrouded Lord made it pretty clear that the Guild *wasn't* involved in these events? And why would anyone mistake Ricard-or-Whatever for some sort of phantom? Widdershins may not have been all that close to him, but she knew full well that the fellow wasn't a warlock of any sort!

"Olgun? What the hopping horses is going on?"

There really shouldn't have been an emotional equivalent to Olgun chewing the inside of his cheek in nervous confusion. Nevertheless, that was precisely the impression Widdershins received.

"Fat lot of good *you* are, then. So are these guys magic?"

Faint and confused, but the answer was a definite *yes*.

"And are they what you sensed before?"

No puzzlement at all, this time. *Absolutely not.*

"Then what—?"

"Oh, my, oh, my! Blood and pain and beautiful songs! They've gone and started the celebration without us, and we shall be greatly put out if there's no more cake to be had!"

The worst wasn't the hideous two-toned voice, that of a grown man and a child speaking in unison, though that alone was enough to make every hair on her arms and neck stand firmly at attention. Nor was it even the figure itself, which scuttled headfirst down a nearby wall using only its impossibly long fingertips, the rest of its body held straight as a board, its coat and hat refusing to fall despite gravity's insistent tug.

No, what caused the blood to drain from Widdershins's face as though it, too, were trying to escape, and made the rapier twitch and vibrate in her trembling fist, was Olgun's silent shriek of absolute terror. She'd sensed the like from him only twice before: once when he'd almost been slain by the wholesale slaughter of his cult, of which Widdershins herself was the only survivor; and once, a few years later and mingled with near-helpless frustration, when he'd done his best to help her face down the demon responsible for that slaughter.

This *creature* she faced now—for, no matter his mostly human shape, human he clearly was *not*—was no demon, or at least not the same sort of demon she'd faced before. But whatever he was, he was enough to scare a god.

A tiny, weak god with only a single worshipper, yes, but a god for all that.

Widdershins sucked in her breath to speak, and was overwhelmed by the scent of peppermint. Somewhere, as though hidden behind the buildings that surrounded them, a chorus of children giggled in the dark.

"Run," she ordered. The two pedestrians, though scarcely able to stand on shaking knees, didn't need to be told twice. The broad-brimmed hat of the creature clinging to the wall shifted as though he watched them go, perhaps deciding whether or not to give chase.

"Don't even think it, Bug Man," Widdershins told him with—she hoped—more bravado than she felt.

"Don't need to." The hat tilted again; this time, the face beneath seemed to be examining Widdershins herself, as well as the men who'd fallen—one directly, one less so—to her unexpected attack. "Girls and boys!" The figure began to chant. "Girls and boys, girls and boys, some for eating, some for toys!"

Widdershins felt the rapier slip slightly in her hand, clenched her fingers in a futile attempt to wipe the sweat off on the hilt. "I, uh . . . I don't think I plan to be either, thanks." And, much more softly, "Olgun, what *is* that?!"

But, other than the sensation that it was very, *very* old, she got nothing but bafflement and fear from her unseen ally.

"Oh, you're *so* welcome!" The creature dropped from the wall, flipping as it fell to land feetfirst on the grass beside the street. "She thinks she has a plan. That's so *cute*!"

The chorus of children cooed, as though having discovered a little, lost puppy.

"Where is *that* coming from?!" Widdershins herself wasn't certain whether the question was addressed to Olgun, the gaunt figure, or the world in general, but it was the creature who answered. And for the first time, he sounded honestly puzzled.

"You can't see them?" he asked.

It was, given the current state of Widdershins's nerves, absolutely the worst answer he could have given. She shuddered and found herself desperately glancing around, despite her best intentions, searching for an army of slack-faced, staring children creeping up behind her in the dark. There were none, of course, but in that moment of distraction, the creature lunged.

Not at her, no. Fast as he moved—and he was unbelievably fast—he might not have crossed the distance between them before she could once again bring up her guard. But Widdershins wasn't his target. Bending neatly sideways, he reached out with those impossibly long, flexible fingers, and snatched up the dark-clad figure who had fallen, a few minutes before, from the neighboring building.

With a single arm, he hefted the screaming man toward his face. Widdershins fell back with a whimper at the rough tearing sounds that followed, and felt the bile rising and stinging in the back of her throat as the body shriveled and dried, in a matter of instants, into a desiccated, leathery slab. (She didn't even notice the cries of agony emerging from the second man, whom she'd earlier stabbed.)

"Ooh, yummy, yum, yum! He tastes a bit of magic, doesn't he? Extra spice is extra nice!" The creature advanced as he "ate," and when he allowed the body to fall, he was finally near enough for the ambient moonlight and the nearby flickering lanterns to illumine the face and figure beneath the flopping brim. "Will you also taste of magic, little girl? Or was this one a special appetizer?"

His features were, other than being grotesquely emaciated, human enough at first glance. The skin was pale; the icy green eyes and ivory teeth gleamed even in the night, as though reflecting a light whose source she could not see. Hair of a filthy, stringy black hung limply from within the hat, the brim of which was stained with a glistening grease.

Her *second* glance—the one in which she noted the figure's cheeks and jaw rippling, as though something moved just beneath the flesh, attempting to distend his mouth in ways it was never meant to flex—was quite sufficient to put the lie to any sense of humanity.

His hands were even worse. His thumbs were relatively normal, perhaps slightly longer than they should have been, but every other finger was hideous. The shortest was a foot long, and all of them were narrow, pointed, twitching, bending in ways and in places they should never have bent. Widdershins couldn't help but think of them less as fingers than as the legs of some monstrous spider.

And that, in turn, stirred up memories in the farthest reaches of Widdershins's mind, the faintest recollections of childhood. But whatever those memories were, they refused to surface on their own, and she wasn't about to take the time and effort to dredge them up *now*.

"Gonna need everything you can give me, Olgun," Widdershins whispered.

His response was a ferocious urge to run.

"Oh, no." Much as a very large part of her agreed, Widdershins stood her ground. "I don't want that thing at my back! Besides, you're the one who pushed me into this in the first place, remember?"

Olgun might have responded to that, had their inhuman enemy not beaten him to it. "And who do *you* talk to, in the silence, in the dark, hmm? You cannot see my friends, so you invent one of your own? How very silly of you."

Widdershins didn't even bother asking how he'd heard the words that she'd barely even formed on her tongue, let alone spoken aloud. "Why don't you step closer, and I'll introduce you?"

The creature's shoulders hunched, his head lowered, his impossible fingers twitched. "I think . . . I would like that."

The unseen children cackled, and the two opponents—one blessed by a god, one utterly ungodly—hurled themselves together in the center of the roadway.

Any observer (and there may or may not have been one; Widdershins had no idea if the man she'd stabbed remained conscious or not) would have seen little more than a blur of movement. The creature advanced in a series of dancing steps and graceful twists, almost pirouettes. Each step *should* have taken him in a different direction from every other, yet somehow he glided toward Widdershins in a perfectly straight line.

For her own part, Widdershins simply charged, propelled by Olgun's energies beneath her pounding feet, carrying her far more swiftly than her steps alone.

Even as they converged, those impossibly long fingers swept through the air, clutching at the young thief's body, but she wasn't there to be hit. An arm's length from her foe, Widdershins dropped to her knees, allowing her momentum to carry her onward. It should have been an impossible slide, across the rough and muddy cobblestones of the street, but she felt the hum of Olgun's power in the air—a power that allowed her to "coincidentally" hit the slickest, smoothest stretch of stone, that smoothed over the worst of the bumps and crevices. Her knees were scraped raw, portions of her hose shredded, but it was enough to carry her beneath her enemy's attack and past him, thrusting her rapier into his thigh as she went.

Or rather, she *tried* to thrust her rapier into his thigh. Despite the swiftness and unexpected angle of her attack, the creature jumped back a fraction of a second before the blade struck home. His leap carried him clear to the nearest wall from which he now hung—again, by his fingertips only, which were stretched out *behind* him. Despite the sudden acrobatics, his coat and hat remained as immobile as ever. His eyes first went wider than any Widdershins had ever seen, then narrowed into glinting green slivers.

"Godly!" It somehow emerged as a high-pitched growl, improbable as the concept might seem. His chorus of children began to wail as though someone had just stepped on their favorite toys.

Widdershins flexed her legs and sprang to her feet, ignoring the pain in her knees. "Noticed that, did you?" *Not much use in trying to deny it at this point . . .* "How'd you enjoy *that*, you creepy critter?"

"I don't think you're fun anymore."

A flex of the fingers sent him hurtling once more across the roadway to land before Widdershins. For several long moments, the air was filled only with the swooshing sounds of blade and digits. No matter how swiftly she attacked, no matter at what peculiar angles she held her rapier, Widdershins couldn't strike fast enough to land a blow. Each and every time, the creature danced nimbly aside or, on occasion, parried with a single finger against the flat of her blade.

For his part, he hadn't laid a finger on Widdershins, not due to her speed—even with Olgun's aid, the inhuman thing was far faster than she—but because the god kept interfering in other ways. A tingle in the air, and her opponent, despite his unnatural grace, skidded briefly in a thin layer of wet mud. A hum that only Widdershins could hear, and her rapier just *happened* to be in precisely the right spot to block an attack that she never would have seen coming. It was very much an evenly matched contest.

For about half a minute, give or take. At which point it abruptly became clear that Widdershins and Olgun were reaching the limits of their combined endurance, and their opponent was very much *not*.

Widdershins slowed, just a heartbeat; her luck faded, just by a hair. And that was enough.

Four of those fingers dragged across her, starting at her left shoulder and running across her collarbone to the neck. She heard a terrible scream, and failed to recognize the voice as her own; heard a ragged tearing, and was scarcely coherent enough to recognize the sound as coming from her clothes and her flesh both. The fingers didn't cut, didn't shred, not exactly. No, they simply fastened to her skin through the fabric, much as they must have fastened to the walls the creature climbed. And when they pulled away, they peeled away narrow strips of flesh with them. Blood coursed down Widdershins's chest, and what tiny portion of her mind remained capable of thought grew nauseated at the sight of tiny banners—made up of twisted strips of skin, strings of muscle, and cloth—that wiggled cheerfully from her attacker's fingers.

She felt the rough cobbles beneath her palms, pressing into her knees, and only then realized that she'd fallen. The film of mud across those stones was mixing slowly with the blood that leaked from her frayed wounds, as well as a small puddle of vomit that she must have coughed up as she stumbled.

"But our little girl cries!" She heard the foul voice, sensed the presence looming over her, and could barely crane her neck enough to look up. The creature was slowly running the stolen strips of flesh—*her flesh*—across its tongue, leaving nothing but dry, wrinkled sticks of leather that it casually tossed to the earth. "Where is her god, to wipe away her tears? Shall I kiss them better, little priestess? I have such comforting kisses. I swear to you that, should you but allow me, you'll never cry again. Never, ever, ever, ever . . ." The figure began to bend, wriggling fingers reaching, reaching . . .

"Olgun . . ."

The tiny god's power surged, flowing through her chest, her shoulder, tingling in the wounds like cold water. It barely helped; far less than it should have, for Olgun had, in the past, relieved the hurt of worse wounds than these. Indeed, the pain surged anew each time it faded, a stubborn, unnatural tide that refused to bend to Olgun's will.

But it helped enough, just enough, that Widdershins could still move—and move far faster than her assailant could possibly have anticipated.

With a hoarse cry she struck, wincing at the sound of steel on stone, and then she rolled upright and ran, staggering and stumbling over her own feet. Laughing maniacally in its dual voices, and joined by the ubiquitous chorus of giggles, the creature began to pursue—only to be yanked abruptly to a halt.

Widdershins hadn't missed, no. She couldn't possibly have slain the creature even if she'd hit it, not with a single weakened stroke. Instead, she had plunged her rapier through the hem of her attacker's coat and wedged it between the cobblestones. That weapon—one she'd carried for years, the one that had brought her into the life of Alexandre Delacroix, thus shaping who she was today—had saved her for the final time.

Abandoning the blade, sobbing as much over its loss as for the agony that racked her, Widdershins dashed around every corner she could, keeping to the darkest reaches, using every trace of Olgun's power not to lessen her own pain, but to hide her trail from one whose senses were far more than human. She was blind to the city around her, deaf to its sounds; only the next step, the next stumble, the next pool of shadow mattered. Her trick would buy her only a handful of seconds, before the creature wrenched the sword free or ripped his coat from the blade. She had to be out of sight by then.

It *had* to be enough.

She needed help; needed a place to collapse, to figure out what to do next. And since she wasn't *about* to risk leading that thing to her friends at the Flippant Witch—nor did she think it probable that the Finders would appreciate her dragging a second monster into their midst—that left her only one option. If she lived long enough to get there . . .

❋

". . . the patrols along the southwest edges of the district." The suggestion was coming from one Major Archibeque, a grizzled veteran with leather-brown skin, iron-gray beard, and a perpetual squint. Technically, he held no greater rank than any of the other majors present at the meeting. Unofficially, as everyone expected him to be promoted to commandant of the Guard when their current leader retired, his words carried a lot more weight than his rank suggested. At the moment, he was leaning over a scarred oaken table, gesturing at it as though it held a map of the city. (It didn't—the maps weren't currently handy, as this had been a last-minute, haphazard meeting—but every man and woman present knew Davillon's layout well enough to get the point he was trying to make.) "It'll mean drawing some manpower away from other quarters, but since most late-night travel comes from the direction of the markets, it seems to me that . . ."

He trailed off with a faint growl at the sound of a fist pounding on the door to the mess-hall-turned-conference-room. "Enter!" Every head in the chamber glanced toward the young constable who appeared in the doorway.

"Apologies for disturbing you all, sirs, but there's a visitor here for Major Bouniard."

Julien rose from his own seat, cast an apologetic glance at Major Archibeque, then returned his attention to the messenger. "A visitor? At this hour?"

"Yes, sir."

"And can't this wait, Constable? I'm rather—"

"She's insisting that it's an emergency, Sir. And she's injured."

Julien's fists clenched. Injured? *She?* Assuming it wasn't a fellow member of the Guard—and the constable would surely have said so, were that the case—he knew pretty damn well who it had to be.

"Major?" he asked.

Archibeque nodded brusquely. "Go on, then. We'll fill you in on what we decide."

Bouniard held himself to a moderate (if stiff-legged) pace as he departed the room and followed the constable, even as every muscle twitched, demanding he break into a sprint. After what felt to be about three or four years of passing along the drab, flattened carpets, and the pockets of greasy smoke belched forth by the cheap oil lamps that were the hallways' main sources of illumination, he finally reached the door to his own office.

"Didn't know where else to put her, sir," the constable said in response to the unasked question. "I didn't think we ought to have a young woman bleeding in the foyer, right?"

"You *did* call for a chirurgeon, I assume?" Bouniard demanded.

"Of course, sir. Not sure why he hasn't arrived, but—"

"Then go see what's taking him!"

The constable recoiled from the abrupt shout, then offered an abortive salute and sprinted away. Bouniard grunted and threw open the door.

Yep, that's who he'd thought it would be.

"Hey, Major," she said weakly.

"Widdershins, I . . . Gods!" It was only as she turned away from his desk, on which she'd been leaning (and probably looking for confidential papers, no doubt) that he saw the sheer quantity of blood plastering her tunic to her skin.

"We've got to stop meeting here," she said with a pale, shaky smile. "I keep mixing with questionable elements like the Guard, my reputation's going to—to . . ."

Julien caught her before she hit the floor, but it was a very, *very* near thing.

❋

From yet another rooftop—one several dozen yards from the action, but near enough to make out the gist of what was going on—three fleshy masks of terror had observed the bloody confrontation. They'd marveled at Widdershins's dramatic entrance, widened at the appearance of her opponent, cringed at the horrid death he'd delivered to the first of the black-garbed pair, and struggled to keep up with the inhumanly swift duel that followed. Some long minutes before, the inhuman creature had freed himself from Widdershins's rapier, yanking it free of the stones between which it was wedged and leaving a ragged tear in his coat. Head tilted and muttering to himself, he'd wandered off—perhaps in pursuit of the fleeing thief, perhaps merely on his way to whatever endeavor might appear next on his itinerary.

And still they gawked, unable to quite believe what they'd seen, until the stench of spilled blood and freshly slain bodies wafted over to them on the gentle breeze.

"Well," Squirrel said, trying to keep his voice from quivering (and, it should be noted, failing miserably). "I guess we have some idea of what's haunting the streets, huh?"

"Are you fucking *joking*?" This from the larger, lumbering thug on the left. "Yeah, we *saw* it, but I sure as hell have no idea what the hell it *is*!"

"For that matter," said the third, "what's going on with Widdershins? Sure, I've heard she's a fast little scab, but *that* . . ."

Squirrel shrugged. "I don't know. Maybe she's a witch. Hell, maybe she's linked to that—that whatever it was. All I know is, we've gotta report all this to Remy, maybe even the Shrouded Lord. They'll know what to do."

"I don't think *anyone's* gonna know what to do."

"Oh, but you're *so* wrong!" All three Finders went stiff, petrified at the voice that drifted over the eaves. "*I* know what to do. I *always* know what to do!"

The wide-brimmed hat hove into view first, followed by the rest of the creature's form, until it crouched upon the shingles, knees and elbows jutting at impossible angles. For a moment only it held that pose, then rose to its feet, seemingly oblivious to the precarious slope at the roof's edge.

"Spying eyes are naughty eyes," the creature scolded, wagging a single, dagger-long finger at them. "They shall perforce have to be plucked."

Unlike his two panicked friends, who immediately bolted for opposite sides of the roof, Squirrel held his ground. It wasn't bravery, not in the least; rather, his own dread caused him to freeze instead of flee. But whatever the cause, it saved his life, at least for a moment.

Their enemy sprang, a single leap carrying him halfway across the roof, and a few sprinting steps were more than enough to catch up to the slower of the two fugitives. Those terrible fingers lashed out, snagging Squirrel's companion at the neck and the right side of his ribs. He screamed, even as Widdershins had screamed, as those fingertips fastened themselves to his flesh.

The creature flexed, swinging his hands until his arms crossed at the elbows, and the victim's scream grew shrill as entire swathes of his flesh simply *unraveled*, peeling away like the outer layers of an onion. The body, glistening in fascinating spiral patterns where raw muscles and organs now lay exposed, convulsed as it hit the rooftop, and the shriek swiftly went silent.

But the thief's murderer wasn't through with him. Allowing the streamers of flesh to flutter away into the darkness, he lifted the twitching body overhead and hurled it just as the other fleeing Finder had begun to clamber over the edge of the roof. The two bodies collided with a dull thump, followed by a second, wetter slap as both hit the ground beside the structure. The sound of children cooing and applauding echoed from the distance. And then, for a moment, there was silence.

The dark figure stared at Squirrel, his head once again slightly tilted as though not quite certain what he was looking at. Squirrel stared back, unable to blink. His entire body shook with the beating of his heart, and he was only scarcely aware of the wet warmth running down the inside of his leg.

"You . . . you . . ."

"I, I?" the creature asked, advancing in one of his peculiar dancer's steps.

Simon swallowed hard. "You don't want to kill me."

"I don't?" The head straightened, then cocked to the other side. "I'm rather certain—entirely positive, in fact—that I really, really do."

"That's—that's because you haven't thought it through. . . ." The thing was closer already, so much closer than he should be.

"Oh, I haven't?" Another surge, and he was *right there*, filling Squirrel's field of vision. His right hand lashed out and those impossible fingers cupped Simon's face—*almost*. They hovered, half an inch from his flesh, close enough that he could feel the wind of their twitching in the scruffy hairs on his cheeks. "And you're going to explain it to me? I'm *so* excited!"

"Um, it's just . . . I can help you! You need someone who knows this city!"

"I do? I seem to be doing fine without one." Again the fingers twitched, and Squirrel twitched with them.

"What about her?" he shrieked.

"Her? Her, her, her? Her who?"

"The girl you just fought! Widdershins!"

The fingers vanished from around his face with a series of rapid snaps. "Widdershins? Her name is Widdershins?"

"It's—it's what she goes by, anyway."

"Goes by? Goes by? A name is a name is a name! Is this hers?"

"Yes! Yes, it is!"

"Widdershins . . ." His mouth moved around the syllables, bending and twisting. "And her god? Do you know her god?"

"I . . . You mean the Shrouded God?" Then, at the narrowing glare, "No! That is, I don't, but I can help you find out! I know people who know her! Know her very well! Know where to find her!"

"I see . . . Little god, tiny god, where have you been? Out and about in a silly girl's skin! Little god, tiny god, where have you been . . ." The figure began capering about the roof, spinning in ever-widening circles—and just as abruptly, after a full minute of rhyming, stopped.

"Very well." A single step, and he once again loomed over Squirrel, blotting out the moon and stars. "You will be my vassal, my guide, my northern star. Tell me what I want to know. Show me where I want to go. And learn all you can about this . . . Widdershins." A fingertip tickled the skin beneath Simon's ear, drawing only a faint line of blood. "You have my oath, Boy-Thief. No harm will come to you, so long as you remain my servant."

"I . . . Thank you. Ah, my lord."

"Splendid!" The creature stepped back and clapped his hands. "We have a friend! Oh, goody, goody!

"Tell me, friend. . . . What's a nice place to find someone to eat around here?"

CHAPTER SEVEN

So wrapped up was Bishop Sicard—apparently in reading the holy treatise that lay open before him across the desk, but more accurately within his own tumultuous thoughts—that he failed to notice the first two knocks on his chamber door. Only the third sequence of raps penetrated the cloud of cotton encompassing his mind. He grunted once, smoothed his bushy beard with one hand while rubbing at bloodshot eyes with the other, and called, "Enter!"

For a moment, Sicard thought that a complete stranger had stepped into his study, even though he couldn't imagine a circumstance in which the guards would have allowed such a stranger to wander in alone at this time of night. He was just rising to his feet, whether to call for help or defend himself he wasn't certain, when the newcomer doffed his ragged cap and filthy cloak to reveal the blond, tonsured head and lanky frame of Brother Ferrand.

"Well." Sicard returned slowly to his chair, struggling to keep a scowl of embarrassed anger from his face. "I see you've got the 'incognito' bit down."

"I assumed, Your Eminence, that wandering around town in a monk's cassock would probably not be conducive to my efforts."

"Right, fine." Sicard waved distractedly at the nearest chair, into which Ferrand allowed himself to slump. "So I assume you've learned something about the young noblewoman?"

"Uh . . ." Ferrand squirmed in the chair, causing the wood to squeak, and coughed once.

"Succinct," Sicard noted, "but not precisely helpful."

"Her name is Madeleine Valois," the monk told him. "Something of a social butterfly. Popular enough at parties, but without many close personal friends that I could find. Nobody actually seems to know her all that well."

Silence for a moment, broken only by Sicard's fingers drumming on the desk. "And?"

"And, well, that's all I've found so far, Your Eminence."

"That's all?"

"She is, as I said, not especially well known on anything but a superficial social level. Shows up at all the right parties, says all the right things, and is otherwise about as forgettable as day-old bread."

"There's something unusual about her, Ferrand. I felt it."

The monk shrugged. "I'm not doubting you, Your Eminence. I'm simply saying that nobody else seems to have noticed."

Sicard grimaced at Ferrand for a moment, then at the small chandelier that hung from the ceiling—as though seeking answers or inspiration from what was, at this hour, the room's only illumination—and then back at the monk once again.

"And this riveting report couldn't have waited until a decent hour?" he asked finally. "I'm fairly certain that nothing you've just told me qualifies as especially urgent."

"That's, um, not precisely what I came to tell you, Your Eminence."

"Oh? Then get to it, man!"

"Well, it seems that there have been a few deaths. . . ."

"Deaths?"

Ferrand nodded. "As regards your, um, ongoing project."

"Bah." Sicard returned to the book on the desk, reaching out for a quill to make a few notes in the margins. "I've heard the rumors, too. Utter nonsense. Just the sort of exaggeration we *expected* from this sort of—"

"All due respect, Your Eminence, but it's not. I'm not speaking of whispers on street corners. I've spoken with City Guardsmen who were at the scene. Who observed the—well, the bodies."

Sicard straightened, slowly letting the quill topple to the desk. "That's not possible, Ferrand."

"Nevertheless . . ."

"My instructions were *specific*!" The bishop was slowly standing now. Papers crumpled beneath his fists on the desk, and his cheeks flushed red above his beard—whether with anger, with shame, or a combination of both, even he couldn't honestly have said. "Nobody was to be killed, or even badly harmed! *Nobody!* Terrorized, yes. Even slightly injured, gods forgive me, to make it all seem real, but not . . . Gods, what are they . . . ?"

"It's not precisely what you think, Your Eminence. Your, ah, 'assistants' weren't responsible."

"I don't understand."

"Two men clad in strange, flowing black garb—including full face masks—were among the dead. I wasn't present when you made the arrangements, but they certainly *sound* like what you've described to me."

Sicard fell back into his own chair with a muffled *whump*. "But . . . I don't understand. Who . . . ?"

"That's what the Guard is investigating." The monk rolled his head back, trying to stretch away some of the tension in his neck. "Rumor going around the Guard is that a young thief by the name of Widdershins was somehow involved in what happened, though few of the stories agree on precisely how."

"Widdershins? That's an odd . . . Why do I know that name?"

"Brother Maurice's report," Ferrand said gently, "of William de Laurent's murder."

The clench of Sicard's teeth was a crack audible throughout the room.

"Maurice swore," Ferrand continued, "that this Widdershins was a friend to the archbishop, that she actually *thwarted* a prior attempt on his life. But he also admits that he knows little else about her, as William dismissed him from the room during the bulk of his conversation with the young woman."

"Could she be responsible for what's happened, then?"

"I couldn't begin to guess, Your Eminence. But if she's involved in this, *and* in what happened with the archbishop last year . . . Well, I find it difficult to write off as coincidence."

"As do I. Is the Guard currently hunting for her?"

"I wasn't able to learn that, I'm afraid."

"All right." Again the bishop's fingers drummed across the desk, this time in a rapid patter much like hail, or the impact of a blunderbuss's lead shot. "If she's responsible for what's happened, then either she's attempting to use our 'haunting' for her own schemes, or she's learned what we have in mind and is trying to prevent it. Either way, she cannot be allowed to continue."

"And if she's not responsible, but involved in some other capacity?" Ferrand asked.

"Either way, we can't afford to have her interfering until we know more."

Ferrand nodded and stood, recognizing the cue when he heard it. "What would you have me do, Your Eminence?"

"Davillon and our Mother Church are only just starting to mend their disagreements, correct? We should make it clear to the brave and noble Guardsmen that such efforts could only benefit if they were to arrest this Widdershins with all speed—and that said efforts could well suffer should they *fail* to do so."

The monk's expression flickered for the barest instant, and Sicard wondered if he was actually preparing to question the propriety of using a Church office to bring such pressures to bear. But instead he finally shrugged, offered a shallow bow, and departed, leaving the bishop alone with thoughts far darker and more brooding than they had been only a few minutes before.

❁

She dreamt of the pain.

It ran deep, burning, searing, itching, aching, no matter how her mind struggled to escape. She dreamt of herself as a child, and it was there. In winding alleys that never ended; on wooded mountainsides; in a cathedral that became the Finders' Guild; in the Flippant Witch, which became a house; while desperately searching for a chamber pot and some privacy in which to use it; when locked in the embrace of a man whose face she couldn't see, and wasn't sure she wanted to know; through it all, the pain remained. Though she never, during or between any of those dreams, fully awakened, she could feel herself tossing and turning, her skin burning with what may or may not have been fever, clammy against the sweat-soaked sheets, trying and failing to find comfort; and the pain remained.

Until, finally, her mind began to quiet, and she felt the balm of Olgun's tranquility, his concern, his protection wash over her. And the pain remained—but finally, it began to lessen.

Consciousness was a sickness, at first, a parasite that she wanted nothing more than to fight off. After a few moments, however, as mind and body adapted to the idea that perhaps waking up wasn't the worst possible fate in all of recorded history, the final fog of dreaming faded.

Widdershins licked lips that were as dry as parchment and opened her eyelids, squinting against the light.

She realized three things in rapid succession. First, that she was not in any room with which she was especially familiar, as the ceiling—apparently rough, cheap stone—wasn't one she knew. She might have thought that she was in a prison cell somewhere, except that most prison cells didn't have mattresses this comfortable, and smelled a lot worse.

Two, that her chest and shoulder hurt a lot. A *lot*. More than she'd have expected, if Olgun had indeed been working to heal her, though certainly less than any normal person would have felt under the circumstances.

And three, her left hand was aching pretty fiercely in its own right. What could she possibly have done to her . . . ?

Oh.

"Robin?"

"Shins! Oh, my gods, you're awake!" The pain in Widdershins's hand actually grew worse. "Guys, she's awake!"

"Robin, you're crushing my fingers. . . ."

"Oh!" The girl's grip slackened, much to Widdershins's relief, but she refused to relinquish her grip entirely. "I'm sorry."

"'Sall right. Where . . . ?" She tried to sit up and fell back, biting back a groan, as her shoulder flared anew.

"Stay still, my dear lady. You need your beauty sleep."

That voice—most certainly *not* Robin's—was quite enough to spur her into doing the precise opposite. She sat up once more, this time ignoring the tightness and the pain, and examined the room over her young friend's shoulder.

She saw Julien first—and, indeed, upon seeing him, recognized from the walls and the worn carpeting that she must be somewhere within the headquarters of the Guard—but it hadn't been he who spoke. So who . . . ?

There. Seated on the edge of the major's desk as though he owned it, a handsome (if rather short) fellow grinned at her from behind a dark mustache and a pair of bluest eyes. His tunic was colorful enough to make the average flower garden seem positively drab, the buckles of his boots were polished to a mirror sheen, and he wore a purple half cape thrown dramatically over one shoulder. Widdershins saw an ostrich plume sticking out from behind him, and knew from experience it was attached to a foppish, flocked hat.

"Renard?!"

Renard Lambert, one of the few Finders whom Widdershins actually trusted (for all that he often annoyed the stuffing out of her), shot to his feet and bowed so low that his bangs nearly brushed the floor. "At your service, most lovely Widdershins."

"What in the name of the gods and all their pets are you doing *here*?"

"Have you noticed," Renard said with a sniff, "that you always greet me that way? It's never 'Wonderful to see you, Renard,' or even just a simple 'Hello,' but always 'What in the name of some silly expression are you doing here?' It's enough to make a gentleman feel unwanted."

"And you, too, I'll bet," she said smugly—which effect was ruined when she couldn't help but laugh at the look her comment brought to his face.

Then, when it became clear that Renard wouldn't offer any additional explanation, she turned back toward the others.

Julien, in response to the unspoken question, could only shrug. "I sent for Robin. I knew you'd want a friend close by—and one who could, ah, keep you company while the chirurgeon worked without, let's say, sacrificing either propriety or modesty." He blushed faintly, as did Widdershins herself.

"I appreciate you thinking of that," Widdershins said.

"Uh, you're welcome. But as for this 'gentleman' . . ." He cast Renard a narrow grimace. "I've no idea. He said simply that he had 'sources' and insisted he was a friend. I'd never have let him stay, but Robin vouched for him."

At Widdershins's puzzled look, the other girl smiled faintly. "I figured, with so many of the Guard out looking for this phantom-thingy, and with Major Bouniard having his own duties to attend to, it made sense to have someone nearby who could protect you in case . . ." Although her voice may have trailed off, the flicker of her eyes toward the wound on Widdershins's shoulder—a wound that, Widdershins only now realized, was swathed in bandages—left no doubt as to her meaning.

"Sources?" she asked Renard, trying not to grin.

"The good major and his fellow officers dislike believing that the Finders have eyes and ears within his ranks, but that doesn't make it any less true. Has been as long as there's been a Guard."

"And you're comfortable just telling me about it to my face?" Julien snapped.

"Seeing as how you've no evidence that I've committed any crime, and thus have no grounds to hold or question me—to say nothing of the fact that I couldn't identify most of our informants anyway—why should I not?"

"Bouniard," Widdershins interrupted, before the argument could go somewhere unpleasant for all concerned, "what am I doing here, exactly?"

"You . . . Widdershins, you came here looking for help. Don't you remember?"

"Well, yes, but I'd have thought—"

"You collapsed," he told her. "It was safer for you to have you treated here, rather than try to take you anywhere else. And I could actually keep your presence quieter here than if I'd had to arrange for constables to help me transport you. I, ah, wasn't entirely sure that everyone in the Guard would understand why I was helping you.

"You're in my office, Widdershins. Have been for nearly a day. I had a mattress brought in, and I've left orders not to be disturbed except in dire emergency."

"Why would you do all this?"

Julien's flush grew even redder, and he actually began to fidget like a schoolboy. "Because you needed me to," he said finally.

Hesitantly, even shyly, Widdershins stretched out her hand. Just as slowly, the major stepped near enough to take it.

"Thank you, Julien." She couldn't quite bear to meet his stare; neither could she look away. She found herself smiling—and all but basking in the smile she got from him in return. Apparently acting without bothering to wait for orders from her brain, her fingers tightened their grip on his hand, and for a moment, she actually forgot the pain of her injuries.

Until, suddenly, a conscious thought actually wormed its way through the wall of surging emotion, and all Widdershins could think was, *Oh, gods, I must be such a* mess! Somehow, the fact that she'd been badly wounded, and unconscious for most of a day, didn't feel like much of an excuse.

It was Olgun—and wasn't it always?—who guided her back to an even keel. A faint surge of undifferentiated emotion, the equivalent of a gentle cough, was enough to grab her attention. From there, she felt as though she were briefly floating in what she could only describe as a pool of calm, cooling the extremes of her emotional turmoil and lingering pain both.

"Thank you," she whispered again, this time too low for any mortal ears in the room—and Olgun could certainly have never doubted that her thanks were for more than just that moment.

Widdershins took a deep breath, felt her heart slow to something vaguely resembling its normal rate, and tore her rapt attention from Julien's face (or at least the vicinity thereof) to take in her surroundings. Indeed, she recognized his office, now, as she'd been there a time or two before. The same rickety chairs; the same cheap desk that seemed about ready to collapse beneath the tectonic shifting of the parchment continents moving about its surface; the same oily lamps that added an acrid tang to the air and had stained the walls a color that wasn't really gray, but wasn't really any other color even more than it wasn't really gray. All that had changed was the mattress on which she now lay.

Well, that and the truly motley assortment of individuals currently gathered in said office.

Individuals who . . . Widdershins blinked, puzzled, wondering if she remained dazed enough to be so severely misinterpreting what she saw. Both Renard and Robin were glaring at Julien Bouniard with a simmering anger; what could, indeed, have almost been hatred! From Renard, Widdershins could have dismissed it. The flamboyant thief, for all his bravado, had to be made a little uneasy just standing here in the heart of his enemy's domain. But Robin? What could Julien possibly have done to earn *Robin's* ire?

Perhaps sensing Widdershins's confusion, if not the underpinning reasons for it, Julien gently released her hand and took a half step back from her side.

"Better count your fingers," Renard warned, casting a sidelong grin at Widdershins that *almost* hid the growl of genuine hostility underlying his words.

"Oh, please," Widdershins huffed. "I wouldn't steal from Bouniard." Her own grin went impish. "Until I was well enough to escape, anyway."

Julien snorted back a laugh. "Whatever issues I may have with your *friend* here," he said, "he hasn't left your side since he arrived. He says he's something important to tell you."

Three faces swiveled toward Renard, then, who blinked, looked askance at Robin, and then back at the young woman on the mattress.

"I trust her," Widdershins said simply.

"I'm sure you do," Renard began, "but—"

"I trust her. Completely. Out with it."

Robin beamed, tenderly brushing a strand of sweat-matted hair from Widdershins's forehead.

"Well . . . All right. Widdershins, there's been some talk going around the Finders."

"Yeah? Wow. Good thing I'm already lying down, or else I'd probably fall—"

"Talk about *you*, my little jester."

"Still not being shocked here, Renard."

"Talk that you just murdered a couple of Finders."

"*What?!*"

It took a bit of time to calm things down after that. Widdershins needed a few minutes to recover from the surge of pain in her shoulder brought about when she shot to her feet (or attempted to). Bouniard had to speak to several of his fellow Guardsmen, assuring them that no, they had *not* in fact just heard someone being violently assaulted within the walls of their own headquarters. And thankfully, by the time all that was done, Robin had recovered most of the hearing in her right ear.

"Who do these people think they are?!" Widdershins was lying back, and her voice was substantially softer, but neither fact was preventing her from giving the rant everything she had. "What am I, the guild's designated scapegoat? 'Something's gone wrong, must be Widdershins's fault!' 'Uh-oh, it's raining, must be Widdershins's fault!' 'Stubbed my toe! Curse that Widdershins!'"

"Uh, Shins?" Robin began. "Maybe—"

"This was supposed to get *better* once Lisette was gone! But *noooo*, I still have a target painted on my soul's butt!"

"Widdershins," Julien said, "I think—"

"All right, so I messed up *one job*! But it was dumb! And it wouldn't have worked anyway, and it would've brought the Guard down on us! And—"

"Widdershins!" Both Robin and Julien, this time.

"Well . . . it's all I've done *lately*. How long can they hold a grudge, anyway?" She crossed her arms with a genuine *hmph*, as though daring anyone to answer. "All right, fine. I've done a lot. So if there's plenty to blame me for, why does the world always insist on getting me in hot water for stuff I *didn't* do, hmm? Seems like a stupid amount of effort to go through, yes?"

Robin, Julien, and Renard all waited, presumably to be certain she was done. Then, as she began to draw breath—suggesting, perhaps, that she *wasn't* done—her fellow Finder spoke up, apparently determined to head her off before she built up any further momentum.

"There's a witness," he told her.

"What?" Not a screech this time, but more of a faint squeak, as Widdershins seemed to deflate or even flatten rather like a mouse in a grain mill.

"Simon Beaupre."

Widdershins was able, this time, to keep herself from sitting bolt upright and stressing her injuries even further. She settled, instead, for squeezing her eyes shut against what promised to become an incipient headache. "Squirrel."

"Squirrel?" Robin and Julien asked simultaneously.

"That's him," Renard said.

"I'm gonna kill him!" Widdershins promised.

Several chuckles answered her. "Maybe not the best thing to say when he's the one accusing you of murder," Renard pointed out.

"Or in front of the Guard," Julien added.

"Oh, both of you shut up." Then, "Renard, I didn't kill anyone, and I don't know what Squirrel's talking about, though I can take a pretty good guess as to why he's trying to blame it on me." Another pause, as she squirmed beneath the questioning expressions of Julien and Robin. "I, uh, sort of interfered with a job he was trying to pull. You . . ." She offered the Guardsman a weak, limp sort of smile. "You, uh, were sort of there for part of it."

Julien's face stiffened. "I think you'd probably better not go into any further detail, before I hear something I'll have to act on."

"Yeah, I was just thinking that."

Robin looked at her, at Julien, at Renard. "Guess there's a reason you thieves don't plan anything with Guardsmen in the room, huh? Umm . . ." It was her turn to wither beneath the weight of several unamused glowers. "Maybe you guys should keep doing most of the talking."

"What the hell have I gotten myself into?" Julien asked the world at large. Widdershins—who knew, for once, when *not* to make a snide comment—just nodded her sympathy.

"I never for a moment believed you a murderer, Widdershins," Renard assured her, with a borderline melodramatic hand over his heart. "More importantly, neither do the Shrouded Lord or the taskmaster."

Widdershins felt the fist that had closed around her lungs relax its hold just a bit, and nearly gasped aloud.

"There's a lot of pressure from the ranks of the Finders to question you—you're, let's say, not popular in some quarters . . ."

"You don't say?"

". . . so I can't promise you that there won't be repercussions. And I'd *definitely* watch my back while out alone, were I you. Actually, I wouldn't *go* out alone, were I you."

"You offering to follow me around, Renard?"

"Well, if mademoiselle wishes . . ."

"Never you mind."

Renard chuckled. "Honestly, though, I think it should blow over fairly quickly. Even most of the Finders who believe you capable of murder don't really believe you'd use witchcraft to do it, so—"

"Stop. Stop right there. In fact, go back a few steps. What are you *talking* about?"

"The bodies. Our people you supposedly killed. They certainly weren't *natural* deaths."

That fist in Widdershins's chest began to clench again. "Dry?" she asked. "Like old leather or parchment?"

She'd already had the attention of everyone in the room, yet somehow it felt as though her audience had grown. "You know about it?" Renard demanded.

"How many?"

"Widdershins . . ."

"Renard, please! How many?"

The older thief sighed. "Four."

Widdershins shook her head. The hair Robin had so carefully brushed away fell right back into her face, though she scarcely noticed. "I only knew about two. Robin, help me sit up, please."

During the few moments it took for her to get settled again, the pillows propped behind her so as to avoid putting any pressure on her wounds, Widdershins's mind was furiously chasing itself in half a dozen different directions. How much could she say here? Who would she have to keep secrets from? Gods, but this had been easier when she didn't mind lying to Julien, but now . . .

She blinked. When had she decided she didn't want to lie to Julien anymore?

Oh, this is bad. . . .

"I ran into—well, into *something*—on the street last night," she began. *Better not mention that two of the Finders were actually masquerading as our local "phantom," not in front of Jul—in front of a Guardsman.* "I don't know *what* it was, but it . . ." She shuddered, and not just for dramatic effect. She found herself clutching at her shoulder with her right hand, though she didn't remember moving. "It did this to me, and . . . Well, you know what it did to *them*."

"Something?" Julien asked, crouching down beside her. "Not some*one*?"

"Trust me, Julien, I can tell the difference."

He nodded, and if he doubted her words at all, no such qualms appeared in his expression or his voice. "Can you describe it?"

"It, he—whichever—was *kind of* human-looking. Frighteningly gaunt, like a scarecrow, with really long limbs. Even longer fingers, like spider's legs or—"

Robin, with something somewhere between a gasp and an abortive shriek, actually lurched back from Widdershins's bedside. Her voice, when it emerged from between quivering lips, was a gravelly whisper. "Spider hands and webs for hair . . ."

"What?" Widdershins, stunned at the reaction and frightened by the sudden pallor in her friend's face, ignored her own pain and reached out to put a hand on Robin's arm. "Sweetie, what is it?"

"Don't you remember, Widdershins? You must have heard it when you were young. I'm sure everyone who grew up in Galice must have!"

The thief frowned, troubled once again by the strange sense of familiarity she'd felt when she'd first gotten a good look at the creature. "I'm not sure what . . ."

Robin took a deep breath, and began.

"Beneath the sun, the roads are man's,
His work, his home, his town, his plans.
But 'ware the ticking of the clock:
The night belongs to Iruoch."

Widdershins's breath caught, and she felt the tingle of a thousand tiny legs across her back and neck. She *did* remember!

"In shadowed wood, in distant vale,
In summer rain or winter hail,
If you alone should choose to walk,
You may just meet with Iruoch."

It was a children's rhyme, nothing but a silly, scary story; one of scores they told each other in the dark, long after they were supposed to have gone to sleep. Just one of many Galician bogeymen.

But he wasn't *real*!

"With spider hands and webs for hair,
A black and never-blinking stare,
A scarecrow's form, a dancer's walk,
There's no mistaking Iruoch."

It didn't seem that Robin could have stopped, now, even if she'd wanted to. With every word, her cadence grew ever more singsong; her voice grew higher, as though she were physically reverting back to the girl she'd been when first she'd heard the words. She shook beneath the weight of a childhood nightmare made very, very real, and Widdershins could do nothing but try to hold her.

"No means to fight, nowhere to run,
Your dreams are ash, your days are done.
No point to scream, to cry, to talk;
Your words mean naught to Iruoch."

Even Julien and Renard were captivated, reaching out to Robin as though to comfort her, even as they clearly had trouble believing that she could possibly *need* comfort, not from something as simple, as silly, as a rhyme. And Widdershins—Widdershins, who now remembered it as clearly as when she herself was a little girl, could only recite the last stanza along with her friend.

"No mortals, magics, blades, or flames,
He only fears the Sacred Names.
Only a faith as stout as rock
Might save your hide from Iruoch."

Robin inhaled once, deeply, as though only now able to breathe, buried her head in Widdershins's chest, and sobbed. Unsure of what else she should do, Widdershins held her tight, casting a worried glance over Robin's head—a glance returned by the other occupants of the room.

"Uh . . ." She cleared her throat and tried again. "Robin, that's not, well, not *exactly* how he looked. His hair wasn't . . ." She tried to shrug, and succeeded only in jostling the other girl's head. "I don't think we've got enough reason to believe that—"

"It's him," Robin insisted, sniffling, and raised her head. "Iruoch's come to Davillon."

"It's nonsense," Julien insisted. "It's just a folktale. A child's rhyme."

"Pure silliness, dear girl," Renard agreed.

Widdershins nodded. "See, Robin? Besides, there haven't been any fairies in Galice in hundreds of years."

"Like there haven't been any demons, Shins?"

The thief actually felt herself wilt. "Olgun?" she asked, scarcely vocalizing. "It's *not* Iruoch, right?"

Olgun's silence was worse than any confirmation he might have offered.

"Oh." Then, somewhat more loudly, "Uh, guys? I don't know if Robin's right about who or what this thing is, but we know it's real, and it's magic, and it's really, *really* not friendly. Does it honestly matter what his name is?"

When nobody offered her any reply more intelligible than a grunt of agreement, she continued. "Jul—uh, Bouniard, can you increase the patrols?"

Julien grinned. "Widdershins *asking* for a greater Guard presence on the street? Are we certain the world's not ending?"

"Keep talking, Bouniard, and you'll wish it was."

The major's grin only widened, and Widdershins had to bite her lip to keep from matching the expression. Trying to force herself to remain on topic, she said, "I don't actually think any of your people could take on Iruoch—or whoever he is—but maybe he won't attack groups."

"My people couldn't . . . ? You have an awfully high opinion of your own fighting skills, I see." Then, his grin fading, "We *already* reinforced the patrols when this whole mess started. We really don't have more constables to spare. But I'll talk to command about trying to concentrate them further."

"All right. Renard?"

"Yes, General Widdershins?"

"Stop that. I need you to arrange a meeting for me with the Shrouded Lord. Or at least with Remy."

Renard's mustache twisted as he frowned. "I can report back everything you've—"

"No. There's . . ." She forced herself not to glance at Julien as she spoke. "There's other stuff I need to talk to them about."

If the Guardsman recognized that Widdershins had all but admitted she was keeping some of the details secret from him, it didn't show on his face.

"Ah. All right, I'll see what I can do."

"And *you*," Julien said, straightening, "are going to get some sleep."

"But I—"

"No. You're still recovering. And frankly, Widdershins, this doesn't involve you. I'm sorry you had to face Ir—whatever this thing is, but you're not a Guard."

"And you have other problems," Robin reminded her softly.

Evrard! Gods, she'd actually *forgotten*! Mortified, she initially wanted to blame Olgun, to accuse him of tricking her into focusing on other issues, but she knew she'd just gotten caught up in it all.

"I want to know what's going on, what this thing is," she admitted. *And why Finders were masquerading as a supernatural thug before the* real *supernatural thug showed up!* "But that's all. I'll try to gather information, but beyond that, I'll stay out of it. Promise."

She swore she could actually *feel* the mattress buckling beneath the weight of their combined disbelief, but nobody challenged her outright.

"I'll stay with you," Robin offered.

Widdershins shook her head. "I need you to manage the Witch, sweetie."

"But—"

"Please, Robin."

Robin stared down at the floor for a moment, then rose. "All right." She leaned down and gave her friend a kiss on the cheek. "You get better quick, though, or I might just take the whole tavern somewhere safer."

"I'll remember that." Widdershins smiled—a smile that swiftly faded as, for just an instant, Robin turned an angry glare on Julien Bouniard. But before Widdershins could be sure she'd even seen it, and *certainly* before Julien himself might have noticed, the girl left the room. Renard offered another low bow, tossed his hat onto his head with a jaunty flip of the wrist, and followed.

When the door drifted shut, and Widdershins realized that she was alone with Julien—Olgun's constant presence notwithstanding—she caught herself preparing to scream for Robin to come back.

This is so stupid! I've been alone with Julien before! I—

He scooted one of the chairs away from the desk, and rotated it so he could sit facing her. The worry he felt for her was so clear in his eyes, it practically obscured their color.

Oh, figs . . .

CHAPTER EIGHT

Renard Lambert felt his back growing tense, his tunic bunching up as his shoulders rose to his ears (or so it felt, anyway). Each step he took was a struggle, and he wondered which would overcome him first: the urge to glance over his shoulder so often he'd probably break his neck, or the burning need to break into a mad sprint for the door.

He did neither, of course—by the Shrouded God and the rest of the Hallowed Pact, he'd walked calmly *into* the Guard station, he'd bloody well walk calmly *out* of it!—but it was a near thing.

The occasional suspicious glance cast his way by passing constables actually helped calm him down, rather than wind up him any further. It wasn't as if the bulk of them knew his face, and even if some *did* recognize him, well, he wasn't currently wanted for anything. (Not because he hadn't *done* anything, of course.) All they knew was that here was a colorfully dressed character wandering the halls, and while that wasn't exactly normal, neither was it automatically cause for alarm. He certainly wasn't about to give them the satisfaction of seeing how nervous the place made him.

Of course, he realized glumly, they might just assume that he was an aristocrat come to bail his daughter, or some other young relative, out of trouble. *I*, he grumbled to himself, *am really not enamored of this whole aging thing.*

Robin—who could indeed have been his daughter, if only just—marched a few steps ahead of him, and kept whatever thoughts she might have had entirely to herself. Her pace, however, was stiff enough that Renard had no doubt she was just as troubled as he, if presumably for other reasons.

Gods, even when he *had* gotten away from here, there was so much to do! He'd picked up readily enough on Widdershins's hint that she had more to tell him, things she couldn't say in front of the major. (And the thief couldn't repress a scowl at the thought of Julien Bouniard, *especially* the thought of Bouniard alone with Widdershins.) He'd certainly have no trouble arranging a meeting with the Shrouded Lord—and he wondered if Widdershins would ever puzzle out *that* particular secret, because if anyone ever did, he knew, it'd be her—but he wanted a couple of days to look into this "Iruoch" matter himself before said meeting. Plus, there was all the usual night-to-night business of the Finders' Guild to deal with, and the mess with Simon Beaupre, and then there was . . . *Bloody hell, it's a wonder I have time to take a piss! If this had been anyone but Widdershins, I never would have taken the time to—*

They had, by this time, passed by the desk sergeant on duty as well as the sentries nearest the entrance, and Robin was pushing open the heavy door to reveal the lowering skies of late afternoon beyond. As she did so, she turned, and Renard couldn't help but note the sour expression she directed not at him but *past* him, back down the hallway from which they'd come.

And he wondered. *I know why* I'm *so damn irritated at Bouniard. I'm honest enough to admit to jealousy. But what the hell has* she *got to be so grumpy about?*

But since he would never be so uncouth as to ask, and since she'd already darted out into the street before he could have done so even if he'd wanted to, his curiosity remained unsated.

❋

For roughly 150 years—or maybe a *little* less time, but Widdershins wouldn't have sworn to it—the thief and the Guardsman just watched each other. Or rather, near each other, neither quite willing to maintain eye contact for more than a heartbeat or so.

"Uh," Widdershins finally said.

"Yes?" Bouniard straightened in his chair, practically at attention.

"You, um, you saw the scene? Where Iruoch killed those people?"

"Not me, personally, but some constables scoured it." He offered no objection to her use of the name Iruoch—less because he'd begun to believe, she assumed, than because, well, he had no better name to offer.

"I don't suppose you found my sword?" she asked, her voice small and miserable.

"Your . . ." He shook his head. "I didn't hear reports of *any* weapons found. Someone must have taken them before our people arrived. I'm sorry."

"If it was Squirrel," Widdershins muttered darkly, "I'll kill him. Then I'm going to find a healer, revive him, and kill him again."

"I didn't hear you," Julien said blandly. "I'm *sure* you just said that you were going to find him and ask him, politely, if he had your blade."

"Yeah. That, too."

Another few decades passed. . . .

"Widdershins, about last week?"

She blinked. What was he talking ab—Oh. *That*.

"I don't know what you're talking about," she said sweetly.

"Uh-huh. The Ducarte estate?"

"Oh. That."

"You're stealing again," he accused her.

"What's the matter, Bouniard? You afraid of having someone out there you can't catch? I'm too challenging for you, maybe?"

"I'm serious. I can't . . . That is, I don't want . . ."

"Don't want what?"

Julien shrugged, looking away.

What could she tell him? That the Flippant Witch wouldn't survive without some "outside income"? That it was all she was good at? That she was *bored*? Somehow, she was pretty sure that none of those would fly.

And why am I bothering to explain myself?!

"Look, Julien. I promise you won't catch me doing anything illegal." It was an old joke between them, but this time, he didn't seem amused.

"I'm serious, Widdershins," he said again.

"You know, I think I almost picked up on that the first time you told me."

"But you obviously aren't."

"Well, no. Wouldn't want you accusing me of stealing your mood, would we?"

More glaring, more silence. A silence that broke as Julien scooted his chair back with a low scuffing across the carpet and began to pace.

"You shut up," Widdershins breathed. Olgun, who hadn't actually been about to say anything at all, continued not doing so.

"Uh, Julien?"

He halted his pacing, his back toward her. "What?"

"Um, given that I've been out for a day, and that you're probably keeping a pretty close watch on what's happening in Davillon . . ."

"Hmm?"

"I was wondering if, well, if you knew who's throwing the next high-society ball or dinner party. And when."

Oh, yeah, this was exactly *the right time to ask him that, Widdershins! Graceful as a three-hoofed pig on a stack of turtles, you are.*

He was facing her again, though his expression couldn't have been any more astonished if he'd just discovered that she'd been smuggling a street mime in her cleavage.

"Have you *utterly* lost your mind?!" The major was too dignified to actually shriek, but only just.

"Uh, maybe? What are my options?"

"I should have arrested you last week! Maybe you'd actually learn something from a few months in gaol!"

"What makes you think I'd have let you hold me that long? You couldn't manage it last time!"

Widdershins couldn't help but laugh as Julien's hand, seemingly of its own accord, dropped down to clutch at the keys on his belt—the keys that she'd used to escape the last time she'd been incarcerated.

Then, deciding that goading him any further was probably neither the wisest nor the most productive course of action, she said, "Look, I'm not looking to rob anyone. I told you, I want to find out more about what's going on in the city, as well as about some problems of my own. Nobody gossips like aristocrats, and nobody has more ears throughout Davillon. *That's* why I want to go; not to steal anything."

"And I should believe that why, exactly?"

"When have I ever lied to—"

"Do you *really*," he growled at her, "want to finish that sentence?"

"Ah, no. No, I don't think I do. Julien . . ." She sighed and finally, steadily met his gaze with her own. "Whatever else I might do, whatever tricks I might pull, I'd never make you complicit in something you wouldn't approve of. I swear it."

His face froze an instant longer and then cracked and softened. "I believe you. Which may say less about your honesty and more about my fracturing sanity, but there we are. The Marquise de Lamarr is throwing a soiree of some sort tomorrow evening—she's asked for a few of the Guard to bolster her own security—but that's probably too soon. Next week, the Baron—"

"No, tomorrow should work." Widdershins swung her feet off the mattress, wincing but refusing to retreat before the pain. "Are my shoes around here?"

"Widdershins . . ."

"Because I'm pretty sure I had shoes when I got in. I really don't go out without 'em all that often. . . ."

"Widdershins, lie down. You're hurt. Give it a few days!"

"I heal fast, Julien. We've been through this."

"Not *that* fast, you don't!"

And it was actually true. Widdershins's shoulder and chest burned, aching far more than she would have expected. Was Olgun's power less effective against such an unnatural wound? Maybe so—but she was doing better than anybody else would have been, even if she wasn't exactly her full self.

And she *sure* wasn't about to spend another night in Julien's office! In its own way, and for its own reasons, the thought scared her as much as Iruoch himself.

"I'll be fine, Julien. And I'm going."

He stood before her, arms crossed. "And if I put men at all the exits, with orders not to let you leave?"

"How many windows does this building have?" she asked smugly. "I'm pretty sure you can't spare *that* many guards."

"Guards on the office door, then."

"Sure. Just as soon as you explain to them that you've had me stashed in here for a day or so. That'll go over *real* well."

"I could arrest you," he insisted, but she knew from the slump of his shoulders that he was starting to surrender. "I can hold you for a while before we have to start worrying about charges and trials and all that."

Widdershins smiled, stood—with only a single wince of pain—and, unconscious of what she was about to do until she was doing it, ran the tips of her fingers across his cheek. "But you wouldn't do that to me, right?"

"No," he admitted. It came out somewhere between a grunt and a sigh. "I wouldn't. Just . . . Be careful, Shins."

"I'm always careful." Widdershins stretched up on her toes and planted a kiss right at the corner of Julien's mouth—not on the lips, no, but not quite on the cheek, either. And then, before either of them could react to what had just happened, she was out the door and gone.

Without, it's worth pointing out, her shoes.

Julien was still standing in that precise spot, staring at the empty mattress and trying to remember how to form a cogent thought, when his door shook with a familiar, military cadence.

"Uh . . ." He shook himself, wishing briefly he had a snifter of brandy available, or at least a bucket of ice water in which to dunk his head. "Enter!"

Paschal pushed the door open, saluted (with the wrong hand, but given his injured arm, that was acceptable), and then looked with some bemusement at the mattress.

When it became clear that nobody would be answering his unasked question, he spoke. "Sorry to disturb you, sir, but I thought you should know . . ."

"Yes, Constable?"

"The thief we discussed last week? Widdershins?"

Demas, does this whole damn city revolve around her?! "What of her?"

"We've orders to arrest her on sight, sir."

Julien blinked rapidly enough that Paschal could probably feel the breeze. "Why? What's she accused of?"

"Not entirely sure, sir. The request came from the bishop's office."

"*What?!*"

"Apparently, due to her rumored involvement in the death of Archbishop de Laurent—"

"She was trying to *save* the man!"

"So I've read in the reports, sir. Nevertheless, given the unnatural events surrounding that tragedy, and given her proximity to what's happening now, they want her brought in until they can determine for themselves whether she's responsible or otherwise involved."

"And we're taking instructions on how to uphold the law from clergymen now, are we?"

The constable's look was more than enough to convey the various meanings that he couldn't, as Julien's subordinate, actually come out and utter.

"Yes, yes, you're right. Well, I can assure you that I have no notion of where Widdershins is at this point in time." *As opposed to what would have happened if you'd shown up five minutes ago. Widdershins, your luck is incredible!* "But I will, of course, keep a lookout and do as we've been ordered."

"I had no doubt of that, sir." Paschal frowned behind his goatee. "Major, I'm sorry to be the one to put you in this position. I know that you're friends with the woman." If there was just the tiniest hesitation before the constable pronounced "friends," well, both men chose to ignore it.

"Bah. It's not as though you gave the order. Better to hear it from you, anyway." Julien took a single step toward the door, then paused. "You do understand, of course, that given all the troubles facing Davillon just now, any hunt for a street thief—however genuine our efforts may be—cannot possibly take priority over other concerns."

"I'm quite sure," Paschal said with an almost straight face, "that nobody could argue that."

Julien nodded once, brusquely, and stepped out into the corridors, his actively not-grinning friend close on his heels.

❋

Not at all unlike his namesake, Squirrel crouched in the branches of a large tree that sprouted alongside the partially paved lane. Between the thickening darkness and the lush foliage of late spring, he was utterly invisible to passersby. (Or he would have been, had there been any.)

But while the world might have been oblivious to him, he was not at all oblivious to the world—much as he might wish he were.

While the smell of the leaves and the fading aromas of Davillon's busy days might have overpowered the distant smell of peppermint, nothing—not even the hands he clasped desperately over his ears—could drown out the sounds emerging from the shop across the way.

"Ooh! Are we playing hide-and-seek? How high am I supposed to count?"

"Help me! Get away from me! *Get away!*"

"Well, that's no good. How are you supposed to hide from me if you're screaming like that? You really have no idea how to play this game, do you?"

"Help me! Somebody, please! Help . . . Oh, *gods*!"

"You're making me cross, now. Here." Squirrel winced at the horrid, wet ripping sound, followed by a gurgle only vaguely recognizable as a human voice. "There! Won't be screaming without one of *those*, will you? *Now* we can play!"

The gurgle sputtered once, then faded.

"Oh. Huh. You're all so *fragile*." The shop's old walls and shuttered windows kept Squirrel from seeing so much as a single gesture of what was happening inside, but he was certain the gaunt creature who was now his master must have shrugged. "But delicious."

Squirrel's whimpers masked the worst of the lapping, squishing, and dry crackling to follow.

But what followed *those*, oddly enough, were a series of crashes and thumps, as though the thing inside was ransacking the shop. And accompanying the not-so-musical tones of a careless search, a cheerful, jaunty whistling.

Eventually, the clattering and the whistling both ended with a satisfied, "Aha! Here we are! Some of those and some of these, some for you's and some for me's . . ."

Wood thumped against stone, and one of the shuttered windows flew open. The floppy hat emerged, followed by the rest of Squirrel's master. He crawled across the wall with only a single hand; in the other, he clutched what appeared to be a bedsheet, tied into a makeshift sack and stained with fresh blood. Where the bricks ended, he dropped to his feet and progressed directly to the tree in which his reluctant servant was concealed.

"Come down, come down! I have surprises for all my good little boys and girls!"

It took every ounce of will for Squirrel to pry his hands free from the bark and force himself to descend.

"Uh, master?"

That mostly human head cocked to one side. "A question, a question! I think I have an answer or two just lying around. Shall we see if they match?"

"Well . . . I was just . . ."

"Oh, no. Never be *just*." A long finger wagged in Squirrel's face. "Never, ever, ever. Understand?"

"Um . . . Yes?"

"Goody!"

"I was ju—that is, I was wondering . . . Was the shopkeep enough for tonight? For, uh, for you? I mean, that wasn't, well, it wasn't exactly quiet, and the Guard—"

"Enough? *Enough?* Silly, stupid child, there is no *enough*, oh, no. Never. The loud old man was stale and dry and not very sweet at all. We didn't come to him for supper."

"No? Then why . . . ?"

The creature's grin widened enough to split his face clear across the middle. With a dramatic flourish, he flung the bedsheet upon the earth, yanking it so that it rolled open as it landed. Within rested an entire array of glazed pastries; brightly colored hard candies; and rich, sticky toffees.

"I told you already, forgetful thief. Surprises for *all* my good little boys and girls! Just as soon as you show me where to find them. . . ."

Squirrel stared in horror at the tempting treats spread out before him, and softly began to cry.

CHAPTER NINE

He'd known it had to be bad.

From the moment Constable Sorelle had appeared in the doorway to his office, scarcely capable of stringing two words together in any coherent fashion, his face fish-belly pale and his eyes wide as carriage wheels, Julien had known that his day was about to become very, very unpleasant. Throughout the journey, as Paschal led him through the afternoon crowds, carving a path through Davillon's bustling streets, he'd contemplated and considered, imagining a dozen and one scenarios, each worse than the last. He'd questioned the constable time and again, but the normally unflappable Guardsman was so distraught that Julien couldn't find it in him to berate the man for his unprofessional demeanor.

He'd known it had to be bad. But not even in the darkest of his imaginings could Julien Bouniard—who had been a member of the Davillon Guard all his adult life, who had been present a few years back at the discovery of the worst massacre in the city's modern history—have anticipated *how* bad.

A crowd had gathered in their path, facing a small courtyard formed by the corners of several modest houses. An angry grumbling pawed at his ears, punctuated by sobs and the occasional gasp. Scattered throughout that assembly were several men and women in the black and silver of the Guard; men and women who *should* have been dispersing the crowd, or otherwise securing the scene, and yet instead were only staring alongside their fellow citizens.

Major Bouniard began to shove and elbow his way through, barking orders and scowling at every constable failing in his or her duty. . . . And then stopped as something crunched beneath his boot. He looked down to study the broken slice of candied fruit, cracked and smeared on the roadway, and initially assumed it was simple litter, unimportant and readily dismissed.

Or so it seemed, until he saw a second sliver of the same confection, as well as an uneven wedge of chocolate, a peppermint stick, a gooey handful of pastry stuck to the brick of a nearby wall . . .

A *trail*. It was a trail of sugary leavings, just as one might find in the wake of a passel of schoolchildren or unsupervised urchins. It led . . . Why, it led toward that same courtyard to which Paschal had been guiding him!

A courtyard whose entranceway Julien could now see. An entryway in which lay a little toy pony, its stitches torn, its stuffing scattered. And beside that, just the faintest scrap of what, beneath the drying blood, might have been the hem of a brightly dyed floral print dress.

"Oh, gods . . ."

Julien didn't have to push his way through anymore. The crowd melted aside, allowing him to pass—now that he desperately didn't want to.

They were all so *small*. It was hard to imagine that they'd ever been anything more than heaps of clothes and flesh, hair and bone; that they'd ever laughed and cried, run and skipped.

That they'd ever squealed with delight over the sweet promises of the scattered candies.

Half a dozen of them. Half a dozen voices that would never laugh again, half a dozen lives that would never be lived, half a dozen families that would never be whole.

Julien literally, physically reeled beneath the enormity of it. He might well have fallen, had he not been near enough to slap a palm against one of the neighboring walls and hold himself upright. Beyond that, however, there was nothing. He did not cry, as many of the crowd, and even several of his constables, were doing now. His gut didn't churn, though several wet and rancid stains on the cobbles outside the courtyard suggested that more than a few of the witnesses had emptied their stomachs over what they saw.

It wasn't that Julien had grown suddenly hard, that he didn't care. It was that, for the nonce, he'd simply been numbed by it all. Later, he knew, it would hit him. He would shake, and he would sob, and he would beg Demas or Vercoule or any other god for an explanation that he knew he'd never receive. But for now, it remained at some small remove, outside him rather than a part of him. He couldn't take it in, not all of it.

And that was good. It meant, for the moment, that he could do his job. Julien allowed himself one second to think *I wish old Sergeant Chapelle were here*, and then forced himself to take in the entire scene.

It took some time to notice, because it required examining the tiny bodies directly, and neither Julien nor any of the others had any desire to do so, but eventually he recognized a peculiar inconsistency. Whatever it was that Iruoch did to most of his victims—draining? drinking? desiccating? Whatever process led to the cracking, parchment skin, the shriveled flesh, the relative paucity of blood . . . it wasn't universal here. Three of the poor children were, indeed, nothing more than bones and dusty leather. But a fourth was, for lack of a better word, *floppy*, as though the process had only been about halfway completed; and the other two were merely murdered (as if that wasn't bad enough), their pale skin showing wounds of the foulest sort, but their bodies otherwise left intact.

Had the creature's appetite finally been sated? If so, had he only slaughtered the remaining victims to indulge some sadistic pleasure?

Or had something happened, something to distract Iruoch from his ghastly repast? Something of sufficient import to draw him away? Julien had no evidence to that effect, but every instinct he'd developed as a City Guardsman screamed at him that this latter possibility was indeed the case.

Thus, when another moment's investigation actually *did* provide the evidence to support that assertion, he was already prepared to act on it.

In the smears of blood on the cobblestones, and small patches of dirt in or alongside the road, Julien found sporadic tracks. The first set was bizarre, puzzling, and difficult to follow. They were more smears than prints, only occasionally taking the shape of a shoe, as though the man who left them behind hadn't been walking so much as skipping, sliding, even pirouetting on his way. These tracks began just beside the partially drained body, which was splayed and broken on the earth. Unless Julien was badly mistaken, it had simply been dropped and abandoned in the midst of—of whatever it was that was being done to it.

A second set of prints, smaller than the first and far more normal in both shape and pattern, joined the first toward the edge of the courtyard. They followed behind—a companion, perhaps, or a servant?—and whoever left them seemed to be making some effort to avoid stepping through the worst of the carnage.

The trail would never be sufficient to lead them to the perpetrators of this ghastly crime. Blood on the boots, patches of mud in the road; such signs would fade quickly enough, especially given the added complication of additional pedestrians on the street. Still, it might continue far enough to give Julien some general sense of direction, maybe even reveal the district into which his quarry had gone.

"Constable Sorelle!" And then, louder, as Paschal continued to gawk vacantly at the scattered remains, "*Constable Sorelle!*"

"Sir!" The constable practically shot from his boots. "Yes, sir?"

"Select two Guardsmen. One is to remain with you and secure the courtyard; the other is to report back to headquarters and summon extra investigators to search the scene."

"Yes, sir. And you?"

"I," Julien said grimly, "will be taking the rest of the unit with me, and we're going to do our damnedest to hunt this monster down and end the gods-damned thing!"

The gathered Guardsmen didn't have to be told twice. Hearing the major's intent, they shook themselves from their fugue and converged on him, whereupon—accompanied by the angry mutters and bloodthirsty encouragement of the crowd—they set out to follow the feeble trail for as long as the gods, fate, or plain dumb luck would allow.

❋

Madame Berdine Jolivet, the Marquise de Lamarr, was not among the wealthiest, most powerful, or most popular of Davillon's aristocrats. She wasn't in disfavor, by any means; she just didn't particularly stand out in high society. At any other time in modern history, any party she might host at her manor would have garnered only a modest attendance, with a few semi-impressive guests, and perhaps a few whispered words of gossip over the course of the following day or three.

But this was *not* any other time in modern history. Not only were Davillon's nobility actively struggling to avoid showing any concessions to (or even awareness of) the city's economic woes, but now the growing threat of some horrid phantom or murderer stalking the streets made the comfort and safety of numbers even more appealing. Tonight, then, a great many private guards from half a dozen different noble houses strode the lawn and the garden paths of the Lamarr estate, and the house itself was absolutely crammed to capacity, and beyond, with aristocrats of every rank and position, to say nothing of the army of servants required to feed and entertain aristocrats of every rank and position. Had Beatrice Luchene, the Duchess of Davillon herself, thrown such a party at this same time last year, it probably wouldn't have boasted as many attendees.

Every space not occupied by people was, instead, occupied by tables. These had long since lost the strength even to groan under the weight of the piled meats and fowls and pastries and fruits, and instead settled for the occasional despairing whimper. Nobody leaned against the walls, despite the press of the throng, because doing so would have entangled them in the hanging banners of Vercoule and other various gods. Dancing was simply out of the question as well, as there was insufficient space for more than a few couples at a time. Despite this fact, Jolivet's hired musicians played on from a balcony above—played on for an audience consisting largely of themselves, since only the most keen-eared members of the throng below could possibly have heard more than every fourth or fifth note.

And as it happened, the keenest of those keen ears was listening for something entirely unrelated to the music.

Widdershins—or, rather, Madeleine—made her rounds of the hors d'oeuvres, the wines, and the various social cliques with as much grace and poise as the overly friendly conditions would permit. Her golden-blonde wig and the expert makeup (designed not so much to enhance her appearance, but to further blur the similarities between each of her two identities) were the same as they always were, but her garb—customarily emerald in hue—tonight consisted of a gold-and-burgundy-trimmed gown rather less full than the hoop skirts that were currently in fashion. Much as she hated the damn things, her failure to wear one now wasn't a stylistic choice; rather, the effort of getting into one, let alone supporting it throughout the evening, aggravated the stiffness in her chest and shoulder that Olgun hadn't entirely healed.

Fortunately, she wasn't the *only* lady present who'd chosen to eschew those monstrously stiff fabric enclosures, so while she wasn't exactly the height of fashion, neither did she particularly stand out. And it meant she was far more comfortable, and far more agile, than most of the women crammed into the Lamarr household.

Gliding through the room (or, more accurately, shoving and elbowing her way through the room with as much courtesy as shoving and elbowing permit), she took a dainty bite of this, a small sip of that, an appreciative sniff of the other; bestowed a dazzling smile or a respectful nod to all who knew her; and otherwise allowed her body to coast through the party-going motions while straining her own ears and Olgun's magics to pick up any words of import.

Unfortunately, while most conversations she overheard touched on Davillon's current woes, she learned precious little that she hadn't already known. Conspiracies regarding the identity of the crazed killer ranged from some sort of demon summoned from the Pit, to a witch preparing for a horrid ritual, to a scheme on the part of city officials to take more power from the private citizens and place it in the hands of the Guard, to the ghosts of the poor who had died during Davillon's financial difficulties. (There were, of course, a few who assumed that *none* of the rumors were true, and that no such attacks or murders had occurred at all, but these were largely excluded from the conversation by those who knew better, or thought they did.)

She learned that the Guard patrols had indeed doubled in size and frequency, that every noble house had hired on extra soldiers of their own, and that—in the face of the murderer's apparent supernatural nature—attendance at religious services had quadrupled in the past week, as people's anger at the Church for its treatment of the city slowly gave way to their need for protection against the ghouls and goblins of the night.

But as to hard facts, believable theories, or actual plans regarding what the city should do about it all . . . well, they were about as common at this aristocrats' party as honest smiles or genuine compliments.

"Why, Mademoiselle Valois! What an exquisite pleasure to see you here!"

"Oh, goose muffins. Olgun, you really need to learn how to make either me, or other people, completely invisible." In a far louder and more cheerful tone, she called, "Baron d'Orreille! As I live and breathe!" And then, once more in a tone far too low to be overheard, "And gag. And possibly retch."

She felt Olgun's chuckle across the back of her scalp.

Charles Doumerge, the Baron d'Orreille—or "Baron Weaselface," where Madeleine was concerned—scurried and twisted his way through the throng so that he might bow obsequiously to her and kiss the back of her hand with thin, dry lips. Since Madeleine couldn't have escaped without Olgun's supernatural aid (aid, it's worth pointing out, that she seriously considered calling upon, despite the need for secrecy and subtlety), she kept the smile plastered firmly to her face and allowed her hand to suffer in order to protect the rest of her.

Doumerge's bony form straightened so awkwardly, Madeleine actually found herself looking for the strings that must surely be puppeteering him. A gray-faced, straw-haired, limp rag of a fellow, Doumerge had attempted to gussy himself up in tunic and trousers of pristine white, a vest sparkling with gold lace, and a broad sash of a wine hue. The last was so near to being royal purple that it not only bordered on insolence, but stuck a toe across that border and mouthed various obscenities at anyone on the other side.

None of it did the tiniest glimmer of good. He remained a gaunt, unimpressive rodent of a man. But he was a man with powerful friends, and who himself hosted many elaborate soirees, and whom Widdershins had successfully robbed more than once, so it paid to stay polite, however difficult it might be.

The baron rose, and Madeleine successfully fought off the urge to find something on which to wipe her hand. "And what do you think of the marquise's party?" she asked, mostly to keep Doumerge from guiding the conversation himself.

"Eh." The weasel twitched his fingers as though brushing off a length of cobweb. "Acceptable, I suppose, for one of her means, but she's clearly trying to rise above her station. I doubt she's fooling anyone with her pretensions to greater wealth and breeding. Or, well, she's certainly not fooling *me*. I suppose I oughtn't speak for those with less refined sensibilities."

"Well," Madeleine breathed, *clearly* hanging on Doumerge's every word (and trying not to cringe as said breath drew his attention, with alarming rapidity, to her neckline). "I certainly wouldn't even consider disagreeing with you, dear baron." *Mostly*, she added silently, *because if I did, I'd probably start by folding you in half like an envelope and shoving your heels up your nostrils.*

She was just trying to think of some polite way to extricate herself from further conversation—which shouldn't have been that difficult, since the two of them weren't precisely good friends or even close acquaintances—but apparently Doumerge was feeling particularly gregarious. (That, or he believed he recognized, in Madeleine, a potentially captive audience for his great social insight.) Even as she drew breath to speak, the baron turned so that he might intertwine his arm in hers. "Come, my dear. I can tell you with complete confidence who's worth being seen with and who isn't. Perhaps I can even introduce you to a few new friends, hmm?"

When the woman who had three separate names, and until recently had made her living entirely through theft, responded with, "I'd be delighted," it was perhaps the single greatest lie she'd ever uttered. She offered her unwanted companion a tight smile, mostly intended to keep her from gritting her teeth, and allowed him to half lead, half drag her through the packed multitudes of high society.

For endless minutes, he prattled on about this lord or that baroness, this marquis or that mistress. Everything from wealth to breeding, from the size of one person's estate to the size of another's debt, from the mismatched colors of one outfit to the fraying wig of another . . . If it could be commented on or gossiped about with any degree of disdain, Doumerge was ready with a wit that was about as pointed and razor-honed as a bowl of soup.

For her part, Madeleine pretended fascination with his droning, nodding or gasping or grumbling in all the right places, and otherwise continued listening for information regarding her *actual* interests. Information that, as before, was proving frustratingly elusive.

She was, however, paying *enough* attention to Doumerge to drag him abruptly to a halt in both midstep and midsentence.

"I'm sorry," she said sweetly. "Introduce me to *who*, now?"

"Gurrerre Marguilles," the baron repeated. "Lord of—"

"I know who Monsieur Marguilles is," Madeleine told him, allowing a touch of frost to condense over her words. "I fear that I find the man rather frightfully boorish, and I've nothing I care to say to him."

Which, while not entirely true, was far safer than saying, *He's met me as someone else, and while I don't* think *he knows Widdershins well enough to see through the makeup, I'm not about to take the risk. Plus, if I have to talk to him, I'll either start crying over Genevieve, or punch him somewhere really rude.*

"Oh. Uh . . ." The Baron d'Orreille, clearly unprepared for Madeleine to have found any fault in one of the few aristocrats whom he himself had deemed as worthy of their time, was plainly at a loss. "Well, I certainly shouldn't be so discourteous as to insist, but—"

"Splendid! I'm so delighted to hear it." Again she cast about her, looking for any sort of distraction (and possibly an excuse to break away from Baron Weasel-face already). "Why don't you instead . . ."

Holy gods! Her breath caught in her throat, and she felt Olgun start, then slowly begin to simmer with a rapidly growing rage.

Here he was, *right here*! Standing beside one of the tables, a glimmering goblet of wine in one hand, he was currently laughing at some witticism or other offered by one of the many blue bloods gathered around him. He still wore mostly darker grays and blacks, though his tunic and his vest were both trimmed in gleaming silver. Here, at this formal affair, neither his traveler's coat nor his tricorne hat were present, but the chiseled, angular features and the black braid were more than enough.

To say nothing of the dark eyes, currently flashing with mirth but capable of such a deep, angry malevolence . . .

"Him!" This time it was Madeleine who dragged the baron through the sea of people, towing him, a captured ship in her wake. After a few steps, she held herself at an angle where she could point out her target without drawing his attention in turn. "Can you introduce me to him?"

"Ah . . . That is . . ." Doumerge flushed lightly, apparently embarrassed to be caught out by the young woman he was so hoping to impress. "I fear that I haven't been formally introduced to the young lord myself, so it would be improper for me—"

"Then just tell me who he is!" She found herself about to stamp a foot in emphasis and forced herself to relax, to remember where—and who—she was at this moment.

"Uh, his name is Evrard, I believe."

Yes, I know *that!* She found herself about to scream. *But what's his full—?*

"Evrard," the baron continued, "d'Arras."

D'Arras? *D'Arras?* As in *d'Arras Tower*?!

Widdershins, who had taken at least some of her mentor Alexandre's lessons to heart, and thus hadn't uttered a single true profanity in about four years, said, "Oh, shit. . . ."

❁

Magali was a serving girl in the Lamarr household, just one of many. Perhaps thirteen years of age, she was round and pretty of face, with just a hint of the beauty that would be hers as an adult. Her honey-colored hair was pulled back in a simple tail, and her entire body was stuffed into a tightly laced gown and corset of formal pearls and golds, despite the fact that few of the partygoers would ever look upon her.

No, because tonight, Magali's duties were all upstairs, tucked away in a few large but secluded rooms about as far from the chatter and tumult as one could get while remaining within the manor proper. Here, a number of beds, sofas, chairs, and tables had been neatly and meticulously prepared, and had far more swiftly been ravaged beyond recognition.

Here is where the children played, and where Magali was officially (hah!) in charge.

Not *many* children ran and played through the suite of rooms. The bulk of the guests who were also parents had, of course, left their sons and daughters at home in the care of servants or relatives (and far more often the former than the latter). But some, for reasons ranging from the age of the child to simple affection to wanting to display their heirs to their fellow aristocrats, had brought their offspring along. And of course, there were the Marquise de Lamarr's own three children as well. In total, then, there were about nine of them, not counting Magali herself—Magali, who was somehow supposed to keep a rein on the little rampaging monsters when, as a simple servant (and a young girl at that), she couldn't really discipline, punish, or yell at them.

"Pierre! Ives!" She was trying desperately, and failing miserably, to keep her voice down to normal levels. "Stop that this instant!"

The two boys in question stuck out their tongues in perfect unison, and continued jumping on the sofa cushions and laughing hysterically at the goose-down blizzard spawned by their antics. In the interim, Marie was in the corner crying (again) over some imagined slight or other, while Chrestien and Alberi had already made an absolute disaster of their clothes, wrestling and punching under the table. (Magali couldn't tell, at this point, whether the boys were playing, or had progressed to an actual fight. She wasn't sure if *they* were sure, either.)

It was enough to try the patience of a saint, a god, or even a saintly god, let alone a thirteen-year-old girl. Magali was, herself, about to break down in tears—that, or start taking a belt to tiny rears, and to hell with the consequences!—when she thought she heard . . .

Yes! There it was again. Barely audible over the chaos, a faint rapping on the door to the main room. It was too much to hope that the party was over already, but maybe some of the parents were departing early? If they'd take even some of the children with them, it might be easier to . . .

"Yes?" Magali called, sidling up to the door. "Who is it, please?"

"We have treats!" The voice that called back was somehow odd, dissonant, but over the clamor and through the thick wooden door, Magali couldn't really make out what was wrong with it. It was probably her imagination, anyway . . . "Treats for the children!"

This hadn't been part of the evening's plan, so far as Magali knew, but she welcomed it. If the brats were busy stuffing themselves on pastries, then at least they wouldn't be cackling and screaming for a few minutes.

Without the slightest trace of hesitation, Magali threw open the door. . . .

CHAPTER TEN

A few frantic moments of intense (and only borderline polite) questioning of Doumerge revealed a number of fascinating facts about the man Madeleine had previously known only as "Evrard."

The remaining core of the family d'Arras had, for roughly a decade, dwelt in the heart of Rannanti, Galice's nearest neighboring—and often rival—nation. (Unconfirmed rumors suggested that, for much of that time, the d'Arrases weren't there to oversee their business interests, as claimed, but were in fact political prisoners—albeit well-treated and lavishly kept political prisoners—held against the possibility of future leverage.) Only a few years ago, the family had finally returned to their homes in the Galicien city of Vontagne, where most of them lived to this day. Evrard himself had arrived in Davillon some few months ago, not long after the death of William de Laurent.

As to why he had come—or indeed, anything else about the young aristocrat—gossip was heavy on speculation but frighteningly light on confirmed fact. Business or pleasure, politics or romantic interest? There were as many theories, if not more, as there were curious ears and whispering mouths to theorize. On only three points were the majority of the tales about Evrard in agreement: First, that he was the only d'Arras to have visited Davillon from Vontagne. Second, that he was not yet firmly attached to any of Davillon's respected citizens, either on a political or long-term romantic level.

And third, that—as he had mastered the blade-play of Rannanti as well as Galicien culture—he was purported to be one of the finest duelists of the modern era.

This last detail was more than enough to convince Madeleine to be grateful that Robin had stopped her from drawing steel on the man. Even with Olgun's aid, he didn't seem the sort of fellow with whom she'd care to cross blades. And the name he shared with the tower that had been the site of her greatest robbery was more than enough to explain his vendetta against her. But what *none* of this told her was . . .

"How?!" It was the fourth or fifth time she'd asked in the ninety seconds since she'd disentangled herself from the Baron d'Orreille and made her way—as rapidly but as unobtrusively as possible—toward the door. "How in the name of Khuriel's left sock did he know it was *me*? Nobody in the Guild would've told an outsider that! *Nobody!*"

Olgun's answering wave of confusion and concern wasn't much of a response, but it was all she really expected.

Time and again, as though it were deliberately conspiring against her, the press of the crowd threatened to shift her back toward the center of the room; and time and again, Madeleine forced herself the other way. The change of outfit, of carriage, of attitude, and of makeup from Widdershins to Madeleine had fooled many people who knew her far better than Evrard d'Arras did, but she found herself absolutely unwilling to take the chance. She was certain, to the depths of her gut and her soul, that if anyone would see through it at exactly the wrong moment, it would be he.

The rich aroma of roast meats and sweet wines was no longer enticing but cloying and overpowering, threatening to choke her. The hum of the throng had become a roar; the laughter, ear piercing and sinister. She wanted to cry, to scream, to punch or throw something. It was all too much, and she couldn't focus, not in the midst of all this. She had to get out, find somewhere private (and safe from discovery), and figure out what to do next.

Finally, *finally* the front door was in sight; the two servants whose job was purely to open and close said door, and perhaps take a cape or a coat from the occasional guest, almost near enough to speak to. Madeleine found herself gasping as though she'd just broken the ocean's surface after a deep and exhausting dive.

At which point, just as freedom was within reach, she learned two things. First, that it wasn't to be that easy. And second, that she'd been wrong: It was *not*, in fact, Evrard d'Arras who would be the one to see through her disguise at the worst possible time.

"We knew you'd be here. We—*he* sensed it!"

"*Squirrel?!* You little bedbug, I should—Gods! What happened to you?!"

Indeed, it was Squirrel, and indeed, he appeared to be someone a plague victim might well cross the street to avoid. His complexion was a sickly gray, nearly transparent, and his cheeks were so sunken that his face seemed little more than skin stretched over skull. His eyes were so bloodshot they had more red in them than white, his lips were chapped and bleeding, and if he'd changed clothes or bathed since she'd last seen him, it clearly hadn't taken. Swathes of his sleeves were actually matted to his skin by dried mud and other filth. It was probably only the overwhelming aroma of the party that kept his own stench from being lethal, or at least leeching the colors from nearby fabrics.

(He was also, she noted, wearing a blade at his belt, but it most assuredly was not the one she'd lost.)

All of which inevitably led to her second question, which was, "And how the frying frogs did you even get *in* here looking like that?"

And indeed, the closest of the guests and servants were beginning to glance their way, raising hands to mouths or stepping back in scandalized chagrin at the sight of what appeared to be a diseased pauper in their midst. Silence rippled outward, crossing the entire chamber, followed rapidly by a second ring of horrified and angry murmurs.

"I sneaked. I do a lot of sneaking now. More than I used to." He giggled, then made an ugly snorting through his nose as he tried to stop. "Maybe even more than you do."

"Uh, yeah." Madeleine glanced around, saw her "fellow" aristocrats backing farther away, and several of the Marquise de Lamarr's guards pushing their way through the thick curtains of heavy fabrics and powdered flesh. "You should get out of here before they get hold of you, Squirrel." *And before you say something to expose* me, *you nitwit!* "We can deal with our own little disagreements"—*and figure out how you recognized me so easily!*—"later on, yes?"

"Yes. Or no. I don't think I should leave. He wouldn't care for that at all."

"He, who?" Before she could ask anything further, however, a warning surge of emotion from Olgun inspired her to glance over her shoulder. The guards were *awfully* close, now. . . .

"Olgun? Would you mind?"

A faint tingle in the air, a rush of power that only she could feel, and several of the guests tripped as they attempted to clear a path for the nice men with swords. The result was a sudden collision of nobility, jamming men and women against their neighbors, and briefly but thoroughly blocking the path.

"Come on, you lunatic." Recoiling even as she did so, Madeleine put a hand on Squirrel's shoulder—shuddering at the faint sense of grit and grease beneath her palm—and started steering him toward the doorway. "Let's get you out of—"

Apparently, even a god (or a god of Olgun's stature, anyway) could be thrown by a crowd as tightly packed and squirming as this one. A handful of men-at-arms he could sense easily enough. But a lone individual? By the time Madeleine felt Olgun's second warning, it was far too late to avoid the encounter.

"Well. I see that even in a host as distinguished as this one, you'll find a way to attract associates of your own quality."

She didn't even have to recognize the voice; she actually recognized the *smug*. "Monsieur d'Arras," she greeted him through clenched teeth, dropping her hands to her sides and turning his way. *Am I even* wearing *makeup here? Seriously . . . !*

Evrard stood some few feet away, the fingers of his left hand idly stroking his chin. The grin that spread above those fingers was openly predatory. "Ah. I see you've puzzled it out. And by what name shall I call you, hmm?"

Madeleine—Widdershins—bit her lip and answered with a glare that would have sent a gorgon crying home to mommy.

The d'Arras scion only chuckled. "It's only, there's so much potential here! I'm not actually sure what to do with this first. Though I will say that it answers certain questions about how you manage to operate as you do."

By this time, not only had they attracted a wide ring of fascinated observers, but the household guards had finally pressed their way to the front as well. There was no way for Widdershins to prevent several dozen people from hearing whatever it was Evrard chose to say next. She swore she could feel the floor falling away beneath her feet. It wasn't so bad as when her life as Adrienne Satti had ended that horrible night all those years ago, but it was uncomfortably similar.

And with that realization, her head abruptly rose. Unblinking, back straight, and voice steady, she said simply, "I won't dance for you, Evrard. Do what you have to do."

Evrard's smile faltered. Clearly, he'd been hoping for something a bit more satisfying. "All right, then. If that's the way it's to be, I—"

Whatever he might have done was halted, however, by a sudden cacophony of shouts. Some surprise, some grief, but largely a chorus of anger, they filtered in through the open door and the nearby windows from some commotion or other on the roads outside.

It was enough to draw everyone's attention from the much smaller and more personal drama that had been playing out before them. The Lamarr men-at-arms dashed for the exit to see what was happening, a great many of the guests trailing in their wake.

"Great timing, Olgun! How did you—?"

Much of Widdershins's growing elation wafted away as swiftly as it had risen at the god's confused reply. "But if *you* didn't, then what's happening out there?"

Before the god could answer, assuming he even *had* an answer, Evrard was suddenly directly before her, utterly filling her vision. "If you think this is going to distract us from finishing this, Widdershins, you—"

"Really?" she breathed, her jaw dropping as she stared over his shoulder. "Not even *that*?"

It's possible that Evrard, who certainly didn't trust the young thief, might have recognized the diversion for what it was—*if* her abrupt look of astonishment had been all there was to it. At that same moment, however, Olgun reached out to tweak the cork on a bottle of effervescent wine sitting, unopened, atop a nearby table. Thus, at the precise instant that Widdershins gawped at nothing over her enemy's shoulder, a harsh *pop* sounded from the same direction.

It was all enough to inspire Evrard to twist his neck in an attempt to see what had snagged her attention—at which point Widdershins kicked him in the groin (again), then kneed him in the face as he doubled over. He made a muffled grunting sort of sound as he hit the floor, something that might, or might not, have been an unintelligible garble of "*Quit that!*"

"I could get used to this," Widdershins observed, though whether to Evrard, Olgun, Squirrel, or nobody at all was unclear.

Actually, no; not Squirrel. Glancing around, she realized abruptly that the wriggly little thief had disappeared at some point during her confrontation with Evrard.

Well, nothing to be done about it now, and she was pretty sure she'd run into him again. Deciding that she probably ought to see precisely what had caused the commotion that had so conveniently saved her from embarrassment at the least, and possibly arrest or even worse, she strode forward to get a better view. Again, Olgun's power reached out, twisting this footstep or tugging at that lace, so that Widdershins had a relatively easy time pressing through the throng.

And after a single, quick glimpse of what was happening, she just as rapidly retreated back into the dining room. A number of the City Guard were assembled outside, led by one Major Julien Bouniard. Widdershins actually would have loved to talk to him just then, to see a friendly face—and that was *all it was*, by the gods, no matter what her heart rate was doing!—but on the off chance that she escaped this mess with her Madeleine Valois guise intact, the last thing she needed was to give any Guardsman, even one she more or less trusted, the opportunity to see through it.

But while she didn't know why the Guard was here, she'd seen enough to know what it was that the constables had found, and what had caused their obvious consternation.

The street beyond the gateway to the estate was strewn with a handful of bodies, bodies that would never have been visible from the house if several of the constables hadn't been gathering them for study and transport. Tabards and weapons suggested that the dead included both Lamarr men-at-arms and actual Guardsmen—probably the men and women assigned to protect the Marquise's soiree. At this distance, Widdershins couldn't possibly begin to determine how they'd died, other than that it was bloody. Olgun might have enhanced her vision enough for her to do so, but that would require her to remain in sight of Julien and the others for longer than she was comfortable with.

Not that Julien and the others were staying outside. Although a few Guardsmen remained behind to watch over the bodies until a wagon arrived, the major himself led the bulk of his squad straight for the front door. The guests fell back as the constables burst in with hands on hilts. Julien Bouniard first began snapping orders to the household men-at-arms, essentially drafting them into his command until further notice, and then demanded to see Berdine Jolivet at once. The marquise herself—certainly not far from the commotion that had disrupted her well-planned evening—began worming her way through the throng. As said throng was too tightly packed to easily give way before her, it took her a few moments to reach the major; moments that Widdershins, in turn, used to back even farther away.

"Olgun?"

But she didn't have to ask. Already, people were "conveniently" shifting and shuffling, moving just enough that Julien wouldn't have a clear line of sight to Widdershins even if he happened to glance in her direction.

At which point, now that she had a few seconds to think and to breathe, it occurred to Widdershins to check behind her.

Yep. Evrard was gone. Apparently, whatever he had in mind, this was no longer the audience for it.

"Well," she sniffed at Olgun, "I hope he's sore enough that it hurt to walk out of here."

She'd expected a chuckle (or rather, the pocket god's emotional equivalent). What she got, instead, was a moment of pensive silence, followed by an abrupt surge of horror and an irresistible urge to make for the stairs.

"Whoa! Olgun, what—?"

Olgun kept tugging at her mind.

"Oh, sure. Suddenly dash out for no reason? That's not exactly the best way to avoid attention, you—"

If Olgun had a voice, per se, it would have risen to a shriek. She swore she could feel phantom hands shoving her toward the steps.

"All *right*! I hope you know what you're doing. . . ."

The staircase itself was a sweeping wing of broad, shallow steps, lush carpeting, and polished hardwood banisters. Widdershins had actually ascended about a third of those steps, one hand lifting the hem of her skirts so that she could walk unimpeded, when the first voice called out for her to stop.

Julien. Of course.

Widdershins proceeded as though she hadn't heard a word of it. A few more steps passed beneath her feet.

"Mademoiselle!" Much harsher this time. "I'm not going to ask you again! Until we've determined what happened outside, we cannot allow anyone to—"

But by that point, Widdershins had gotten far enough up the stairs so that, after a tingling in the air to indicate Olgun's assistance, she could more than smell the faint ambiance wafting down from above.

Blood. And peppermint.

"Oh, no . . ." Widdershins broke into as much of a run as the combination of stairs and skirts would permit. "Hurry!" She barely had the presence of mind to stick with her slightly higher-pitched "Madeleine" voice, scarcely caring anymore if Julien identified her or not. "*Hurry!*"

Nobody below knew what she knew, of course, or even understood what was at stake. But there could be no mistaking the genuine tremor in her voice. Instantly not only the constables, but the Marquise de Lamarr and a huge swathe of her guests, were following her up the stairs. Slowly at first, but spreading rapidly, nervous gasps and horrified mutters spread through that portion of the assembly who already knew precisely what was so important about the upper floor.

Widdershins dashed across the balcony above, whipping past a gold-framed portrait of Berdine Jolivet's grandfather and setting a light banner of Vercoule swaying and flapping in her wake. By the time she reached the door from which the awful scent emanated, the fastest of Julien's constables was pounding along directly beside her, his expression one of puzzlement and a growing fear to which he couldn't put a name.

She felt sorry for him.

The door flew open; Widdershins could never afterward remember whether it was she or the constable who'd shoved it. After a single shocked instant, she could only look away, her back pressed to the wall in the hall outside, and sob into her open hands. The constable, all professional detachment washed away, was huddled over across the open doorway, struggling not to retch.

She'd expected the bodies, ever since she'd first detected the horrid combination of odors. She'd even expected their dried, cracked, and shriveled condition, though that expectation had done little to prepare her for the experience of actually seeing them. But she did not, *could* not, have anticipated that there would be so many.

Or that they would be so *small*.

The corpses had been laid out and positioned as neatly as you please. Some reclined on the sofas, blankets tucked up under their chins. Others sat at the tables, hands resting on cups or saucers. Still others sat cross-legged on the floor, board games open between them. One, larger and presumably older than the rest, clad in a formal gown, was carefully leaned against the inside of the doorframe, as though observing the rest.

On the far wall, huge and uneven letters, scribbled in green wax crayon, read:

Where, oh where, is your little god now?

The hallway around Widdershins began to fill with a rising flood of humanity, and by the time it occurred to her to suggest that the constables shut the door and not permit the parents to see what lay within, it was far, far too late.

Never, in a life filled with trouble and difficulty, had Widdershins ever heard screams and cries the likes of which now echoed through her mind, blazing trails of memory that might never fade. She clapped her tear-wet hands over her ears and clenched her teeth until her jaw pounded, yet she couldn't begin to drown them out. Each sob, each shrieked and grief-drenched name, was a dagger in her gut.

Widdershins knew to whom, precisely, that taunting message was delivered. And if it wasn't her fault that Iruoch had killed, it was, at least, because of her that he had killed *here*.

"Where were you? *Where were you?!*"

She finally looked up, drawn by the despairing cry. One of the guests, a young noblewoman in a gown of white and gold, her wig askew and her makeup smeared into multicolored whorls, was pounding with both fists on a constable's chest. The poor man was trying to explain, but between the horror of what he'd seen and the emotional onslaught, he appeared to have forgotten how to form complete syllables.

Many of the assembly, the Marquise de Lamarr included, had shoved their way into the room, unheeding of Julien's protests. Some had fallen to their knees beside their sons and daughters; some stood in the chamber's center, unable to bring themselves any nearer the malformed bodies.

But many of the others, whether or not they'd had children present (as, indeed, most did not), turned toward the Guardsmen as though summoned by that one woman's cry, a sudden fire igniting in their expressions. Several of the mourners within rose as well, and began converging on the protesting (and rapidly paling) constable.

"My lords and ladies, please!" Julien stepped forward, his palms out, until he stood beside his beleaguered soldier. The other constables, with more or less subtlety, swiftly converged on their commander. "I assure you that we're doing everything we possibly can in order to—"

"*Everything you can?!*" It was the same woman screaming, but the expressions on all the faces around her suggested that it could just as easily have been any one of them. "Ives is dead! My baby—my baby's gone! What good is 'everything you can do' *now*?!"

Widdershins could *hear* the sound of fists clenching, of feet shuffling forward as the mob (and it *was* a mob, now) drew ever nearer the Guardsmen in their midst, packed themselves ever more tightly into the stifling hall. The soldiers themselves stood, as best the confined space allowed, in a rough circle, their backs toward each other. Julien continued to reason, even to plead, with the aristocrats, but his words were bumblebees in the face of a gale, blown away before they even had the chance to fly. The angry, ragged breaths of the assembly were a hot and humid gust, but it was far more than these that caused every man and woman in uniform to sweat.

Should the dam burst, should the partygoers boil over from misdirected anger into violence, the Guardsmen weren't numerous enough to fight them off without the use of weapons. Yet if the constables were to draw steel on a crowd of grieving aristocrats . . .

Widdershins huddled at the edges of the throng, forcing herself to breathe. Every impulse in her body urged her to push forward to Julien's side, not to allow him to face this threat alone. (Or rather, without her, since the presence of the other constables more or less made any real definition of "alone" inapplicable.) But what could she do? The presence of one more warm body wouldn't avert the crowd's fury, and any sudden action on her part might very well provide the spark to set the whole thing off. She found herself dancing from foot to foot as she struggled to make up a mind that was as tumultuous and confused as the situation in which she found herself.

A tingle in the air, another surge of Olgun's power, and Widdershins felt her hearing both expanding and narrowing, a sensation with which she was becoming quite familiar. And she heard, with a sense of abrupt relief that was nigh a physical blow, the sound of boots and voices and shouted orders on the pathway through the estate's front lawn.

More constables, presumably having accompanied the corpse wagon for which Julien's men had earlier sent. For the second time in minutes, Widdershins—who normally saw the silver fleur-de-lis as nothing but a nuisance—might just have been saved by the immaculately timed arrival of the Davillon City Guard.

"I assume," she whispered to Olgun, "that you won't be too jealous if I offer a quick prayer of thanks to the Pact later?"

Olgun's relief, a close match to her own, was answer enough.

"Do you think you can . . . ?"

Her voice trailed off, but her vague gesture toward the packed hallway was more than enough. Again she felt the air around her grow charged, felt Olgun reaching out to the furthest limits of his power, catching the sounds from below, carrying them, augmenting them.

For an instant, just an instant, *everyone* nearby, rather than Widdershins alone, could hear the sounds of the approaching soldiers.

With a single, communal exhalation that was half-breath, half-sigh, the mob deflated. Shoulders slumped, half-raised fists fell, and eyes that had burned themselves dry in anger once more began to glimmer with tears. And if the Guardsmen, too, were seen to sigh—albeit in utter relief—well, they could hardly be blamed.

Widdershins was already moving, heading not for the stairs or the door but for the nearest unobserved window. She hadn't, as Madeleine, done anything wrong, but she couldn't afford the time it would take to answer questions right now (to say nothing of the risks involved if Julien himself should interrogate her). Now that the immediate danger had passed, there was far too much to do.

The first step of which was a visit to the Finders' Guild. Neither the Shrouded Lord nor the taskmaster had summoned her for the meeting she'd requested, but this could no longer wait. They'd see her now, because she wasn't prepared to give anyone a choice in the matter.

Iruoch wanted to make this personal, did he? Fine, then. "Personal" was something with which Widdershins had a *lot* of practice. . . .

❋

Gods damn it all, how did she keep *doing* that?!

Evrard d'Arras stalked furiously along the avenue, though his determined pace was somewhat unsteadied by the ache that radiated from his privates, as well as the bloody handkerchief he pressed on occasion to his reddened nose and split upper lip. Although he was obviously wounded (if only mildly), and dressed in the finest fabrics, he hesitated not an instant before turning his steps toward Davillon's less-reputable quarters. The pockets of illumination through which he moved grew more sporadic as functional street lamps became ever more rare, and the eaves protruding from the buildings grew worn and filthy, but Evrard would have welcomed it, had he noticed it at all. A part of him *hoped* that he might be confronted by some ragged robber, or perhaps even the same fiendish creature he'd briefly faced a few nights previously. He'd have given much for the opportunity to legitimately run someone through right about then.

An opportunity he was *supposed* to have had before now.

As it happened, nobody disturbed him; in fact, of the few people he *did* encounter on the streets at such an hour, most of them very consciously moved to clear his path. He couldn't help but notice the garb on the pedestrians was beginning to run to extremes: The majority of them were either dressed in tattered outfits that were little more than rags, obviously too poor to have anywhere else to go no matter how dangerous the darkness got; or else were wrapped in blatant finery, the servants of men and women so rich that they could afford to send their lackeys out on errands regardless of the perceived hazards.

The contemplation of all this bought Evrard perhaps a minute and a half of distraction before his mind returned to his objective and his cheeks once more began to burn.

He'd underestimated her. Aggravating as it was to admit it to himself, and despite the many warnings from his informant not to do precisely that, he'd underestimated the tenacity, the skill, and the patience of the wretched little thief. Everything he'd done, everything he'd *threatened* to do, even the various slurs and insults he'd hurled across her face like a leather gauntlet—words that, though he'd never have admitted it, made him feel soiled and dishonored for speaking to a lady, no matter how lowborn—and still she'd refused to act as she was supposed to.

The first time, well, she'd had her friend to restrain her. So be it, that sort of thing was to be expected. But tonight? The arrival of the bloody Guard at *precisely* the right moment to prevent him from pushing the matter, lest he draw unwanted attention? Had she arranged that? And if so, by every member of the Hallowed Pact, *how*?

Well, so be it. Evrard had planned to be patient about this, meticulous, to turn the screws ever so slowly tighter until the woman called Widdershins—no matter how much self-control she might have—could react in the only human way left to her. But no more. Her stubbornness, the growing discord in Davillon itself, and (had Evrard been honest enough with himself to admit it) the burning shame and humiliation of her various assaults on his person had all combined to convince him that it was time to jump straight to his final ploy.

She already believed the worst of him, so she'd readily believe that he would do everything he threatened. And if even the threat was enough to besmirch his own personal honor, well, it was worth it if it enabled him to restore his *family's*.

The night had grown aged, or rather the morning had already been birthed and was struggling to take its first steps, when Evrard marched up the handful of stairs and hurled open the front door. Before the wood had even finished rebounding from the stone, he had his rapier in his right hand, a small flintlock pistol in the left. The thunderclap of the shot, followed instantly by the crack of the ball embedding itself in the stone and mortar of the hearth, was more than sufficient to draw every eye in the sparsely populated tavern. Various mugs and tankards thumped down across a smattering of tables, a few of them sloshing their contents over the scarred wood.

"I assume," he announced, his tone calm but carrying, "that nobody here cares to be hurt." A flick of his wrist beneath his coat and the pistol he'd just discharged was replaced by a second, loaded and ready to fire. "Good. I don't care to hurt anyone. So let's keep this friendly, and we can all leave satisfied."

"What . . . ?" The voice was small, clearly frightened. "What do you want?"

Evrard smiled as the girl appeared from around the bar, impressed despite himself that she had the courage to face him, rather than cowering in hiding. "Robin, was it?" he asked, not unkindly.

Her short brown hair bobbed in a single, shallow nod.

"Good. What I want, child, is for you to come with me." Then, as the blood drained from her face, "I've no intention of hurting you—just so long as you make no trouble for me. I simply require the honor of your company for a few hours, nothing more."

A red-bearded server began to advance from the back of the room, his hands clutching the base of a broom as a makeshift cudgel, and several of the customers rose to their feet, fists clenched.

"Admirable," Evrard said. "You have worthy friends, Robin. Believe me when I tell you that I'd truly hate for you to lose any of them." His expression changed not a whit, his friendly smile never faltered, but both the rapier and the flintlock rose by a fraction of an inch. . . .

"Guys, stop!" Her steps were awkward, her knees locked, but Robin emerged and made her way reluctantly toward a fate that she imagined would probably be far worse than Evrard actually intended. "Don't get yourself killed over this. Please."

"You're a wise young woman," Evrard assured her under his breath. "I truly don't intend to harm you, if it can at all be avoided."

"Doesn't matter."

The aristocrat couldn't help but blink at that. "No? And why would that be?"

"Because either way, Widdershins will kill you for this."

"Ah. That, dear Robin, is *entirely* the point."

CHAPTER ELEVEN

She'd begrudged every wasted minute, every unnecessary step from the Lamarr estate to the hidden, but somewhat less than secret, headquarters of the Finders' Guild. As light and sporadic as the traffic might be, she resented every pedestrian on the road, the extra fractions of seconds it required to sprint around them.

So distracted was she that, even though she'd spent the entire run with her skirts gathered in one fist (as otherwise she might well have tripped on them), it took Olgun to remind her, as the pawnbroker's hove into view, that she was dressed and disguised as Madeleine Valois. And while more than a few of the Finders knew that Widdershins had an aristocratic guise that she used to case the homes of the rich and powerful, not many of them knew the precise details of that disguise, or by what name she went.

Grumbling further about the delay, Widdershins ducked into a small walkway that ran behind several of the nearby shops. Stepping over a pile of refuse that looked (and smelled) as though it might, at some point last week, have been a head of cabbage and a few other vegetables, she carelessly stripped off the gown, revealing portions of the sleek black leather that was her "working uniform." The rest she acquired from the small sack that had also hung hidden beneath her skirts, so that in less than a minute, she was more or less Widdershins again. The wig and the gown were crumpled sloppily into the sack—she didn't expect to wear that precise outfit again, lest it bring to mind anyone's memories of Madeleine speaking to Squirrel at the party—while a barrel of rainwater from a few days previous was sufficient to remove the bulk of her makeup. (She realized that a few smears and smudges surely remained, but while these might draw a few sidelong looks or even some mild mockery, they weren't enough to identify who she'd been just moments before).

Finally, she removed a main gauche dagger, with a silver wire grip and a ring protruding from the hilt for extra protection, and strapped it to her waist. It was something she'd picked up on a job about two years ago and hadn't gotten around to selling. She'd never expected to use it, really, but she hadn't yet purchased a replacement rapier. She knew she should, knew that she might well regret not having a sword at her side, but she hadn't been able to bring herself to do so. It would have meant a final acknowledgment that she'd lost Alexandre's blade, and that was one admission that she couldn't quite face.

Although there wouldn't have been room to hide a full-sized rapier in her disguise anyway.

The bag itself she stuffed behind said rain barrel, hiding it with a few slats of wood from what had previously been either a second barrel or a large box. It wouldn't stand up to any sort of meticulous search during daylight hours, but Widdershins was pretty sure that she'd be retrieving the sack before dawn—and *completely* sure that very few people would ever have much reason to search this particular alleyway, night or day.

Thus suitably attired, Widdershins marched across the road and pounded on the door. The hidden panel had barely scooted open when she announced, "Widdershins. Member. I've every right to be here, and I don't want to hear it. Open the stupid door."

Eyes blinked, skin crinkled, the panel slid shut, and—after a prolonged stretch in which Widdershins was starting to become convinced that she would have to pick the lock—the door creaked inward. Her chin forward and nose in the air as though she'd never for a heartbeat doubted that her way would be cleared, she cast a single nod toward the woman currently guarding the door, steadfastly ignored Olgun as he softly laughed at her, and proceeded into the guild's twisted hallways.

Her plan, which had begun as something to the effect of "Barge in on Remy or the Shrouded Lord and make them listen" had by now evolved into the much more intricate and political plan of "Knock politely first, *then* barge in on Remy or the Shrouded Lord and make them listen." Whether either of these plans would have panned out, in their original or modified forms, became a moot point, however. Just as Widdershins was stalking past the heavy door to the guild's chapel, the iron portal slid open to reveal a handful of flickering candles around the feet of the idol to the Shrouded God.

And, somewhat more importantly, the priestess Igraine Vernadoe silhouetted against that dim and dancing halo.

"A moment of your time, Widdershins." It was *not* phrased as a request.

Widdershins gave an instant's thought to blowing it off and continuing on her way, but she decided—even without Olgun's warning—that offending one of the Finders' top-three leaders, *particularly* one who was already harboring more than her share of suspicions, was not the best path to either success in her current endeavor or a long and happy life in general.

"Sure thing," she said, turning on her heel and stepping so swiftly into the shrine that Igraine had to retreat a frantic step to let her pass. "Whatcha need?"

"Don't you think this charade has gone on long enough?" Igraine demanded.

"Uh . . . What?"

"Still playing? How foolish do you think I am, anyway?"

"What are my choices?"

The priestess's skin, naturally dark-hued to begin with, went almost mahogany, and her mouth twisted in a scowl. "I know there's something unnatural about you. I've warned you of this before."

"Yes, but—"

"And this *thing* that's stalking Davillon? I know you're involved with it. I've heard the tale you told Lambert."

"But I—"

"And now we hear that the Church is pressuring the Guard for your arrest? You expect me to believe that's a coincidence?"

"Wait, they're doing what?" Widdershins was rapidly starting to feel that she'd been thrown completely from the saddle of a wildly bucking conversation. "When did *that* happen?"

"Obviously, they've determined some link between you and these events. Maybe due to your involvement with de Laurent's death, I don't know. But I *do* know that it's time, and well past time, for you to tell us *precisely* what's going on in Davillon, and what your part in it might be. At which point, I'll know whether to advise the Shrouded Lord to have you killed or just expelled."

Widdershins only realized that she'd narrowed her gaze at the priestess when the floor and the ceiling went blurry. "What happened," she asked softly, "to 'I have nothing against you personally, Widdershins'?"

"That," Igraine said, her shoulders stiff, "was before it became blatantly obvious that we had something not only supernatural but murderous haunting our streets—and before we lost several of our own Finders to it. I've told you before, I know there's something *off* about you, something unnatural. I haven't determined how you're involved in all this, but between what's happening now and your complicity in the demonic attack against the Guild last year, I've no doubt whatsoever that you *are* involved."

"Fine! I was just on my way to see the Shrouded Lord, and explain some of this to him. You're welcome to come along and—"

"I think not. You'll tell me—*everything*, not 'some of this'—and I'll decide which parts of it need to be brought to his attention, and which fall under my purview as priestess."

"Uh, no." Widdershins cast an exasperated glance ceiling-ward and turned toward the door. "Tag along or not, but I'm going."

Igraine clamped a hand down on Widdershins bicep. "I *said*—!"

The priestess swallowed whatever the rest of the sentence might have been, very nearly along with her own tongue. Her reflexes augmented by Olgun's power, Widdershins swiveled away from Igraine even as she stepped *toward* her, yanking the taller woman off-balance. For an instant Widdershins stood with her back toward the tottering Igraine, and then the thief stuck a leg out behind her, between the other woman's own, and shoved with her elbow. Igraine toppled backward with a faint screech—only to find that Widdershins, with blatantly unnatural speed, had actually pulled away and spun around to *catch* her before she hit the floor.

Except that what Igraine felt in the small of her back, supporting a good amount of her weight, was not Widdershins's hand, but the pommel of her main gauche.

"You realize," Widdershins said, her tone casual, "that if I hadn't held the dagger point *down*, you'd be dead now?"

"The thought had occurred to me," Igraine croaked, staring up at Widdershins's face, and the idol of the Shrouded God beyond. It peered back at them both, as indifferent as ever.

The priestess's weight was beginning to become awkward, given how precariously balanced she was, but Widdershins refused to let the strain show in either her expression or her voice. "So you see how this proves I'm not the enemy here, right?"

"Proves . . . You *attacked* me!"

"Actually, you grabbed me first." Then, before Igraine could protest, "Look, if I'd wanted to kill you, you'd be dead, and I could tell whatever story I wanted, yes? And if I had something to *hide*, I wouldn't have attacked you at all, because I wouldn't have wanted you to know what I could do. So *obviously*, since I went this far but didn't hurt you, it can *only* mean that you can trust me."

Igraine looked dizzier now than she'd been when she was actively in the process of falling over. "I wouldn't know how to *begin* to argue with that."

"Good, because honestly, I don't know what half of it meant."

"Can I get up?"

"Oh, sure." Widdershins clasped Igraine's arm with her free hand, moved the fist holding the dagger (the pommel of which had certainly left an impressive bruise in the priestess's back, but otherwise hadn't harmed her in the slightest), and helped leverage the woman to a more or less upright position.

Igraine coughed once, then did what she could to smooth out the new rumples in her cassock of office. "You're awfully fast," she noted.

"I've been told that."

"Do you really think that assaulting me was the best way for you to make your case?"

Widdershins blanched, though she tried her best to keep it from her face. What *had* she been thinking? True, she'd never even considered actually striking with the blade, but even so, she'd just been so *furious* . . .

"That wasn't an assault," she said in a tone far lighter than her roiling emotions. "That was roughhousing. *Maybe* a tussle, if we're being generous in our definitions."

Despite herself, Igraine found her jaw tensing once more into a scowl. "You don't take *anything* seriously, do you?"

Widdershins met her stare without so much as blinking. "It's because I take the important things seriously," she said, "that I know not to take *you* seriously." And then, once more before Igraine could make the retort for which she was clearly drawing breath, "I'm going to see the Shrouded Lord now. You're welcome to join me. After I've told him what I need to tell him, if you want to lodge a complaint, be my guest."

This time, though the priestess huffed something that might or might not have been a word, she made no attempt to stop Widdershins as the thief made for the door. Instead, she followed close behind—though not, Widdershins couldn't help but note, ever quite stepping within reach.

"Yeah," Widdershins admitted in a voice that was even less than a whisper, agreeing with Olgun's unspoken remonstration. "Maybe it *was* dumb to show off in front of her. But she already sensed you, you know, or *something* about you. This way, at least she also knows I can take care of myself and I won't put up with her nonsense!"

Olgun somehow didn't seem convinced.

A few quick turns through hallways lit by the ubiquitous cheap lanterns (and thick with the equally ubiquitous oily smoke), and the two women—carefully keeping at least an arm's length between them—faced the door to the Shrouded Lord's audience chamber.

Today, Widdershins couldn't help but worry, *is going to turn out really embarrassing if he's not here after all this.* Then, with a shrug that drew a puzzled expression from Igraine, she took a few more steps and nodded to the sentry standing beside the door.

"He in?"

She kept her sigh of relief subtle when the fellow nodded, and reached past him to knock on the door. A voice called out for her to enter, and she did just that.

No matter how many times she saw it, Widdershins couldn't help but be impressed at the effect. The Shrouded Lord's peculiar gray garb really did blend perfectly with the heavy smoke that always wafted through the room, as well as the similar cloths laid across his chair and table. It truly made the man appear to be a vaguely phantasmal, disembodied presence.

Of course, part of the effect might have come from the fact that the fumes always made visitors' eyes water something nasty, but hey, who was going to complain about it?

"Well." A vague sense of movement, and the sudden appearance of a pair of white orbs in the haze, was enough to indicate that they had the man's attention. "There's a pair of women I didn't expect to see keeping company."

"It wasn't by choice," Widdershins announced cheerfully.

"Ah. And do you care to add anything to that, Igraine?"

"No, my lord, I think Widdershins summed it up fairly well."

The Shrouded Lord chuckled, but only briefly. "Widdershins," he said, his voice serious once more, "Lambert told me of your wish for a meeting, but I haven't sent for you. You really need to learn to be more—"

"I'm sorry about that—uh, my lord," she added swiftly as, even through the haze, she could see him tense at her interruption. "But something's happened that can't wait." Then, taking his silence for permission to continue, Widdershins began recounting the events of the evening. By the time she neared the end, she found herself rushing, tripping over her own words, in her haste to get it all out so that she could stop remembering. She hoped the other two would attribute the redness in her eyes to nothing more than the cloying smoke.

When she was done, both the Shrouded Lord and Igraine remained silent for several moments more.

"I'm sorry," the Shrouded Lord said finally, "that you had to witness that." Was that genuine sympathy in his voice? Widdershins thought it very well might be. "And you're absolutely correct, that this makes the issue rather more immediate. But I'm curious as to why you seem to feel that this is *our* responsibility."

Somehow, Widdershins didn't think that saying *Because Iruoch's singled me out personally, and since I can't do this without your help, I intend to drag you into it whether you like it or not* would go over all that well. It would, if nothing else, require explaining a lot of details—such as, oh, say, the matter of her own personal deity—that, Igraine's suspicions notwithstanding, she'd just as soon not divulge.

What she said, instead, was, "Weren't you the one *asking* me to look into this just a few days ago?"

"Indeed, I was—because I wanted to be certain that we couldn't be blamed for what was happening. But now that it's become clear the perpetrator is truly something supernatural, and kills indiscriminately, I don't believe there's any further risk of misplaced accusations."

"Except," Widdershins countered, "that the Guild *might* still appear to be involved. Did Renard tell you everything I told him about my encounter with Iruoch?"

Igraine snorted at the name, and threw a look at the Shrouded Lord that Widdershins couldn't begin to interpret, but the master of the Finders' Guild nodded. "Some of us aren't entirely sold on your notion as to who and what this creature is, but yes, I know everything you told Lambert."

"Well, there was some stuff I didn't think I should tell him in front of Jul—uh, Major Bouniard."

"Yes, he indicated that as well."

"All right, so . . ." Widdershins took a deep breath, and then regretted it instantly as she spent the next twenty or thirty seconds choking on the smoke. With the exception of a faint tapping of fingers against armrests, the Shrouded Lord waited patiently for her to recover.

"So," she said again, her voice rough, "you know that Iruoch—or *whatever* we want to call him," she added with a sneer at the priestess, "killed two Finders?"

"I know." All humor was gone from the Shrouded Lord's voice. "Aubin and Raviel."

"Raviel? Was *that* his name? I could have *sworn* it was two syllables. . . . Uh, that probably doesn't so much matter right now, does it?"

"Not to any great extent, no."

"Uh, yeah. Well, the thing is, my lord, they weren't just in the wrong place at the wrong time. I mean, they were—I don't think you could argue that being caught by Iruoch is ever in any way the *right* place . . ." She grinned faintly, and then, as both the Shrouded Lord's and the priestess's glowers threatened to actually light her on fire, she rushed ahead. "But my point is, they weren't just out and about. They were pretending to *be* Iruoch!"

"*What?!*"

And, simultaneously, "That's nonsense!" from Igraine.

Widdershins raised a hand. "Hold on. I don't mean they were pretending to be Iruoch *personally*. I just . . . You know how, for the first few weeks, nobody was ever actually killed, or even badly hurt? And it was only in the last few days that our brand-new monster began leaving shriveled bodies behind it?

"Well, I think that's because, until a few days ago, Iruoch—*or whoever*—wasn't even *in* Davillon! The earlier attacks were Aubin and Raviel!"

"This is the stupidest thing I've ever heard," Igraine snapped. "I don't know what you're trying to—"

"Igraine, a moment." The Shrouded Lord leaned forward in his seat, a motion made visible only by the swirling and darkening of the smoke before him. "Widdershins, this is a serious—to say nothing of utterly bizarre—accusation. What's your reasoning?"

"Just that I *saw* what the two of them were doing before Iruoch arrived, my lord. I don't know *how* they were doing it, but they were definitely masquerading as something unnatural. They were terrorizing their victims, without actually robbing them. And the descriptions that we've been hearing of our 'phantom'? They don't match Iruoch, but they *do* match what Aubin and Raviel were wearing!"

"I find this entire supposition to be awfully shaky," Igraine protested. "You're drawing a lot of conclusions from *one* encounter, and that's assuming it happened the way you claim it did!"

"All right, then," Widdershins challenged. "If you have a *better* way to explain why the attacks suddenly turned lethal and blatantly magical, and why our guys were dressed as ghosts and tormenting pedestrians, I'm dying to hear it. My lord, can we possibly have some chairs, and maybe refreshments, brought in? I just *love* story time!"

"You impudent little—!"

"Igraine, enough! Widdershins, you will speak to your priestess with more respect. Is that clear?"

Widdershins bit her tongue just before saying *In this room? Nothing's clear!* "Yes, my lord."

"Good. I agree that this scenario sounds improbable—but if it *is* true, and if others make the connection, it could indeed spell a great deal of trouble for us." The Shrouded Lord reached behind him and yanked on one of several ropes. Widdershins didn't hear any bells chime, but a moment later the door slid open and Remy Privott entered the chamber.

"You sent for me, my lord?"

"Yes, Taskmaster. I want to know what Aubin and Raviel were working on the day they were murdered."

"Hmm. I think Golvar was on shift that day. If they were on Finder business of any sort, he'd be the one to ask." Then, after a long and pregnant pause, "So, uh, I imagine you want me to go ask him."

"Your imagination is impressive indeed."

Remy offered a shallow smile.

"While you're at it," the hooded figure continued, "put out the word that I want Simon Beaupre brought to me as soon as he can be found. Our little Squirrel is apparently keeping some very poor company."

"Right. I'm on it." With that, Remy was gone as abruptly as he'd appeared.

"So," the Shrouded Lord said, his wide grin evident in his voice despite being hidden behind layers of smoke and fabric. "Is there anything else you ladies would care to discuss while we wait? Perhaps you'd care to tell me what it was you were doing before you arrived at my door?"

Widdershins and Igraine traded glances, and shook their heads as one.

The following minutes passed in brittle silence.

❋

It was over an hour later, just as the combination of acrid smoke and awkward quiet was about to drive Widdershins from the chamber, when a heavy tapping on the door finally heralded the taskmaster's return. Remy seemed clearly bemused—no, more than bemused, positively befuddled, very nearly stunned—as he entered. His entire bald pate, from his eyebrows to the nape of his neck, was furrowed in contemplation.

"My lord," he began, "perhaps we ought to consider some, ah, *adjustments* to our process of reports and assignments."

The Shrouded Lord blinked languidly through the holes in his mask and looked a question first at Igraine, then at Widdershins, both of whom just shrugged. "I take it," he said, "that you've learned something?"

"Uh, yeah. Yeah, you could say that."

"And are we to learn it, too? Or are you merely bragging?"

"Oh! Sorry. Well . . . It didn't take me long to track down Golvar. He was in the map room on the second level, talking—well, it doesn't matter. Point is, I found him, and we had ourselves a little chat.

"So, seems that some weeks ago, a guy approaches Golvar and asks to hire on some of our boys. This guy's doing all the stereotypical 'you can't know who I am' horseshit: hooded cloak, baggy clothes, whispering voice, the works. Real amateur hour, right?

"But he's offering a hefty bag full of five- and ten-mark coins, and he's got all the right answers to Golvar's usual questions. He wants to hire six or eight Finders, and they've got to come in pairs who are accustomed to working together."

"And," Widdershins piped up, "if I guessed that one of those pairs happened to consist of Aubin and Raviel . . . ?"

"Heh. You wouldn't be wrong."

"So, what," the Shrouded Lord asked, "was the job?"

"Well," Remy answered, "the guy wouldn't say exactly. But he'd satisfied Golvar that this wasn't some trick of the Guard, and that it wouldn't be targeting anyone on our 'don't touch' list. So when all he'd explain was that he needed these guys for some long-term con game, Golvar didn't press any further." Then, as though feeling the need to defend his fellow Finder, "He wasn't breaking any rules . . ."

The partially obscured guildmaster waved a hand in dismissal. "Go on."

"Anyway, so Golvar gathers the boys and offers them the assignment, and of course, they all take it. Long-term job with that kind of up-front? Who wouldn't? But Golvar, even though he doesn't much care what the actual job is, he decides he really wants to know who the boys are working for. So he has one of his people—not someone involved in the job—follow Monsieur Hooded-and-Oh-So-Mysterious, until he's able to identify him."

"And?" Widdershins finally asked after a sufficiently dramatic (and obviously expectant) pause.

"And," Remy told them, "turns out the guy's name is Ferrand. *Brother* Ferrand."

Igraine choked on an errant wisp of the room's thick smoke, and even the Shrouded Lord recoiled. "'Brother'? As in . . ."

"As in, my lord. Brother Ferrand is the personal assistant to His Eminence, our city's very own Bishop Sicard."

"Aha!" Widdershins straightened, practically bouncing in place. "I *knew* there was a reason I didn't like the guy! He—uh . . . Yeah." Staring sheepishly at her shoes—and very much away from the astonished expressions surrounding her—she returned to slouching against the wall.

Again a great many moments came and went, lived and died, trooping mutely past as everyone present wrestled and debated with their own thoughts. (Or, in Widdershins's case, with her own thoughts and those of her incorporeal patron.)

"Just to be clear," the Shrouded Lord said eventually, "Golvar hired out six Finders for a confidence job to a *member of the clergy*, and this didn't seem unusual enough for him to think it worth reporting? Isn't this precisely the sort of thing you're supposed to stay on top of, Taskmaster? What sort of discipline are you enforcing, exactly?"

Remy's entire head went so red, Widdershins was convinced it was turning into some sort of root vegetable. When he spoke, the words were sharp and jagged, having had to drag themselves out from between his teeth. "My lord, nobody has violated any of the rules. I had no reason to think that Golvar was keeping anything from me. And Golvar maintains that he was planning to report all this, but saw no reason why he should consider it urgent."

"And," the Shrouded Lord added, "I imagine he was looking for some way to turn his knowledge of Church involvement to his advantage. And perhaps the deaths of Raviel and Aubin also made him somewhat reluctant to come forward?"

"Even if that's true, my lord, he came clean willingly enough when I confronted him with it. Like I said, maybe we ought to reconsider some of our policies—but none of them were broken here. Bent a little, maybe, but—"

"Fine, fine. You're right; there was no reason for Golvar to believe the job was anything of particular import. We're only just now theorizing about its possible connections with this 'Iruoch,' ourselves. But he *should* have come forward with it as soon as he learned that two of the men involved were among the dead. Please make it clear to him, Taskmaster, that any such lapse in the future will be met with severe repercussions."

Remy bowed, albeit stiffly.

"And draw up whatever modifications you feel we should make to our procedures. We'll discuss them next week, and implement those with which I agree."

"Understood, my lord." A second bow, rather less rigid and reluctant than the first, and Remy—clearly having recognized the dismissal for what it was—once more retreated from the chamber.

"I assume," the voice said from within the smoke and hood, "that I needn't point out to either of you that the timing of this 'con job' coincides neatly with the start of the initial, nonlethal attacks on Davillon's citizens?"

"I'd noticed that," Widdershins said flatly.

Igraine was chewing on her left thumbnail. "It doesn't prove anything," she muttered obstinately. Then, with a sigh, "But I admit, it's certainly suspicious. If nothing else, we should look into it enough to ensure that we do not, in fact, receive any of the blame for what happened next."

Widdershins smiled sweetly. "I bet that hurt you to say. You look like you just swallowed a monkey."

"Widdershins . . ."

"A *poisonous* monkey."

"That will do, Widdershins," the guildmaster warned.

"Yes, my lord."

"So what are we thinking?" he asked, shifting in his chair. "Is this some scheme of the Church as a whole? Something Sicard has put into motion? Or is Ferrand acting on his own? Igraine? You'd know better than the rest of us. . . ."

The priestess nodded and began to pace, leaving whorls of haze in her wake. "I think we can rule out the notion of this being officially Church sanctioned. They have other resources on which to draw, without taking the risk of involving *any* outsiders, let alone a bunch of Finders.

"But as to whether this is something put in motion by Sicard or Ferrand—well, I can't imagine what *either* would have to gain, and it's not precisely in character for either a bishop of the Pact or a brother of the Order of Saint Bertrand, so I'm at a loss."

Widdershins raised her hand like a schoolgirl. "So what's stopping us from finding out?" Then, beneath the weight of twin glowers, "Well, I mean, how hard can it be to spy on a couple of clergymen? Shouldn't be *too* hard to follow them long enough to figure out what they're up to. And besides, if this is something they started, maybe they'll have some idea of how to *stop* it, yes?"

"Much as I hate to say it," Igraine admitted, "I haven't any better ideas."

"Well, if you hated *that*, you're going to *loathe* this . . ."

"Oh, gods . . ."

Widdershins offered a shallow smile. "I think we should bring the Guard in on this." And then, "Uh, Igraine? If your jaw drops any farther, we'll actually be able to see your brain. . . ."

"Widdershins," the Shrouded Lord asked, his voiced vaguely strangled, "are you *completely* insane?"

"This is even a question?" Igraine muttered.

"Maybe," Widdershins admitted readily. "But I'm also right."

"I await your efforts to convince me," the guildmaster told her, "with breathless anticipation."

"That'd be the smoke, I think. But, uh, it's just . . . Even if we learn something, Sicard and Ferrand will just deny it, right? If we don't have some pretty unimpeachable witnesses, we can't exactly make use of whatever we learn. I mean, I'm assuming the Finders' Guild isn't planning to just 'disappear' the bishop, so we need a way to handle this legally, right? Right?"

Then, having not exactly gotten the unambiguous agreement she was looking for, she hurried on. "Plus, what's the point of working to show that the Finders' Guild isn't responsible for what's happening—that we even tried to help *stop* it—if nobody *knows* about it?"

"Maybe *I'm* going mad," Igraine said to the Shrouded Lord, "but she's actually making sense."

"Oh, good," he replied. "I was worried it was just me. Widdershins, I hear what you're saying, but . . . the Guard? Really?"

"I'm pretty sure I can get them to give us a fair hearing. I have, uh, friends . . ."

"Yes." The Shrouded Lord's voice once more went flat, even frosty. "Yes, you do." He heaved a sigh, made ragged by the fumes in the air. "Very well. Widdershins, you'll contact your . . . friend. Igraine, you'll accompany her."

"I—what? My lord—"

"This isn't open for discussion. You're a priestess of a god of the Hallowed Pact. Your word will carry some extra weight, if we do indeed have to make accusations against the bishop or his assistant."

Igraine bowed her head. "As you wish."

"Good. I expect the two of you to cooperate. And I'll be sending along someone to provide extra muscle, in case things go poorly."

The priestess smirked tightly. "'Muscle.' By which I assume my lord means 'babysitter'? Widdershins, I don't believe he trusts us to get along."

"I am shocked at such an insinuation. Truly scandalized. Possibly appalled, even."

The pair of them aimed matching grins and wide, innocent looks at the smoke-wrapped figure.

"Get out of here," he ordered, "before I come to my senses and realize what an abominably bad idea this is."

The pair of women bowed, still oddly in unison, and turned. They had just about reached the door when, "Widdershins, Igraine?"

Two necks twisted as they both looked over their shoulders.

"We don't know what we're dealing with. We don't know who this conspiracy entails, other than that it's someone highly placed in the Church—a Church, I would remind you, that is not especially popular in Davillon at the moment. We don't know what their masquerade was intended to accomplish, or why it appears to have gone so horribly awry. Be careful—not just for your own sake, but for the Finders. This city is desperate for a scapegoat for our recent woes. Let's not volunteer for the position, hmm?"

Two deep nods, doubling as final bows of farewell, and they were gone.

CHAPTER TWELVE

The hum of conversation slithered from several of the rooms they passed on their way, and the halls were, if not *full* of Finders going about their business, then at least sporadically occupied. Plus there were the occasional guards, the chime of bells indicating that someone had failed to pick the pocket or slit the purse of a practice mannequin, even the hiss and spit and crackle of the oil lamps.

Yet, to Widdershins, it felt as though she and her reluctant companion were traversing the entire length of the Finders' Guild sanctum in utter silence. Whatever thoughts the priestess had, she hoarded them to herself as if they were pure gold and uncut gems.

For a time, Widdershins felt that allowing said silence to linger was the best option, but eventually . . .

"I'm not the enemy, Igraine."

"Hmm?"

Widdershins shrugged without turning or pausing in her stride. "I know you don't trust me."

"Why, whatever gave you *that* silly idea?"

"Call it a hunch. I'm just sensitive that way. But look, I'm really not. I'm loyal to the Guild. I always have been."

"And that's why you led a demon into our halls last year, is it?"

"Didn't have a choice. I know you think there's something weird about me, but I'm no traitor and I'm no danger to the Finders. I'm not responsible for what's happening out there on the streets, and I really am trying to stop it. The sooner you get that, the happier we'll both be."

"I don't *think* there's something weird about you, Widdershins. I *know* there is. I sensed it even before I heard the rumors of your impressive physical feats—to say nothing of that little display of inhuman speed you put on for me earlier. The presence of the unnatural is one of the first things priests of the Pact learn to sense.

"But," she continued as Widdershins drew breath to speak, "as far as what's happening now, I *do* believe you. Or, rather, I'm willing to entertain the possibility that you're telling the truth. You'll have to be satisfied with that."

Widdershins finally halted, albeit only for a few seconds. "The Shrouded Lord trusts me. Why don't you?"

Igraine's face twisted briefly into an expression that Widdershins couldn't possibly interpret—though she saw, among other things, a barely suppressed amusement hidden within—and then went blank just as swiftly. It was, then, Igraine's turn to shrug and march on ahead, and Widdershins's turn to trail behind, her thoughts once more her own.

They stopped briefly by the priestess's own quarters. Widdershins stood outside the door, tapping her foot, twiddling her thumbs, grunting occasional sarcastic comments to Olgun, and otherwise fidgeting for what was probably less than ten minutes, but she herself would have sworn included two or three changes of season, and possibly a birthday. Finally, however, the door swung open and Igraine reappeared. She had abandoned her cassock of office for men's trousers, a heavy coat, and a pearl-hued tunic that perfectly offset her dusky skin. She carried no sword, but the pair of flintlocks and the small truncheon that she wore openly on her belt, to say nothing of the small dagger hilt protruding from her right boot, were evidence enough that she didn't care to be disturbed.

"You sure you're ready?" Widdershins asked flatly. "You don't need to stop by and pick up a blunderbuss, or a battleaxe? Maybe a cannon?"

"As soon as you're through being foolish," Igraine said, "we can be on our way."

"Nah, let's be on our way *now*. We don't actually have that much time."

The priestess blinked, opened and closed her mouth twice, and then began walking.

As they finally approached the exit, Widdershins saw immediately that someone was present up ahead—someone other than the sentry on duty. She couldn't help but grin, despite every effort she made at sculpting her face into an expression more serious.

"Heading out for a walk, Renard?"

The foppish thief grinned and smoothed his mustache between thumb and forefinger. "I thought this would be a good night to show off the new ensemble." He twirled, displaying hose and half cloak of deep indigo, tunic of forest green.

"You look like a peacock," Widdershins told him.

"Well, but is it a *handsome* peacock?" Then, after waiting for Widdershins to oblige him with a chuckle, he bowed his head. "Priestess."

"Lambert. I suppose it's you who the Shrouded Lord has asked to accompany us?" Her voice sounded oddly atonal as she asked.

Renard bowed more deeply. "I am to be of service in any way that I can. And of course, other Finders shall be made available if we should require them."

"Very well." She sounded, if anything, resigned; Widdershins wondered briefly if the priestess didn't have something personal against Renard. Then again, it wouldn't surprise her. On the one hand, Renard did rub many people the wrong way; and on the other, Igraine—at least in Widdershins's own experience—developed personal objections to many people on a fairly regular basis. "So, what," Igraine continued, "is our first step?"

She directed the question at Renard, who looked to Widdershins, who shrugged. "Well, if we're supposed to bring the Guard in on this . . ." Renard raised an eyebrow at that, but chose not to interrupt. ". . . then I should probably speak to my friend alone. It'll be, uh, easier to convince him."

"You are *not*," Igraine protested, "about to tell us to simply wait here!" She didn't add *After you let me go through all the trouble of changing*, but Widdershins heard it anyway.

She was tempted to say yes, just to watch the reaction, but, "Nah. I don't think Ju—Major Bouniard would be all that reassured if I asked him to accompany me back here. Why don't I get you settled in at the Flippant Witch, make sure there's a private room ready for us to talk, and then you can relax *there* while I fetch our own personal officer? Igraine, you can fill Renard in on any of the necessary details while you're waiting."

Neither Igraine nor Renard looked thrilled at the notion of just sitting around, but since neither of them had any better suggestions, either, they both reluctantly acquiesced.

❋

Widdershins was already moving ahead, striding through the darkening streets as though the city couldn't possibly throw anything unexpected at her. (And who knew, after all she'd been through, or claimed to have been through, maybe it couldn't.) Renard followed a few paces behind, and barely glanced over as Igraine appeared behind him.

"I'm not convinced this is a good idea," she said.

"Why not? I've been to the Flippant Witch. It's nothing to crow about, but it's not a *bad* little—"

The priestess sighed. "That is *not* what I meant, and you know it. Aren't you at all concerned that she'll figure it out?"

Renard's voice dropped to something barely above a whisper. "That I'm the current and oh-so-enigmatic Shrouded Lord? Were you planning to tell her?"

"Certainly not!"

"So what's the worry?" he asked with a shrug. "She and I have been friends for years, and it's never been an issue."

"So, of course, you'll give her every additional opportunity to catch you in some slip?"

"She's my friend," he said again. "And these are events of more than a little importance to the Guild. I think my participation is justified."

"And *I*," Igraine said, with as much fire in her voice as she dared allow, "am not certain that your judgment is entirely sound where Widdershins is concerned."

"I don't know what you mean." Enough ice dripped from each word to chill an entire punchbowl.

"Lambert . . ." And more quietly, "My lord, you *must* know that the priesthood is growing concerned about your obvious attachment to—"

"Don't call me that in public, no matter how quietly."

"All right, but—"

"And this conversation is concluded."

Renard quickened his pace to walk beside Widdershins, making sarcastic comments about this sight or that as they progressed. Igraine, for her part, fell back a few steps with a shake of her head and a second, worried sigh.

❋

Narrow lanes grew broad, and rough buildings grew slightly less rough, as the trio made their way from the squalid Ragway quarter into the more widely used, if not necessarily more opulent, Market District. The scents of the various food vendors, though closed for the evening, permeated the air, soaking into the mud, the bricks, and the clothes of even those pedestrians who passed through only briefly. It was a route that Widdershins knew like the inside of her own eyelids—better, actually, and it was a stupid expression, anyway, since she couldn't really have described the inside of her eyelids even on a bet—and despite the severity of their overall situation, she found herself scarcely paying attention along the way.

Broad lanes narrowed once more, here at the very edge of the market. Widdershins rounded a shadowy corner to come face-to-face with the shallow steps and rough wooden door of the Flippant Witch—and the sudden weight in her gut suggested that the world now had her *absolute* attention.

The plan had been to leave Renard and Igraine here while she went to fetch the Guard.

The fact that the Guard was *already here*, as evidenced by three men and women in the black-and-silver tabards, sporting the fleur-de-lis, could not *possibly* be an indication of anything good.

Renard, Igraine, and even Olgun called for her to stop, to observe, to think, but she was deaf to them all. She was sprinting before she was even consciously aware of her intention to move, physically shoving through the assembled Guardsmen before they'd entirely registered her presence. (She never felt the tingle in the air as Olgun reached out to hide her approach for an extra few seconds, for if he had not—had the constables seen this woman charging them from the darkness—one might well have drawn a blade or a pistol and struck before anyone knew what was happening.)

Arms reached out as she burst into the common room, grabbing her from behind and holding her in place. Widdershins lashed out blindly, screaming something—she thought, later, that her words had been panicked questions as to what was happening, but she was never sure—and things might still have gotten ugly had not two voices called out together for the constables to let her go.

The first was Gerard, the red-bearded fellow who'd been with the Witch since long before it had fallen into Widdershins's possession. The second was a Guardsman with pale mustache and goatee; a sliver of Widdershins's mind recognized him as a companion of Julien's, though she couldn't for the life of her remember—or, frankly, care about—his name.

The brief jostling by the constables, however, combined with the sight of Gerard's flushing cheeks and bleary gaze, was enough to snap her back into some semblance of restraint. "What happened?

What happened?!" She heard the shrill edge in her voice, felt tiny little teeth chewing at the already-frayed edges of her self-control; heard it, felt it, and *hated* it, but was as powerless to stop it as she was her own heartbeat.

"Widdershins," Gerard began, "I—"

"Where's Robin?"

"I didn't know what else to do," he said, gesturing helplessly at the gathered constables. "We couldn't find *you*, and I didn't think it was safe to hesitate, and—"

"Oh, gods, *where's Robin?!*"

"Mademoiselle?" The blond constable stepped closer, one hand raised. "We need to—Mademoiselle, please?"

But it was Renard who stepped in, laid a hand on Widdershins's wrist, and whispered, "You can't help her like this."

She froze, actually raised a hand to her cheek as though he'd slapped her, and nodded. "I'm sorry. I'm sorry, everyone." She inhaled once, deeply, then faced the constable—and if he, or any of the others, noticed the violent trembling of her clenched left fist, they chose not to remark on it.

"I am Constable Paschal Sorelle," he told her. He didn't ask her name; clearly, he already knew. "Your man here reported a crime, and we've come to investigate."

"A crime? Robin . . . ?" *Keep calm, keep calm, keep calm . . .*

She felt a slow but steady torrent of soothing emotions from Olgun, enough—*just* enough—to enable her to maintain her composure. Had he been tangible, she'd have kissed him.

Paschal nodded. "Your friend Robin has been abducted, mademoiselle."

"I couldn't stop him!" Gerard sobbed, stretching out a hand to lean against the nearest table. "I wanted to, but . . ."

It never even occurred to Widdershins to ask *who*. Had Robin been murdered, there might have been options, but kidnapped? She had no doubt at all.

"I'll kill him. I'll *kill* him!" She spun, backhanding a carafe off the table with that same trembling fist. Several of the constables, as well as Igraine, leapt back to avoid the sloshing wine and shattering ceramic.

"I take it," Sorelle said blandly, "that you believe you know who did this? Ah . . . Hmm. I'll take that glare as a 'yes.' You realize I can't permit you to—"

"Don't. Just *don't*. Gerard? Was . . ." Widdershins cleared her throat, tried again. "Was she hurt?"

"No. Not when they left, anyway."

"Good." The knot in her belly didn't disappear, but it loosened a touch. "Good, that's something. All right, the first thing we need to do is—"

"The first thing *you* need to do," Renard said quietly, "is go with the nice constable. Talk to Bouniard. There's a lot that needs doing. *I'll* get Robin."

"If you think for one second—!"

And, simultaneously, from Sorelle, "The Guard cannot allow you to make this into some personal—"

"One at a time! You," Renard said, pointing at Sorelle, "patience. We'll explain in a moment. And you"—here he grabbed Widdershins by the shoulders and steered her over to the bar—"need to listen."

The constable looked as though he might follow and demand to participate in the conversation, but he held his ground, scowling.

"Renard, it's *Robin*. I can't just—"

"Listen," he said again, his tone low but sharp. "We need you to talk to Bouniard. Nobody else is going to be able to convince the Guard to help us deal with Iruoch."

"I don't *care* about Iruoch right now! I—"

"And when he kills more children? Will you care then?"

Widdershins slapped him. Renard clearly saw it coming, and just as clearly held himself rigid rather than avoiding the blow.

"That's not fair," she whispered, tears rolling down her cheeks.

"No," he agreed. "It's not. Widdershins, I'm not an idiot. I know—a *lot* of us know—that you can do things, sometimes pretty amazing things, that most of us couldn't even attempt to duplicate. Even if you *weren't* the only one who could bring the Guard and the Guild together on this, you might be the only one with a chance of stopping that creature."

At any other moment, the revelation that Renard knew more of her secret than she'd suspected would have elicited at *least* a comment, if nothing more. Now, she just nodded. "But I can't just—"

"Widdershins, why do you think Evrard's doing all this?"

"D'Arras tower," she spat. "Why else?"

"No, I mean, why is he threatening you? Taunting you? Abducting Robin?"

"I . . ." Widdershins blinked. "I assume he's trying to goad me into doing something stupid."

"Precisely. You've heard of Evrard's skill as a duelist?"

"Yes, but—"

"He's noble blood. You're not."

"So?"

"So by custom, he can't challenge you to a duel. All he can do is sic the law on you, and for that, he needs proof. But if *you* challenge *him* . . ."

Widdershins's jaw dropped, and she swore the Flippant Witch must have shifted off its foundations. "All of this is because he wants me to attack him? Because it wouldn't be *proper* for him to draw *first*?!"

Renard shrugged. "I can't say for sure, of course, but that'd be my guess."

"But . . . That's *stupid*! If he attacked me, he could just *say* it was self-defense! Who'd argue it?"

"Aristocrats," the foppish thief said, "have a twisted sense of honor. I've never really understood it, myself."

"That's because it's *dumb*, Renard!"

"Could be."

"So I let you do this," she said slowly, "it means we get that much closer to stopping Iruoch, *and* we make sure Evrard doesn't get what he wants."

"Precisely."

"But Renard, it's *Robin*."

"I know." He reached out, took Widdershins's right hand in both of his. "I know she's practically a sister to you. I swear to you—I *swear* to you, on the Shrouded God and the rest of the Pact—I won't let him hurt her. I'll bring her back safe."

"You were just telling me what kind of an amazing, renowned duelist he is. . . ."

"Indeed." Renard's teeth gleamed in the lantern light. "But he's one man, whereas I . . . I am a Finder."

For the first time since she'd spotted the black-and-silver assembly outside her tavern, Widdershins smiled, if only shallowly. "How will you find him?"

"The same way you would have. He *wants* you to come to him, so he won't make it difficult. If he's not staying in one of the various properties owned by the d'Arras family—probably a tenement or a warehouse, I'd wager—I'll be shocked."

Widdershins nodded. "I don't like this. I understand, but I don't like it. Renard, if he's hurt her . . ."

"Then he'll regret it. Briefly."

A second nod, followed by a chaste kiss on Renard's cheek, and then Widdershins squared her shoulders and turned to address Constable Sorelle.

❋

Said constable was, to judge by the seemingly involuntary twitching in his jaw, not entirely convinced by anything she had to say.

"You're insane," he told her finally, which certainly seemed to confirm said assessment.

"Look, Constable, if you'd just take me to see Julien, he—"

"Major Bouniard," Sorelle said stiffly, "is more than a little busy at the moment. And even if he weren't, you're asking me to escort a known thief to him, while abandoning an investigation—to say nothing of leaving said investigation in the hands of a personal, civilian vendetta—in order to deliver to him some ludicrous story about a Church conspiracy behind a string of murders that you claim were committed by a figure out of fairy tales. Is that, more or less, the gist of it?"

"Uh, well . . ." Widdershins offered a broad, shaky smile. "Not *exactly* . . ."

"Oh? What did I get wrong?"

"You're not leaving the investigation in the hands of civilians. It already *is* in the hands of civilians."

Sorelle spun, taking in every corner of the Flippant Witch, but the young woman's dapperly garbed companion had seemingly vanished. The constable muttered something that Widdershins pretended not to hear.

"How the hell . . . I have constables at *every door*! How did he . . . ?"

Widdershins spread her hands. "We're better than you guys. Uh, no offense."

"I believe I'll choose to take some, if it's all the same to you. I'm supposed to be *arresting* you, Widdershins!" he growled in a softer voice. "I'm trying to find a way around it, mostly for Major Bouniard's sake—feels wrong to nab *his* friend while we're investigating *your* friend's abduction—but you're not making it any easier!"

"Uh-huh," Widdershins said. "Arresting me. At *whose* request, again?"

"The . . ." Sorelle blinked. "The Church."

"And what does *that* tell you?"

"It does *not* tell me that they're part of some murderous conspiracy," he insisted, but he sounded just a tad less certain of himself.

"Constable?" The voice emerged from over Widdershins's shoulder. "I am Igraine Vernadoe. You know the name?"

"I've heard it spoken a time or two. Read it a time or two more."

"Then you know what position I hold?" When he nodded, she continued, "As a priestess of a god of the Hallowed Pact—and he *is* of the Pact, regardless of what you might think of him—I'm prepared to swear to you that Widdershins is speaking the truth as best we understand it. This is a threat against us all. We *must* speak to Major Bouniard."

"I'm just . . . I'm not . . ."

Widdershins sighed and drew her dagger. Sorelle's blade was halfway free of its sheath, and they heard the other constables reacting as well, before it became apparent that she was holding the weapon out to him hilt first. With a suspicious glance, he took it. "What are you—?"

But she wasn't done. From the pouch on her belt came her primary set of wires and lock picks; from hidden niches in boots and gloves and even wound into her hair came several more. She sensed Igraine's startled look, and even Olgun's disapproving glower.

"There," she said, handing those over to an equally startled Sorelle. "You can search me, if you want, but that's all of it."

"I . . . What . . . ?"

"I surrender myself into your custody, Constable," she told him formally. "But only on your word as an officer of the Guard and a gentleman of breeding that you'll deliver me to Major Bouniard, and nobody else, for interrogation."

"You're *that* serious about this?"

"You're the one holding my dagger and my tools, Sorelle."

"All right." Sorelle nodded to the other constables. "Colette, you're with me. The rest of you, continue taking statements and seeing what evidence you can turn up. Madame Vernadoe, you may accompany us if you wish, for the moment."

"How generous. I do indeed wish."

Widdershins offered Gerard a wan smile and a whispered, "We'll get her back," and then the two constables and the two Finders were on their way, leaving behind them a crowd of Guardsmen and witnesses who were even more puzzled than they had been before.

CHAPTER THIRTEEN

Widdershins hadn't been making an empty brag with her comment to Sorelle. While obviously not every Finder was "better" than every member of the Guard—were that the case, none of the thieves would *ever* be arrested, save from meanest luck—it was certainly true that the more skilled Finders could readily avoid detection by the *average* constable. That was, indeed, how Renard Lambert had departed the Flippant Witch without being noticed, despite the presence of watchers at every obvious exit.

It was *also* how every man and woman present, whether constable or otherwise, managed to overlook the spy on their periphery.

Again, this shouldn't be taken to suggest either carelessness or incompetence on anyone's part. Widdershins and the other Finders were heavily focused, first on their mission, and second on the discovery of the Guard's presence at the tavern. The constables themselves were attending primarily to their investigation (as well they should have been), and then to the presence of known criminals in their midst. That someone might have been hanging from the eaves of the Flippant Witch, cloaked in the shadows away from the street lanterns and listening through the half-shuttered windows, was a thought that simply—and, one might argue, reasonably—had never occurred to any of them.

All that said, and even allowing for the fact that he'd always been among the best at going unnoticed, Squirrel found the whole thing almost too easy. He hung beneath the eaves, and never once felt the tremor or cramping of muscles. No matter what dance steps the moon and the clouds followed, or where the constables wandered below, the shadows never once threatened to reveal his presence. The night itself was his coconspirator, and he found himself even more afraid than he had been.

What, precisely, was his association with Iruoch *doing* to him?

He overheard it all, Squirrel did; perhaps not every single word, but more than enough for him to understand what was happening within. He thought, long and hard, of simply running. He didn't even have a destination in mind, just the nigh-overwhelming desire to hit the ground, pick a random direction, and go until he couldn't go any farther.

But of course, he did no such thing. It wasn't even his fear of Iruoch's wrath that kept him tied as tightly as any leash, though of course that was part of it. It was, instead, his fear of himself.

If he abandoned his "master," if he broke free of his self-inflicted bondage, it would mean that everything he'd done for Iruoch, every horror he'd aided the creature in perpetrating, was meaningless. It would mean that he had been free *not* to participate in the nightmares of the past week.

That the indelible stain on his soul was not just Iruoch's, but well and truly Simon Beaupre's.

Once Widdershins, Vernadoe, and the two constables had departed, and the remaining Guardsmen had congregated inside, Squirrel allowed himself to drop from the overhang. A split second spent on hands and knees, and then he was off down the road. He struggled to keep himself to a casual walk, but the sidelong glances he got from the sporadic, rushed passersby suggested that his stiff-legged, twitching gait wasn't quite doing the trick. Still, given the maelstrom of conflicting emotions that churned from his belly to the base of his skull, it was the best he could do.

He passed, at one point, a storefront with actual glass windows (it was, he thought, a jeweler's of some sort, though he couldn't be sure), and he practically leapt in fear from the reflection that loomed beside him. His eyes and his cheeks were sunken pits in a skull-shaped field of waxen, corpse-gray. Dirt and oil plastered his hair to his scalp, save where occasional tufts jutted out at irregular angles. His clothes, whose original colors he'd long since forgotten, held enough dirt to begin a small garden—or, more aptly, a shallow grave.

He looked . . . Well, he looked like someone that he himself, even in his hungriest and most miserable days, wouldn't have bothered to mug.

Squirrel found that thought oddly droll, and spent the next minutes of his walk struggling desperately not to break into hysterical giggles. The effort occupied his mind until he finally found himself standing before the house, and all thoughts of laughter were purged, perhaps carried away by his sudden sheen of sour perspiration.

It was a modest structure, boasting only a single story. The shingles were rough and somewhat mildewed; the bricks of the walls, old and cracked; the parchment windows, stained and torn. Nothing, other than the fact that the small garden outside was somewhat more overgrown and less well kept than those of its neighbors, marked it as in any way different from the other houses that stretched away to either side.

Nothing on the outside, anyway. Alas, for the family that no longer lived here—that no longer *lived*—the inside was something else again.

Squirrel went around to the back and let himself in, recoiling against the stench of decay. It wasn't particularly strong, as Iruoch hadn't left much intact to rot, but still pervasive enough to fill the household.

The master himself sat cross-legged on the dining room table, licking with violent tenacity at the inside of a child's shoe.

"You don't want to waste even the tiniest portion," he said in his awful twin voices, responding perhaps to Squirrel's unspoken question. "Not when there are so many children starving in this world—who will certainly die before we can get around to eating them." He tittered briefly, then tossed the shoe over his shoulder, where it landed perfectly amidst the shrunken, desiccated remains of the house's former occupants. "Sing me a song, my young thief. Tell me of little girls and the littler gods that live between the folds of their deepest dreams."

"Uh . . . Well, I found her. I mean, I knew she'd go back to the Witch *eventually*, so I, um . . ."

"Found her. Yes." Iruoch slowly drummed the spidery fingers of one hand against his cheek, occasionally rustling the floppy brim of his hat. "As you said you would. *Not* an accomplishment, silly boy. *Anybody* can do something that's so easy that anyone could do it."

"Um . . ."

"You may be impressing my friends"—and right on cue, the distant chorus began to *ooh* and *ahh*—"but you're not impressing me. I want you to impress *me*."

"Well, I—"

"Impress me! *Impress me!* Now, now, *now!*"

"I know what they're planning!" Squirrel shrieked.

"Oh, *do* you?" Iruoch applauded twice. "That's a *little* impressive. Well, don't leave me in suspense."

Squirrel nodded, trembling, and spoke for several minutes. As he neared the end of his recitation, Iruoch placed his hands on the table, lifted himself upon them, and—still seated, his legs crossed—began to walk himself back and forth across its surface on his fingertips.

"The thief and her god, the Church and the Guard," he muttered as he "paced." "Alone they're no danger, together . . ."

"They're hard?" Squirrel offered hesitantly after a moment of silence.

Iruoch ceased his peculiar pacing and swiveled himself about on his fingertips so he could face his servant. "I was going to say 'they might be a bit of a problem.' What's with the rhyming?"

"I, uh . . ."

"Still, I've never met a problem I couldn't eat." Iruoch flexed his fingers and shot to his feet, coming to rest beside the table. At no point in the graceful arc did his coat so much as flap. "Thieves and

Guards and Churchmen, with—what do you think? Butter? Cinnamon? Or perhaps a sprinkling of random passersby?"

"I think we should lie low," Squirrel said.

"Lie low? *Lie low?!*" Iruoch took a single staggering pace sideways and was abruptly directly before the quivering thief. "Cower and hide, cower and hide, draw the curtains and stay inside? Let the citizens brush us aside, feast on nothing but swallowed pride? This is your 'suggestion,' my little morsel?"

"I . . ." Somehow, Squirrel didn't think that pointing out the rhyme would be an effective use of breath. "You're great and powerful and all that . . ."

"I knew this already."

"But, I mean, *all* of them? Priests, Finders, the Guard, and Widdershins's, uh, personal god? I just think it'd be smarter to—"

"I. Don't like. Cowards." Iruoch was looming over Squirrel, their faces nearly touching—enough so that Simon could *see* the twitching and writhing of *something* beneath the creature's lips. "And I think you've been just about as useful as you're ever likely to be. . . ."

"You can't," he whispered.

"Can't? *Can't?*" The distant children began to weep. "Not my favorite word, oh, no, not at all!"

"But you swore . . ." Squirrel was sobbing now.

And just that swiftly, Iruoch drew himself up and stepped away. "I did, didn't I? An oath is a promise is a vow is a bargain. I swore that no harm would come to you . . ."

"For as long as I served you," Squirrel breathed, his heart pounding.

"Yes, yes. And I will not break that oath, no."

The boy's shoulders slumped in relief.

"Simon?" the fae said thoughtfully.

And tightened once more. Iruoch had never, *never* used his name before.

"Yes, master?"

Iruoch's face literally stretched, distorting itself outward to contain his impossible smirk. "You're fired."

Squirrel squeezed his eyes shut and wailed—even as a part of him, the tiny surviving sliver of his soul, welcomed what was to come.

❋

". . . and, Vercoule, who among all the gods, has chosen this, Davillon, as his favored city. To all these, and more, we offer our gratitude, and our devotion, and our most humble prayers."

This, the bishop's favorite holy litany, was now familiar to a huge swathe of Davillon's populace. Sicard invoked the same divine names (with perhaps a little variation, so as to avoid offending any of the more minor deities of the Hallowed Pact) in each of his services—and with each service, the Basilica of the Sublime Tenet grew ever more heavily attended. As the terror of the city's murders spread, and with it the fear of some supernatural agency at work, more and more of the people forgot their anger at the Church's treatment of Davillon (or, more accurately, allowed their worry to overshadow said anger). They sought comfort in the words of the priests, and the protection of the houses of the gods.

At this particular service, despite the fact that the day was just now dawning outside, the pews supported enough prayerful rears that the wooden planks, perhaps having grown accustomed to lesser loads, offered the occasional squeak or groan in counterpoint to the bishop's words. Perhaps only one of every five or six seats remained vacant, and a great many of the attendees were dressed not in their finery, but in workday clothes. The implication—that church attendance was once again considered, by some, to be an everyday event—was unmistakable.

"In times as trying as these," Sicard said, tugging at one sleeve of his cassock to remove a stubborn wrinkle, "it does us all good to recall that the gods of the Hallowed Pact watch over those who honor their names. Let me recall to your memories a tale I'm sure you've all heard before, involving the cavalier Verrell d'Ouelette and his seemingly impossible quest to slay the Charred Serpent of Lacour. . . ."

The sanctuary itself was lit in a rainbow of colors, resplendent in the thin shafts of light that speared through, and were cheerily rouged and shadowed and otherwise made up by, the stained glass windows. And indeed, for most of the audience sitting in that rain of colors, the tale was aptly chosen, for it told not only of one of Galice's greatest folk heroes, but specifically of how the gods protected and guided him through his most troubled days.

But it was not this to which *everyone* in the audience reacted, no. For Widdershins (who was largely dressed as herself, not guised as Madeleine, though she'd thrown a less conspicuous green tunic over her leathers), the bishop's choice of stories was more interesting for other reasons. While he was not a primary character in the tale, d'Ouelette also made a brief appearance in "The Princess on the Road of Beasts"—perhaps the most popular of the fairy tales in which Iruoch himself played a part.

It was, most probably, coincidental—d'Ouelette popped up in a *lot* of Galice's stories—but she found it apt, if not actually ominous.

"You know," she whispered, leaning so that her nose was just about inside Igraine's ear, "Iruoch doesn't actually behave much as the stories portray him. He's . . . wilder."

The priestess glared and raised a finger to her lips.

"Oh, like you haven't heard *this* story before," Widdershins huffed. But when that brought nothing but a second glare—as well as several irritated murmurs from the others seated nearby—she sunk into her seat, crossed her arms, and contented herself with an impatient, but *silent*, sulk.

It was a sulk that continued unbroken, save for the occasional subvocal snide comment to Olgun, until the sermon and the final benedictions were completed. At that point, Widdershins and Igraine stood with the rest of the human tide rising around them and let the milling worshippers slowly filter by them.

"Anything?" Widdershins asked, once more directly into her reluctant companion's ear.

"No. No, nothing. If he's consorting with any sort of unnatural entities, they haven't left a mark on his soul."

Igraine might not have said *Unlike yours*, but Widdershins heard it clear as the cathedral's bell.

"All right," the thief said. "Go join the others outside. I'll try to follow him, but if he slips by me, one of you needs to keep him in sight until I can catch up."

"Yes, Widdershins. I was present when we went over the plan the first time."

"So go be present when we execute it."

Igraine snorted something and joined the departing worshippers. Widdershins returned to her seat. Several other parishioners were also lingering, offering their own prayers or perhaps waiting for an audience with Sicard, so she didn't look particularly conspicuous. All she had to do now was wait and . . .

"Your pardon, mademoiselle."

Widdershins craned her head around, looking over her shoulder. Behind her stood one of the ceremonial Church guards, normally assigned only to the protection of eminent clergymen such as Sicard himself. His uniform was almost clownish, replete with baggy pantaloons, steel breastplate and helm, and an old-fashioned halberd that was probably too big to even function as a genuine weapon in any room more confined than the sanctuary itself.

The pistol and dueling sword at his waist were another story entirely, however, and his expression suggested that he clearly meant business.

"Uh, yes?" Widdershins asked with a shy smile.

"His Eminence wishes to see you. Now."

"Umm . . ." *Oh, figs!* "Of course. Up on the dais, or—"

"He'll await you in his office."

Widdershins forced herself not to frown. *How could he possibly—?*

She felt a brief flash from Olgun. *Of course. Igraine sensed me. Archbishop de Laurent sensed me. I just never thought he could pick me out of a crowd, from so far . . .*

"Mademoiselle, I really must insist."

Run? Fight? Not without drawing a *lot* of attention—and probably losing their only chance at learning what Sicard was up to. She sighed once and rose to her feet. "Of course. Lead the way."

As they started across the room, the rapidly diminishing crowd thinning out before them, she saw Igraine watching from the doorway. Widdershins tried to shrug without being obvious about it, but the guard bustled her around behind the raised platform before she could see if the priestess understood.

They proceeded into a curving hallway half-hidden behind the dais. The sea-green carpeting here was thin enough that their footsteps echoed, albeit only faintly, between the narrow walls. They could hear voices from up ahead and from various rooms they passed, but never clearly enough to make out more than the occasional syllable.

Finally, they approached a door somewhat larger than the others, with the Eternal Eye symbol of the entire Hallowed Pact embossed in silver at—appropriately enough—eye-level. Just as the guard raised his fist to knock, Widdershins said, "Please tell the bishop I'll see him now."

The fellow's clean-shaven face twisted her way. "Are you trying to be funny?"

"I'm not trying one bit," she answered cheerfully. "It all comes naturally."

The guard grumbled something, knocked, and pushed the door open at the response from within.

Framed beyond the portal stood Sicard himself, still clad in the silver-trimmed ceremonial robes he wore for his sermons. Very little of the chamber was visible behind them, but Widdershins had the faint impression of a third person present. Probably the monk, Ferrand, if she'd had to guess.

"Well," Sicard said, "I don't believe we've ever been formally introduced, but I imagine you would be Widdershins?"

Widdershins blinked. *How much does the bishop already know about me?* Even Olgun felt more than a little startled. "Uh . . ." She gave some thought to denying it, then decided it wasn't worth the effort. "You imagine correctly, Your Eminence.

Sicard stepped back, gesturing for Widdershins to enter. "Martin, please ensure that our guest is unarmed, and then see that we're not disturbed."

She might still have time to run. Gods alone knew what Sicard was capable of, what his schemes were, how much of the recent bloodshed was, indirectly or otherwise, his doing. Being trapped with him in his own chambers, unarmed, didn't precisely seem to be the pathway to a long and prosperous life.

Bah! I can take care of myself! And there was so much she needed to learn . . .

Widdershins smiled once more at the guard—Martin, apparently—and held out her arms. The guard's efforts were professional, but thorough. He located and confiscated not only Widdershins's main gauche, but a few smaller blades she had secreted on her person. "Well," she said to Olgun in her not-even-a-breath voice, flinching as the office door slammed behind her, "that could have gone a little better, yes?"

Struggling to keep the doubt from her face, Widdershins smiled, nodded in response to Sicard's gesture, and moved to take a seat. The office was large and well furnished without crossing the line into opulent. Several chairs with thick cushions stood around a marble-topped table, upon which sat several glass carafes and a number of narrow goblets. Bookcases lined one wall, a few tasteful portraits (presumably of saints or other holy figures) the opposite. Across from the door, a large window allowed the early-morning sun to illuminate the room. Before that window stood a desk with a chair, but it seemed rarely used, suggesting that the bishop preferred to sit at the table.

Sicard lit a chandelier hanging above that table and waved. Ferrand—for it was, indeed, he who Widdershins had noticed—drew the heavy curtains, so that the newly kindled flame became the room's only light.

"We don't have *many* passersby in the courtyard," the bishop explained, "but nonetheless, I'd hate for anyone to spot us talking and get the wrong idea."

"No, of course," Widdershins muttered. "Couldn't have that."

Sicard took a seat across from her, with Ferrand hovering behind him. "Wine? Juice?"

"Uh, no, thank you."

He nodded and poured himself a goblet of a rich, sweet-smelling vintage. "So, tell me, young lady . . . What, precisely, did you hope to accomplish here?"

"I beg your—"

"Please, let's not insult one another's intelligence, hmm? Your *last* visit here was about studying me, so that's not why you came back. It certainly wasn't to hear my sermon. Were you hoping to spy on me, or simply to attack me outright?"

Widdershins felt her jaw trying to unhinge itself again.

"Your plan *was* one or the other, was it not?" Sicard pressed.

"Um, of course not," she lied.

"Of course not." Sicard chuckled. "Widdershins, a man doesn't reach my position without learning the ins and outs of intrigue. You wouldn't last five minutes in the political wrangling I've seen."

"William wasn't like that," she muttered.

Sicard's smile fell. "William de Laurent was a great man. One of the best I've ever met. But he left his footprints on enough backs and shoulders on the way up. We *all* do.

"And *you*," he suddenly roared, his wine threatening to spill across the table and his pristine cassock, "haven't the right to speak his name!"

Widdershins couldn't help it; she actually recoiled, sinking back in her chair against the unexpected surge of fury. Even Brother Ferrand jumped a little, and his expression was ever so slightly wild.

"What . . . What are you talking about?" she asked.

"You know damn well! I have no idea what your vendetta against the Church may be, little girl, but it ends now!"

"Vendetta? *Vendetta?!* I've done nothing—!"

"We know you were involved in Archbishop de Laurent's murder—"

"I was trying to *save*—!"

"I've read Brother Maurice's report. It's confused and spotty, and leaves out far more details than it includes. I doubt his conclusions, frankly."

"But—"

"*Especially* since you're so obviously working to sabotage us *now*, as well!"

"I never—"

"Is it something personal, thief? Something in your past? Or is this a move on the part of your heathen god?"

Widdershins, who had by now realized that Sicard didn't intend to let her complete a sentence any time soon, clamped her mouth shut and tried her best to burn a hole through his forehead with nothing but the power of her stare.

"Oh, yes, I know about him," Sicard continued. "Not his name, or where he comes from, but I know he exists. I felt his presence the first time you entered my church. Between what I read of Brother Maurice's report—"

"The one you doubt?" Widdershins growled, but the bishop didn't hear.

"—and everything else I've dug up on you, it would have been only a matter of time before I pieced it together even if you *hadn't* appeared in my church this morning. And of course, now that you're right here, I can just about *see* him! How you kept his presence from de Laurent—"

"He knew," Widdershins said, relishing the chance to interrupt. "William understood. He approved."

"Nonsense!" Sicard was practically spitting. "And your own actions put the lie to any such ludicrous claims!"

"And what actions would those—"

"You're a *murderer* as well as a thief!"

"If you interrupt me one more—Wait. You think I'm *what*?"

"Oh, yes, I know. I made certain, *absolutely* certain, that nobody would be hurt! *Nobody!* Everything was proceeding as well as I could have dared hope, with nothing but a few scrapes and bruises. And then, you! You stick your nose in, and now Davillon has blood running in the streets!"

Widdershins realized she was standing, as was Sicard, and wasn't certain when either of them had risen. Brother Ferrand virtually vibrated in place, as though torn in multiple directions at once.

"You think *I* killed those people? Me? Gods, *why*?"

"There's nobody else involved who—"

"It's not me, you idiot! It's Iruoch!"

She hadn't meant to just blurt it out, but at least—other than his heaving breath—she'd finally silenced the shouting old goat.

When he finally did relocate his voice, Sicard didn't seem certain what to do with it. "What . . . You . . . Did you just say 'Iruoch'?"

Widdershins struggled to control her own breathing, her own temper, and sat back down. "I did."

"Iruoch's a fairy tale, you stupid girl! A story!"

"Like the cavalier d'Ouelette?" she challenged.

"A story," he repeated. "One of many I tell, to make a point. To teach. It doesn't mean I believe them, any more than my adult parishioners do. If you think I'd accept for one instant—"

"Look, you don't have to believe that he's *literally* Iruoch! But there's *something* unnatural hunting Davillon, and it sure as figs isn't *me*!"

"Ridiculous. You—"

"Ah, Your Eminence." Ferrand sounded as though he'd rather cover himself in salt and dance for the lions than get involved, but he did so nonetheless. "I *have* been keeping an ear on what's going on, and it's true that there's definitely some sort of magic involved in these murders. The bodies—"

"That just proves that her heathen god has given her powers of witchcraft, Ferrand! She's the only murderer involved! She—"

By which point, Widdershins's patience, already stretched so far it would ache for days, snapped. With a sound somewhere between a grunt and a shriek she lunged from her seat, calling on Olgun's aid as she moved, less in control now even than she'd been when confronting Igraine in the shrine of the Shrouded God.

One hand on the edge of the table was enough to vault her across the room, not at the bishop, but at Ferrand. Her calves crossed around his knees and she twisted as she fell, sending him crashing to the carpet. It wouldn't hurt him much, except maybe his pride, but it would keep him out of the way just long enough . . .

Sicard was already recoiling, hand reaching for the staff of office leaning on the back of his chair, but he might as well have been swimming through cobweb. Widdershins was back on her feet—or, more accurately, one foot. The other rose, then fell in a heel kick atop one of the carafes, shattering it across the marble. A simple cartwheel, and she came up directly beside the bishop, one arm wrapped around his neck, the other clutching a curved length of broken glass that had previously been the decanter's handle. Her hand should have been bleeding all over it, but Olgun's will had allowed her to avoid every other shard on the tabletop.

It was all over before Widdershins's chair had finished its slow topple to the floor.

"If I were the murderer you believe me to be," she hissed into the pallid clergyman's face, "you'd be dead. And I'd be out that window in another three seconds."

At which point she dropped the makeshift weapon and was in the process of righting her chair before the guard outside had finally shaken off his shock at the abrupt eruption of sounds and thrown open the door to see what was amiss.

"Brother Ferrand tripped," she said to the sentry's stunned face.

"He did no such thing!" Sicard's voice lacked the certainty it had held only moments before, but if he was having doubts now, it wasn't stopping him. "I want that creature in chains!"

"Well," she said softly to Olgun, already beginning to flush with embarrassment at her brief lapse of control. *What in the name of the gods is* wrong *with me? First Igraine, now Sicard?* "That probably wasn't the *smartest* thing I've ever done. That argument worked so well with Igraine . . ."

Martin approached, one hand on his pistol, and she was just trying to decide if it was worth resisting when Igraine herself appeared in the office doorway. Paschal Sorelle was beside her.

And *they* were followed by Julien Bouniard! Even though she'd known he was nearby, watching in case the bishop had slipped by her, she couldn't repress a gasp of relief (or *was* it just relief?) at the sight.

Julien, for his part, took one look at the broken glass, a second at Widdershins, and then just shook his head.

"I don't know what *you're* doing here, Major," Sicard said, far more calmly. "But you couldn't have picked a better time. This woman is a thief and a—"

"You can save it, Your Eminence," Bouniard said. "We heard all of it." Then, when the bishop and the thief both gawped at him, "When Igraine saw you being escorted into the back, we improvised. Cup against the bishop's window. Thank you for pulling the curtain, by the way. Otherwise, you'd have spotted us in a second."

Sicard was scowling, his jaw working, no doubt trying to recall if, in the heat of the moment, he'd said anything too terribly self-incriminating.

Widdershins was only too happy to help. "Which means," she crowed, "they heard you admit that *you* arranged the initial attacks! Before the people actually started dying!"

"That doesn't justify your attack on me," he insisted, though he'd begun to pale. "Major, I intend to press charges with the full weight of the Church."

"And you have that right," he said. "Of course, in the process, Igraine and I will have to testify to what we heard—and of course, if we make such a claim in court, we must inform the Church as well."

"Why are you aiding this girl?!" Sicard demanded. "She's a murderer!"

"Actually," Bouniard told him, "she's not."

"I—what?"

"She has, in fact, been assisting us in our attempts to *stop* the creature committing these crimes."

"Creature? You don't honestly—"

"Yes, Your Eminence, I do. I've seen its handiwork—including the injuries Widdershins suffered the first time *it tried to kill her*."

"She could have faked—"

"No. She couldn't."

Sicard literally fell backward, and it was only sheer luck that the chair was near enough to catch him. "But . . . William de Laurent? She—"

"I was there for some of those events as well, Your Eminence. She did everything she could to *save* the archbishop. And she lost her own closest friend in that mess."

Widdershins turned away, memories of Genevieve—and, spawned by those, a new flare of concern for Robin—briefly overwhelming her.

"I was so sure." Sicard's palms were shaking as though abruptly stricken with palsy. "I was *so sure*. It *can't* be because of us, we made *certain . . .*"

"What *exactly* did you do, Your Eminence?" Julien asked, not unkindly. But the old man—growing visibly older by the moment—seemed unable to answer. The monk knelt beside his master and held his trembling hand.

"Why," Widdershins couldn't help but mutter, "does everyone want to blame me for everything?"

She hadn't intended to be overheard, but by one pair of ears, she was. "Because you're secretive," Igraine said. "And you're impetuous. And you do find yourself near the center of trouble far more often than is good for you. And because some of us can sense that there truly is something abnormal, even unnatural about you. But mostly because you really, really annoy people."

Widdershins couldn't think of a better reaction than to stick her tongue out. "Igraine?" she asked a moment later in a whisper, careful that nobody else in the room might hear. "Is what you heard really enough to start an inquiry? I mean, he only kind of touched on—"

"We didn't hear a damn thing, Widdershins," she answered as quietly. "Cup against the window? We barely made out every fifth word."

Olgun somehow *emoted* an "Eep!" and Widdershins stared through horror-widened eyes. "You mean . . . ?"

"We just came running when we heard things get messy, and hoped that you'd gotten *something* useful from him."

Widdershins couldn't tell whether she wanted to sob or hit someone, and was just deciding that she needn't choose one over the other when Sicard coughed once and straightened his shoulders.

"All right, Major," the bishop said. "I don't know what's happened, or where things went wrong, but I never intended for anyone to suffer. I'll tell you the whole story."

"*Would* you? Oh, splendid!" Every head in the room flinched in mounting dread as the door to the office slowly drifted open once more, admitting that awful, dual-toned voice. "I just *love* a good story!"

CHAPTER FOURTEEN

"Where *is* she?"

Robin watched from her seat—a comfortable, cushioned chair in the center of the room—as her captor paced as if *he* were the one caged. Her prison wasn't especially arduous; in addition to said chair, she had access to a table with an array of juices, cheese, and pastries, as well as a chamber pot if nature should demand its due. The only sign of her captivity at all was the manacle about her wrist, and the length of chain attached to it. Bolted to the leg of the table, it allowed her a substantial amount of freedom, though not enough to reach any of the four walls of the cavernous, and largely empty, chamber. A storage room or a warehouse, no doubt.

For his own part, Evrard passed to and fro beneath one of the room's rows of windows. A second table supported a carafe of wine and several loaded pistols; he'd spent substantial time with the first, and relatively little with the second.

"You could've left her a note, you know," Robin told him, lifting a goblet of fruit juice to her mouth. (The cup was flimsy, a lightweight wood—very obviously provided because it would prove utterly ineffective as a makeshift weapon.)

Evrard ceased his pacing long enough to glare.

"No, really," Robin continued. "I mean, if you *wanted* her to find you, then you could just—"

"She'll find me," he snapped. "My family only *owns* a few properties in Davillon."

"Like the tower?" Robin asked innocently.

"You're pushing it, child!"

Maybe she was; maybe she should just keep her teeth together. Robin was no Widdershins. Not a fighter, not brave, not . . .

But she also wasn't stupid, and damn it all, she wasn't just some tool to be used and thrown away at need!

"I don't think so," she said, trying with only debatable success to work a touch of steel—a touch of Widdershins—into her tone. "You're not going to hurt me, Evrard."

"So sure of that, are you?" His own goblet, of equally flimsy wood, cracked in his hand, sending rivulets of purple cascading across his fingers.

"Yes. Come on. You practically begged Gerard and the others not to make you shoot them when you abducted me. Hell, you *apologized* when you snapped this stupid cuff on my wrist!" She jingled the chain for emphasis, as if he could possibly have thought she meant some *other* manacle. "The food, the drink . . . You're not exactly a traditional kidnapper, you know."

"I'm not a kidnapper!"

Robin just looked at him.

"I'm *not*."

She held up her wrist and once again shook the chain.

Evrard growled something unintelligible. Turning back to the nearer table, he lifted the carafe of wine and began to pour, then flinched as the liquid dripped through the cracked vessel. With a grunt he tossed the useless cup to the floor and took a large and very unaristocratic gulp from the decanter itself—a decanter which was, Robin couldn't help but note, already half-empty.

"Classy," Robin said. Evrard pulled a second, smaller chair out from the table and slumped into it.

"I'm no kidnapper," he insisted again, sulking.

"My chain and I would like to debate that."

"Gods *damn* it! This is all *her* fault, you know!"

"Who? Widdershins?"

Evrard's lips actually peeled back from his teeth at the sound of that name. "Who else?"

"This is *her* fault, is it? Maybe she paid you to kidnap me? There are easier ways of firing me, if that's what she—"

"This isn't a joke!" Evrard was again on his feet and again pacing, though this time it was toward and away from his less-than-willing guest, rather than parallel to the windows. "I didn't want it to come to this. She was supposed to . . ." He stumbled to a halt, then shrugged. "I thought that surely *this* would do it. But no, apparently your precious Widdershins won't even put herself out for her so-called *friends*!"

"She'll be here!" Robin realized she was screaming and forced herself to calm. "You don't know her. She'll be here, and you'll wish she wasn't."

"I doubt it." Evrard shook his head and returned to the carafe of wine. "I don't believe anymore that she has even *that* much honor."

Robin didn't remember rising to her feet. "*Honor?!*" She was shouting again, and this time couldn't be bothered to care. "You're talking about honor? *You?!* You threatened to destroy her life! You *kidnapped me!* And over what? A few stolen treasures that your family hadn't bothered even to *look at* in a decade or more? What gives you the right to impugn *anyone's* honor?"

The carafe shattered against the wall, leaving a series of divots in the wood and a blotch of wine that gave the impression of someone having just swatted a two-foot mosquito. "What *else* would this be about, you stupid little girl?!" Evrard, too, was shouting, his fists clenched and shaking. "Everything I've done has been to erase the stain on my family's honor! A stain left by your precious *Widdershins*!"

"Oh, right." Robin looked meaningfully at the shackle on her wrist, at the wine stain on the wall. "Mother and Father would be *so* proud of you right now, wouldn't they?"

For a moment, Robin really thought she'd gone too far. With a strangled cry, Evrard was across the room and looming over her, his arm raised for a brutal backhand blow. Robin whimpered and fell back, cringing away from the coming pain . . .

But the blow never fell. For long seconds Evrard hovered, his face twisted—and then his shoulders slumped and he fell back. Robin, who could see him only blurrily between squinted lids, forced her eyes all the way open.

Evrard blinked slowly, just once, and then he made his way once more to the far table. "Let's just hope you're right," he said, "and she gets here soon. I want to get this over with."

Robin couldn't help but nod in heartfelt agreement. And as neither of them had anything more to say, they waited in silence, each lost in his or her own tumultuous thoughts.

So lost, in fact, that when Robin next blinked herself out of her near fugue and glanced around, the oil lamps that provided the room's only illumination, set roughly equidistant around the chamber, were beginning to gutter. But that meant . . .

Hours. It'd been *hours* since she and Evrard last spoke. Hours in which Widdershins had failed to appear.

Those guttering flames grew suddenly broad and bleary through Robin's unshed tears. She wouldn't give up; she *wouldn't*! And yet . . .

She couldn't quite repress a startled shriek as Evrard appeared in her peripheral vision, his approach heralded by the ominous echo of footsteps—a sound she had utterly missed until he was *right there*. Perhaps he'd come to the same conclusion—that Robin's usefulness as bait had proved sorely lacking—because his stare was hard, his hand darting into a heavy leather pouch at his belt. Robin recoiled, squeezing herself back into the chair, as that hand emerged, clutching . . .

A key?

Robin held her breath as Evrard knelt for an instant at her side. A slight jostling, a loud click, and the manacle around her wrist fell away. By the time she rose, carefully rubbing and poking at the slightly chafed skin, he was already stepping away once more.

"Go home," he told her, unwilling or unable to meet her gaze. "I don't—"

Pistol shots shattered the nighttime silence in the streets beyond the warehouse. The wood of the window shutters cracked and splintered as lead balls punched their way through, hurtling upward to embed themselves in the ceiling with a shower of dust and splinters. Robin screamed as something heavy slammed into her, knocking her to the floor. Except it wasn't some*thing* at all, but some*one*.

Evrard. Evrard was actually lying atop her, shielding her with his own body.

Not, they both realized at roughly the same moment, that it'd been necessary. The pistols had clearly been aimed upward, intended to fly over the heads of anyone within the chamber. Neither Robin nor Evrard himself had been in any danger, save for the risk of shallow cuts from flying shrapnel.

A diversion, then? If so, it had done its job well, for by the time Evrard had climbed back to his feet, his ruby-hilted rapier unsheathed in his right hand, it was already too late.

The door hung open, the lock apparently having been picked, and two men clad in blacks and grays had darted through, one to either side of the door. Both held muskets, aimed steadily at Evrard's breast. A third dark-garbed intruder—this one female, to judge by the shape, but otherwise similar to the first two—had crept in from one of the entrances at the back, and now stood at the rear of the chamber. She, too, had her weapon locked squarely on the young aristocrat.

"Well," Evrard said, his focus flickering from one to the next, "I suppose I should have seen this coming." He stopped and faced a fourth figure, who was only now appearing between the two men at the door. "Too much to expect for you to come alone, wasn't . . ."

His teeth came together with an audible click when the new arrival revealed itself to be not Widdershins at all, but rather a short dandy in bright tunic and hose, a half cape slung over one shoulder, his mustache perfectly trimmed. He wore a hat with an ostrich plume and a rapier at his side, and in his right hand he clutched a flintlock pistol.

"You're not Widdershins," Evrard said, his voice almost accusatory.

"Goodness, no. I believe if I were, you should never entice me to leave the house." He bowed low. "Renard Lambert, at your service. Robin? Are you injured?"

"No," she said, her voice quavering as she crawled a few feet from where she'd fallen and then stood. "No, I'm fine. Is . . . Where's Widdershins?"

"I fear the good lady couldn't attend. I've come in her stead."

"Hah!" Evrard shook his head. "I knew the woman had no honor, no loyalty! She—!"

"You would do well, monsieur, to be more careful about insulting people whose friends have loaded weapons pointed at your heart."

Evrard, apparently, felt there was some wisdom in that, as he fell silent.

Renard directed his attention once more toward Robin. "Come on, girl. Over here."

She obeyed, her limbs moving mechanically, but her lips were pale, her jaw quivering. She felt the wet warmth of tears on both cheeks, and couldn't be bothered even to wipe them off. She knew she ought to be grateful, to be delighted that rescue had come (even if it was starting to look as though she might not need it), but any joy was swiftly overwhelmed and drowned beneath a rising tide of despair.

Widdershins didn't even bother to show up.

"So what now?" Evrard asked. He might as well have been discussing plans for dinner, so little did he seem to care anymore. "Did she send you to kill for her, as well?"

"Any killing I do, monsieur, is entirely for me," Renard retorted. "And you are simply bitter that Widdershins found a way around your snare."

"By abandoning her friends," Evrard spat, his every fiber radiating contempt.

Robin actually *saw* Renard's finger tighten on the trigger, saw his face go hard; she swore she even saw the weapon's hammer tremor with anticipation, though of course that wasn't possible, was it? At the last second, however, the fop relaxed his grip with a loud sigh. He studied the aristocrat standing nigh helpless before him, then Robin's tear-glistening face.

And whether he directed his answer to one, the other, or both, Renard spoke once more.

"You doubt her," he said softly. "But you've no reason. It took every argument we could muster to persuade her not to come. I've never seen her so worried as she was about you, girl. And had it just been a matter of this idiot's trap, not every god of the Pact could have held her back."

"Then why?" Robin asked softly, but her question was lost in Evrard's own.

"And I presume I'm supposed to ask, then, what it *was* that kept her away? Fine. What, pray tell, could that have been? A theft she couldn't pass up? A rendezvous with some lover?"

Again the leather of Renard's gloves creaked, again his weapon almost discharged. "She's a little busy," he hissed, "working with the Guard and the Church to keep the creature stalking our streets from *murdering any more children*!"

Although it was Robin who was standing beside the thief as he shouted, it was Evrard who physically recoiled. "What? She . . . Why?!" Apparently, it never even occurred to him to doubt Renard's story—presumably because it was so very unlikely that there would be no point to concocting such a ludicrous tale. "What's her involvement with that . . . *thing*?"

Renard blinked, perhaps at the implication that Evrard himself knew more about Iruoch than he should, but merely shrugged. "None at all, other than the desire to stop it."

And Robin could only laugh through her tears at the expression on the gobsmacked aristocrat's face. "I *told you* you didn't know anything!" she crowed.

"All right," Evrard said, clearly struggling to recover. "So what now?"

Renard apparently caught something—a flicker of an eyelid, a shifting of Evrard's weight—that Robin herself had missed. "Now, you don't even think it. Even if you could reach the table before the four of us shot you down, you'd die before you could fire off more than one of those pistols that await you so tantalizingly beyond reach."

Evrard offered a faint grin in exchange. "But you're going to shoot me anyway, are you not?"

"Well," Renard admitted, "that's not entirely impossible, but—"

Robin had never, in her life, seen anyone move so fast (although it must be pointed out that she'd never witnessed one of Widdershins's supernatural feats). Literally between one of Renard's words and the next, Evrard was whirling, the air around him whining in pain as the hem of his coat and the tip of his blade both sliced their way through it. Wobbling in an awkward arc, the ruby-hilted rapier spun through the intervening space and plunged through the small gaggle of thieves gathered by the front door. It wasn't much of an attack—rapiers not, by and large, being designed for use at a distance—but the sheer speed and ferocity of the throw sent Renard and his two companions cringing away from the flashing steel. For the barest instant, the four gun barrels aimed at Evrard had been reduced to one.

That one, the musket held by the woman covering him from behind, discharged with a deafening clap, but Evrard was already sprinting. The ball flew harmlessly through empty space, vanishing finally into the wood of the far wall.

A fusillade of three more shots came rapidly after the first, as Renard and the others recovered, but hitting a moving target with a flintlock weapon was tricky at the best of times; when it was moving as swiftly and unexpectedly as Evrard, well, far better marksmen than these three Finders could have been excused for missing the mark.

Renard was already forward, the others close on his heels, steel sliding from the sheath at his waist. They needed to close the distance fast, before Evrard could take advantage of the pistols that lay, loaded and waiting, on the table.

Except that Evrard wasn't *going* for the pistols. Without slowing down or breaking stride, he leapt, using the table as a stepping stone to the row of windows beyond. Old wooden shutters disintegrated beneath his shoulder, and the aristocrat was tumbling out into the dusty road, leaving only astonished faces and angry mutters behind him.

❋

Renard smiled gently as he returned to Robin's side, sheathing his blade and bending to retrieve both the pistol he'd dropped in his haste, and the weapon the aristocrat had hurled his way. "Ready to go home?" he asked.

She gave him a single nod. "You didn't chase him."

It wasn't precisely a question, but Renard decided to accept it as one. "The gunfire probably already drew more attention than we want. A bunch of us chasing a lone man down the street? Even assuming he didn't pick us off one by one, it would certainly have gone ill for all of us. You're safe; that's the important bit."

"Important to *some*."

Renard didn't think he was supposed to have heard it, wasn't sure if Robin had even realized she'd spoken aloud. He frowned, glanced about himself to make certain that none of the other Finders were within earshot, and leaned in as though examining the girl's chafed wrist.

"Everything I said to that popinjay was true, Robin. The only reason Widdershins didn't come herself—"

"I know." Robin managed a brief and feeble smirk at the sound of *Renard* calling anyone "popinjay," given that the man dressed as though he were paying court to the daughter of a rainbow, but otherwise her demeanor, and her haunted expression, changed not a whit. "I know why she couldn't be here."

She didn't add the *But still* aloud, but Renard heard it all the same.

And in a veritable bolt of inspiration, Renard completely understood.

"You love her."

Robin's face became stone—no, not even stone, but *ice*. All of it, that is, save for the two burning splotches of red in her cheeks.

"Shut up. *You shut the hell up!*"

Renard glanced over his shoulder, raised a hand to signal the puzzled Finders to remain where they were, that this was no difficulty he couldn't handle on his own.

"You don't know what you're talking about! You don't know *anything*!" She'd lowered her voice, but what the rant lacked in volume, Robin was more than making up for in sheer vehemence. "Don't you *ever* say that again, you bastard! Me? *Widdershins?!* That's not . . . I mean, that wouldn't be even remotely . . . She's not . . ."

The dapper Finder had never really been all that close with Robin. She'd never been anything to him but Widdershins's friend, and the girl who helped Widdershins oversee the Flippant Witch. Nevertheless, he reached out and took her gently by the shoulders.

For an instant, Robin stiffened, as though she would run, or even strike at him—and then the ice cracked. Her arms wrapped around his chest, the tears she'd been battling earlier soaked his doublet.

"You can't tell her!" Robin sobbed. "Please, Renard, you *can't*!"

"Shh. Hush. I won't say a word, I promise."

He twisted his neck around until it ached, struggling to meet the gaze of his companions without relinquishing the embrace. When he was certain he had their attention, he deliberately tilted his head toward the chair to which she'd been chained and carefully mouthed the words "It's all too much."

He was relieved when the Finders nodded and looked away, making themselves look busy while the girl recovered. Let them believe the lie; it was better for everyone.

"Come on, Robin," he said kindly as her shaking finally began to subside. "Let's get you home." He took her wet sniffle as agreement, and slowly began to disentangle himself from her grasp.

"Renard?"

"Yes, my dear?"

She hiccupped once. "How did you know?" she whispered. "How did you know how I feel about . . . ?"

He had no reason to answer truthfully. In fact, so far as Renard was concerned, honestly was rarely, if ever, a virtue. Yet somehow, the notion of lying, or even refusing to answer, just felt *wrong*.

Smiling sadly, he brushed a tear from her face with a single gloved knuckle. "It takes one to know one, kid."

Robin's eyes widened, and then—thank the gods!—so did her own smile. "Your secret's safe with me," she assured him.

"I know it is, Robin."

The thief's hand on the serving girl's shoulder, they led the small, ragged group from the warehouse, toward home.

CHAPTER FIFTEEN

The shape—for indeed, a *shape* is what it was, not a person, not even a creature—appeared from the top of the opening doorway, revealed slowly as though extruding from the ceiling itself. The deathly gaunt limbs; the impossible, elongated fingers; the twitching flesh around the mouth; and of course that hat, and that coat, whose flops and folds refused to conform to either the movements beneath them or the pull of gravity itself. Iruoch descended into the church hall, entered the bishop's chambers with a single, careless stride, and nobody moved to stop him.

Nobody but one.

Had she been a bit more calm, a bit less enraged, and indeed a bit less frightened, Widdershins might have noticed that Iruoch was not moving *quite* as he had in their first meeting. His steps were ever so slightly less certain; his arms and shoulders spasming with a faint and sporadic twitch. His jaw clenched tight, and he squinted as though he peered directly into the noonday sun. Widdershins might have noticed, and might have wondered.

But she didn't. She noticed nothing, nothing at all, save Iruoch himself. She saw the creature appear in the doorway, and swore there were bloodstains remaining on his hands, his lips. She heard the distant laughter of that ghostly chorus, but in her mind reverberated only the terrified cries of murdered children.

All the frustrated rage and simmering guilt she'd felt since that awful discovery on the upper floor of the Lamarr manor—all of Olgun's own fury, caused by the sheer, diseased *wrongness* of the faerie's presence in this city of mortals—came together, a spark and tinder, erupting into a spiritual conflagration.

No communication, no requests, not even at the instinctive level of the rapport the thief and her god had developed these past few years. Today they acted, and they acted as one.

Iruoch had only just begun his second step into the room when Widdershins appeared above the shoulders of the others. A leap that should have been utterly impossible without a running start carried her over their heads. She tucked into a tight ball as she tumbled, barely enough to keep her from striking either the stone ceiling or the marble table. Broken glass crunched beneath her feet and one knee as she landed in a crouch, yet the shards failed to penetrate even the fabric of her hose, let alone her skin. Although she stared straight ahead, locked on Iruoch, her hands lashed out to each side, snagging the flintlock from the belt of the Church guard, and dragging the rapier from Constable Sorelle's scabbard.

The others gathered in the chamber hadn't even finished their gasps of astonishment when the pistol ignited with a deafening crack, and not even Iruoch was fast enough to avoid the shot.

The ball tumbled through the creature's filth-matted coat, through the flesh and bone of the shoulder beyond, and fell with a dull thump to the carpet in the hallway. A cloud of cinnamon-hued dust puffed from the wound and drifted to the floor in a flurry of flakes—flakes that resembled nothing so much as blood long dried to near powder. The ball, fresh and new when it was fired, was coated in years' worth of corrosion.

Ghostly children wailed in a chorus of pain, and Iruoch's face was a mask of utter astonishment. His jaw and cheeks flickered as those peculiar muscles—or whatever they were—twitched and flexed beneath the skin.

"*Ow!*" He really and truly looked as though his feelings had been hurt as much as his flesh. "That was—"

Widdershins kicked, and a small shard of broken glass from the carafe arced across the room—again, with impossible, unnatural accuracy—slicing for Iruoch's throat. He raised an arm fast enough to shatter the missile; several strips of shredded coat and skin dangled from wrist to elbow.

"That was—" he started again.

The flintlock—which Widdershins had hurled less than a heartbeat after kicking the glass—careened off his forehead, sending him staggering.

"That was—"

Widdershins lunged forward with a piercing cry and skewered the creature with Paschal's rapier, literally pinning him to the door.

"*Quit it!*" he shrieked at her. His breath was a waft of waste and blood, like the feces of an incontinent vampire. It punched through the miasma of peppermint that surrounded him, making Widdershins gag.

Gag, but not fall back. Grunting, she twisted the rapier, widening the wound. More dried blood—or whatever the dust in Iruoch's veins might be—sifted out across his boots, and hers.

"Would you just *die*?!" She heard the murderous hysteria in her voice, and a part of her *welcomed* it.

"Hmm . . ." Iruoch cocked his head aside and actually tapped one of those horrific fingers against his chin. And then, "Nah!"

Eight fingers clenched tight, wrapping and *re*wrapping themselves around Widdershins's wrist until it was encased in two or three *layers* of flexed digits. She felt his skin searing her own, felt it pierce the fabric and stick fast to her flesh, and she couldn't repress a shudder.

Slowly, methodically, Iruoch straightened his arms, pushing her back. The blade slid obscenely from his body, the once-pristine steel now rusted and pitted.

She'd hurt him—she *knew* she'd hurt him! She saw the pain in his clenched jaw, the wince as the sword slid free. But even as she watched, that agony faded. The small stream of dust pouring from his chest stuttered and stopped as the wound . . .

The ragged edge of the wound shaped itself into a mass of tiny fingers that slowly interleaved with and clenched one another, stitching the injury closed. And the gashes on his arm, the hole in his shoulder, already gone.

Yes, she'd hurt him. But not nearly, not *nearly* enough.

"You're a *really* good dancer," Iruoch told her with a manic grin. "But it's *my* turn to lead, now."

Iruoch's fingers flexed—not his shoulders, not his arms, but the fingers alone—and Widdershins hurtled back across the room, bowling over Constable Sorelle and Brother Ferrand in her flight. They fetched up against the desk with a painful clatter, a roiling heap of limbs and fabric and badly bruised flesh. Blood smeared the carpet around Widdershins's wrists, where the creature's touch had once again peeled layers of skin from her flesh, but she scarcely noticed the pain. Her ears filled with the sounds of desperate combat as someone fired off a second shot, as swords and bludgeons leapt from scabbards, as those still standing converged on the monster in their midst—but this, too, she was aware of only peripherally, as something happening at a great remove, lacking any immediacy.

Around her, cocooning her, insulating her from the world around her, was a despair so thick it was tangible; a despair partly her own and partly Olgun's, though she couldn't begin to guess where one left off and the other began.

Everything. She—*they*—had hit Iruoch with absolutely everything they had, everything they could muster. And he'd laughed it off. Oh, she'd made her mark, made him bleed to the extent that he *could* bleed, but nothing more.

She felt the weight around her shift as one of the men with whom she'd collided—she neither knew nor cared which—hauled himself up and to his feet. She was now free to move, and so she did, rolling over and curling into a tight ball, face pressed to the leg of the bishop's desk. As the earlier rage had seemed to come from beyond, to belong to someone else, so too did the hopelessness nipping and gnawing on the edges of her soul. For a moment, Widdershins—who had watched the slaughter of two dozen of her fellow worshippers, who'd lost the two people closest to her barely six months ago, who had faced not only betrayal but a *literal* demon without giving up—Widdershins surrendered. Eyes squeezed tight against both sight and tears, she abandoned the world to do as it would. To do with *her* as it would.

But only for a moment.

It wasn't the peculiar music of combat that dragged her back, kicking and screaming, to herself. It wasn't the cackles and nonsense rhymes of the creature she so hated, nor the grunts and groans of pain from her allies—not even when she recognized, with a faint spark of concern, Julien's voice among them.

It was, in his own way, Olgun. It was *always* Olgun.

It was Olgun's acquiescence; the sense of resigned despondency that flowed through her, merging with and augmenting her own. She'd given up—and so had he.

He could not fight without her, no longer had it in himself to try. If Widdershins surrendered, so did Olgun.

And she knew, as she pried her eyelids open and dragged herself to her feet, that she couldn't do that to him.

The scene before her was just about as awful as she could have expected. Julien was slumped against the wreckage of one of the bookcases, half-covered in fallen texts and tomes, struggling to pick himself up. Blood drenched the left half of his tunic and had even soaked through his tabard, though Widdershins couldn't clearly see the injury itself. Brother Ferrand held the bishop's staff of office and was jabbing it as a makeshift spear, but proved unable to get close enough to do any good. Paschal, who no longer had a rapier and whose injured arm would have prevented him from using it to full effect if he did, was struggling desperately to stay out of everyone's way while he fumbled through reloading his flintlock. The Church guard—Martin, was it?—hung limp from the wall beside the door, where he'd been pinned with his own broken halberd. Portions of his face hung in tattered ribbons: a blotch of carnage that was a near-perfect match to one of Iruoch's inhuman hands.

Iruoch himself crouched on the very edge of the table, a position that *should* have sent the furniture toppling, but of course did nothing of the sort. He lashed out in all directions, turning his head at impossible angles to keep a watch on every one of his opponents, but they had learned—though too late for some—to stay well beyond his reach. The phantom children giggled, and Iruoch himself was chanting, "Monks and soldiers, thieves and priests! Toys and games and snacks and feasts!"

All this she absorbed in an instant. What took her longer to grasp was what the two priests were doing—and, more importantly, the implications.

Sicard and Igraine both stood perhaps seven or eight feet from their enemy; he by the desk, not far from Widdershins herself, she near the portraits, opposite where Julien had fallen. Both stood with their holy icons raised, reciting prayers and paeans to the gods of the Hallowed Pact. Sicard's emphasized Vercoule, of course, while Igraine's were devoted mostly to the Shrouded God, but both were broad enough to encompass other divinities as well.

And they were *working*! This was no magic as Widdershins understood it; she saw no flashes of light, felt no power such as when Olgun worked his miracles through her. But Iruoch cringed and flinched from them as they spoke, turning his squinting face away.

That, then, brought back to mind the sights she'd failed to absorb earlier: Iruoch's abbreviated steps, his apparent discomfort upon entering the chamber. "It's the church," she whispered to Olgun, her voice shaking from all that had happened, all she'd seen. "Gods, that stupid rhyme was right!"

No mortals, magics, blades, or flames; He only fears the Sacred Names.

Maybe the unnatural aura of this unholy creature of the fae was enough to make even gods recoil in discomfort, but the same was true in reverse. *That* was why he'd focused on Widdershins and Olgun, why he'd taunted her specifically with his murder of the young nobles. They alone, among all he'd encountered, were . . . Well, a threat if they were lucky, but at least an irritant.

So maybe, if the two priests could just hold him for long enough . . .

As if mocking her for daring to plan, to hope, Iruoch chose that moment to act. He leapt from atop the table, flipping around so that his feet connected with the ceiling. There he hung, if only briefly, his coat still falling from his shoulders to his ankles in defiance of all natural laws. His spidery fingers closed on the nearest chair and tossed it across the room with brutal force. Sicard grunted, wood splintered, and the bishop fell, bleeding from an ugly gash across his forehead.

A second flip and Iruoch stood upon the carpet, stalking with stiff but inexorable steps toward Igraine. Apparently, whatever power the priests might have held over him together could not be maintained by one alone. The Finder began to sweat, and her voice grew louder, but the creature would not slow.

"Ready, Olgun?"

The god's reply, a muffled surge of doubt and hesitation, was not precisely reassuring. Nevertheless, Widdershins felt the familiar not-quite itch of his power flowing through her, suffusing her, brightening the air around her. One deep breath, to steady herself; a second, since the first was rather less effectual than she'd hoped; and Widdershins lunged.

No weapon in hand, no blade or even bludgeon held before her, she crashed into Iruoch as though catapulted, only steps away from Igraine. Guided by Olgun's touch, she struck, again and again, her hands a blur. She punched, bare-handed, at the creature's head; jabbed stiffened fingers into the soft spots at his throat, under his jaw, under his ribs, even at his eyes. Her intent wasn't to kill, not even to cripple. Widdershins was no brawler, and though she'd survived more than one fistfight in her time, she wouldn't have known how to render such blows fatal even if she'd tried. No, her goal was diversion. Her goal was *pain*.

Her goal was to strike Iruoch with every iota of power Olgun could give her, counting on the touch of his divinity itself to accomplish what blades of steel and balls of lead could not.

And to a degree, it worked! With every blow, Olgun's power swelled through her, overwhelming the faint burn Widdershins felt with even the briefest contact against Iruoch's skin. He flinched from every punch, every jab, every slap, crying out as he had not done even when shot through the shoulder or skewered through the chest. For the first time, he truly appeared uncertain of what to do, of how to react to the not quite mortal, not quite divine assault.

She couldn't take the time to plan her next attack, or even to think at all. All sense of technique was gone, all grace abandoned. She struck, again and again and again, a blur of violence, not daring to let up for so much as a heartbeat. Someone was yelling Julien's and Igraine's names, ordering them to get everyone else out, and Widdershins never realized it was she herself who shouted. She could only hope that the sound of shattering glass and feet tramping on wood—presumably the desk—meant that they were, indeed, making their escape through what had previously been the bishop's courtyard window.

Still she pounded on the creature she hated more than anything else in the world, until her hands were numb, her knuckles bleeding, her fingernails ragged. Had she been able to continue thus for minutes more, it's possible she might have done Iruoch permanent damage.

But she couldn't. Not even Olgun's influence could grant Widdershins the level of endurance she'd need to beat this murderous faerie to death. Gradually but inevitably, she slowed; her strikes coming less frequently, less powerfully. It was only a little, but it was more than enough.

Iruoch screamed, a primal sound bereft of meaning, and hurled Widdershins off him with both hands. She felt a brief sensation of freedom, until her flight was rather rudely—and quite abruptly—interrupted by the ceiling. She groaned, coughing up a dollop of blood-tinted spittle, and then a second, larger mouthful as she slammed back to the floor.

Some few paces away, Iruoch was rising to his feet, and whatever sense of humor (however cruel and twisted) normally occupied a portion of his expression was utterly absent. His eyes were impossibly, inhumanly wide; his teeth ground together with such impossible force that they visibly twisted and swayed in bloody sockets.

"Time to go somewhere else, yes?" Widdershins mumbled. The swell of agreement from Olgun was almost strong enough to lift her off the carpet under its own power.

"Oh, good. I'd hate for us to argue at a time like this." A brief grunt of exertion and she was up and running, diving through the shattered remnants of the window before Iruoch could even begin to draw near.

The world spun around her (and *not* in the direction she was tumbling), as exhaustion threatened to yank her back off her feet. She managed, if awkwardly, to roll upright and stagger forward. The courtyard, a simple square lawn with a variety of flowers in neat rows around the perimeter, was empty, suggesting that the others had wisely continued their flight.

Well, empty but for . . .

"Julien?!"

He was heading back her way, his left hand clutching the bloody wound in his side but his right wrapped about the hilt of his rapier. "I wasn't about to leave you alone to—"

"Chivalry later!" she shouted as a dark silhouette appeared in the bishop's window. "Desperate fleeing now!"

They fled.

Stumbling, leaning, and sometimes falling against each other, Widdershins and Julien passed through the narrow archway at the far end of the courtyard, shoving the thin, ivy-decorated gate from their path with enough force to loosen the squeaking hinges. They rounded the corner of the church, Widdershins propping herself up against the wall when it appeared that both of them might fall. She scraped her palm against the stone a time or two, and didn't even feel it; just another ember in what was currently a bonfire of pain.

The others awaited them in the road beyond, and a sorry band they made. Only Igraine and Paschal hadn't been wounded in the fray, and the constable, of course, still wore a sling from his earlier injury. Brother Ferrand, limping from where Widdershins had plowed into him, carefully supported the bishop, who was struggling to focus past the blood that trickled from his scalp wound. The monk was tugging on Sicard's sleeve, trying to entice him into flight, but apparently the bishop refused to leave the others behind.

It was almost enough to make Widdershins believe he was genuinely sorry for what had happened.

They were, the lot of them, the only people in the street. The crowds that should have been present—not just parishioners lingering after morning services, but the early ebb and flow of the day's traffic—were absent. Dropped baskets and parcels littering the street, as well as the occasional abandoned wagon and confused-looking draft horse, suggested that the lane had been rapidly abandoned.

Probably due to the gunshots and other sounds of violence from within the church, Widdershins decided. Which meant they could probably expect a Guard patrol within a few more minutes, for all the good they'd do.

"There!" She pointed a shaking finger toward the nearest wagon, a dilapidated thing of rough wood and cracked wheels, hitched to a particularly bored-looking roan. The horse flicked its mane at the sound of her approach, offered a flat and largely uninterested glance, and then returned its attention to whatever sorts of daydreams the average Galicien beast of burden preferred.

"Uh . . ." She could feel Julien's disbelief, but it was actually Brother Ferrand who voiced the first overt objection. "I, um, I don't think that we can outrun the creature in *that*. Maybe—"

"Would you just *go*?!" Widdershins shouted at him. And as none of the others had any better ideas, they went.

Widdershins reluctantly pushed away from Julien—yanking his rapier from its scabbard as she did so, and ignoring his yelp of protest—and jogged unsteadily ahead, reaching the wagon a few seconds before any of the others. "Just go with it," she gasped to Olgun. "We—"

"There!"

She didn't know who had shouted the warning, but a quick glance back was certainly enough to tell her *why*. Iruoch was emerging from around the corner to the courtyard and moving toward them with his usual erratic, impossible pace. At least he was actually on the *ground*, not the church wall, but his jumbled dance steps put the lie to any pretense of humanity he might otherwise have made.

Widdershins lashed out with Julien's rapier and Olgun's power. Hemp and leather parted beneath the edge of the blade—an edge that, really, shouldn't have been keen enough for such a neat slice—and then, ignoring the startled cries of her gathering companions, she carelessly dropped the weapon.

Not that it would have done her much good anyway. No, she bent forward, her numb and exhausted fingers a blur as they worked, and prayed that Olgun could keep her moving fast enough to make this happen.

A few more seconds, just a few more . . .

She heard the patter of rapid footsteps cease with a crunch, saw a shadow fall across her, and knew without looking that Iruoch had leapt toward her, arms outstretched. With a final desperate surge—the very last bit of strength that either she or her god could muster—she, too, took to the air, bounding not out of the creature's path, but directly toward him!

They collided in midair, and the startled faerie didn't quite have time to grab at his enemy before they both tumbled once more to earth, each landing in a crouch, staring intently at one another.

"What," Iruoch asked, head cocked sharply to one side, "was *that* supposed to . . ."

He blinked, peering over Widdershins's shoulder toward the horse; toward the rope harness that no longer led to the wagon, but instead stretched across the ground toward the two opponents. One of those spindly fingers rose to poke at the awkward noose of hemp that now lay around his neck.

Widdershins stood, smiled, and raised the strip of leather reins that she'd cut free at the same moment she'd sliced through the rope.

"Oh, phooey," Iruoch said.

Widdershins turned and snapped the leather, with a whipcrack, across the animal's chestnut haunches. A startled whinny and the horse was off, galloping through the abandoned streets. The rope snapped taut, and Iruoch, too, was gone, dragged across the dirt and cobblestones behind the animal's mad dash.

Again she turned, this time into a rising tide of disbelieving stares. She shrugged and tossed the rapier in a gentle arc toward Julien. He caught it awkwardly, apparently unable to tear his gaze from Widdershins to the blade.

"We really need to go," she told them.

She got nothing but a few scattered blinks for her trouble.

"No, really," she insisted. "That's only going to buy us a few minutes. We need to not be here when he gets back."

More blinking, more staring.

Widdershins threw up her hands, grumbled something, and then proceeded down the street at a brisk pace, trusting the others to fall in behind her.

They did, but by the time they'd reached the Flippant Witch quite a few blocks away, the others hadn't said a word.

And they were *still* staring at her.

CHAPTER SIXTEEN

Nor was there a great deal of discussion about what had just happened immediately *after* they arrived, because Widdershins and Robin had spent a good twenty minutes just holding each other and alternating between laughter and tears.

Given that it remained early in the morning, and thus outside normal business hours for an establishment of this sort, the tavern was empty of customers. The group had pushed two of the tables together for use as a makeshift hospital bed. Igraine and Ferrand, using torn linens for bandages and various spirits—the cheaper ones, naturally—as disinfectants, had done their best to treat the various and sundry injuries. They couldn't do much about the deep bruises or other aches, but the gash on the bishop's head, the wound in Julien's side (thankfully shallower than it had first appeared), and the torn skin on Widdershins's arms had all been cleansed (with only a modicum of screaming and threats) and tightly wrapped.

The common room now smelled fiercely of alcohol, sweat, and greasy smoke; it was lit only by a handful of lanterns, as all the shutters were tightly latched, and was already growing uncomfortably warm. Widdershins and Robin sat side by side on one of the longer benches; Julien on the "operating table"; Renard on the bar, where he'd helped himself to a jug of something or other; and the others in the tavern's various chairs. The Finders who'd accompanied Renard on his rescue mission (for which Widdershins had already tearfully thanked him about a thousand times) loitered on the streets outside, where they could shout a warning if danger approached.

And, not coincidentally, where they couldn't overhear any of the private discussion within.

Sicard studied one of the dancing flames and mumbled to himself, while most of the others waited with greater or lesser displays of patience for Widdershins and Robin to wrap up their reunion. Robin had, by this point, pretty much narrated the entire experience, but Widdershins—in addition to constantly apologizing for catching Robin in her mess, however unintentionally—was having real trouble grasping some of the finer details.

"He was just letting you *go*?"

Robin couldn't help but laugh. "Yes, Shins. Same as the last eighteen times you asked."

"But . . . he was just letting you go?"

"Which," Renard interjected from atop the bar, "doesn't in any way diminish the extent of my own accomplishment in rescuing her."

Both women did him the courtesy of a quick smile.

"Seriously," Robin continued. "I really got the impression that he was in over his head, and he knew it. I'm not defending the man," she added quickly at Widdershins's abrupt scowl. "Just trying to understand him."

"Well, after I murder him horribly," Widdershins said, "you can understand him all you want."

"Could you please see your way to saving the death threats for a time when Paschal and I aren't around to hear them?" Julien asked plaintively.

"Which reminds me," Renard said, hopping down from his perch, "I have something for you." He reached back behind the bar and presented a gleaming blade to Widdershins with a dramatic flourish. "I believe you're short a rapier, mademoiselle. I hope you'll find this a satisfactory replacement."

Widdershins's eyes gleamed as she recognized the weapon as Evrard's own. "You're a treasure."

"So good of you to notice."

"I . . ." She took the weapon from him, then stopped. "Renard, this sword had a ruby in the pommel."

"Did it? Oh, my. I can't imagine what might have happened to it."

Widdershins gawped at him, and then laughed. "Well, I'm sure it cuts just as well without it."

"I was almost certain it would."

"If we're all through catching up," Igraine snapped at them, "perhaps we'd be willing to spend a minute or two discussing what to do about the unkillable monster?"

Widdershins bent over and kissed the top of Robin's head—utterly missing the incongruous flicker of sorrow that crossed the younger girl's face as she did so—and with a whispered, "I'm really glad you're safe," rose from the bench. She carefully lay Evrard's rapier aside until she could recover her old sheath, and moved to stand in the center of the group.

"All right," she said aloud. "Let's discuss. I'd say, first and foremost, that His Eminence has some explaining to do, yes?"

Sicard slowly, even sleepily, dragged his attention away from the lantern. "Yes," he said softly. "He does."

"Your Eminence," Ferrand said, "you don't have to—"

"I think I do, Ferrand. I think explanations are the very *least* of the debt that I owe." He smiled, an expression with no joy or humor in it whatsoever. "I know that it's a bit cliché to begin one's confessions with 'I never meant for anyone to get hurt,' but it's the gods' honest truth. I really didn't."

He paused, perhaps to allow for any questions or interjections of disbelief. When he got none, he went on. "You must understand, my position here was . . . awkward, at best. Some might even call it untenable. The first bishop assigned to Davillon in years, and how did my tenure begin? In the shadow of the murder of Archbishop William de Laurent, and the Church's retaliation against your city.

"I don't . . ." He coughed once, shook his head. "I don't pretend that what the Church did was right. We're supposed to be above such pettiness, but we're human. I know that their—our—efforts at directing trade to other cities, at discouraging travel here, caused nothing but suffering to a population that largely didn't deserve it.

I may have been a newcomer to Davillon, but I couldn't stand seeing what was happening.

"Of course the people turned away from the Church and from the gods in their anger, and who could blame them? But I knew they were only harming themselves spiritually. And I knew that I could never convince my brothers in the clergy to lift the interdiction so long as Davillon's citizens were so openly hostile to the Church, no matter how justified that hostility might have been. So I . . ." Again he stopped, his voice choked.

It was Julien who first put it together, or at least first enunciated his understanding. "So you decided to give the people a reason to turn back to prayer. Back to the gods."

Sicard nodded miserably. "It seemed so simple, really. Make the citizens think they had some sort of unholy terror stalking their city, something the Guard was helpless to confront—no offense, constables—and what else would they do? It would take some time, of course, and it would hardly change *everyone's* mind, but it would get people back into the pews. And once *that* was done, I had hoped I could use their return to the flock as an argument for the Church to cease interfering in Davillon's economy."

Widdershins knew her entire face was incredulous, and saw clearly that hers wasn't the only one. "How by all the happy hopping horses did you think you could make that *work*?!" she demanded.

The bishop shrugged. "It honestly wasn't that hard. Obviously, a mortal adversary wouldn't do the trick, but it doesn't require much sorcery to make something *appear* far less natural than it actually is. And it *was* working! During the first few weeks, nobody had been seriously hurt—I know there were a few minor injuries, but that was unavoidable—and the rumors were spreading! Church attendance was higher than it had been in months! Until . . ."

"Iruoch," Robin said with a shudder.

"Until Iruoch," Sicard agreed. "My friends, hate me if you must—perhaps I deserve it—but I swear to you, I *swear* by every god of the Hallowed Pact, I *did not* summon him! I didn't even believe he *existed*! I truly don't know why—"

"I think I do," Widdershins said softly.

Well, she certainly had everyone's attention *now*, Sicard's included. She cleared her throat. "I'm only speculating, you understand . . ."

"Speculation's more than the rest of us have," Julien encouraged. "So by all means . . ."

"Uh, right. Well . . ." She exhaled softly. "Most of you won't know this, but the gods are shaped, in part, by our beliefs. What we think of them, how we worship them, that sort of thing."

A number of puzzled looks and startled breaths met that pronouncement, but none so dramatic as Sicard's violent gasp. "That . . . How could you *know* that? That's a philosophy debated at only the highest levels of the clergy!"

"I told you," Widdershins said, and she couldn't keep just the tiniest trace of gloating from her tone, "that William de Laurent trusted me more than you believed."

"So I see," the bishop whispered.

"Anyway," she continued, "so our own thoughts and beliefs and feelings influence the gods, and lots of creatures in myths and fairy tales are attracted to human emotions, yes? Fear, or love, or whatever? So I think . . ." She looked at Sicard, and this time there was no gloating, only sympathy. "I think, indirectly, maybe you *did* summon Iruoch, Your Eminence. I think the fear you created, everyone's belief that there was something very much like him stalking our streets already . . ."

Sicard paled. "He felt it. That fear, that belief, made us susceptible to him. *Called* to him. And he answered."

Widdershins nodded. "I think it drew him to us. I'm sorry."

The bishop lowered his head and began to weep. Ferrand rose and limped to his side, placing a comforting hand on his white-robed shoulder.

Flames hissed and spat, footsteps and hoofbeats slunk through the windows from the street outside, and Renard took occasional sips from the bottle he'd commandeered. Beyond these, however, no sounds interrupted Sicard's grief. After several moments of respectful silence (or near silence), however, Julien finally said, "Your Eminence . . ."

The bishop raised a flushed and tear-streaked face.

"I'm so sorry, but I fear that time is rather a precious commodity at the moment." When Sicard nodded, he continued, "I'm just wondering, *how* did you pull off your, um, false haunting? As you yourself said, a few mundane thugs in frightening dress wouldn't have been enough on their own . . ."

"No, no, you're right." Sicard cleared his throat, sucked in a last, wet sniff, and straightened in his chair. "The practice of magic isn't part of priestly training," he said. "We gain certain advantages due to our communion with the divine—particular insight, the occasional portent, and abnormal luck in certain ventures if the gods approve of our actions—but nothing that the layman would recognize as sorcery.

"We *do*, however, learn *about* magic. Not how to cast spells, but their history, how to recognize them. Normally, this is so we can discover the presence of hostile witchcraft or other dangers, but for those of us willing to take the time, and with sufficient discipline, it does give us a leg up on learning certain magics of our own."

He stopped, frowning slightly at the array of expressions before him. "Not *all* magic is forbidden by Church doctrine, you know. Only spells that are directly harmful, or that call on unnatural beings who are not servants of the gods themselves."

"We understand, Your Eminence," Julien assured him. "Nobody was questioning you."

Which was patently false, of course, but they all chose to let it go.

"Anyway," Sicard continued after another few breaths, "one of the spells I'd come across and actually mastered involves briefly linking two individuals on a semispiritual level. It allows them to not only coordinate their efforts and their awareness, but to share a portion of their skills and physical acumen with one another. Strength, endurance, nimbleness, and so forth. I've used it mostly to aid my priests and assistants in performing particularly long or complicated religious observances."

"Good gods," Renard breathed. "What a pair of thieves—or Guardsmen, or duelists, or soldiers," he added swiftly in response to an array of glowers, "could do with that sort of spell! How have such magics not already been claimed for military use?"

Sicard smiled shallowly. "I haven't been precisely open about the fact that I have this spell, save with my most trusted associates." He absently patted Ferrand's hand. "I chose to use it so my 'phantoms' could coordinate from a distance, appear to be the same creature in two places, and so they could perform feats of climbing and agility that no normal person could accomplish unaided. I figured that, along with the proper theatrics, would be enough to create the desired illusion. But I never expected them to need it for genuine combat, and honestly, I'm uncertain of its military applicability. It takes many minutes to perform, so it can't be invoked swiftly or in emergencies, and it doesn't last long. Further, the recipients share in their discomfort as well."

Widdershins nodded in understanding, remembering how one man had fallen from his perch in agony when she'd stabbed the other.

"I've never seen anyone *severely* injured, let alone slain, when under the spell's effects, so I can't say for certain what would happen to his partner, but I can't imagine it would be anything pleasant."

"Still," Julien insisted, "it seems we ought to be able to find *some* use for it. It's not as though we have a lot of options, and we haven't done so well against Iruoch as is . . ."

"I assure you," Sicard said, "even two men drawing on each other's strengths wouldn't make an appreciable difference against that creature."

"Two normal people, no," Igraine said thoughtfully, chewing on a thumbnail. "But what about two of *her*?"

Widdershins squirmed in her chair and looked about ready to bolt. "I'm not sure what you—"

"Widdershins," Igraine said in what was, from her, a surprisingly gentle tone, "I think we're past that now, don't you? Everyone here has heard tales of your unusual abilities, and we saw them ourselves back at the church. I've told you long before that I can sense something off about you, and I'd be surprised if His Eminence hadn't as well."

Sicard nodded.

"We need to know what our resources are," the priestess continued, "if we're to have any chance at all."

Widdershins shifted and again felt herself tense, as if to run. She cast her gaze at Robin, but the girl could only stare back, as uncertain as Widdershins herself.

"Olgun?" she whispered desperately.

Even he didn't know. She could feel it from him immediately. He wasn't sure what she should tell them, had no idea how Sicard's magics might interact with his own.

But she felt something from him, as well. Trust. Olgun trusted her. Whatever she decided, he'd support.

Widdershins sighed, and leaned forward in her chair. "I . . ." She realized her voice was shaking, and held out a hand toward Renard. Without having to ask what she meant, he slapped the bottle into her waiting palm. Widdershins took a few loud swigs, ignoring the trickle of alcohol running down her chin. "I'm sorry," she said then. "I've told almost nobody the whole story, and . . ." She cast about helplessly. "I'm not going to demand oaths in the gods' names or anything. I just need . . . I need to know that you won't tell anyone. None of you. Please."

Renard and Robin—though the girl knew most of what was to come already—nodded instantly. More slowly, Igraine, Sicard, Ferrand, and Julien followed. Only Paschal hesitated. "What if . . . ?"

The major coughed once, and the constable nodded. "Yes. All right."

"His name is Olgun," Widdershins said—and with those words, it felt as though one weight had lifted from her shoulders, to be replaced by a second. "He's—well, he *was*—a god of the northmen. Not part of the Pact. I worship him, and he . . . he protects me, as best he can. He works with me. He's . . ." She smiled, knowing how this would sound. "He's my friend."

Olgun beamed at her.

"Don't let it go to your head. You're annoying sometimes, too." And then she couldn't help but laugh, not at Olgun's response, but at the looks she was getting. "I know I sound crazy, but . . ."

"No," Igraine said, seemingly unaware that she was shaking her head as though she would never, *could* never, stop. "No, I believe you. Now that I know what I'm sensing, it's so clear."

"To me as well," Sicard added. "But I don't understand. No god should be granting that much power to any one person. How powerful *is* this Olgun?"

"He's not, really," Widdershins admitted. "He's just more focused. I . . . I'm his *only* worshipper."

The bishop, the monk, and the priestess all rocked back as though struck. "I've never even *heard* of such a thing!" Sicard gasped. "This is astonishing!"

"How could it even *happen*?" Brother Ferrand demanded. "To *any* god, let alone a northern deity who should have no presence here at all?"

Widdershins took a deep breath; if any revelation would cause her problems, it was the one yet to come. It wouldn't mean anything to most of the others, but to the Guardsmen in their midst . . .

Robin crept forward and took Widdershins's hand. The thief smiled at her, and bulled ahead.

"Olgun's worship was brought to Davillon by an explorer," she told them. "There were—there were a number of us, for a while. The others . . ." She cleared her throat, blinked away a few tears before they could form. "The others were slaughtered a few years ago. Only I survived."

Julien went abruptly pale, his hands clenching on the arms of his chair. *He's put it all together. . . .*

"Your Eminence?" Igraine asked. "How does that change things?"

"I honestly don't know," the bishop replied. "It depends on so many factors. When Olgun grants her his power, is he changing *her*, or the world around her? Will the spell even serve as a proper conduit? There are so many details to . . ."

Widdershins let the conversation drift away from her. She didn't need to hear the details and the discussions, the philosophy and the debate. It wouldn't mean anything to her anyway. Gently disentangling her hand from Robin's, she rose and wandered to the far side of the room, to stand stiffly before the shrine that she'd left standing in honor of the late Genevieve Marguilles.

She wasn't alone long, as she knew she wouldn't be. She heard the squeak-snap of a floorboard behind her, saw his shadow darken the white cross of Banin atop the stone.

"You're Adrienne Satti," he said gruffly. It very clearly was *not* a question.

"That was the first night I ever saw you, Julien," she whispered, hugging herself against a sudden chill.

"Saw . . . ?"

"I was hiding in the rafters when the Guard showed up. Too afraid to come down, too afraid you wouldn't believe a word I had to say."

"I don't know if we would have," he admitted. "But . . . Gods, Shins, you should have said *something*! Over two and a half years . . . Certainly nobody's going to believe anything you have to say about it *now*!"

"Nobody?" She turned, gazing up into his face. He was close, closer than she would have thought. . . . "Not even you?"

"Widdershins . . . Adrienne . . ."

"Because, after all this, if *you* honestly think I could possibly have killed all those people, all my *friends* you—you don't—"

"Widdershins? Don't be stupid."

Her jaw dropped.

"Of *course* I know you didn't do it, you little idiot." His grin widened beneath his mustache. "I'm violating every oath I ever took by keeping this secret—except for the one about upholding the gods' justice. I know the law won't give you a fair chance, so the law can go hang."

"Wow." She squeezed his hand in hers. (*And oh my gods, when did I even* take *his hand?!*) "I bet that was really, really hard for you to say, you righteous Guardsman, you."

"Not as much as you'd expect," he said, sounding vaguely bemused.

"So . . . What now, Julien?"

She knew it was coming, saw it in his face the instant she asked. Something akin to terror ran its fingertips down her spine as he leaned in, and she was frozen, trying to decide which way to run, when his lips touched hers.

At which point all thought of running—at which point all *thought*—was utterly lost, trampled into the dust beneath the sudden violent pounding of her heartbeat. She knew she made *some* sort of sound, though whether it was a cry or a gasp or a moan or some bizarre crossbreed of all three she couldn't possibly tell. And then there was nothing but his taste on her tongue, the fabric of his tabard and the muscles of his back beneath her grasping hands.

Where things might have gone from there, Widdershins had no notion—and, she realized with another surge of strangely delicious fear, didn't *care*—had Julien himself not pulled away after about two or three decades. "We're, uh, not exactly alone," he whispered with a peculiar hitch in his voice.

"What?" she asked dreamily, her expression utterly unfocused. And then, with a quick blink, "Oh! Um . . . I, um . . ."

As Widdershins appeared to be too busy turning red to actually form a cogent sentence, Julien simply smiled, gave her hand a final squeeze, and moved to rejoin the others, all of whom were very palpably *not* looking in the couple's general direction.

Widdershins coughed once, ran her fingers through her hair (which didn't need brushing), told Olgun to shut up (though he wasn't saying anything), and, shoulders straight and chin jutting, strode over to the others.

Had she been less preoccupied with what had just happened, or with covering for what had just happened, or with the homicidal faerie haunting the city, she might have noted Renard grinding his teeth, or Robin's red-rimmed eyes—but odds were that even if she had, she'd never have correctly interpreted them.

"So," she said, dropping into an empty chair and practically *daring* anyone to comment. "Have we decided anything?"

"Um . . ." Igraine coughed delicately. "His Eminence and I have discussed the magic in question, and we're fairly certain that you *could* briefly share a portion of your—that is, Olgun's—gifts with someone else."

"Well, that makes things easier! I mean, I'm not sure that even two of me would be enough to take on Iruoch, but it's certainly—"

"There's also substantial risk," Sicard interrupted, "that whoever linked with you would also suffer irreparable damage in the process. He'd be tapping into a divine power that wasn't intended for him. It's not inconceivable that it could cause the body to burn from the inside out, or become so stressed that even a small scratch could prove fatal."

"Oh. Uh, that's less good, then."

"It is."

"Then what—"

"I'll do it," Brother Ferrand said softly. Then, after giving the chorus of objections and protests a moment to subside, he continued, "I'm aware of the risks I'm taking. But you must understand, I've been part of this from the beginning. I aided His Eminence in his efforts. If there is any blame to be had for calling Iruoch to Davillon, I share in it. Bishop Sicard must cast the spell; he cannot be a part of it. I can."

"Ferrand," Sicard said, "are you certain?" He sounded as though he might cry again.

"I am, Your Eminence. I *must* do this. Please."

Sicard bowed his head. Widdershins felt a gentle waft of sorrow from Olgun. "It won't be your fault," she assured him. "All of which is well and good," she continued more loudly, with a brief smile of respect to the monk, "but it's not sufficient. As I was saying, even two people who can do what I can do may well not be enough. We need more."

"I can only link people in pairs," Sicard said. "If we had others with your abilities—or even others who were more highly skilled than we are—I could work with that, but I cannot join more than one person to you."

"Can we just overwhelm the creature?" Constable Sorelle asked. "I saw him take injury from a pistol, if only briefly. If we were to gather enough Guardsmen—or even Guardsmen and Finders together . . ."

Igraine and Sicard both shook their heads. "If Iruoch is drawn to emotion, as we believe," the priestess said, "then he's certain to sense people's presence, however well hidden. If he feels there are enough of us to threaten him, he'll simply wait for a more opportune time. We have to keep the group small. Major Bouniard, have you any particularly skilled fighters in the Guard? Anyone whose presence might make a difference?"

Julien frowned. "My men and women are good, no doubt, but . . . Well, none that are so dramatically more skilled than myself that they'd tip the balance." He shrugged. "Guards have to fight, but it's not *all* we do, so we can only train so much. . . ."

"I know who we need," Robin told them weakly. "So do you."

Widdershins, at least, did Robin the courtesy of not pretending any confusion as to whom she meant.

"Are you *completely* out of your mind?!" she demanded (which, honestly, probably wasn't substantially more courteous than if she *had* pretended confusion as to whom Robin meant).

"Can you tell me I'm wrong?" Robin asked.

"Yes! Yes, I can. You're wrong! You're *so* wrong, there aren't enough syllables in the word 'wrong' to encompass how wrong you are!"

"Um, what are we talking about, here?" Sicard asked mildly. The two young women ignored him, if they even heard him at all.

"I'm not," Robin said, "and you know it."

"Robin . . ." Widdershins stood and put her hands on the younger girl's shoulders. "He's our *enemy*. He hates me. Gods, he *kidnapped* you!"

"No, really," the bishop said. "Who are we—?"

"And he was going to let me go," Robin reminded her.

"That doesn't excuse—"

"No, it doesn't. Shins, I'm not suggesting that he's suddenly our best friend or anything. But I spoke to him. I *listened* to him. I don't pretend to understand his code of honor, but I know he *has* one. Under the right circumstances, I think he can be trusted."

"Under the right circumstances, so can the average trapdoor spider!" Widdershins snapped. "What does that—?"

"How many people told you about him, did you say? Said that he's one of the greatest duelists alive today? Not just in Davillon, but in all Galice? If you're looking for someone good enough to make a difference, while keeping the group small, you know you won't find anyone better suited."

"Ugh!" Widdershins threw up her hands and began to pace, just a couple of steps in each direction, before her friend's chair. "Robin, I don't think you know what you're asking."

"Is *anyone* going to fill the rest of us in?" Sicard asked, his tone starting to grow petulant. Renard leaned over and began whispering in his ear.

"I know this is more important than anyone's personal grudges," Robin continued relentlessly.

"Yes, but—"

"It's more important than your pride, Shins."

"This isn't about *pride*! This—"

"It was important enough that you sent someone *else* to save me."

Widdershins stumbled to a halt, nearly tripping over her own feet.

Was *that* what this was really about? Was Robin testing her, to see if she'd do as much as she'd demanded of others, put the needs of the moment above her own feelings? Was the girl maybe even punishing her, if only a little?

And . . . After all that had happened, didn't she have the right to want to know?

"All right." The words were bile on her tongue, actually burned the back of her throat, but still she coughed them up. "All right, Robin. I'll try to convince him. But if he kills me, you're the first one I'm haunting."

Robin smiled, if only faintly.

"Start planning," Widdershins told the others. "I'll be back soon." One last, brief glance—lingering, perhaps, on Julien's troubled brow—and she was gone.

❁

That this particular suite of rooms was nicer than the average house in Davillon would have come as no surprise to any visitor. Quality (read: ostentation) was the hallmark of the Golden Sable mansion block, located at the fanciest end of Rising Bend, scarcely more than a bowshot away from the estates of Duchess Beatrice Luchene herself. What *might* have surprised such a hypothetical visitor was the *size* of the suite; it was substantially larger than those same average houses. A combination sitting and dining room opened up into numerous hallways, which in turn led to almost a dozen additional chambers. The carpeting was thick and plush enough to have silenced the hoofbeats of a mule (and yes, said mule could potentially have fit through the door, while carrying saddlebags stuffed with unnecessary luxuries). Chandeliers hung from the ceiling, their glass and crystal adornments glinting like stars in the light of their many candles, and the overall stench of the city was cloaked by pomanders hanging near the numerous doorways.

One of the rooms farthest from the front door, however, was utterly unlike the others. In this chamber alone, the carpet had been pulled up, the bulk of the furniture removed, the window covered by a sturdy square of wood. Several straw-stuffed mannequins stood along one wall, and heavy bags of sand hung at random intervals from the ceiling. Through it all, currently clad only in a pair of heavy hose, Evrard d'Arras twisted and spun, lashing out with rapier and dagger (the former of which was rather less ornate than the one he'd so recently lost). Straw flew and sand poured in torrents, yet so precise were his strikes that the bags barely swung or twisted as they opened to his blades. Sweat poured from Evrard's face, but he found that the growing knot of frustration—and, if he'd been more honest with himself, confusion—in his belly refused to loosen.

Finally, cursing in disgust, he stalked across the room and grabbed up a pair of towels—the first for his face, the second to ensure that no particles of sand clung to the steel.

"Jacques!" Evrard hadn't brought any of his family's servants with him to Davillon, but the Golden Sable included a few valets and maids as part of their amenities. "Jacques, some wine!"

He'd completed cleaning the weapons and replaced them on the wooden rack, present beside the door for just that purpose, before it occurred to him that his shout had not been answered.

"Jacques?"

Another pause, another failure to respond. Evrard frowned thoughtfully. He'd never been particularly fond of the valet with whom he'd been provided, but neither had the man ever failed in his assigned tasks before today. The fellow *probably* just hadn't heard him—but then again, despite the size of the suite, it'd be the first time, were that the case.

Casual and unhurried, Evrard finished toweling off, retrieved the frilled tunic he'd left hanging on the edge of the rack and pulled it over his head, and once more lifted the rapier from its niche. Blade held before him, relaxed but ready, Evrard proceeded into the hall.

His footsteps, utterly silent on that veritable lawn of carpeting, had carried him past the bedroom, the bathing chamber, the dressing room, and several closets when he found himself in one corner of the sitting room. To his left was a mahogany table on which he kept a great many of his items for going out: rings, buckles, his hat, and several pistols. Beyond was a hallway leading farther back into the apartment, boasting doors to either side, culminating in a large window.

Leaning against the wall beside that window was a chair that someone had dragged from the dining room. And seated casually in that chair, her ankles crossed before her . . .

"Hello, Evrard," Widdershins said.

❁

She couldn't help but smirk, even through her simmering anger, when the aristocrat jumped—however faintly—at the sound of her voice. She saw his entire body twitch, subtly but vaguely in the direction of the table.

"No point," she told him. "I unloaded them."

He froze, glanced at the flintlocks, and nodded. "Of course you did." He flexed his wrist, just enough to tilt the rapier in his fist. "I can be down that hallway in seconds."

"Yep. And I can be out that window in less. At which point, I haven't wasted anything but time and breath, and you never find out why I'm here."

"I suppose you expect me to believe that it's *not* to kill me?"

"Kind of a stupid way to go about it if I were, yes? Announcing myself and putting you on your guard?"

"Maybe. Maybe not. Honestly, I don't understand you at all, Widdershins."

"That," she hissed through clenched teeth, "is an understatement."

They both waited, letting their glares conduct the duel that their bodies were avoiding.

"How did you find me?" Evrard finally asked.

Widdershins scoffed. "You're a visiting blue blood who spends more on a month's rent than the Flippant Witch pulls in over a good couple of *years*. How did I find you? I *asked*."

"Ah. And Jacques?"

"Tied up in the kitchen. Unless you're talking about a *different* stuck-up servant, in which case I have no idea."

"Ah," he said again, then gestured with his chin. "And my sword? Are you planning to return that?"

"This?" Widdershins's hand dropped to her waist. "This isn't your sword."

"No? It looks an awful lot like—"

"Your sword," she explained patiently, "had a ruby in the pommel. This one doesn't. Ergo . . ."

"I see." A scowl, and then more silence. Finally, "Why are you here?"

"I—Did you *really* set out to destroy my life, and to kill me, over a *theft*?" she demanded.

It was clearly not what she'd been about to say. "It wasn't just 'a theft,' damn it! You broke into my family's ancestral home! You took heirlooms that had been with us for generations!"

"And which you hadn't touched, or even *looked* at, in over a decade," she pointed out.

"Utterly immaterial. This was about family honor!"

"Oh, I see." She couldn't possibly have masked the scorn in her voice, even if she'd bothered to try. "So threatening to take away my *dead best friend's* tavern, kidnapping an innocent girl . . . These are about honor, are they?"

Evrard's face flushed, but he couldn't *quite* meet Widdershins's eyes. "Why," he growled again, "are you here?"

"I need your help."

Evrard burst into a belly laugh, doubling himself over—it was probably more luck than anything else that he didn't stab himself in the forehead with his rapier—and even Widdershins couldn't quite keep the grin off her face. "Yeah," she said when his fit had finally subsided. "I know."

"All right," he said, wiping away tears of near hysteria with the back of his hand. "I'm listening."

So he did, and Widdershins spoke. She didn't keep much from him—only some of the details of Olgun and their relationship—and over the course of her narration, the last of the humor faded from his face.

"There are some," he said carefully, "who would call me crazy for even *considering* that you might be telling me the truth."

"There are," Widdershins agreed. "There are also some who would call me crazy for coming to you with this kind of story if it wasn't entirely true."

"There is that. But—"

"And if you'll trust me just long enough to come with me, His Eminence, the bishop, should confirm it. Unless you think I've got *him* in my pocket, too."

"Suppose," he said slowly, "I'm *not* prepared to trust you even that far?"

Widdershins sighed loudly. "Do you think I want to be here, Evrard? Do you think I want to be talking to you, instead of dropping something heavy on you from a very great height? We *need* you!"

"Why should I help you?" He asked it as an honest question, with no challenge in his tone.

"You're not. You're helping all of Davillon. You're helping a whole bunch of people who'll be slaughtered by this creature if it's not stopped."

"And why do you think that matters to me, either?"

"Because you care about your family's honor. And because you were about to let Robin go."

"Damn it . . ." She knew she had him wavering, could literally see the indecision working its way across his features. "Widdershins, I don't know . . . I—"

"When this is all over," she pressed, "assuming we're all still around, I'll challenge you to your stupid duel."

"Will you, now?"

"I swear it. Time and place of your choosing."

"And my rapier?" he asked, apparently just to be ornery.

"This isn't your rapier. But if I'm dead, you're welcome to take it."

"All right . . . All right." He somehow seemed to nod with his entire body as the decision was made. "Just let me get properly dressed."

Widdershins smiled brightly. "Don't forget to untie the valet on your way out."

CHAPTER SEVENTEEN

"I don't know," Widdershins hedged, her fingertips trailing across a dusty stretch of old, cracked marble. "This is starting to feel a little disrespectful, don't you think?"

Sicard turned slowly away from his painstaking preparations, accompanied by a melodious popping in his back and cracking in his knees, and sighed. In the tone of a man repeating himself for the umpteenth time, he said, "The creature is most uncomfortable on hallowed ground, so we require just such an advantage. A cramped space, with lots of surfaces to climb, favors him over us, so the church would be inappropriate, even disregarding the danger to innocents. This truly is our best option, Widdershins. I think the families would understand—and I *know* the gods will."

Widdershins frowned even as she nodded, glancing around once more at the array of tombstones and burial plots stretching away in every direction. They had set up shop at a crossroads of the footpaths that wound between the rows of resting dead, and Julien had stationed members of the Guard at the entrance to dissuade mourners and visitors from entering, but she still didn't feel as though they were even remotely alone.

She knew, also, that she should be upset that—despite his high-sounding justifications—Sicard had chosen the Verdant Hills Cemetery, which serviced workers, craftsmen, and other citizens of moderate means, rather than one of the wealthier, upper-class graveyards with which he'd probably have been more familiar. (He'd told them it was so Iruoch wouldn't have the mausoleums on which to climb, but Widdershins wasn't sure she bought that logic.) *Should* have been upset, except that she could only give thanks, however ashamed she might feel of herself for it, that neither Genevieve's nor Alexandre's graves would be impacted by what was to come.

His Eminence, apparently realizing that no further questions or objections were forthcoming, returned to his efforts, laying out a broad circle of various herbs and incense, fine links of silver chain, small two-faced mirrors, and other esoteric components for his forthcoming mystical endeavors. Widdershins, in turn, tore her gaze off the stretches of thick green grass and sprouting flowers, the meticulously carved stones and raised patches of earth, and studied her motley allies instead.

No Robin; Widdershins had shouted and ordered and eventually threatened to tie the girl up until she swore to remain behind. The thief understood her friend's burning need to help, but really, she could have done little except put herself, and the others, in greater danger. Similarly, no Constable Paschal. Julien had stationed him with the other soldiers at the gate, to ensure that no innocent mourners wandered into danger, but the man's injured arm would have made him a liability in the battle to come. He knew it, of course, which is why he'd swallowed his pride and accepted the "lesser" assignment.

All of which left, in addition to Widdershins herself (and Olgun, of course): the bishop, who would be responsible for the casting and maintaining of the enjoining incantation; Igraine, who would do what she could against Iruoch, but served primarily as Sicard's assistant; Brother Ferrand, who would share (as much as the spell would allow) in Olgun's power; Evrard d'Arras, who stood off on his own, shoulders stiff and chin raised against the mistrustful glares constantly lobbed in his direction; Renard Lambert, resplendent in his usual finery, who had won the coin toss and would be linked to Evrard, in order to share his dueling acumen; and Julien Bouniard, whose own loss of that coin toss had probably rendered him relatively useless in the coming confrontation and had sent him into a furious sulk, though he was doing his damnedest not to show it.

And they were supposed to not only stand against Iruoch, a creature from myth and fairy tale who had already taken everything Widdershins could throw at him—twice—but to destroy him. It would have been laughable, if it wasn't quite so terrifying. Despite her every effort to remain upbeat, Widdershins found herself looking again and again at the various grave plots around her and wondering if her own final resting place would be so neat and tidy.

So preoccupied was she in her grim ruminations that she almost missed it when Renard suddenly pushed away from the tombstone against which he'd been leaning and strode purposefully to Evrard's side. Only Olgun, metaphorically tapping her on the shoulder and pointing, was enough to draw her attention. Worry wrapping her fingers into fists, she sidled closer to listen in.

". . . threats you're planning to make," Evrard was saying, not even deigning to face the shorter man, "you needn't bother. Widdershins asked me to be here. Our personal issues can wait until later."

"Maybe yours can," Renard replied. "Maybe hers can. But *I* wasn't consulted, and I made no such agreement."

Still Evrard refused to turn, but Widdershins didn't miss—and Renard could not have missed—the slow slide of his hand toward the hilt of his rapier. She felt her breath catch.

"What would you have of me, then, Monsieur Lambert?" the aristocrat asked.

"A token, nothing more. A sign that you can, at least while our interests coincide, be trusted."

"And what form might such a token take?"

"Just this, Monsieur d'Arras: the name of the man who told you that Widdershins was responsible for the theft at your tower."

That same gasp, trapped a moment earlier, now exploded from Widdershins's throat. In all the chaos, all the other priorities, she'd *completely* forgotten that was even a question!

"You didn't just stumble across that information," Renard was pressing. "While it wasn't precisely a secret within the Guild, it's not the sort of thing any of us would speak of in public."

Widdershins couldn't keep out of it any longer. "And Genevieve's will! You knew enough to question the veracity of the will! Only someone with contacts deep in the Finders would have known enough to do that!" If she realized that she'd just more or less confirmed to Evrard that the document was, indeed, a forgery, it happened too late for her to swallow the words.

"And what if," Evrard asked them, "I choose not to reveal my sources at this time?"

"Then, Monsieur d'Arras, you either prove all the rumors of your skill by killing me—and thus do without me in the coming battle—or I *disprove* them by killing you, and His Eminence links me with the major instead of you. But I'll not put my life, or Widdershins's, in the hands of a man I cannot trust even in the face of a common foe."

Evrard pursed his lips in thought, and then nodded sharply. "I owe this person nothing. I made no oath of secrecy, and I knew from the beginning that she had her own purposes and agenda in telling me of what happened."

"She?" Renard snarled. Widdershins just scowled.

Of course. Who else could it have been?

Another nod. "She. A woman with hair like the reddest leaves of autumn, and a notable limp. Her name was—"

"Lisette," Widdershins hissed. "Lisette Suvagne."

"I see I wasn't wrong in assuming the two of you had some past history," the aristocrat said blandly.

"A bit." Widdershins sneered. "Did she tell you that the *reason* she hates me was because I got to your tower before *she* did?"

All traces of humor faded from Evrard's face. "She . . . No, she *neglected* to mention that detail."

"Thought she might have. Renard?"

"I can't speak for the Shrouded Lord," Renard said, an odd inflection to the words. "But I'm fairly certain you can count on the Finders' Guild making every effort to hunt her down. Even after she was removed from the Guild, she should have known that her oaths remained binding—*especially* as a former taskmaster!"

"It won't help," Evrard said. "She's not in Davillon. Or, well, she wasn't when we last spoke."

"We have reach," Renard said, though he refused to expand any further on the topic. What he *did* say, some moments later, was, "Thank you, Monsieur d'Arras. That answer was more helpful than you know. Shins, you should have killed her when you had the chance."

"I'm getting that, yes."

"Would that be when you gave her the limp?" Evrard asked.

"As a matter of fact, it—"

"His Eminence is ready," Igraine called to them.

All thoughts of the traitorous Lisette instantly forgotten—well, *most* thoughts of her, anyway—the three of them, along with Julien Bouniard and Brother Ferrand, gathered around the kneeling priests.

"We'll start with Messieurs Lambert and d'Arras," Sicard said. "I know how long the spell's effect is supposed to last, but I do *not* know how the presence of Olgun might alter such details. So I'd prefer to link Widdershins and Ferrand second, in case the incantation is foreshortened." He paused briefly. "Ferrand, are you certain about this? You're not required to—"

"I'm certain, Your Eminence."

Sicard sighed. "I knew you were going to say that. Very well, if everyone but Lambert and d'Arras would kindly step back . . . ?"

So they did, while Renard and Evrard knelt before the bishop. Sicard began to chant in a language predating modern Galicien. At times, both his hands rested on his subjects' heads, while at others he would reach down for the mirror, or the silver chain, or even for the incense and herbs that currently burned and fizzled in a small iron brazier, wafting a sweetly floral scent across the cemetery.

"I don't like this," Julien said from just behind her.

"I think you may have mentioned that," Widdershins told him, leaning back against his chest and reaching down to lightly clasp his left hand in hers. "A time or two. Or three. Or eighty-seven thousand."

"I'm serious, Shins. I'm no use to you if I'm not part of this spell. We should—"

"Julien, we *have* been through this, you know."

"Yes, but I haven't won, yet."

Widdershins laughed softly. "Now you're starting to sound like me."

"Oh, gods. That's *all* I need."

She slowly faced him, let go of his hand so she could cup her left palm against his cheek. "You'll do what you can. And it *will* help me to have you here, no matter what."

"And when this is over?" he asked her softly.

He sounded sure, *so* sure, that there would *be* an after. Widdershins wasn't. She stretched up on her toes and kissed him, oh so briefly, then spun away to stand where she could watch Sicard casting his spell.

Where she wouldn't have to ponder the answers to Julien's questions, spoken or unspoken.

It was perhaps ten or fifteen minutes later when the two men rose, staggering and staring first at their own hands, and then at each other, as though not entirely certain of what they were seeing. Sicard took a moment to sip from a small bottle and to restock the herbs in his brazier, while Igraine nodded for Widdershins and Ferrand to step forward.

"You ready for this, Olgun?" Widdershins asked softly. And then, "Heh. Well, if it makes you feel any better, neither am I."

"Are you certain he'll come to us?" Igraine asked as the pair of them crouched in the dust. "This is a lot of wasted time and effort if he doesn't."

"You want me to lay odds, Igraine? I can't." Widdershins shrugged. "But he was able to sense me at the Lamarr estate from halfway across town, and he definitely considers me a threat, now. I think, if there's effectively two of me, it'll attract his attention pretty quick."

"I think it would attract *anyone's*," Julien stage-whispered from off to the right. Several of the group chuckled, and Widdershins found herself unaccountably blushing.

"Are we doing this, or what?" she demanded.

"We are," Sicard told her. "Try to relax. Breathe evenly, think calming thoughts, and . . . Um, please ask your god not to do anything at all . . . well, not to do *anything*, really. I can't begin to guess what might happen if he interferes."

"I don't think I need to. He *can* actually hear you, you know."

"Oh. Uh, yes, of course." The bishop took a final deep breath. "Very well. Let's begin."

For all that the incantation seemed to go on indefinitely, when the effect finally came over her, it was nigh instantaneous. One moment, Widdershins was kneeling in the dirt, wishing she could scratch her knees, irritated at the bishop's sweaty palm on her head and his constant droning in her ears. The next, she was listing to the side, barely keeping her balance, as her senses and her mind went to war over a conflicting array of perspectives.

It wasn't as though she were actually in two places at once, not precisely. She saw the world from only one perspective, as always. What she had, instead, was two parallel tracks of recent *memories*. At any given second, she was staring at the bishop, or a nearby tree, or the array of tombstones. But one heartbeat later, she could recall not only that vista at which she'd been looking, but another angle on the cemetery, from somewhere off to her left: a different tree, a different side of Sicard, or even—gods, even *herself*, flailing around and trying to catch her balance. She didn't see what Ferrand saw, but she *remembered* seeing what he'd just seen.

The earth lurched beneath her feet, her stomach heaved, and Widdershins wondered how her sanity—how *anyone's* sanity—could stand up to this.

Sicard continued to chant, his voice growing rough and jagged, and the world began to steady, her thoughts to cease their drunken capering and once more fall into some semblance of order. As if controlled by an expert stagehand, a thick curtain swayed shut between her own perspective and her memories of what Ferrand saw—or had seen, or whatever it was. She still received the occasional muffled sound or brief glimmer of light, but it was a minor distraction at worst, easily ignored. Only if she deliberately chose could she peek through the curtain and share in the monk's own experiences.

"Well . . ." Widdershins staggered to her feet and reached out a hand to help Ferrand in doing the same. "Did the earth move for you, too?" she asked him.

Ferrand opened his mouth, shut it, and looked away, blushing.

"It *seems* to have worked normally," Sicard said, also rising. "But I can't be sure. . . ."

"I don't know," Ferrand said. "I don't feel any different." Then, at Widdershins's startled look, "I mean, no, that's not . . . We're linked. I can remember what she sees, what she hears."

"Which, incidentally, is creepy," Widdershins added. Only then did she realize how dry her mouth was, and reached out a hand for the bishop's flask. He handed it over without question.

"Uh, yes, that's one word," the monk agreed. "But I mean . . . Well, I thought I would feel your, um, your magics, or Olgun's power, or something. But I don't—"

"That," the thief said just a tad smugly, "is because he's not *doing* anything."

"Uh . . ."

"Olgun?" Far too softly for the others to hear, she continued, "Olgun, are you all right?"

The waft of emotion Widdershins received in reply was a good-humored, teasing contempt at the very idea.

"Well, *excuse* me, Your Divinitiness! Some of us *aren't* used to more than one point of view at a time! Guess that's why *you're* the god, and *we're* just poor little . . . *Ooh*, you're impossible! It's not too late for me to trade you in, you know. I bet I could get a whole *herd* of good-quality horses for . . ." It was right about then that Widdershins realized her voice had risen, and that she was being very studiously examined—possibly to determine which asylum would best suit her—by more or less everyone else present.

"What?" she challenged. "You talk to your gods in your ways, I'll talk to mine in mine."

Oddly, that didn't seem to assuage any of them.

"Fine. Ferrand? Pay attention." Widdershins sprinted for the nearest tree and leapt. Soaring past the first layer of branches, she finally wrapped her fingers around a particularly thick bough close to twenty feet above the grass. She swung, the bark refusing to bite into her skin, and flipped backward, clasping another, higher branch with her knees. There she hung, her hair dangling, arms crossed over her chest, and smiled at her audience. The air around her hummed and crackled with the touch of Olgun's power.

Brother Ferrand himself had literally staggered back and slumped to the ground, sitting against the side of a weather-worn grave marker. "My gods . . ."

"Well, one of them," Widdershins said. At which point, rather belatedly, a thought occurred to her. "Olgun? If Ferrand's drawing on your power—even through the bishop's spell—does that mean he's likely to start including you in his worship when this is all over with? And if he does, what does that mean for you and me?"

She was somewhat less than comforted to interpret the god's response as indicating that he wasn't sure. Of course, Olgun could always refuse to accept a mortal's worship—but the longer he remained Widdershins's god alone, the more he risked dying if something should happen to her.

Widdershins couldn't repress a surge of white-hot jealousy at the idea, and she was ashamed. Was it fair even to ask that of him? Could she—?

"Shins?" Julien called. "Are you, uh, coming down any time soon?"

"Oh. Yeah." Widdershins relaxed her legs and let herself slide from the branch. She slapped a quick hand against the trunk to slow her fall, as well as to twist her around feetfirst, and landed in a crouch among the bulges of the tree's roots.

"Thank you," the major said. "My neck was starting to hurt."

"You didn't *have* to keep staring at me up there, you know."

"Actually, I—"

"I remain less than thrilled," Igraine interjected, her voice marinating in impatience, "that we're supposed to just wait, now."

The others nodded, though several scowls suggested that the priestess was not the only one unhappy with this stage of the plan.

"Didn't you just have this conversation?" Julien demanded. "If you've got any idea of how to find Iruoch when he could be anywhere in Davillon, I'd be delighted to hear it. Otherwise—"

"No, I don't have any such idea!" Igraine snapped. "But we're risking an awful lot on the idea that the creature not only senses Widdershins and Brother Ferrand, but that he doesn't suspect it's some sort of trap to begin with!"

"It doesn't matter what he suspects," the Guardsman said. "You heard Widdershins. She's the only real threat Iruoch's faced since he arrived! If he thinks he feels *two* people with her power, he *has* to investigate!"

"I heard what Widdershins said, yes. I'm just not convinced that—"

The sudden flutter of songbirds taking flight was lost in the sudden, "*Get down!*"

It was Julien who shouted, as a shadow blotted the sun from the sky, a grotesque missile plunged into their midst, but there was little else he could do. By the time he'd even begun to move, Renard Lambert had dived forward, spurred on by expertly trained reflexes borrowed from Evrard. He slammed into Widdershins, knocking her from the path of the falling object—for indeed, it had been she, of everyone in the group, at whom the attack had been aimed.

(That she could probably have gotten herself clear—with Olgun's speed if not her own—was not the point. Julien, though clearly relieved that she was unhurt, was just as clearly horrified that, as he'd anticipated, he'd proved all but helpless in the face of their impossible enemy.)

The rest of the band leapt aside as best they could, seeking cover, shielding their faces and heads against the worst of the shrapnel. The body of the poor horse to which Iruoch had been tied—now limbless and headless—crashed to the earth, where it had been hurled with inhuman strength. On impact, a row of twine stitches poorly sewn into its belly burst open, splaying a handful of viscera-soaked rocks and bricks in all directions. Several voices cried out—Widdershins couldn't tell precisely whose—as some of those revolting projectiles drew blood or bruised flesh. The acrid stench struck nearly as hard, making her lungs burn and her chest ache.

Or maybe some of that ache was Renard laying limp across her ribs.

Widdershins squeezed out from beneath him and rolled to her feet, drawing her blade and searching intently for the source of the attack.

It didn't take her long.

He should have been a *little* less disturbing, a little less fearsome, viewed in the bright sunlight of midday. Instead, if anything, he was worse. He moved across the cemetery with that hideous, spastic, sideways gait, each stride seeming to take him in a different direction yet always ending up one step nearer his destination. But his *shadow* . . . Iruoch's shadow, regardless of which direction he moved, regardless of what position the sun might hold at his back or side, *always* pointed directly behind him, as though he were literally dragging it along by its heels.

And on occasion, it would reach a single trembling hand across the earth toward any who stared at it for too long, as though pleading with them for help. . . .

As he drew nearer, Widdershins and the others began to hear the ubiquitous phantom chorus that surrounded the creature. They were cooing over the tombstones, making ghostly "*oooooh . . .*" noises at each other, punctuated with the occasional shrill giggle.

Renard, Julien, Igraine, and Evrard drew their pistols and fired. The thunderous crack was deafening, the wall of smoke opaque, but it was little more than a gesture of defiance, and well they knew it. Iruoch twitched—an inch this way, an inch that—and if any of the balls struck their target at all, they did so without notable effect.

"Oh, but that was a nifty trick with the horse!" his twin voices called out. "Bravo, bravo! Actually, it was kind of fun! Down the street, past hooves and feet . . ." His grin grew wide, his cheeks bulging. "But of course, horsey couldn't run forever. And *so* many nice people gathered around me when he stopped, to see if I was hurt. They were all really . . . sweet."

Widdershins felt nauseated.

Another step, and another; with each, Iruoch allowed the tips of his fingers to dangle across the top of this tombstone or that, as though casually drawing a line of profanity across the sacred ground. At the fourth, however, he jerked away with a faint hiss, glaring at the offending marker—but Widdershins could not see any reason why, and the creature's course otherwise remained unchanged. He was now less than ten yards distant, and still none of the group had moved to engage.

"But what is it you've done, silly little girl, with your silly little god? What song are you singing, that came to me across the streets and rooftops and . . . Oh." For just a moment he halted his forward pace, head tilted, staring first at Widdershins, then Brother Ferrand, then at Evrard and Renard, and finally at the bishop.

"Really?" The creature sounded genuinely disappointed. "That's all, then? Tricks and strands of simple, mortal magic? Mortal magics I've already seen?" He raised a hand, pointed with one long digit as though he were poking each of them in the chest with every word. "That. Is not. Exciting. To me."

With that devastating pronouncement, Iruoch actually turned his back on them all and began to walk away. And damn it all if, for the briefest instant, they weren't inclined to let him go.

But only briefly.

It was Evrard, of all of them, to free himself of that peculiar lassitude. "Very well, then," he announced, freeing his rapier with a dramatic flourish. "Then let us endeavor to make things more interesting." He broke into a charge, feet crushing the emerald grasses, and Iruoch turned once more to meet him.

The aristocrat held the blade lowered like a lance, his attack surprisingly clumsy and straightforward for one of his supposed skill, and the fae creature easily sidestepped, lashing out with two fingers for the back of Evrard's exposed neck . . .

But Evrard was no longer there. Even as his awkward charge had carried him adjacent to his opponent, he dived, turning his momentum into a sideways roll across the lawn. His shins caught Iruoch at the ankles and yanked his feet out from under him, sending the gaunt figure sprawling.

Or so it should have done—to anyone human. Iruoch landed not on his back, but on his fingertips. For a single blink they held him upright, stiff as a plank, staring up at the sky. Then they flexed, all eight of those spidery digits, launching him upright once again. Evrard, wary and more than a little stunned, had rolled back to his feet and carefully circled, blade at the ready, just beyond reach.

If the creature's impossible recovery had shocked the duelist, however, it had also spurred his allies into action. Crying out with a single voice, Widdershins and the others who were linked by the spell converged on their enemy, with Sicard, Igraine, and Julien trailing behind, hoping to make themselves somehow useful. The Guardsman brandished his blade, the two priests their amulets sculpted into various holy symbols of the Hallowed Pact.

"Olgun? Let's do this." The tickle across her skin, the blown kisses of distant candles, wasn't quite the same as she was accustomed to. It felt as though it had picked up an odd current, as though portions of Olgun's power were flowing through her on their way to somewhere else. Again she saw Ferrand's eyes go wide, and she actually shared briefly in his confusion, but for all that, the young monk kept up. His wrists twisted, spinning the bishop's rod of office like a quarterstaff before him.

Iruoch clearly heard them coming; with a creaking of old wood, he rotated his head completely around to see them. And he laughed.

Evrard lunged, but even his vaunted prowess was too slow. Iruoch lifted his knees straight up, yanking his feet off the earth so he abruptly dropped. He landed once again on his fingers, spread wide beneath him. The blade passed harmlessly over his head, and the creature thrust his legs back down, standing straight once more.

But his hands were no longer bare. Long strips of grass and clods of earth clung to his spindly fingers, seemingly stuck fast.

A flick of the wrist, and those globules of soil hurtled toward Evrard's face. The aristocrat craned his neck, flinching away from the missiles, and in that split second it was Iruoch's chance to lunge.

Had he succeeded in wrapping Evrard entirely within his grip, the man would already have been dead, ripped apart in ribbons of flesh and blood. But the duelist was *almost* quick enough to avoid the attack, despite his momentary blindness. He retreated swiftly, practically leaping, and Iruoch caught only the end of his left arm. Still he screamed, despite himself, and Widdershins winced in sympathy. She'd felt the touch of the murderous fae before, felt her skin rip beneath it. She knew that, lacking Olgun's aid in healing, Evrard would be feeling the pain of that clutch for a long time to come.

Iruoch bent backward at the waist, hurling Evrard over him by that captive arm. Ferrand ducked beneath the living projectile, but as Iruoch had thrown him directly at Widdershins—who had, herself, been rushing forward in a dead sprint—she wasn't quite so lucky. She twisted, so that what might have been a bone-shattering impact was instead only bruising, sending them both tumbling over each other across the grass.

But it wasn't the pain of the attack, or even the undignified sprawl in which she and Evrard found themselves, with his head flopping dazedly across her chest, that disturbed her. No, it was the sudden consternation she sensed from her partner in the bishop's spell. Shoving the aristocrat aside, she looked up just in time to see Brother Ferrand's headlong pace slow so abruptly that he stumbled over his own feet. Iruoch casually backhanded him aside, and it was neither magic nor the monk's skill, but blind luck, that allowed the staff to take the bulk of the blow. Ferrand staggered and fell, but he was merely winded, rather than crippled or dead.

Even before Widdershins could ask herself, or Olgun, why Ferrand had stumbled, why he'd slowed, she understood the answer.

The spell linked him to *her*, not to Olgun. He shared in *her* strength, not the god's. And that meant that only when Olgun was *actively* exercising his divine influence, however limited, on Widdershins's behalf . . . *only* then, and at no other instant, could Ferrand himself draw upon the power of the god.

How long could Olgun maintain a *constant* flow of power, without needing time to rest and recover? A few minutes, at best? Not long enough; not since the hallowed earth of the cemetery didn't seem to be any more than a mild inconvenience to their enemy, not if he had the wherewithal to actually *use* the terrain against them as he had done. Every advantage they possessed was suddenly taunting, slipping away, promising far more than it could deliver.

Renard had moved past her as she struggled to stand, engaging Iruoch with a display of swordsmanship the likes of which he'd never before exhibited. Blades flashed and Iruoch swayed, sidling from the weapon's path here, parrying with a finger against the flat of the blade there, but Renard continued to press. It wasn't enough to have one chance in a million of beating the creature—odds were it wasn't even enough to *survive* him for long—but it allowed the others to recover their bearings.

Muttering a brief summary of what she'd just figured out—not because anyone could hear her, but so that Ferrand would *remember* hearing it, thanks to their peculiar link—Widdershins once again darted forward under Olgun's power. Her own sword glinted in the sun as it darted and struck, but she took only a few small shreds of Iruoch's cloak for her trouble. Ferrand, for his own part, succeeded in landing a brutal knock against the creature's knee, but the resulting limp lasted for only for a fusillade of heartbeats before it vanished.

Time and again the four of them sought to converge on Iruoch, pinning him between them in the hopes of dishing out enough injury to slow him down, if not destroy him. And time and again, he evaded their every effort, either sidling out from between two of them faster than they could react, or even leaping *overhead* to land some yards distant. Never could they manage to attack him in more than pairs—or, if they were *truly* lucky, a trio—before he found a way to disengage. Thanks to their inhuman speed, Widdershins and Ferrand had both landed the occasional blow, and even Evrard had gotten in a good thrust while the creature was distracted, but none of the wounds had lingered. Iruoch appeared as healthy, and as fresh, as the moment he arrived, whereas the humans—even drawing on each other's strengths, to say nothing of Olgun's—were growing tired.

The grass around them was trampled flat, the dust kicked up in hovering puffs. Anyone who observed the ground afterward would have believed a pitched battle with dozens of soldiers must have taken place here. But for all they darted to and fro, parried back and forth, ran and twisted and slashed and lunged, it remained meaningless.

Iruoch and the chorus of ghostly children never ceased their cackling and giggling.

Evrard slashed, the creature sidestepped, and Widdershins abruptly dived. Rolling beneath the aristocrat's arcing sword, she came to her feet only inches from Iruoch, thrusting her own blade clear through his belly. For the first time in what seemed forever, the laughter ceased. A twitch of pain racked his face, but Widdershins had no time to savor her victory, however minor. While she easily ducked below the swipe of fingers that she knew was coming, neither she nor Olgun were fast enough to avoid the knee that followed. Her head ringing, blood coursing from a split lip and one nostril, Widdershins tumbled back to fetch up against the side of a tombstone. Iruoch moved as though to follow, but Evrard and Renard closed in, weaving a wall of steel, buying her a moment to catch her breath.

She glanced up, puzzled, as Ferrand reached out a hand to help her rise. "I'm not much good while you're out of it," he reminded her, smiling through a purple-mottled jaw.

Blinking to clear the spot and splotches from her vision, Widdershins took in the scene before her. The two swordsmen were falling back, step by rapid step, scarcely able to slow Iruoch. Julien and Igraine had reloaded their pistols, searching in vain frustration for a clear shot and all too aware that it wouldn't help even if they found one. Sicard held his silver Eternal Eye amulet before his face in a trembling fist, breathing heartfelt and ever more desperate prayers across its surface.

Widdershins watched the bishop's mouth moving just beyond the icon, as though entranced. Then, as if abruptly unaware of the urgency of what was happening around her, she turned toward the tombstone against which she'd been hurled. It was very similar to all the others in the cemetery—very similar to the one Iruoch had, abruptly, pulled away from as he approached.

Much was embossed in the hard granite: names and dates, of course, ivy and leaves and growing things . . . And the symbols of the various gods to whom the fallen had been most closely devoted.

Whether it was the mystical link between them or a more mundane understanding, Ferrand nodded sharply. "Will it be enough?"

"Bet it'll slow him down, at least," she said.

"Will *we* be enough?"

"The three of us will. Olgun?"

She swore she could sense the god taking a deep breath, bracing himself against—against whatever spiritual surface he might have had to brace himself. "On three," she told Ferrand.

"One."

The two of them laid their hands upon the headstone, one on each side, gripping as tight as the broad and relatively smooth surface would permit.

"Two!"

They burned with the surge of Olgun's power, infusing flesh, muscle, bone. Between the two of them, the heavy granite rocked easily within its shallow foundation of soil.

"*Three!*"

The tombstone wrenched free of the earth, dripping dirt and beetles and strands of root. Again, Olgun's power flared within them and they were running, faster even than they had before, when unencumbered by hundreds of pounds of stone.

Widdershins felt Ferrand's exhaustion as a lapping tide against her calves even as she struggled to repress her own. A quick glance his way, and she nearly dropped her side of the stone; his cheeks were pale and hollow, his brow glistening, as though he'd gone for nights with neither sleep nor food over the span of the last minute. She wondered if she looked half that badly off, if she'd even feel it if she were.

Iruoch saw them coming, of course. But just as he began to step back, Evrard and Renard redoubled their attack, pinning him into place for an extra few seconds . . .

With a twin scream not entirely dissimilar from the creature's own voice, Widdershins and the monk slammed the makeshift battering ram into the creature, leading with the holy symbol of Geurron along the topmost edge.

Bone and granite cracked in an ear-rending duet. The phantom children gasped and fell silent, even as Iruoch screamed. Widdershins pushed forward, onward, until her enemy collapsed, pinned to the earth beneath the weight and sanctity of the carven stone.

"Now! While he's down!" She struck as she cried out, thrusting with the tip of her blade, aiming for the face, the neck. Around her, the others did the same with sword and staff, struggling, hoping, praying that they could actually *kill* the damned thing before it had the opportunity to recover.

They failed.

Continuously shrieking, his face coated with the dried powder that might or might not have been his blood, Iruoch tensed, bringing his knees up and his elbows down. The tombstone cracked across the center and fell away in two distinct halves. One tumbled to the earth with a dull thump as the fae twisted to his feet. The other, lacking any of the symbols he found so agonizing, he clutched in a single inhuman hand.

"My turn . . ."

Ferrand reached out, trying to hook Iruoch's arm with the curved end of Sicard's staff—and Iruoch spun and drove the chunk of stone down, shattering the monk's knee into a mangled wad of torn flesh, ripped tendon, and splintered bone.

With so horrific an injury, even a normal man might well have succumbed to shock. Already under the strain of the bishop's spell, laboring to channel a divine strength that was never his, Ferrand's body simply surrendered.

He fell limp to the blood-soaked grass. And Widdershins felt her throat trying to rip itself open from within as she screamed.

CHAPTER EIGHTEEN

Fire and ice warred for dominance in the nerves of her leg, making the entire left side of her body lock up in agony. Sparks burst inside her; her own thoughts stabbed at her; her memories singed the edges of her mind. Her vision—or what little she could make out through the blurring and twisting of the inner fire—constricted, a tunnel, then a pinprick in a field of black. Through it, all she could see, now, was Ferrand's slack face, and she knew without a doubt that the spell was dragging her down into death alongside him.

Except it didn't. She felt the grass under her cheek, little things crawling in the soil, the sun beating down on her neck. She heard the swish and clatter of blades, the grunts of exertion, the bishop's broken voice calling Brother Ferrand's name.

Her leg ached, but it was a dull, distant sort of pain, the last lingering remnants of an old injury. And where she'd felt that peculiar connection, that strange echo of Ferrand's memories lurking just behind a thin curtain of concentration, she now sensed only . . .

"Olgun?!"

Despite his lack of anything resembling a head, she sensed what could only be a nod.

"You cut the link?"

Another nod, along with an emotional gust suggesting, in no uncertain terms, that it hadn't been even remotely easy.

"Thank you." She sucked in a deep breath. "How are we doing?"

Before the god could answer, she heard a grunt of pain and felt a few warm spatters of blood across her outstretched hands.

"Oh. That good?" Widdershins forced her eyes open and craned her neck to see.

The combatants drew ever nearer to Sicard and Julien, despite the best efforts of the aristocrat and the thief to hold the line. Renard was bleeding furiously from his left arm and shoulder, where Iruoch's touch had ripped strips of skin from his body. It hadn't slowed him much—not yet—but he winced in pain with every step. Evrard didn't seem much better off, favoring the same spot on his body, even though it bore no visible injury. Iruoch seemed to be playing with them as much as battling them, casually brushing their blades aside, sometimes feigning a lunge at one or the other without bothering to follow through.

Igraine Vernadoe stood between the two groups, shouting prayers and malisons, her icon of the Shrouded God raised high. It was brave, no doubt, but if it had any appreciable impact on Iruoch's advance, Widdershins couldn't see it from here. The glistening sweat on the priestess's forehead, which *was* visible to Widdershins, suggested that Igraine didn't expect much good to come of her defiance, either. Since neither she nor Julien still held their pistols, Widdershins assumed that they'd taken their shots during the brief moments when she was insensate on the lawn.

And speaking of Julien . . .

"—better idea?!" the Guardsman was shouting, shaking Sicard by the shoulders. Clearly, any courtesy or respect he'd normally have felt inclined to show the bishop was long gone.

Widdershins grunted, trying to rise without drawing Iruoch's attention, and strained to listen in on the argument. Her ears tingled as Olgun lent a hand to her efforts.

"Even if she *wasn't* too far away and too busy," Sicard was insisting through clenched teeth, "it takes ten or fifteen minutes to cast! This'll be long over before—"

"You can *try*! I can't just stand here *useless* like this!"

The bishop shook his head, and it was only Olgun's power that enabled Widdershins to hear his muttered reply. "It didn't help Brother Ferrand much, did it?"

"Gods *damn* you, we have to do *something*! We—"

Widdershins felt the roiling tumult of Olgun's emotional shouting, strained to make sense of concepts too complex to be easily conveyed. "What? I don't . . . But . . . Are you sure? All *right*, you don't have to *yell*! Julien! Your Eminence!" She winced even as she raised her voice, knowing she'd just announced to Iruoch that she was up and around. "Just start casting!"

"But—," Sicard began.

"Trust me!"

"Trust her," Julien insisted. "Do it."

The bishop jogged back to where he'd left the iron brazier and began scooping up the last of his stock of herbs and incense. Julien trailed behind, his rapier drawn, watching the ongoing melee.

"Awake, awake, our little girl's awake!" Iruoch actually clapped his hands with glee as he bent over backward and stepped to the left, allowing both Renard's and Evrard's blades to pass harmlessly through the space he'd just vacated. "Oh, I'm *so* happy!" He straightened with impossible speed, a living catapult snapping upright, with one arm outstretched. The creature's palm slapped against Renard's wounded shoulder, sending him tumbling—and screaming—across the grass, leaving a serpentine trail of blood behind him.

"If you're not awake," Iruoch continued, his voice dropping in mock disappointment, "you don't actually *feel* anything." The fingers of his left hand twitched and flexed, parrying even the fastest and most ornate of Evrard's thrusts. "And *that's* no fun at *all*!"

The children booed at the very idea.

"Yep, I'm awake!" Widdershins scooped her rapier up from where it had fallen, slashed the air before her a time or two. "Not feeling anything, though. Why don't you come get me?" Even before the creature took a step, she had begun to fall back, retreating with a slow but steady pace, trusting Olgun to warn her if she was about to back into an obstacle of any sort.

"Aww . . . Step and dance and run away, thiefie doesn't want to play?" Iruoch took a pace toward her, a second, and then, "Thiefie thinks I'm really, really stupid."

Rotating so swiftly that it should have neatly snapped his knees, Iruoch bounded back toward the others. Evrard took a desperate swing, but again caught nothing but the hem of the filthy coat. The creature landed beside Igraine, flinched away from the holy symbol, and then kicked her in the gut with the toe of his boot. The priestess doubled over, tumbling to the earth and spitting blood-tinged vomit.

Their trick with the tombstone, and the mass of injuries they'd inflicted, *had* left some enduring effect. His leap was less steady, his pace not quite as swift as Widdershins remembered it. Even so, as she broke into another run, ignoring the growing pain in her sides and the exhausted patina that lay across every one of Olgun's emotions, she knew that she could never reach the creature before he reached Julien and Sicard.

The volume of the bishop's incantation grew louder, the tension in the major's shoulders more obvious, but neither of them could do anything but press on, and hope.

Because she'd told them to. Because they trusted her.

"Olgun! Olgun, it has to be now!" She was gasping, forcing each word out between harsh breaths and pounding steps. "It has to be *now*!"

The god's power lashed outward, a whip of sheer, stubborn *intent*. Widdershins had never felt anything quite like it, and stumbled as she ran. She felt her god reach out, snagging the raw strands of the mystical link that were only beginning to form around Julien, the earliest stages of Sicard's spell. She felt him grasping the remnants of the prior spell that clung to *her*, the broken link that had joined her with the late and lamented Brother Ferrand; felt him sculpting it beneath his intangible touch, forcing it into a new form.

And she felt the two ends, of the two distinct but similar incomplete magics, touch and fuse into one.

Sicard could not have done it. Olgun could not have done it. But together, they forced the magics to meld. In perhaps a tenth the time it should have required, Widdershins and Julien were joined.

Again she felt a brief moment of disorientation, of overlapping memories and shared experiences, but it was gone half a heartbeat after it began. Widdershins had experienced the effect once already, and knew better how to work through it—and because she knew it, so, too, did Julien.

Iruoch was two steps away from him when Julien rose, faster than a striking serpent, and plunged his sword through Iruoch's throat.

It wasn't enough to kill the creature, not by far, but Iruoch stumbled to a sudden halt, gagging and coughing up rusty powder. He staggered back, pulling himself off the blade, hands clutching briefly at the wound.

Again Julien struck, the tip of his sword moving too swiftly even for Iruoch, and two of those spidery fingers tumbled through the air in an almost graceful arc to land, flopping and twitching, in the dust.

Everyone—Iruoch included—fell silent and stared at the thrashing digits for a moment, until they swiftly decomposed with a puff of grayish, peppermint-scented powder. Several of the beetles boring through the nearby soil abruptly metamorphosed into bright scarlet moths. They fluttered away on the summer breeze, their flight paths awkward and very, very confused.

Slowly, gradually, Iruoch turned to gawp at Julien. "Those were two of my *favorites*!"

"Um . . ." Julien sounded utterly at a loss. "I'm sorry?"

Iruoch lunged; the Guardsman parried. Back and forth, step and cross-step . . . And then, before the creature could even begin to wear his opponent down, Widdershins was there.

Finally, *finally*, it looked as though they might have a chance. The two of them shared not only in Olgun's gifts, as Widdershins and Ferrand had done, but in Julien's skill and experience in the Guard. Not only her speed, but his training, allowed them to block strokes that might otherwise have laid open their flesh; to stab through the tiniest openings in Iruoch's own defenses. Blood, both dusty and liquid, flew—but for the first time, there was far more of the former than the latter.

Renard and Evrard hovered around the edges, lunging when an opportunity presented itself but mostly keeping Iruoch from easily retreating out of the others' reach. Widdershins and Julien shared a grin—quite literally—at the thought that this might soon, finally, be over.

But again, Iruoch's implacability dashed those hopes even as they began to sprout. Yes, they pressed him hard, far harder than they had; yes, his injuries were many, slowing him down. Still, *still* they could not land any crippling or killing blows. Still all but the worst of his wounds knitted themselves closed in moments, the ragged edges interlacing with and grasping at each other. Widdershins tried every trick in her repertoire, from head-on dueling, to tumbles and twists that would shame an acrobat, to balancing on and bouncing off the tombstones and tree branches like a rubber ballet dancer. No technique worked better than any other.

The mortals verged on exhaustion, propped up only by the strength they borrowed from one another, or from Olgun. And the god, too, teetered on the edge of collapse, his energies coming more and more sporadically to even Widdershins's most urgent need.

And ultimately, as everyone knew they must, Widdershins and Olgun stumbled together once too often.

She'd just twirled aside from another of Iruoch's grabs, then kicked off with one foot against a drooping old tree in hopes of coming back at him before he was prepared. She twisted in the air, blade coming sharply down—and Iruoch sidestepped the blade and caught her. His injured hand wrapped her wrist, fingers and stumps digging into her flesh, holding her rapier at bay. The other closed around her neck.

"It always makes me a little sad," he said conversationally, his shoulders leaning this way and that as he dodged her friends' attacks, "when I outgrow a playmate."

Widdershins tried to thrash, and could not. Tried to speak, and couldn't force so much as a squeak through her throat. Blood pounded in her ears, and her chest began to burn.

"If it's any consolation to you," Iruoch continued, "there are *plenty* more people for me to play with in your beautiful city. I know it's a consolation to *me*."

Her skin burned where his fingers lay across it. She could feel it *tear* as he moved, feel the blood welling up. Her hand spasmed, dropping her rapier. She wondered why the others had ceased attacking, wondered where Julien was, and only realized when her sword fell away that they now hung above the ground. Using the tips of the same fingers that clutched at her throat, Iruoch had climbed over a dozen feet up the trunk of that tree. There was nothing the others could do.

She couldn't move, couldn't breathe. *Olgun, I don't want to die this way. . . .*

Through eyelids that she struggled to keep open, she looked down past Iruoch, past his feet that dangled perfectly straight, parallel to the trunk. She saw Julien running toward them, saw him leap, felt the faintest surge of Olgun's power. But she felt how weak the god had become, knew that Julien couldn't possibly reach them. . . .

But what he swung at them was not his rapier at all, but Bishop Sicard's staff of office, which Ferrand had been using as a bludgeon.

The curved end of the crook hooked around Iruoch's arm. Widdershins had the brief satisfaction of seeing the creature's jaw go slack before the weight of Julien's body yanked them both off the tree.

They hit the ground and rolled apart, bark and skin clinging to Iruoch's fingers. Widdershins sucked in an agonizing breath, and it was only the fact that she couldn't stop her desperate gasping that kept her from screaming at the agony in her wrist and her throat. She rolled to her knees, coughing and choking. A hand closed on her shoulder, and she almost lashed out before she recognized Sicard standing over her, offering her a sip from his flask.

She reached for it, wheezing—and then saw the bishop's face go white, his lip begin to quiver. And she felt . . .

A sudden surge of fear, overwhelming, held at bay only by the memory of the life he had just saved. . . .

Pain, roaring, screaming pain, the tearing of flesh, the breaking of bone, the bursting of a beating heart. . . .

Delight that, at the last, he'd overcome his doubts, his hesitations. That she'd known, before the end.

Widdershins . . . Adrienne . . . I love you. . . .

A final surge of magic, as Olgun gave almost everything he had left to once more sever the link before it was too late.

And Julien Bouniard was gone.

No screams. No tears. Widdershins rose, everything inside her absolutely numb. Iruoch stood some yards away, Julien's rapier jutting obscenely through his chest—he seemed scarcely even to notice it—and Julien's broken body hanging from a two-fisted grip.

Casually, dismissively, Iruoch tossed the corpse aside. It bounced once, wetly, off the tree trunk and then slammed to earth. Evrard and Renard stood close, their own blades trembling with fatigue.

"Now," Iruoch said, gripping the hilt of the rapier between two fingers and slowly sliding it from his body, "perhaps we can—"

Widdershins reached back and shoved Sicard aside, ignoring his startled yelp. Hands held at her side, empty of any obvious weapon—though one fist was clenched around something that glinted in the sun—she strode steadily up toward the creature she hated more than anything else in the world. As she clearly was not attacking, didn't appear armed, Iruoch let her approach.

"Was there something?" he asked lightly as the sword finally sprung free from his torso with a moist *pop*.

"Yes." *Olgun, I need you to stand for just a moment more. . . .* "Heal *this*!"

Widdershins sprang forward, opening her fingers to reveal the silver Eternal Eye amulet she'd yanked from the bishop's neck as she'd shoved him, and jammed it hard into the slowly closing wound left by Julien's blade.

Iruoch's scream rose above the graveyard, the twin voices undulating across a dozen octaves. He collapsed to his knees and instantly began scrabbling at the flesh of his chest, hurling desiccated, lightly smoking chunks of muscle and bone aside as he worked desperately to dig the holy symbol from his body. Widdershins calmly, resolutely watched his efforts, even waving off the others as they approached with weapons raised.

Finally the silver—now tarnished and pitted—flew free, and Iruoch gasped in relief, seemingly oblivious to the gaping hole in his chest.

A hole through which Widdershins reached, her hand tingling with the last inklings of power that Olgun had to give, and grasped Iruoch's shriveled, unbeating heart.

He looked down at the arm jutting into his chest, then up into the face of the woman who'd killed him.

"Well . . . Darn."

Widdershins yanked. The voices of the children wailed once in the distance, and were gone. Iruoch's body fell at her feet and exploded into a puff of dust that flew, with utter disregard for the wind, up into the open sky. In her fist, she held only an undulating mass of maggot-white sludge.

It smelled of peppermint.

"It's over, Shins," Renard gasped from behind her. "You did it."

"Yes." Her voice was raw, gravelly, every word a stab at her aching throat. "It *is* over, isn't it?"

She staggered a few steps, fell to her knees beside Julien's body, and willed—even *begged*—the tears to finally come.

But she was too exhausted even to mourn.

EPILOGUE

My dearest Robin,

I'm telling you all this in writing because, to be entirely honest, I don't think I have the strength—the courage*—to look into your face while I say it. I know how you're going to feel, and I'm so sorry.*

I'm leaving Davillon. The last thing I want is for you to feel I'm abandoning you (or Renard, or anyone else). But I have no other choice. Everyone I love is here, but this city is poison to me right now. First Genevieve and Alexandre, now Julien . . . I need to get away from the ghosts, Robin. I need time, and I need peace, and I cannot find either here.

You won't be left to fend for yourself, or the Flippant Witch. I've reacquired the ruby that Renard took from Evrard's rapier,

Renard choked, his hand reaching for his belt pouch of its own accord, but he stopped his fingers from so much as untying the clasp. If she said she'd taken it, she'd taken it, no matter how impossible it seemed. He couldn't help but smile, though his lips quivered as he returned to the note.

from Evrard's rapier, and hidden it beneath the floorboards under the bed in my room upstairs. There's a sack of coin and some other valuables from prior jobs in there as well. Ask Renard to fence them for you. He'll grumble about it, but he'll get you a fair price. It should be more than enough to keep you comfortable, and the tavern running, for a year or more.

I hope, by then, that you'll be doing enough business for the Witch to support itself again. Bishop Sicard swears *he's not returning to Davillon until he's convinced the cardinals to lift this stupid Church interdiction on the city, and Igraine says she thinks he might actually pull it off. If he manages it, things ought to return to normal (whatever normal looks like anymore). If not—if you wake up one morning and we've got some new guy as bishop—well, I guess it means things didn't go so well. But we do what we can, right?*

You shouldn't need to worry about Evrard. After that day in the cemetery, he refused to call in my promise of a duel. He said it was just for the time being, that it wouldn't be honorable to take advantage, but he sounded unsure. If I had to guess, I'd say he was questioning the whole vendetta. Maybe he's actually got a soul after all? I suppose fighting side to side against a monster of nightmares might tend to bring that out of one. Even if he does *decide to follow through, though, he should have no reason to bother you while I'm gone. (And if he does, I bet you could talk Renard into dealing with him for a reasonable fee.) Keep an eye on him if you see him, but don't lose any sleep over it.*

Tell everyone there that I'll miss them. Don't forget that we still need to deal with that leaky barrel on the rear left, under the green bottles. Trust yourself; you were always better at running the place than I was.

And please don't hate me. I know you may not believe it right now, but I couldn't bear to lose what family I have left. I just need time to deal with it all.

I will *be back someday. I promise.*

My love to Renard, and all my love to you, Robin. Be strong for me, and maybe I'll remember how to be strong, too.

—Shins

The letters blurring, Renard blinked a time or three and twisted in the chair, wincing as the movement pulled at the slowly healing gashes across his left shoulder. Carefully, he handed the note back to a red-eyed, flush-cheeked girl who truly looked as though the entire world had turned against her.

"I'm sorry," he told her. It didn't really seem the right thing to say, but it felt less wrong than anything *else* he might have said.

"How could she *do* this, Renard?" Robin's words traveled on a voice that staggered, rubbed raw by grief. "How could she do this to m—to *us*?"

The thief leaned over the table, cupping her hand in his. "I know how you look up to Widdershins," he said. "I know how highly you think of her. She's one of the strongest, most capable people I've ever met. But Robin, she's just a girl herself, still. And she's dealt with more in the past year than anyone should ever have to. This? This isn't about abandoning you, or me, or anyone. This is about running and pulling the covers up over her head, and praying that the monsters will go away for just a few minutes.

"There's no logic to it. It just is." Again he smiled. "Hell, she probably thinks she's *protecting* us."

"If she goes away," Robin said miserably, "we can't help her."

"I know. Gods, I know."

"Do you think she's telling the truth?" she asked him, the tears beginning to fall once more. "Do you think she's coming back?"

Renard rose and stepped around the table so he could hold the sobbing girl in a tight embrace—and so he wouldn't have to offer her an answer that he honestly didn't know if he could give.

❋

The shadow darted along the outskirts of Davillon, flitting between the torches and the lanterns, invisible in the deepest night. It was equally as silent as it was unseen; the hooting of the occasional owl, the screech and hiss of an alley cat, and the faint susurrus of the early summer breeze might have disturbed the quiet, but nothing of the sprinting figure ever did.

It barely slowed as it reached the outer wall, scaling the surface as easily as if someone had provided a winding staircase for the figure's convenience alone. A quick hop over, a glance to ensure that none of the sentries were anywhere nearby, and then down the other side to land on the dew-moistened grass.

Had Widdershins known that she was less than a hundred yards from the spot where Iruoch had climbed that same wall on his way *into* Davillon . . . Well, it probably wouldn't have made a difference.

She fretted over the burning anger she'd felt, the unnatural temper that had compelled her to hold a blade, however briefly, to Igraine and Sicard both. That her fury had been ignited by guilt over Iruoch's murders, and by Olgun's own discomfort at the creature's presence, she was all but certain; nonetheless, she felt the need to keep away from her friends until she could be *absolutely* sure she was back in control.

But that was an excuse, and she knew it. Mostly, she was running from the pain, and she hated herself for it—but still she would run.

For long moments she maintained her crouch, a heavy satchel slung over one shoulder, and stared back the way she'd come. Davillon was her world. It was all she'd ever known. It was home to everyone she'd ever loved.

It was the source of every wound and every hurt she'd ever received, in her flesh and her heart and her soul. The former might heal, but the latter never would—not here, anyway.

And then, finally, she forced herself to stand, to turn her gaze toward the highway that stretched out before her, winding its way through the dark and gently waving trees, toward an unknown and previously unimagined horizon. She'd never been there, never even come close. She wondered what lay beyond it.

"We're coming back, Olgun. Davillon doesn't get rid of us *that* easily."

The god offered her the courtesy of a polite snicker.

Arguing the merits of her own sense of humor—and the obvious lack of a divine equivalent—Widdershins started down the open road, the city and everything she knew slowly fading into the distance behind her.

ABOUT THE AUTHOR

Ari Marmell would love to tell you all about the various esoteric jobs he held and the wacky adventures he had on the way to becoming an author, since that's what other authors seem to do in these blurbs. Unfortunately, he doesn't actually have any, as the most exciting thing about his professional life, besides his novel writing, is the work he's done for Dungeons & Dragons and other role-playing games. His published fiction includes both *The Goblin Corps* and *Thief's Covenant* from Pyr Books and a variety of novels with other publishers including *The Conqueror's Shadow* and *The Warlord's Legacy*. The Widdershins novels are the only ones intended for the YA audience, at least so far; but if you liked this novel, you'll probably like his others. Just don't tell your parents for a couple more years.

Ari currently lives in an apartment that's almost as cluttered as his subconscious, which he shares (the apartment, not the subconscious, though sometimes it seems like it) with his wife, George, and two cats who really need some form of volume control installed. You can find Ari online at mouseferatu.com and follow him on Twitter @mouseferatu.